Jack of Hearts

For

John

With best wishes

Jim

Jim Moss
26 Feb 1999

JACK OF HEARTS

Jim Moss

BRIAN-GUNNER BOOKS

A Brian-Gunner Book

First published in Great Britain by Brian-Gunner, 1995

Copyright © Jim Moss 1995
All rights reserved

Cover artist Kevin Knott
Cover designer Lydia G. Goldstone

The right of Jim Moss to be identified as the author of this work has been asserted by him in accordance with the Copyright, Designs and Patent Act 1988.

This book is sold subject to the condition that it shall not, by trade or otherwise, be lent, resold, hired out, or otherwise circulated without the publisher's prior consent in any form of binding or cover other than that in which it is published and without a similar condition including this condition being imposed on the subsequent purchaser.

ISBN 0 9525948 0 3

Typeset by Deltatype Limited, Ellesmere Port, Cheshire.
Printed in Great Britain by Gwasg Dinefwr Press, Dyfed

Brian-Gunner Books
18 Penmon Close
Blacon
Chester
Cheshire CH1 5SS

I would like to thank for their great help

Rosetta (my wife) Jackie Cridland, J.R., Janice Ramage, Lydia. G. Goldstone, Mansel Edwards, Kevin Knott, Joan Newby, John O'Toole, Kevin Jones.

For Grandad and the children

The moon came out of its doors,
to pour gold on the dying day.
The paths of pleasure are wide open,
for a young boy, with no tolls to pay.

Welsh bard Harri Phillips (A breeze from the mountain)

FOREWORD

Whilst all the facts are accurate to the best of my knowledge, I categorically state that I have never had any involvement with the art of witchcraft – either black, or white.

I have never been involved in the taking, or, the distribution of drugs, in any shape or form.

All characters and locations in this novel are fictitious.
THANK YOU.
The Author.

The Author,
Jim Moss was born in Hertfordshire, and educated at the Chester College School. He has previously published two children's books, and now resides in Chester.

Chapter One

As she rose to her feet, Miss Bull's left fist smashed onto her cluttered wooden desk top and sent pens and pencils bouncing.

'Brats!' she roared. 'As far as I'm concerned you're all nothing but a bunch of maladjusted brats!' Her voice echoed around the sparsely covered white walls.

Miss Bull, her name describing her perfectly, smacked the plastic ruler threateningly into the palm of her chubby hand. Her huge frame slowly stomped down the aisle between the desks. Her piggy-like eyes, set in fleshy folds, surveyed the silent classroom. The atmosphere was one of simmering hatred, kept in check only by Bull's ruthlessness. Young lips were bitten and teeth clenched as the teacher's harsh voice once again cut the air. 'I may be new here, but I know what's what! The authorities may like to believe that you are simply poor little highly emotional children, but I know better. You're badly behaved maladjusted brats!'

Bull's ruler struck Jacky Dooley's desk hard, causing Jack to jump. She watched, relieved, as the woman raised it again and rested it gently on her own shoulder.

Her bottom lip protruding cruelly, Bull thrust out her hefty chest, straining the buttons on her navy-blue cardigan to bursting point. 'And you, Dooley,' she hissed. 'You will not floss your teeth again in permitted toilet time.'

Jacky Dooley, Jack to her friends, was an out-and-out tomboy. She couldn't help but allow a spluttered snigger to escape her.

Johnny Cross, nicknamed Adder, because of his darting snake-like tongue, and Bobby Queen, one of the bonniest of the girls, both followed suit.

Miss Bull's instant response was to bring down her ruler hard onto Jack's desk, but she accidentally caught Jack's fingers as she did so.

The unsuspecting fourteen-year-old let out a squeal of shock. Miss Bull strutted back and forth alongside Jack's desk, still loudly laying down the law. 'You Dooley, will behave yourself at Stonewall House, and you will obey – is that understood?'

Jack Dooley lowered her pretty, lightly tanned face as she defiantly twiddled with her pen. Her voice was just a whisper but held a note of sarcasm. 'Yes, Miss.'

Miss Bull's forehead crinkled into an angry frown as she again thrashed Jacky Dooley's desk top with her ruler. 'Yes Miss what, Dooley?'

Jack eased her chair away from her desk with her boot and shuffled uneasily. 'Yes Miss . . .' her voice became bolder and raucous.

'Yes Miss – up your bleedin' nose Miss with a rubber hose, Miss you perverted old bag.'

The classroom erupted into pandemonium, as Jack Dooley suddenly leapt to her feet and rammed her head into Bull's fat belly.

Miss Bull gave vent to a surprised grunt, reeled backwards, and after groping wildly for a handhold, landed with a thud and a screech onto the pale-tiled floor.

As she writhed on her back, her legs clawing the air like those of a dying fly, to rapturous cheering from her classmates, Jack Dooley fled from the room.

As Bull, crimsoned with rage, puffed, wheezed and wriggled, her long black pleated skirt slipped high above her waist, revealing tree-trunk like thighs and an expanse of white bloomers.

As taunting fingers pointed at the luckless woman, Jack Dooley's loud voice drifted back through the corridors. 'Bull's a filthy old cow, she tried to get fresh with me in the toilets, she's a perv! Bully's – a – pervert.'

She slammed Stonewall House's giant oak door behind her for the last time. Stonewall House, a stone-built prison-like school, which looked out over the tidal waters of the River Denny, was situated only a mile from the sprawling Bedford Housing Estate where Jacky Dooley lived.

Stonewall House stood like a monument of cruelty in Jack's eyes. Three years on, she would see it from the bus on her way into the nearby city of

Balchester. Over two years of Jack's young life were locked inside those cold classrooms. Stonewall House was now an empty, overgrown shell of misery, and one day, Stonewall House would hopefully, die.

In the morning's cool autumn mist, Scouser Danny Black, stood sadly and silently in the pretty little graveyard of Melvern Church. Even though Danny's small family and a few of his grandfather's friends were present, Danny Black stood head bowed and alone. Danny had always been a loner, and at his grandad's funeral he wanted to be left in solitude with his thoughts.

The three giant hollowed-out yew trees, birdsong and the ancient church formed part of a scene he would always remember. At the grave side as the words of committal were pronounced, Danny Black composed himself and stood in silent dignity. Grandad Harry would have wanted him to bear himself with dignity.

Danny drew himself up to his full muscular five feet ten inches. His hawk-like pale blue eyes unblinkingly scanned the graveyard. His searching gaze passed over the masses of beautiful cut flowers which decorated many of the recent graves, to concentrate on the daisies and buttercups, wild all around. Grandad had been Danny's instructor in nature lore now he was dead, and it was a sad, sad day.

At this present moment in time, Danny completely

lost himself in thought. The solemn, murmured condolences and farewells of the small congregation passed by him, unheard. After the last consoling pat on the back, he stooped and plucked a buttercup and daisy.

The frail figure of an old man stood silently behind one of the trees, watching him.

Danny brushed the flowers with his lips before gently tossing them into the newly dug grave. 'I'll see yous, Grandad,' he sobbed, breaking down at last, and his thoughts jolted back to what he had learned of his own origins.

Danny's mother had finally, told him, when in a drugged drunken stupor, that his father was a West Indian cricket supporter who had come over to England to watch them in the test match series. He had fathered Danny and after drunkenly admiring his new son, he had staggered from the hospital ward, never to be seen again.

Danny's mother had once been pretty, with long blonde hair. Her father, Harry Evans had never got over the death of his wife, at the young age of thirty-five – he remained a widower for the rest of his life.

Julie Black, Danny's mother, was a junkie through and through. She had gone through the whole scene, from pill popping and cocaine, to die in the end from a massive overdose of heroin. To her, chasing the dragon was the right way to bring up her mixed-blooded little bastard. It was no wonder that Danny Black hated the world from the word, 'GO!'

Debt-collectors called, a shoplifting court case

was due soon and being on a suspended sentence – well, it was good-night Vienna, goodbye Danny, and after finishing off the bottle of vodka, it was in with the needle and goodbye world.

Danny's grandfather had come to live with them six months before Julie's death, when Danny was just fifteen. It was Harry Evans who, with his love of nature, country rambles and firm discipline had managed to wean Danny Black off glue-sniffing and mild pot.

Danny, now, never smoked cigarettes and only drank an occasional pint of beer. He spent more time these days keeping fit, and practising the basic martial arts technique that his grandfather had taught him. Also he enjoyed preparing his vegetarian meals and trying to score with women.

Now Danny was living alone, with just his empty dingy flat in Toxteth to go home to. He didn't resent the fact that the colour of his skin was much darker than most, because he had plenty of friends around him in Liverpool who were also coloured.

But this morning he stood, sunk in sadness, his long black curls swept by the breeze.

Startled, he swivelled sharply as a bony hand tapped him on his broad shoulder. He stared coldly into a pair of old wrinkled grey eyes that peered at him from behind dainty gold-rimmed glasses. The spectacles balanced on a thin pointed nose above a small neatly-trimmed moustache.

On the old man's head was perched a checked deerstalker. He quickly stepped back a pace at

Danny's speedy turn, then he leaned forward, with both hands clasping his cane-top.

'Sorry to startle you, young fella.' His words poured out as if rushing from a burst dam. 'Freddy Haddock's my name, Merlin they call me – born and bred in Wellington, 28 Carter Street. Born in 1917 and did fifteen years in the army – number 3653594, sir! Served with your grandad I did, and proud to do so. We kept in touch, even when he went back to farming up in the Welsh hills.'

Freddy Haddock paused and licked his lips, then shook his head.

'Distressing thing, your Grandad Harry's death, most distressing,' he went on rapidly. 'Freddy Haddock's my name, Merlin they . . .'

Danny Black wiped the last tear-drop from his eyelashes, raised exasperated eyebrows, sighed impatiently and put up a large pleading hand. 'Hang on a minute me old mate, are yous a full shullin' – or what?'

Freddy Haddock grunted and stretched himself to his maximum five feet five inches, deestalker and all, and his moustache twitched with annoyance.

'I'm a full-a-bob as you'll ever see young fella. You're Harry's grandson, your name's Danny Black, isn't it?'

Danny opened his mouth to answer but Freddy, after blowing his nose lustily into his handerchief, was now continuing rapidly.

'I called at your flat when news reached me of

Harry's death. I only live in Balchester, twenty miles away that's all – got told by an army pal.' He suddenly let loose a shrill whistle from between his teeth as he aped a startled blackbird's alarm call.

Danny's eyes brightened as they followed the bird's prompt flight – he was beginning to take to old Freddy.

'It's on the bottom branch of the yew tree to your left,' he said confidently. 'And it's a blackbird.'

'Eh what?'

'The blackbird you whistled at,' replied Danny. 'And don't crush the snail by your right shoe, or squash the greenbottle on your arm.'

Freddy Haddock quickly glanced about him and smiled, knowingly.

'Huh!' he retorted. 'You're as smart as your grandfather was, young fella.'

Danny dropped down onto a nearby headstone and Freddy did likewise.

'I was sorting out me grandad's funeral an' that – that's why I was out when you called.' He brushed down his dark blue suit, slipped off his black tie and tucked it into his jacket pocket – the sun was gaining strength.

Freddy tucked his hand inside his tweed coat pocket and produced a large brown leather wallet. He muttered under his breath as he flicked through an assortment of personal papers and banknotes. At last, with a grunt of satisfaction, he drew out a folded sheet of paper.

'Ah, here it is, the last letter from your grandfather.' Mumbling, he zipped through the neat handwriting, his head moving from side to side as if he was watching tennis on a TV rewind.

He poked a finger skyward. 'Ah, here we are.' He read aloud. 'In the event of my death Merlin, please see to it that Danny Black receives my silver pocket watch, any money that I may have left and Steeleye.' He quickly glanced up into Danny's eyes. 'I'm his executor, you see.' Freddy hurriedly gabbled the rest.

Danny's face broke into a puzzled frown as Freddy Haddock replaced the letter.

'Steeleye!' he exclaimed. 'Merlin! Who or what the hell is Steeleye? And why did he call you Merlin. Merlin was an old wizard wasn't he?'

Freddy shuffled as he shifted his position. He looked down, then up, and smacked his lips.

'Steeleye, young fella, was your grandfather's best friend in the army.' He gave a wry smile. 'Apart from me that is. As for the name Merlin, yes, he was a wizard at King Arthur's court and your grandad gave me that nickname because I know the odd nifty trick or two.' He leant forward heavily on his silver-topped walking cane. 'Your grandad and Steeleye between them could see off German guards for us without a peep – wiped out nearly half an outpost once. With your Grandad Harry and Steeleye in tandem the result was spurting German blood and broken heads.'

Danny winced, Grandad's war stories never mentioned Steeleye, spurting blood and broken heads – only charging in single-handed and cutting down three hundred Germans with his machine-gun. Or, there were the times he'd crawled onto the tops of enemy tanks and dropped hand-grenades inside their cockpits – never any talk of the bloodthirsty stuff.

He broke off and looked round as a single-decker bus approached the graveyard. As it slowly drew to a halt, Freddy glanced at his watch and panicked.

'That's my bus young fella, I'll have to hurry. It goes out in one minute – on the hour.' He slid off the headstone, produced a pen, dug deep for a grubby piece of paper and jotted down his address. He pressed it into Danny's hand, before shuffling briskly away towards the wrought iron gate, swaying slightly as he went.

'Freddy Haddock's my name, Merlin they call me. Born and bred in Wellington . . .' his words died on the wind.

Danny strode quickly towards the yews. 'Hey! Merlin, what about Steeleye?'

Freddy stopped by the bus, puffing hard. His cane waved at a passing aeroplane as he turned. 'Try his bedroom floorboards,' he called. 'Keep in touch dear boy, keep in touch.' The bus coughed and spluttered before drawing away.

Danny stood, hands on slim hips, as his keen eyes watched Merlin's deerstalker disappear behind a twenty tonner with its horn blaring.

'Tin soldier,' Danny muttered to himself. 'He's definitely a tin soldier.'

Back home, Danny knelt in Grandad Harry's bedroom. His hands trembled as he unwrapped Steeleye from the grease-soaked cloth.

A surprised whistle escaped his lips as his fingers stroked the cold steel of the specially adapted crowbar. Its lever end had been cut to a point. Four inches above this, a short chain was fixed to a large swivel.

The whole weapon was attached to another swivel, connected to a thick, studded leather wrist strap. Both teeth of the claw were also finely pointed, and at the centre of the crook, there was welded a two inch wide circular piece of steel, for straight-thrusted jaw breaking.

Steeleye was an awesome fighting tool, and after strapping it to his wrist, Danny spun the weapon around for the first time in years.

During the first day or two, Danny emptied his flat, giving the furniture to a down-and-out paper-thin smackhead, along with some good advice that just went up with a smoke-ring of blow and a sour mouthful of gibberish.

Steeleye's slender five pound body nestled at the bottom of his rucksack, beneath his few clothes and personal possessions. Danny Black closed Liverpool's door behind him with finality.

Jack Dooley stood, silent and solemn-faced, on the freshly cut grass verge that surrounded the play area, only fifty yards from the River Denny. She drew long and hard on her cigarette as her searching brown eyes strained to pierce the morning's autumn mist, to get a better view of Stonewall House. A homeward trekking snail's shell cracked beneath the unwitting pressure of her desert boot. She glanced down, cursed its stupidity and toed it to one side for a passing bird's breakfast.

'It's a lovely school, Mrs Dooley,' the sweet-talking welfare officer had said, while sipping tea in Daisy's kitchen.

'It's a special school and the teachers are well trained to look after highly emotional young girls like Jacky.'

Remembering, Jack threw down her fag-end and ground it angrily into the wet grass. 'Bullshit!' she muttered, bitterly.

'Die, you lump of stone crap.'

She'd heard about it from her father, Ben Dooley, who was a local builder working on the site, and she had risen early especially, to come and see.

As the giant mechanical digger's bucket hovered in the air, creaking like a hand attached to a deformed metal arm, Jack gave vent to a few more of her grievances against mother nature and stepped forward a few paces to witness the execution. The mist was still thick.

Dried powder-like mortar and plaster belched into the air, and as the bulldozer's shining blade smashed into another of the lower walls of Stonewall House, Jack Dooley's pearly white teeth were bared in a grin of sheer happiness. As the bulldozer retreated, its blade scraped as it dragged the ground level.

As the next high-backed waggon's air brakes hissed, the digger's bucket shook violently while its engine revved. The metal arm lurched forward and lunged downward before coming to a shuddering halt in mid-air.

'Hey! you!' a heavy-chested frame, clad in a sweat-soaked T-shirt, below a wide bristly chin, leaned out of the machine's cab. He tipped back his hard yellow hat and shook a sledgehammer-like fist at Jack.

Jacky Dooley sniffed, gave the driver a hard brown-eyed stared and raised her head a trifle, to acknowledge his urgent shout.

'Yeah you, you crazy or something? Get away from there before you get yourself killed. They're damned dangerous these machines.'

Jack shuffled her feet, pulled up her leather jacket collar to fend off the river's cool mist and backed away a few paces. No way was she going to miss the final breath being crushed out of Stonewall House.

A rising breeze had slowly started to thin the mist and the early sun was beginning to turn the river into a vast sheet of dancing sparkling diamonds. Circling seagulls screeched loudly as a rat scurried over the wet rocks, while a row of weeping willow braids lazily dragged themselves through the black smelly mud discarded by dawn's high tide.

After the last wall had easily succumbed to the

bulldozer, the engines deadened and the four workmen departed to their small cabin for their tea break.

Danny Black had arrived in Balchester two days earlier, with his rucksack, and Freddy Haddock's address in his wallet. He had obtained digs in an attic bedsit on the fringe of the city. Nothing fancy, but it was tidy and cleaned once a week, with the linen changed once a fortnight. He shared a tiny galley kitchen with a pretty eighteen-year-old barmaid, who rented the next room. The toilet and bathroom were shared by the six tenants.

By chance, Danny had met Ben Dooley in a city pub. Dooley had told him of the vacant labourer's job on the Stonewall House demolition site.

Ben Dooley was a middle-aged man with long greasy black hair, about Danny's height but much slimmer. He was a hard self-centred man.

Danny and Ben Dooley had been burning shrubbery, trees and timbers, on the far side of the remains of Stonewall House, and neither had seen Jack observing operations.

Jack Dooley, a slim five foot three, ambled across the ground, and with a sigh and a smile of satisfaction studied the heaps of rubble. She pulled out her cigarettes from her grey trouser pocket and lit up, drawing in deeply, then blowing out a stream of smoke. Suddenly she stopped dead. Her smile rapidly disappeared as she swooped down to pick up a broken-handled mug from out of the debris. As she read the large crimson letters stamped across the mug, Miss Bull's hectoring voice returned to haunt her. The letters spelt the word 'maladjusted'. Jack bit her lip, her expression taut as her grip tightened fiercely on the mug.

'Maladjusted! you're all branded maladjusted now, for the rest of your miserable lives.'

Jack's eyes gleamed with hatred as she fingered the letters on the mug. Her bitterness boiled over. 'Maladjusted my arse!' she yelled at the top of her voice. Then she let fly, hurling the mug into the river. It made a splash, bobbed up and down a couple of times, and sank beneath the gliding water.

At Jack's outburst, two hard yellow hats appeared around the cabin door.

Sledgehammer Fist stepped out and stood legs astride.

'I thought I told you to keep away from here – now get lost!' Two more men appeared from the cabin, they were Ben Dooley and Danny Black.

Jack stood her ground as her irate father walked over to her.

'I told you last night girl, didn't I?' he rasped. 'I told you not to come here.'

His words travelled unheeded past Jack's ears – her eyes were silently communicating with Danny Black's.

Ben Dooley gave Jacky's shoulder a shake and glanced worriedly behind him at Sledgehammer Fist.

'You heard the man, he's the foreman, now get off home. And tell your mother I'll be home at half-five sharp for my dinner, I've got a darts match tonight.'

Meanwhile, inside the cabin, a workman flung the local rag down on top of the squeezed-out tea bags and empty crisp packets.

'It's about time the coppers did somethin' about all of these devil worship rumours,' he growled, loudly enough to be heard outside, 'especially if they think kids could be involved.' There were murmurs of agreement.

Outside, Danny cocked his head, robin-style, his straight gaze magnetising Jack. She ignored her father and, as Sledgehammer Fist ushered Danny back to work, she defiantly held her ground until Danny had disappeared from view. Then, with a contemptuous glance at her father, she tossed her cigarette butt at his feet and turned away, her lip curling with resentment.

'Divvy,' she muttered, and set off running for home with her long black tresses blowing like the mane of a wild pony at the gallop.

Chapter Two

A week later, after the Stonewall House job, Danny stood with his mouth agape, next to the pigman on the badly run-down Banner Estate. One good look at the crumbling cottage was enough. He pointed his finger in disbelief as he let his rucksack fall to the ground.

'A few weeks' work!' he exclaimed. His eyes darted from the rotten window-frames, with several panes of cracked glass, over the half-empty weathered brickwork joints, to the many gaps in the slate roof.

Ben Dooley had passed the job on to Danny after the Stonewall House demolition work had finished.

'It'll be a nice little earner for you,' he'd said. 'The job's got to begin straight away, so I'll give the main contractor a ring to tell him you're starting. He's on holiday in Scotland. Anyway,' he'd added, with a snigger, 'you'll enjoy working in Cheshire, all that countryside – seeing you're so fond of the birds and the bees.'

Danny Black had agreed, living in the cottage with three meals a day and a hefty wage packet at the end of each week was a tasty offer. The job was supposed to be small, by the looks of the place it would take months!

Bill Drew, a sixty-year-old giant of a man stood legs apart – his half-mast pants settled an inch above his size twelve boots.

He held the two large metal buckets of pigswill, one in each of his dinner-plate hands. He rocked back on his heels a little, a tangle of white hair poking through his grubby white string vest. He wore his battered trilby tilted at a rakish angle.

'What's up with thee lad, can't thee do job, or what?' he boomed.

Danny let loose a sharp sarcastic laugh. He nodded towards the cottage. 'A' yous still living in that? I wouldn't let pigs live in there.'

Bill Drew threw back his large head and guffawed.

'Pigs already do lad, in the other half of the cottage – reet next to where you'll be sleeping.' With a grunt, he rattled his swill bucket handles and made for the cottage with long springy strides. He summoned Danny to follow with a curt nod. 'Come on then lad, pigs must be fed.'

Danny snatched up his rucksack and scuttled after him, his Scouse voice rising high in protest as he caught him up.

'What d'you mean, mate, sleep by the pigs – come 'ead you've got to be kidding.'

Bill gave him a withering glance and strode on.

Danny scampered after him, one foot tripping over the other. He realised that even Steeleye would have a job breaking this man's head. The big man halted by the tangled wild growth of climbing roses and bee-swamped honeysuckle that smothered the broken trellis around the kitchen door.

Danny, eager to forget about his promised sleeping quarters, glanced appreciatively at the purple thistles, and the small red dead-nettles, with the sun-worshipping dandelions, that spangled the long grass in the untended garden.

Bill Drew's ancient black and white flea-bitten mongrel, with the dying flat bark, greeted them on tottering legs. As Danny patted old Sal, he glanced skywards and hearkened to the near invisible dot of a skylark in full song. His eye caught the wobbly pot on top of the chimney stack, which needed repairing; he sighed – Danny hated heights.

Bill banged down his swill buckets and poked his head inside the door. He yelled then, louder than ever.

'Mabel! there's a lad 'ere to start work on cottage and new piggery, come on woman, present theeself.' He pointed to a large derelict outhouse, which adjoined the bedroom of the cottage where Danny was to sleep. 'That's new piggery lad when you've done it – and quicker the better, smells getting pretty bad, it even comes through the cracks in the damp walls.'

Danny winced, the aroma was already reaching his puckered nostrils from inside the cottage, and each passing minute was heading towards night, and the prospect of sleeping next to the pigs.

An elderly woman's round, rosy face suddenly appeared at the kitchen door. She beamed at them, showing a solitary, black, pickle-stabbing tooth, and her mass of grey hair was matted and dirty. Her grubby, flower-patterned frock hung loosely to her knees and her feet were encased in a pair of mud-splattered wellingtons.

'You've got the swill then, Bill,' she said, casting a saucy smiling eye over Danny's handsome face.

Danny shuddered at the flirtatious look, and hurriedly glanced away – the dancing white butterfly in his line of vision certainly looked prettier.

Bill Drew grunted impatiently as he picked up the swill buckets and shoved them at his wife. 'Here's pigswill Mabel, feed pigs first and then feed the lad 'ere, then he can start work.' He cocked a teasing eye at Danny and heaved a sigh. 'I'm off to empty bog can lad, it'll be your turn tomorrow so you'll be best fixing drains first.' He spread his hands to a foot apart. 'There's turds in there this big, they're snapping at the bog seat like crocodiles.' Then, ducking his head, he stepped inside the cottage and lumbered away to fetch the toilet can.

By now, Danny was beginning to feel slightly sick. Mrs Drew grabbed him by the arm and pulled him eagerly into the kitchen. She bent over him as she pushed him onto a wooden stool by the littered table, revealing a good deal of her large bra-less bosom which bulged out of her low-cut dress and nearly smothered him.

He sniffed her smelly cleavage and cringed. Undeterred, Mabel stroked Danny's face fondly. 'You wait 'ere me dear,' she ordered excitedly. 'I'll be back when I've fed the pigs.' With a last, 'I want your body look' at Danny, she heaved her fat little form away from him, and went swaying out of the kitchen.

Through the small panes of the kitchen window, Danny noticed Bill Drew returning after emptying the toilet can. He felt trapped between a sex-starved lioness and her unsuspecting but formidably burly mate. He'd seen and smelt enough. He snatched up his rucksack, leapt to his feet and fled out of the kitchen door, past an astounded Bill Drew, who stopped in mid-stride, swinging the empty bog can. He scratched his head in bewilderment.

'Well I'll be buggered,' he muttered, as Danny let the garden gate slam shut and rushed away.

Bill was still a bit shell-shocked as he sat astride the kitchen stool with his personal ladle at the ready. Mabel shook her head and sighed as she served up a dish of steaming stew. 'That's right Bill, 'e just upped and made off like a bat out of hell – can't think for the life of me why!'

Bill Drew dipped a great chunk of bread into the stew and then slurped it down. 'Aye, thee's reet Mabel,' he muttered between mouthfuls. 'They're a strange lot, city folk.'

After a good hour's walking, the early September cloud had thickened and rain was falling steadily, making the day seem completely friendless to Danny. He stopped and pulled up the hood on his black anorak to shield himself from the weather. He felt a momentary surge of pleasure at the sight of the web of wet glistening pearls that clung to the hedgerow. Then he frowned again, realising that the tenner and the few pence that he'd just shoved back in his pocket wouldn't go far – perhaps he should have stuck it out on the Banner Estate. But he then thought of the lustful Mabel and let out a burst of laughter.

He glanced down at his sturdy walking boots and then set off again along the winding country lane, whistling and singing, 'We love yous Liverpool, O yes we do . . .'

The night's torrential rain had ceased, giving way to rays of bright morning sunlight, which dazzled through the gleaming windows of the Dooleys' council-house.

Jack, who was the Dooleys' middle daughter, sat head bowed at the freshly tidied breakfast table, sleepily listening to the radio. Earlier, she had, as usual cleared away the empty beer cans and dirty ash-tray which her father had left cluttering the kitchen table – the girls and their mother, Daisy, were all sick to death of cleaning up after the drunken foul mouthed slob. Another night of bitter fighting between Ben and Daisy, had left its usual mark of misery on Jack's face. At seventeen, Jack was accustomed to her father's violent ways. Nevertheless, it had been a long hard night, she thought and wondered whether to get up and switch the kettle on.

The warm sun stroked her lightly tanned face and a glimmer of a smile flickered in her eyes, as Daisy walked in wearily, Stumpy, Jacky's three-and-a-half-legged Jack Russell terrier, at her heels. Daisy was shrouded in a long blue dressing-gown which reached down to the tops of her fluffy mules. With a deep sigh, she eased herself into a chair. Fumbling in her pocket, she pulled out a packet of cigarettes and a lighter, and lit up with trembling fingers. Aiming a stream of smoke at the lampshade, she finally looked directly at Jack. Her swollen mouth broke into a twisted half-smile.

Jack, who hadn't even undressed from the night before, studied Daisy anxiously.

'Are you all right Mam?' she asked gently. She nodded towards the ceiling. 'I don't know why you put up with him! Can't you get an injunction out on him, or something?'

Daisy knocked the ash off her cigarette and drummed on the kitchen table with restless fingers.

She glanced nervously at the wall clock, Ben Dooley would soon be surfacing. 'It's not that simple, love; last time, when you were little, I tried that. He wouldn't give me a penny and when he was drunk he'd break the injunction and give me hell, at least now, he does give me some money.'

'Ha!' snorted Jack. 'And borrows most of it back every week for his ale and slags.'

Daisy puffed long and hard on her cigarette. 'Anyway, our Sophie's only thirteen and he worships her – Gods knows what he'd do if I tried to get another injunction out on him.' She shrugged with an air of defeat. 'Perhaps one day, when you kids have all gone, I'll try to get shut of him for good.'

Jack planted her elbows on the table and cupped her chin in her hands. 'But that's damn stupid, Mam,' she reasoned. 'It could take years, he could have knocked you senseless by then – anyway, if you do it now we'll all stick by you, our Rosie earns good money in that masseuse job.'

Daisy shook her head. 'But Rosie's getting married to John next year, love – she'll be Mrs Andrews then, not Rosie Dooley. We can't expect her to give us money, she'll have her own life to lead.'

Jacky sighed, nodded, and got to her feet. 'I s'pose you're right Mam – the kettle's boiled, I'll make you a cuppa. I'll have to try harder to get a job, and then if things do get worse and they throw the old bastard in prison, it'll help out.'

Stumpy was by now hopping and squeaking agitatedly by the kitchen door, bursting to perform his morning ritual, amongst the building materials that were stacked around the back garden.

Daisy stepped across the red quarry-tiled polished floor to let him out. 'Off you go, Stumpy,' she urged, her slim body swaying in the cold breeze as she opened the door. Stumpy shot out, wagging his short tail rudder-style.

Returning to the table, Daisy sipped at her tea. Hearing sounds from upstairs, she tensed and ran a trembling hand through her dark shoulder-length hair already tinged with grey – Ben Dooley had risen.

The noise of water running was quickly followed by loud hawking coughs as he smoked his first cheroot of the day. Daisy's lip curled with loathing and her hands gripped her cup tightly. 'Go on Dooley,' she drawled disgustedly, 'choke yourself to death, and give us all some peace, you drunken pig.'

She'd wished for years that he'd just curl up and die.

'Daisy! Daisy!' Dooley's voice roared down the stairs.

'Make sure my breakfast's ready will you, I'm five minutes late for work already.'

It was only seconds before he appeared, and Jack thrust a plate of scrambled eggs on toast under his nose.

Ben Dooley slouched over the table, shovelling his food down, his bristly chin smudged with egg, his narrow dark eyes taking everything in, as he glanced round the room. They glinted with long-held resentment as he surveyed the smart redecoration job that Jack had done for her mother.

The cream venetian blind matched the pale flowered wall paper almost to perfection. The small but charming kitchen had once been adorned with matching wall-plates and other cheerful knickknacks. But in his drunken violent rages Dooley had destroyed most of them, now, the females were just content to keep the place clean.

A smug smile crept around the corner of his thin harelip – his women did him proud – he had them just where he wanted them, so he thought.

As his cold eyes rested on Jack, she bravely controlled an urge to rush out of the room. Instead, she stared silently at the slice of toast in her hand.

Her father gulped tea noisily from his mug, he leaned across the table and stabbed his fork at her.

'Sauce girl!' he barked. 'Pass the sauce – the brown 'un.' There were times when Jack Dooley would have frozen at her father's command, as if shot by a bullet, but no more. Her lips clamped together, she glared at Dooley.

Daisy's face took on a worried look. She breathed a hushed sigh of relief, as Jack slowly pushed the sauce bottle towards her father. He impatiently lurched forward, grabbed it and with a snarl, turned it upside down and shook it violently.

Daisy and Jack watched with weird fascination as three large blobs of sauce shot out, practically covering what was left of his eggs. Dooley cursed under his breath, scraped most of the sauce away and bolted the rest of the food down in swinish fashion.

Just then Rosie Dooley came in. She was a petite twenty-one-year-old, her long golden hair enhanced with highlights. She was the eldest of the Dooley girls and slightly taller than Jack, with a more sensual cast of face.

Her wide sea-green eyes, with long curling, lashes, were particularly beautiful!

'Hi Mum, hi Jack, any toast and marmalade going? I'm starving!'

Rosie was almost tiresomely cheerful in the mornings. She gave Ben Dooley a quick, flashing scrutiny and then sat at the breakfast table, crossing her legs.

Dooley's leering eyes inspected Rosie's body as she sipped her tea, taking in every curve of her long slim legs, to where her baby doll nightie clung to her smooth, dimpled thighs. Daisy noticed his prurient stare and, trying to ignore it, rose to her feet, and busied herself clearing the table.

Jack sprang up to help, while Rosie scowled and snapped at him. 'Nearly finished?'

Dooley leered and carried on eyeing his daughter's body.

'And what lucky man's going to be under your soothin' touch today Rosie?' he mocked. 'Some politician? a bank clerk, or one of those gents wanting special services?'

Rosie went crimson with rage, while Jack and Daisy both stiffened. Rosie and her father at loggerheads was an explosive situation. Rosie leapt up angrily from her chair. Her eyes blazed as she confronted him, hands on hips.

'Oh shut your mouth Dad, will you! I'm a professional masseuse, not some sleazy prostitute.

For your information, I happen to love my work – okay?'

Behind Dooley's back, Daisy nodded towards the door in a mute plea for Rosie to let things drop and go and get dressed for work.

Jack provided a diversion as an item of local news came over the radio.

She pulled a hideous face at Daisy and exclaimed, 'Oooooh, the local Satanists are at it again. Maybe they'll come for you Mam,' she teased.

As Daisy wriggled irritably, Jacky planted a kiss firmly on the back of her neck. 'God, I love you Daisy Dooley.'

'Stop it Jack!' Daisy scolded, breaking free. 'All that black magic stuff makes me shudder – I'll never forget when they found poor Sandra Cross's dead baby in the canal with all the blood drained out of it. And supposedly half-eaten by a human being, yuk! it makes me heave.'

'There isn't anything in it really, Mam,' said Jack, as she swatted a fly which had just landed on the draining board. 'God! I hate flies,' she commented, sweeping it into the waste-bin.

Rosie, having calmed down and finished her tea, cast a final glowering look at her father and walked out, her hips swaying as she went.

Ben Dooley grunted, scraped back his chair, and picked up his lunch bag from the top of the fridge. As he glanced at Jack, he thought how pretty she was, like Daisy, Rosie and little Sophie, yet she was such a tomboy. She dressed like a lad and she could turn her hand to many a man's job around the house – it bugged him. He liked females to know their place. He turned and half opened the back door.

Stumpy, eagerly squeezed through the gap and rushed to Jack for his usual toast crusts.

Dooley turned again and decided to teach Jack a lesson. He'd lit a cheroot, and as the heavy odour filled the room he remarked in spiteful tones, 'Jacky! you'll be coming with me this Saturday – I've got a couple of doorways to brick up at Woodcock's farm. You 'elp your mother enough, you can give me some help for a change.' Jack looked at him with a frown.

'I'm not going to Timberdick's farm, he's a pervert. Anyway, I'm going to town on Saturday with Bobby.'

Daisy attempted to shush her, but Dooley's voice growled menacingly. 'Now that's what you call a pervert, the girl's as bent as a banana, and I've heard she's on the dope.'

Jack bit her lip hard – so, what if Bobby was gay and liked a blow, she was still one of her best friends. Defiance surged through her, tautening every nerve. 'I'm going to town with Bobby,' she hissed. 'You don't bleedin' well own me.'

Dooley angrily brandished his lunchbag at Jack and commanded, 'you'll do as I say girl, while you're under this roof.'

Daisy buried her face in her hands, she'd had enough arguing through the night and was close to tears.

Jack's heart thudded as she retaliated.

'I'm not going to Timberdick's. Last time you took me there all the old beak-nosed pig did was try to chat me up. His bull should have finished him off, instead of leaving him with just a gammy leg.'

Dooley's expression was murderous. 'You'll do as I say,' he roared. 'And that's the bloody end of it.' He nodded darkly at Daisy. 'Dinner at half five,' he ordered, without the slightest hint of affection.

Jacky suddenly stretched out a clenched fist and slammed her heels together. 'Heil Hitler!'

Daisy held her breath with apprehension as her husband turned on his heel and stormed out, slamming the door behind him with a resounding crash.

Stumpy had prudently stayed put throughout the row in his 'air-raid' shelter under the table.

Jack uncurled her fingers and formed her own two-fingered V-shaped salute towards her father. 'Fuck off, Arsehole.'

Chapter Three

A couple of hours after escaping from Mabel Drew, Danny Black secured a lift from the driver of a petrol tanker. When he was ready to get out, he leapt down and offered the driver his last fiver. The man shook his head. 'Thanks mate, keep it, you need it more than me.' He directed Danny to Balchester, and with a farewell grin, revved up and pulled away, amid a cloud of stinking fumes.

Danny walked steadily on for about half an hour, admiring the countryside, until he reached the village of Oakfield. This consisted of a scattering of thatched cottages and a small post office and store which catered for the village, farms and many fishermen who visited the River Denny.

After buying a fresh apple from the cheerful lady behind the counter, he walked on happily munching, until he found himself at the meadow gate which led to the river – the lady in the store had directed him well. He could see the many oaks trees she'd spoken of lining the riverbank, near to where the ancient ford had been used by Romans and travellers through the centuries.

But it was the sweep of golden buttercups, which shimmered down to the river, that took his breath away.

He climbed over the wooden gate, dropped down into the field and trod gently through the flower spangled grass until he came to the River Denny.

A friendly fisherman glanced up from watching his trotting float, to point him downstream for his destination.

At Oakford, the river narrowed and was shallower as it sped over sandy gravel beds. There were stretches of long green streamer weed, with channels between, where silver dace and grayling in abundance fed hungrily. Voracious chub lay in wait for falling grubs in the deep slow glide beneath the overhanging broad-leaved trees on the far side of the river.

After walking for a brief spell, Danny came to a peaceful, spacious clearing between a triangle of giant oaks. He dropped his rucksack and scanned the clearing approvingly – it was deserted and a perfect place to train. He quickly stripped off to the waist, dug deep into his rucksack and with a jerk brought out Steeleye. He watched it glint in the sunlight that shone through the foliage, then strapped it to his wrist and set the crowbar spinning. As he breathed in deeply, the Danny Black who wouldn't hurt a fly unless he had to, became a warrior. He gave vent to savage yells and cut the air with lightning strikes until finally, with a victorious scream, he sank Steeleye's razor-sharp claws into the enemy's neck – an oak tree branch. He was beginning to realise why his grandfather had never told him about the lethal weapon, and only used it in the war. The satisfying ferocity he had felt was almost frightening to him.

Packing Steeleye away, he carried on practising his own style of fighting, phantom punches, movements with the speed and ferocity of a cornered jungle beast, until at last, primed to the hilt and sweating, he stopped.

He went to swill his face in the river's refreshing clear water. Then he dressed, scooped up his rucksack, and carried on downriver.

It was just before midnight on the same day, Friday, when he finally halted and looked across the vast area of meadowland towards Balchester's distant night lights. He cut away from the peaceful river and walked across the fields, weaving in and out of the lazing cows as he went.

The barn which he came across well heaped with hay bales, looked a snug enough place to sleep for the rest of the night. His rucksack made a good pillow and he slumbered beneath the squeaking bats that circled the moonlit building.

By seven o'clock the next morning Ben Dooley had risen, smoked his first cheroot of the day and drunk his first mug of tea. He was up early as there was work to be done at George Woodcock's farm. He poured himself more tea and strode to the open hallway door. 'Jack! Jacky!' he bawled. 'Come on girl, you've got ten minutes to get ready. I warned you again last night that you were coming to Woodcock's with me – now move yourself, I'm just going to load up the van with what I need.' He paused then yelled, 'd'you 'ear me girl?'

Jacky blinked a few times and wearily eased her head from beneath the pink-flowered duvet.

'Yeah, yeah I can hear you.' Her drowsy reply barely reached her father's ears.

He grunted in response, dropped his empty mug in the sink as he passed, and slammed out of the back door followed by Stumpy.

Jack instantly slid back under her duvet, only to be disturbed again by Rosie from the bed opposite.

'Come on Jack,' she advised, 'you know what he's like when he doesn't get his own way.' She recalled how her father had dragged Jack feet first from her bed, the last time she'd disobeyed him.

Jack mumbled a string of obscenities as she resurfaced.

'I suppose you're right,' she sighed, and noticed as she sat up, that Rosie was reading what looked like a letter and there was a dreamy expression on her face. 'What's that you've got?' she yawned.

Rosie looked up, smiling. 'It's a poem from John,' she murmured, tenderness in her voice, 'he gave it to me last night after our meal at the "Flamingo". It's going to be wonderful being married to him, he's so considerate and romantic.'

Jack frowned as she slipped from beneath the

duvet. 'All that hearts and flowers stuff is rubbish, if you ask me, men are all the same, like him downstairs – pigs!'

'You're wrong, Jack.' Rosie hugged her poem to her chest.

'There *are* some decent men around, one of these days, you'll meet one, mark my words.'

'I won't hold my breath,' Jack retorted, slipping on her dressing-gown. She patted off to the bathroom for a quick shower, leaving Rosie to read her poem again and dream.

When Jack got back, Rosie was brushing her hair in front of the dressing-table mirror.

'I wish you'd wear some of the nice clothes I bought you sometimes,' she remarked, as Jack hurriedly donned jeans and a checked shirt. 'I'd look daft going to the farm in frills,' Jacky retorted.

'You know I don't mean now.' Rosie was about to go on but her sister interrupted her.

'Before you start, I don't want a boyfriend and I hate floundering around in skirts.' She tugged on her desert boots and hurriedly attacked her thick tousled hair with a brush.

The beeping of a car horn sent Rosie to look through the window at the street below. 'Mmm,' she sighed as she watched Lance, the good-looking boy from next door, climb into the passenger seat of the green Ford. 'He's a nice lad Lance Roberts, isn't he Jack? – and he's got a good job at the steelworks.'

'He's okay,' came the cool reply. 'He comes to the canal dump with us sometimes when he's not on shift, he's a bit of a smart arse but he's all right – as a mate.'

'Uh – huh,' Rosie responded hopefully.

They were both startled by their father suddenly pounding up the stairs.

'Trying to wind me up are you Jacky by keeping me waiting?' he roared, outside the door.

Rosie snatched up her purse, opened it, grabbed some coins and rammed them into Jack's hand. 'Here you are, luv, get yourself some fags, you'd better hurry.'

'Ta sis,' Jack gave her a hug, 'I love you a lot.' She ran to the bedroom door. 'I'm coming,' she yelled to Dooley. Her father, at the top of the stairs, snarled. 'Hurry girl, for God's sake! If I lose Woodcock's work through you I'll bloody well . . .'

As Jacky shot out of the room he retreated, still cursing under his breath as she followed him downstairs and out of the house.

Little Sophie, whose room was opposite, slept on undisturbed, her long thick auburn hair spread out across her pillow, a scattering of tiny freckles on her delicate skin. She hugged her giant pink teddy bear lovingly, one little bare foot peeping from beneath her duvet. She was watched over by a wall full of pop star pictures, fronted by Michael Jackson in a scene from 'Dangerous'.

Outside, as her father's old blue transit van started up, Jack sat head bowed and tight-lipped – as far as she was concerned, it was going to be a silent trip to George Woodcock's farm.

Danny Black opened a bleary eye and looked over the top of the bales which had been his bed for the night.

The white sheepdog, with the large black patch covering its right eye, bounced around below him, swishing its tail and barking relentlessly.

'Sweep! Sweep! What's up with you, you daft beggar?'

Farmer Woodcock, a lanky middle-aged man, came limping into Danny's view. His left leg was stiff and swung out in a half-circle with every step he took. He stopped abruptly, and stared at the intruder with dark hooded eyes. He scratched his scanty grey locks at the sight of Danny, and cleared his throat. 'Who are you? – and what are you doing in my barn?' he demanded. Still holding Danny's gaze with his own, he snapped his fingers. 'Heel Sweep!'

Sweep promptly obeyed.

There was a strangeness about this man of few words, thought Danny, some quality he couldn't define. He threw down his rucksack, swung his legs over the bales and dropped the full eight feet to the floor. He straightened himself and faced Woodcock. He couldn't help but notice how the farmer's distinctive eagle-beak-like nose twitched slightly every time he spoke.

'I'm Danny Black, and I slept in your barn because I was tired after walking the last twenty miles to get to Balchester.' He whistled through his teeth to Sweep who wagged his tail in response.

Woodcock's eyes flashed. 'Heel Sweep.'

The sheepdog settled down again, motionless.

'You're not English are you?' asked the farmer, after scrutinising Danny closely.

Danny stared back at him, it was a brave man who commented on his colour.

'No I'm not,' he answered, a note of rising anger in his voice. 'And if yous going to be blunt about it, I'm a half-caste. West Indian dad and a Welsh mum.'

Woodcock's eyes widened in momentary surprise – he liked a man with spirit.

'And why've you come to Balchester?'

'I'm looking for a job.'

'What kind of job?'

Danny shrugged his shoulders, 'Anythin' really. Labouring – an' a bit of building – concreting, flagging and stuff like that.'

Woodcock rubbed his finger and thumb thoughtfully down the bridge of his nose.

There was a brief silence, except for Sweep's heavy panting. Woodcock slipped his slender hands into the pockets of his expensive tweed jacket.

'I could do with an extra pair of hands on the farm,' he conceded, in more kindly tones. 'You can live in and I'll pay you fairly. But,' he warned, 'I'll have no clock-watchers working for me, the choice is yours.'

Danny, who had eyed him steadily throughout the confrontation, showed his appreciation. He smiled, displaying a glint of white teeth.

'I'll take the job,' he agreed, bending to pick up his rucksack. 'Mister . . . ?'

'Woodcock – George Woodcock, you can call me George.' The farmer turned and snapped his fingers to bring Sweep to his feet.

'Follow me, young sir, we'll gather the cows for milking and when I take them to the parlour, I'll show you the house. Tell my wife that I sent you and she'll give you a room.' He swivelled about and limped away. 'Come Sweep!' Sweep followed obediently – and so did Danny Black.

After walking for a minute or two, Woodcock apparently feeling the need to break the silence, began abruptly, 'tell me Daniel, do you . . .'

Danny broke in. 'Danny – my name's just Danny, not Daniel.'

Woodcock managed a slight smile. 'H'm, do you have any family or friends in Balchester, Danny?'

'No, me mum an' grandad are dead and most of me mates are in Liverpool.'

'You come from Liverpool then?'

'Oh! yeah, I do know one man in Balchester, he's called Merlin, Freddy Haddock is his real name though. He was in the war with Grandad.'

Woodcock stopped and exclaimed, 'Merlin! that's an odd name to give a person.'

Danny gave a bark of laughter. 'Merlin is a very odd man, which reminds me, I'd better call on him while I'm here.'

They halted at the gate which led to Woodcock's cowfield.

'And there's someone else I've met,' Danny went on. 'I did a bit of demolition work with a builder called Dooley, on the other side of the city.'

Woodcock seemed somewhat surprised. 'Ben Dooley?'

'Yeah.' Danny slapped the rear end of a large friesian, whose full udder was swinging. 'That's the man.'

'Ha, he does my work as well, in fact he's due this morning.'

'Is he?' Danny grimaced. 'Good, I'd like to see him again about a certain pig-man.'

The farmer gave him a puzzled look and carried on rounding up his cattle, with the help of the energetic Sweep.

As he ran a hand through his dark curls, Danny studied Woodcock's farmhouse with relief. It was a splendid building, and nothing like the Drews' shack. It was a newly renovated large, white cottage, with neatly tended gardens and an orchard to the right of it. Just outside of the garden fence, there was a small shallow pond, where two small girls, of about five and seven, were happily feeding bread to the squabbling ducks.

'That's my house,' Woodcock announced, as the cattle made their way to the milking parlour. He pointed towards the duck-pond. 'And those are my daughters, Elizabeth and Susan. You'll probably find my wife in the kitchen – I'll see you at breakfast.'

He then gave a small grunt of pain, evidently his

leg was troubling him, slammed the yard gate shut and headed for the parlour.

Danny gazed after him and scratched his head. Surely he was a bit old to have two such young daughters, he speculated. He shrugged and strode briskly towards the farmhouse.

At the open back-door Danny halted, to stare admiringly at the trim figure and cascade of long dark hair of the young woman within. Her short skirt showed off her shapely legs and small elegant feet. As she buttered slices of toast, she had her back to him and was half-watching the portable TV on a small corner shelf just above her head.

Danny coughed to attract her attention, wondering if she could possibly be Woodcock's wife.

She dropped her knife onto the worktop and turned sharply. 'You startled me,' she exclaimed, frowning.

His breath caught in his throat, her pretty oriental face took him by surprise. If this was Mrs Woodcock, she must be at least twenty-five years younger than her husband, he surmised. She quickly regained her composure and flashed an amused glance at him as he stood there speechless.

'Can I help you?' she asked, with a trace of impatience in her voice as he still stared at her with dazzled eyes.

'I – er – I was told by – er – Mister Woodcock – that you'll fix me up with a room,' he stammered. She waited with raised eyebrows for more.

He rubbed a hot hand over his face. 'What I mean is,' he went on. 'He's given me a job.'

'Aaaah, I see.' Her face lit up with a warm mischievous smile which further mesmerised Danny. She moved a little closer and studied his face with thoughtful dark eyes.

He somehow guessed that she knew men well, and found himself hoping that he would pass muster with her.

To his relief she gave him a welcoming handshake. 'Danny Black,' he introduced himself.

'Su-Ling Woodcock, we always believe in being on first name terms with our workers – now follow me please Danny, and I'll show you to your room.'

She spoke English exceptionally well he realised and wondered which Eastern country she hailed from. She was about to lead the way when she suddenly stopped and directed. 'Oh no boots or shoes in the house please, Danny.'

In apologetic Scouse accents he responded. 'Oh – yeah, sorry, I never thought, cow muck an' all that.'

She waited patiently while he untied the laces and kicked off his boots. He saw with embarrassment, that Su-Ling's notice was caught and held by the sight of his big toe, peeping from a hole in his grubby white sock.

She smiled rather impishly and bade him. 'Come along Danny.'

Following her through the long expensively equipped kitchen, Danny's gaze took in the beautiful oak wood units, the fancy tiled floor and walls, and the sparkling row of hanging copper based pans.

As they climbed the wide thick-carpeted staircase, his attention concentrated on Su-Ling's voluptuously swaying hips.

A mad excitement began to churn in his body – it was if she knew that he fancied her and was deliberately acting seductively. Halfway up, however, he suddenly halted, distracted from Su-Ling's sexy buttocks by the sight of three elaborate shotguns, mounted between paintings, on the plush decorated wall. The centre one was a beautiful painting entitled 'A Fox In Winter-Time' by Ronaldo Lancastrio – a rapidly rising local artist of the highest potential.

He was particularly impressed by the middle gun, with the delicate gold engraving. Fascinated, he reached out to stroke the weapon, from the stock to the tip of the barrels. He didn't like guns – Grandad Harry had been wounded in battle by one, when only a boy of sixteen – yet they cast a strange spell on him, perhaps because of the knowledge that they could take a life with just the simple squeeze of the trigger.

Su-Ling stopped and half turned. 'Aah, my husband's shotguns. The one you're looking at is the one he blew the bull's head off with.'

Danny stared at her, and a curious stillness came over his face.

'Is something wrong Danny?'

'Eh, no – yous a' kidding aren't you.' He gave a short sharp laugh. 'Blew the bull's head off?'

She looked a little vexed. 'I am most certainly not kidding. That's why my husband limps so badly. He has a side full of steel pins after the bull gored him.' She tossed a careless hand. 'So, he blew the brute's head off.' She turned and carried on climbing the stairs.

'Follow me please, I have breakfast to prepare yet for my girls and George.'

Bemused by what she had told him, Danny obeyed.

They reached the landing, where Su-Ling led him to a small bedroom at the far end, which was next to one of the two indoor toilets.

'Your daughters are very pretty,' Danny remarked, trying to erase the bull story from his mind. 'I saw them by the duck-pond a little while ago.'

'Yes, we love them very much, but my husband would like a son to carry on the farm, and his name of course.'

He smiled and nodded. 'Understandable.'

As Su-Ling tidied and patted the already neat bed, Danny looked round at his new home. The bed was a single divan, with a simple blue quilt. A thick unpatterned blue carpet covered the floor and there were two country landscapes on the walls. It was clean, plain, and simple, with a small curtained window which looked out onto the duck-pond at the rear of the house.

Danny put his rucksack down in the corner of the room next to a small wardrobe. Glancing up, he found Su-Ling sitting on the edge of the bed; her skirt had slipped high above her knees, revealing more of her shapely legs.

'It's a comfortable bed Danny,' she murmured, 'you should sleep well.' Her lovely eyes showed surprised annoyance, as he made for the door with an agitated, 'I'll just get a swill, Mrs Woodcock, if that's OK?'

She slipped quietly off the bed. 'Of course it is Danny. We'll expect you downstairs for breakfast directly.' She squeezed herself between him and the wall, her body pressing tightly against him for a brief instant before leaving the room.

Danny let loose a relieved sigh at her departure — she was certainly hot stuff. He made his way to the bathroom with his mind working overtime.

Sexy she might be, she probably put it about like that the whole time, but he wanted to keep his head, not like a certain bull.

They were a quarter of a mile from Woodcock's farm, when Ben Dooley blew out a cloud of cheroot smoke, and turned his head towards Jack.

'Well, that's what I got told in the "Coach and Horses" last night,' he growled. 'That your friend, Bobby, has been done for possessing cocaine.'

Jacky shuffled uneasily and carried on twiddling her fingers — she'd had her ear bent for the entire journey.

'An' it's the last time I tell you, Jacky, you keep her out of my 'ouse and you stay away from her – d'you 'ear girl?'

As Dooley's van swung into the muddy lane, which led to Woodcock's, a muffled defiant agreement emerged from her lips.

Dooley's old transit van spluttered to a halt in Woodcock's farmyard. He shoved his dark bristled chin at Jack, his eye rock-hard. 'I'm just gonna see Woodcock about the work he wants doing.' He slid back the van door and flicked out his cheroot stump. 'I won't be a minute, you start unloading the van.' He nodded to some outbuildings. 'You can put everything over there – I know we've got a couple of those doorways to brick up.'

Jack didn't reply as her father slammed the van door shut and strode off towards the farmhouse.

In response to Su-Ling's message, George Woodcock grunted and folded his newspaper, before slapping it down on the breakfast table. He pushed himself up from his chair, swung out his lame leg, and limped irritably towards the hallway door.

As Danny skipped off the bottom stair, he only just managed to stop himself from bumping into Woodcock.

The farmer slowed, nodded silently to him, and carried on to the front entrance – he'd told that bloody oaf, Dooley, time and again, to use the back door.

When Danny entered the kitchen, Su-Ling quickly

directed him to his chair, where a bowl of dry cornflakes was already waiting.

Elizabeth and Susan, who sat opposite him, giggled and whispered as they competed for their new lodger's attention.

Su-Ling glanced at him occasionally. Her smile was bland, there was a lustful gleam in her eyes.

As he ate, Danny laughed and teased the little girls, but it was an uneasy laugh. While he enjoyed Su-Ling's subtle advances, at the same time, trying to ignore them.

Dooley nodded at Woodcock. 'Thanks very much George, I could do with the extra work.'

Woodcock summoned Sweep with a shrill whistle, and walked away to sort out Danny's first job.

As she dropped the last two bricks on top of the stack, Jack turned back towards the van and stopped suddenly, a look of surprise spreading over her face when she saw Danny heading towards her.

Danny halted in his tracks, a few yards from Ben Dooley. His eyes met Jack's and lingered, a powerful magnetism kept them gazing at each other, unusual between two people who were only silently meeting each other, for the second time.

Chapter Four

'Jack! Jacky!'

For a few moments she stood transfixed by Danny's gaze, only her father's shout jolted her back to reality and she went to join him.

'Anyway Danny,' went on Dooley. 'I'm sorry about that duff job at the pigman's.' He lit a cheroot and turned to Jacky.

'Jacky, this is Danny Black, he . . .'

'I know who he is,' she broke in, 'I saw him at Stonewall House, you told me who he was then.'

Dooley snorted, irritably, but Danny stepped forward, smiling.

'Hello Jack, it's nice to meet you.' He held out his hand. She raised her eyebrows and stared at him in silence.

'Well!' her father barked. 'Answer the man.'

Jack sketched a curtsey. 'Oh sor-ry, forgive me for forgetting my manners.'

Dooley clenched his fists, his voice rising in anger. 'Don't you lip me girl or I'll bloody well . . .' he caught Danny's look of surprise at his sudden outburst and tried to compose himself.

Satisfied at having upset her father, Jack gripped Danny's hand and shook it firmly.

At that moment, her heart warmed to him. 'Hi!' she muttered. She was a little taken aback to realise how much nicer looking he was close to, and she contemplated his well-structured face with pleasurable appreciation.

As Dooley ran out the cement-mixer's electric lead towards the outhouse, Jack gave a quick, frank smile.

'I don't understand why you're here, my old man mentioned that you'd left Balchester.'

Danny laughed. 'I did, but the job turned out to be a bit too smelly. I was on my way back when I met George Woodcock. He's given me work – for now anyway.'

Jacky curled her lip. 'Huh!' she retorted. 'He's a weirdo, a perv.'

Danny raised his eyebrows. 'But he seemed . . .'

'Jacky!' Her father's loud shout intervened. 'A' you helping me or not?'

She half turned and nodded, in a distracted manner. 'OK! OK! I'm coming.' She flashed Danny a quick glance. 'I'll have to go, but I'll probably see you again while you're here – bye now.'

Turning, she sauntered reluctantly towards Dooley. Danny tugged thoughtfully at his ear lobe as he watched her walk away. 'See yous now,' he called. He gazed after her for several seconds before striding off towards the garden tool-shed. His first job for

Woodcock was to tend the allotment, pull carrots and cut a couple of cabbages.

By lunch-time, the hot sun had reached its zenith in the cloudless sky.

Danny was stripped to the waist, and as he hoed weeds, his glance slid past the red flowering runner bean frame, to the farmhouse kitchen beyond. The distance was not great, and without straining his eyes, he could clearly see, through the window, Su-Ling preparing a meal. Every so often he would catch her surreptitiously watching him. His heartbeat quickened as, for a brief instant, their eyes met and held.

Danny could feel the heat rising in his cheeks and, as Su-Ling broke the contact and disappeared from view, he gave a small sigh and carried on with his work.

With a satisfied grunt, Dooley slotted in the last brick to seal up the first doorway. He cut off the excess mortar and threw down his trowel. He glanced at his watch, it was 12.30, time for his dinner break.

By van, the Red Lion pub was only a couple of minutes away, and he always relished their beer and hot meat pies.

As Jack emerged from the side of the outhouse, with another bucket of water taken from the large barrel, Dooley walked to his van, lit a cheroot and opened the door.

'Jacky!' he called. 'You stay 'ere and load up the

other doorway for me, 'an clean up the mess around the finished one will you. I won't be long. I'll bring you back some crisps or somethin'.'

Jack put down the bucket and scowled. That meant he'd be away for at least an hour, and tipsy when he returned, which always made him worse.

Once her father's van had disappeared from sight, she sat down on a small pile of bricks and rested her back against the wall. She lit a cigarette and thoughtfully blew a stream of smoke-rings, determined to make the most of her father's absence. She closed her eyes and relaxed, listening to the merry chirping of birds, and wondered what her friend, Bobby, was up to at this moment in Balchester shopping centre.

After a while she roused herself and rose to her feet. She cleaned up the mortar droppings and bits of bricks around the doorway first, and then started loading up one of the two doorways in the larger of the outhouses.

She knew she had time on her hands, so left half of the bricks for later, and wandered inside the outhouse. It was empty, except for piles of well-used straw littered about, a broken pitchfolk and a few old horseshoes hanging on one of the walls. At one end, a few low brick walls formed cubicles, which had been used by animals at some time or another. But it was the other end which attracted Jack's attention. There was a padlocked solid wooden door, which surprised her a trifle, because there was no window on the outside to signify the room's existence.

She strolled over to the door and fingered the padlock; to her surprise, it sprang open. There was no door handle, so she unhooked the lock and swung open the heavy creaking portal. Cautiously, she peered into the small dark room. She listened intently for a moment, and satisfied that the room was empty, searched the nearby wall for a light switch.

She gave a small squeal as a large black spider scampered over her hand.

Locating the switch, she breathed a sigh of relief and turned on the bare light-bulb.

She peered in, then entered, closing the door quietly behind herself. As she stole around the room, she studied the stacks of old household items, some of which were pre-war. But it was the old chest, only partly visible beneath a couple of wooden chairs and several light shades, which caught her interest more than anything else. She quickly removed the chairs and shades, stooped, and raised the chest lid.

As she rummaged deep down beneath piles of old books, she came upon a neatly folded black blanket, engraved with a gold pattern. Lifting it out, she discovered there was something wrapped in it. Kneeling on the floor she unfolded it, to reveal what looked like a bishop's mitre, with a cat's eye in the centre. There was also a small blood-red cross, wrapped in a robe of mauve silk.

The gold engravings on the blanket could now be

clearly made out, they were *all* the signs of the Zodiac, engraved in a kind of esoteric pattern.

Jack gazed reflectively at the objects for a few moments. She chewed her bottom lip, as a chilly sensation crept up her spine, she'd seen things like this in lots of films about black magic and witchcraft. Then, with a mystified shrug, she wrapped everything up as it was before, and carefully packed it back in the chest.

As Danny Black pulled carrots, a sudden scratching behind him caused him to turn sharply, his fighting fists automatically at the ready.

He looked at the baby grey squirrel, grinned and relaxed. As it scampered along the top of the thin trellis fence it sensed Danny's swift movement and stopped dead, cheekily raising its paws to its mouth.

Sweep, who was padding in front of Woodcock towards the allotment, noticed the playful little squirrel. He broke into a fast run, reached the fence and tried to climb up it, barking and whining with frustration.

Danny watched amusedly as mother squirrel scurried along the fence top to collect her baby. They both streaked back along the wooden tightrope and disappeared up the trunk of a nearby silver birch tree.

Woodcock halted beside Danny and scanned the allotment. He mopped sweat from his temples with a white handkerchief, before taking the plastic bucket full of fresh carrots and cabbages which Danny offered him.

'You've done a good job,' he muttered and nodded towards the farmhouse. 'Just compost the rubbish, put the tools away and then come to the house – Su-Ling will have cooked you a meal timed for about 1.30.'

Danny smiled, as he wiped his brow with the back of his hand. 'Right, I'll make sure I'm there.'

Woodcock snapped his fingers sharply. 'Come Sweep.' Sweep, living in hope of the squirrel's return, reluctantly left the fence and loped after his master, who was going to inspect Ben Dooley's work.

Jack had just finished re-stacking the chairs and lampshades on top of the chest when the door suddenly creaked.

The light went off, plunging the room into darkness, except for a sliver of daylight from the doorway.

Jack went rigid with fear as a large shadow moved towards her. She nerved herself to spin round and gave a gasp of relief.

'Oh – oh it's only you Mister Woodcock. What did you turn the light out for? I thought, I thought . . .'

'Thought what young woman? About how you shouldn't be in here?'

His voice was low and somehow threatening, and Jack couldn't help but turn her face away from the distinct smell of garlic on his breath, as he loomed up close to her.

'This room is full of my father's personal things – not even the men who work for me are allowed in here – the door is always padlocked.'

Woodcock's tone sharpened as he went on. 'How did you get in here? Break the lock? In any case, your father's working on the outhouse door – not in here.'

She could see the whites of his eyes, and there was something wolfish about his stare that made her shudder.

'The door wasn't locked, honest, the padlock was only pushed to – not snapped,' she babbled. 'I was only looking around that's all – I'm sorry, OK? I'm sorry.'

She could hear Sweep's heavy panting.

Woodcock leaned over and placed a hand either side of where she was backed against the pile of chairs.

He was breathing deeply. 'Well now that you're here we shall make good use of the circumstances – you're a very pretty young woman.'

Jack laughed nervously. 'Th – that's very nice of you Mister Woodcock, but I've got to go and help my old man.'

'Come, come, you know what I want, don't you?'

His excited hands quickly closed in and slid over her small firm breasts, squeezing them painfully before travelling on down to her waist.

She stiffened and shook her head vigorously. She choked down her fear and yelled at him. 'No! stop it or I'll tell me dad.' She tried to push past him, but Woodcock was much taller and stronger, he had her cornered. As he probed and eagerly fingered her zip, a deep throaty chuckle escaped him. 'Are you asking a price? If so I'll pay handsomely for the full service.'

She gathered saliva and spat it in his face. 'Get stuffed you filthy pig.'

Woodcock wiped his face on his arm, his voice, still low, shook with temper. 'If you don't do what I want, I'll tell your father that I caught you snooping and stealing, and I'll give him no more work. I give him lots of work every year. I don't think he'd be very pleased – do you?' He leered down at her. 'Now,' he added sharply, 'why don't you be sensible? I won't hurt you.' He was shaking and panting hoarsely, as he clumsily tried to undo her zip. As her trousers' hook fastener snapped, she felt sick. She screamed loudly, dug her nails deep into the back of his hands, then lashed out hard with her right boot, catching him squarely on his lame leg.

'Piss off, you dirty old bastard, and I couldn't give a toss what you tell me ol' man.'

Woodcock roared and clawed painfully at his leg. For a few stunned seconds he gawped at Jack, his jaw sagging, and then he found his voice. 'You'll pay for that, you wait and see.' His face twisted with rage. 'Damned bitch.'

She pushed herself up and smacked her shoulder hard into his face, sending him crashing to the ground. 'Get stuffed, pervert!' She gripped her slipping pants and fled past Woodcock and Sweep, who seemed to think it was all a game. She tugged the heavy door to, picked up the padlock, hooked it through the hasp and staple and snapped it shut. She checked it, and hurriedly left the outhouse.

Once outside, she fastened her pants as best she could, and sped across the farmyard – next stop was going to be Balchester shopping centre and stuff Ben Dooley – and his work.

Her emotions finally overcame her, and as she ran tearfully past Danny, he threw out an arm to try and stop her.

'Hey! Jacky! what's wrong with yous – where are you going?'

Jacky lashed out blindly, knocked his arm out of the way and carried on running. 'Oh get lost, you're all the same, filthy pigs!'

To his surprise, she ran on out of the farmyard gate and into the lane.

His eyes hardening, he stared after her, silent with shock.

On the few occasions when he'd seen Jack, she'd never been so upset and hostile.

As he watched her disappear from view, Su-Ling ventured out of her kitchen. 'Danny,' she called. 'Oh Danny, dinner is ready.'

Startled, he glanced at his watch – it was well past 1.30. He dashed towards Su-Ling. 'I'm sorry I'm late, Su-Ling, I'm coming. Hell shit,' he muttered under his breath. 'My first day and I'm late for piggin' dinner – Woodcock is going to be pleased.'

Ben Dooley pushed his face close to the windscreen. His eyes widened then squinted in exasperation – it was definitely Jacky running towards him. He quickly wound down the window and slowed the van to a snail's pace. 'An' where the bleedin' 'ell d'you think you're going, girl?' he snarled.

She came to a halt, panting for breath. 'Balchester.'

'You're bloody not, get in the van.'

'No, I'm not going back to Timberdick's again – ever. He tried to rape me in the outhouse.'

Dooley smacked a fist onto the steering-wheel. 'Get – in – the – bloody – van! Never mind the bloody rape you little liar. If I lose this work I'll 'ave your flamin' guts – d'you 'ear!'

She shook a defiant head and sprinted away. 'I told you, I'm going to Balchester, so piss off and do what you want.'

Dooley stopped the van and half opened the door. 'Come back here, now!' he roared. 'I know damn well George Woodcock wouldn't lay a finger on you.'

Jack ignored him, quickly climbed over the closed gate, dropped down into the field beyond and raced off. She knew that a couple of fields away she'd come to the many acres of meadow land which fringed the city.

From there, to reach the busy streets, it was just a simple case of crossing the suspension bridge which spanned the River Denny. And, hopefully, she'd find her friend, Bobby Queen, in the 'Fox and Hounds' pub or the coffee house.

Dooley cursed her and slammed shut the van door before turning over the engine.

After pulling into Woodcock's yard, he climbed from his van and was walking briskly towards the cement-mixer, when he suddenly stopped in his tracks.

Woodcock's raging voice reached his ears, loud and clear.

'Dooley! Su-Ling! Danny!' There was loud banging, as he thumped and kicked at the padlocked door of the outhouse room.

'Get me out of here, someone – anybody!'

As Dooley looked aghast at the outhouse, his mouth dropped open. His thoughts flashed back to Jack's recent outburst. He slapped his forehead in despair. 'Oh shit! – I'll kill her,' he muttered, through gritted teeth. 'I'll flamin' well kill her.'

'Su-Ling! Dooley!' The shouts went on.

He raced towards the outhouse. 'Coming George, I'm coming.'

After a few seconds he reappeared and ran to the van to fetch his crowbar – Woodcock had the only padlock key in his pocket. Crimson in the face, Woodcock erupted from the outhouse room, followed by Sweep. He gripped Dooley's arm and pulled him close.

'Where's your daughter Dooley?'

Dooley looked down at the ground. 'She's gone to Balchester – George, she said that you . . .'

Woodcock stabbed his chest with a finger. 'She's robbed me Dooley, your damned daughter robbed me.'

Dooley's expression changed to one of incredulity. 'I don't believe it – she wouldn't dare.'

'Believe it! I caught her snooping in my dead father's belongings and things are missing, valuable things. I won't have thieves working for me. Finish bricking up the other doorway and then come to the house for your money. I won't call the police this time, but you'll do no more work for me.'

Dooley ground his teeth – he'd bloody well slaughter her.

'OK George.' He hung his head. 'And thanks for not getting the law, it's appreciated.'

Woodcock grunted and strode away towards the farmhouse for a very late lunch.

As he started throwing cement and sand into the cement-mixer, Dooley seethed. 'Oh you're in for it now my girl – God! – are – you – in – for – it!' he hissed.

To allow for Danny's vegetarian diet, Su-Ling had prepared him extra vegetables. He'd already polished off the last potato, as Woodcock took off his shoes and drew on his slippers.

As Su-Ling put his meal before him, he offered no response to her question as to where he'd been. He ate silently, thoughtfully rolling every pea and sprout with his fork before devouring them.

Danny, now up to apple-pie and custard, felt a shade uncomfortable at the silence, so looked up at Su-Ling and remarked, 'I didn't notice your little girls when I walked over.'

She picked up his empty plate and turned towards the sink. 'No, Ament has taken them to the River Denny to feed the swans, and then she's taking them shopping. Ament's our au-pair, she's Egyptian and very good with the children. She's also very beautiful. As well as that, she's an accomplished falconer, so don't be surprised if you see her in the fields with her hawks.'

Danny listened intently. He scooped up a spoonful of pie and cast a thoughtful glance at Woodcock. A young lovely Thai wife, a beautiful Egyptian au-pair, God, this bloke was lucky, considering his age and his ugly mug.

Woodcock cut and stabbed a piece of beef with his fork.

'Danny!' he ordered. 'When you've finished your meal, you can spend the afternoon preparing an area of ground by the outhouse for concreting – we'll put your talents to the test. I'll be there myself, I've a new padlock hasp to fix on one of the doors, so I'll mark it out for you.'

Danny nodded and carried on eating, his thoughts returning to the enigma of Jack's recent strange behaviour towards him. When he had finished, he enquired, with a diffident air, 'I was wondering –

would it be all right if I give my friend, Freddy Haddock a ring?' As he looked at Woodcock, he corrected himself. 'Merlin, I mean.'

Woodcock stopped eating and forced a tiny smile. 'Ah, your friend with the peculiar name. Su-Ling, show Danny where the phone is please.'

'Thanks,' said Danny, as Su-Ling beckoned him to follow her. Woodcock carried on eating.

Su-Ling led the way to the opulent lounge. As she pointed to the telephone, she smiled, that seductive smile, which he was beginning to find so very difficult to resist.

He thanked her, and made a point of gently placing his hand on her shoulder. She made no protest, and a dangerous excitement surged through him. He'd only ever made love to English women. What would it be like with this exotic foreigner, he wondered?

As Su-Ling backed slowly away, closing the doors as she went, Danny couldn't help but notice the flush of colour which touched her cheeks, giving them a soft delicate glow.

He took out the grubby scrap of paper with Merlin's telephone number and address on it, reached for the phone and then dialled, hoping his friend would answer.

He tapped his fingers impatiently on the glass-topped coffee-table. At last, on the seventh ring, Merlin responded breathlessly, his words coming out in short bursts.

'Haddock here – Fredrick Haddock, Merlin to my

friends. Army number 3653594 – who's speaking please?'

'S'me Freddy.'

'Who's me?'

'Me, Danny Black – Harry's grandson.'

'Harry who?'

Danny slapped his forehead. 'Harry! who yous was in the bloody war with.'

'Aaaah, that Harry – yes yes I remember now, how are you young feller?'

'Fine, fine, you . . .'

'You'll have to speak up I can hardly hear you.'

Danny flung an exasperated glance at the fancy artexed ceiling. 'Fine! fine! I'm doing fine. You told me to keep in touch after my grandad's funeral, so I am.'

'Yes I remember.'

'Well I'm living here in Balchester now. I'm working on a farm, living in. So I thought I'd give you a ring to see when I can meet you.' He paused a minute. 'A' yous all right Merlin? you sound puffed out.'

'You disturbed me, I was upstairs researching – damned stairs, I should move to a bungalow.'

'Researching?'

'Yes, yes dear boy – Egyptian mythology and witchcraft, they're my hobbies, great fun, along with looking after my roses.'

'Sounds charming.'

'Quite exciting actually.'

Danny heard the distinctive slurp of a drink down

the phone, followed by the smacking of lips. Merlin went on. 'Haven't you heard yet?'

'What?'

'There's been rumours spreading like wildfire here about satanic goings-on.'

'Yeah, I did hear a bit about it when I was working on a demolition job on the other side of Balchester. Don't know much about it though.'

Merlin coughed, cleared his throat and slurped again.

'Fascinating stuff. Right! when are you popping over to see me? – I think you've got my address, I'm in every day next week.'

'OK I'll call one night after work.'

'Right, I'll expect you next week then. I'm off now back up those damned stairs to my Scotch and mythology.'

Danny laughed. 'Whisky! at this time of the day! yuk!'

'Medicinal dear boy, purely medicinal.' He forced a small dry cough. 'Bye now.'

'But Freddy, what time shall . . .'

The phone clicked and burred. Danny hung up and smiled. He shook his head – it was nice to talk to old Merlin again.

'That's right Danny,' added Dooley, as he turned from his bricklaying. 'Nine years ago Woodcock had nothing. He left Balchester after his first wife died, mysteriously, I might add, and flew off to Thailand for three months. Then we heard on the grapevine that he'd moved on to Egypt for another couple of months. Next thing, he arrives back home with Su-Ling as his wife, and forks out thousands of pounds for this place – no-one could believe it.'

Dooley shielded his mouth with his hand, looked carefully around and whispered. 'Rumour 'as it that Su-Ling was a prossy in one of those big Bangkok hotels, you know, where they dance naked on the stage an' all that.'

Danny was enthralled. 'What about the Egyptian girl?' he asked.

'Well, all we know is that two years later she appeared as a seventeen-year-old au pair for their first kid – she's been here ever since, playing with her bloody hawks.' He stroked his stubble thoughtfully. 'I've noticed though, that sometimes she disappears for a couple of days and she always has a briefcase with a small luggage case. You know, the type you see the gangsters carrying their banknotes in.'

Dooley pointed his trowel at a small pile of half-bricks. 'Pass me one of those, will you Dan.'

Danny obeyed, swooped and passed him a half-brick. Then he asked, in puzzled tones, 'Where'd Jack go? She flew past me, and it looked like she'd been crying.'

Dooley scowled at him as he placed his spirit-level against the wall. Before answering, he straightened the small lump in his brickwork by knocking it out with his trowel handle.

'She went home,' he snapped. 'She said she felt

bad – I saw her in the lane on my way back from the pub.'

Danny looked perplexed. 'She ran bloody fast for someone who was supposed to be ill,' he mused. He didn't push the issue, but when Woodcock came to mark out the area of ground which was to be dug out and hard-cored, Danny noticed that not a word was spoken between him and Dooley.

As he held the end of the measuring-tape for Woodcock, Danny's eye was caught by three full-blown yellow dandelions. He thought to himself how cheerful a colour they were and how, if people didn't know they were regarded as weeds, and had to buy them at a florist's shop, they would value their beauty a lot more.

As the jukebox in the 'Fox and Hounds' thundered out rave music, Jack searched for a glimpse of Bobby Queen through the haze of melting chocolate-flavoured smoke – the dopeheads, who were littered about in various stages of oblivion, were in full swing this afternoon.

Fat Man, the red-headed slob, who happened to be the son of a local councillor, was the resident pusher, and revelled in his position of authority over the mindless doped zombies. He swigged his double vodka and tonic and made a beeline for Jacky Dooley. The gold rings on his fingers glinted, as he waved his arms frantically and shouted loudly over the noise to her. 'Jack! Jacky darling! it's so nice to see you.' He straightened his blue-spotted cravat and slid a hand inside his expensive leather coat. 'Can I interest you in an eighth, darling, it's about time you learnt how to live it up a bit.'

He laughed, his wide mouth spreading from ear to ear. He swept the room with his small chubby hand. 'See, see how happy everybody is – pure paradise, now, can I . . .'

Jack waved him aside, her gaze continually searching for Bobby until it came to rest on the long bar.

Pete, behind the bar, was probably the only clean person in the place, apart from herself.

Her glance swung briefly to Fat Man's grinning face.

'Stick your shit up your arse Fat Man – I've got better things to spend my money on than stupid cannabis,' she snapped.

Fat Man chuckled and staggering slightly, spread his hands pleadingly. 'Scag! Jack? What about some Scag – it's the best heroin, and for you . . .' He bowed, and swept his arm to the dirty floor, as low as his rippling paunch would allow. He sniggered, as he eyed Jack's attire. 'For you, such a distinguished lady, a wrap at rock-bottom price.' His laugh was contemptuous. 'Or perhaps you should see Miko for a tab of acid for washers.' He pirouetted in a ridiculous fashion.

'Oooh, we would be a devil then – wouldn't we?' Jack grimaced, pushed past him and headed for the bar. 'Get stuffed, dickbrain,' she mocked. 'You know I don't touch the shit!'

Fat Man turned and wobbled away. He might have lost this time, but he'd nail her, even if it meant a free sample – expensive but . . . it'd be worth it in the long term.

Jack went on and shook her head at poor Joey, a matchstick of a heroin addict, with two till ten feet, who in all weathers wore an ankle-length black raincoat. For shoplifting it was most accommodating – and every little helped. 'Hi Jack – Jack . . .' He staggered past, his eyes mesmerised by the two wall lights that seemed to be dancing all over the place.

'Hi Joey.' She sighed. 'Take care, man.' Too late, he was already swimming with the sea of dope smoke.

She ignored the slobbering greasebag, with his hand up the giggling blonde's miniskirt, and leaned on the bar. Pete, the hefty bearded barman ambled over. 'How are you doing Jack – want a drink?'

'No ta Pete, I'm only looking for Bobby Queen – she been in?'

'Don't know luv, honest. I've only been on an hour. Hang on though, Miko might know, he looks like he's been here a while.' He walked along to the motionless heap slouched over the bar. He gripped Miko, who was on cloud twenty-two, by his blond spiky hair, and jerked his head back. 'Hey Miko, you seen Bobby today?'

Miko wasn't amused, just incapable. 'Hey fuck you man, what the shit d'you think you're doin?'

'Watch my lips – have – you – seen – Bobby Queen today?'

'I think I sold her a couple of tabs.'
'When?'
'I dunno maybe a couple of hours ago.'
Jacky shoved her nose close to his wobbly head. His eyes were spinning like Catherine wheels. 'D'you know where she went?'
'P – piss off an' leave me alone.'
Pete shook Miko's head again. 'Come on, come on, think man, while you're still on this planet.'
'I think she was with Adder, I – dunno, somethin' about a dump.'
Jack waved a hand at Pete. 'S'OK Pete I know where they'll be. Ta mate.'
Pete dropped Miko's head. It cracked on the bar, causing Miko to groan before taking off back to his planet.
'Bye Sweetie Pie,' Fat Man called, as Jack went weaving through the staggering and loitering figures.
She met his sickly grin.
'Next time my little lady,' he shouted. 'Next time – eh?'
Jack mouthed an obscenity and waved two fingers high in the air. She closed the door, leaving the ranting acid music and swirling drugged smoke behind.
Outside, in the bustling street, she stopped and laughed to herself at the sight of the babbling Yankee and Chink tourists, whose cameras were eagerly clicking away as they photographed the

sixteenth century pub. If only they knew, she thought, if only they bloody well knew.

She set off briskly for the canal dump.

Chapter Five

As Woodcock handed Dooley his day's payment, the stony silence that followed their short farewell conversation was for him, one of smug satisfaction, but for Ben Dooley it served to increase his anger against Jacky.

He kicked despondently at a stone with his boot. 'I'll be off then, George,' he grunted. 'I'm just sorry we're having to part on these terms.'

Woodcock nodded, and as Dooley walked away from the farmhouse he closed the back door and smiled triumphantly to himself – he'd teach Dooley's brat to reject his advances – and as the lustful devil himself he would, eventually, one day, enter her, and she'd feel the full might of his penis – by God! she would.

As he walked towards his van, Dooley counted his money from Woodcock, tucked it into his pocket, and then glanced at his watch. It was only half past four, so he had a good hour to enjoy a beer in the 'Lord Tennyson' before he went home to tackle Jacky – she'd probably still be in Balchester now anyway.

The 'Lord Tennyson' was a large low-roofed pub, near to the canal dump. It was split into two rooms, the bar-room being a lot smaller than the lounge.

Dooley's haunt was always the bar, where he revelled in playing the big shot whenever he had plenty of money in his pocket.

By half past five, he was merry, after topping up on his dinner-time session, and Jack's behaviour at Woodcock's farm only occasionally crossed his mind, that was, until Docker and his two cronies swaggered into the bar.

Docker was of medium height, but stocky. He was an ex-murderer, who'd served his time, and then, at the age of thirty, had moved onto the Bedford estate. As he stood legs wide apart, at the bar, he stared at his reflection in the large mirror and ran his hands through his greying hair down to the tip of his neat pony-tail. He nodded at Boots, his right hand man, a tall bald wedge-shaped negro, who always wore cowboy boots, hence his nickname.

Boots quickly ordered a round of drinks.

Brown Trilby, with the Mexican moustache, followed up by purchasing three batches.

Docker and his cronies never worked but lived well – drinking at dinner-time but at night eating at the best Indian and Chinese restaurants in Balchester. It was rumoured across the estate, that on his arrival in Bedford, Docker had soon set up a small protection racket with the smaller shops on the estate, and in some of the shops which fringed

Balchester – but as yet, nobody had dared to tackle him about it.

He turned and leaned his back on the bar, swigging his lager at the same time. There was an impish smile on his face as his gaze swept the room. Yes, Dooley would be easy meat for a bit of fun, to set the early night rolling.

Dooley was now in a reasonably happy mood, and noisily banging down his dominoes. He was laughing loudly and in mid-conversation, when Docker's fearful voice caused a silence to descend on the bar. 'Well I reckon the way she dresses, Dooley's daughter's either a lesbian or a badly got-up transvestite.' Boots, whose gruff voice always tailed off with a high squeak, chipped in by snapping his fingers. 'Correctsville Docker.'

'Dead on Dock' agreed Brown Trilby.

Dooley sensed that all eyes were on him. He desperately tried to keep his own conversation going, but to no avail. His face had whitened, and his knees knocked together. How he wished now that he'd never shouted his mouth off on previous occasions in the Tennyson, he was no match for a hard case like Docker.

Docker nodded to his mates, so that they followed him further along the bar to settle within a couple of yards of Dooley's table – his evening was just beginning.

Daisy Dooley threw the first log of the evening onto the fire to back up the coal. The late summer nights were becoming chilly, so the grate was once again in use.

Sophie was sprawled out on the fluffy white rug in front of the crackling fire, with her chin cupped in her hands, watching TV.

Stumpy sat next to her, roasting himself.

Rosie, opposite, stretched out on the red settee, flicking through the daily tabloid, occasionally muttering some comment about the contents.

'Dad's late Mum,' Sophie remarked, her eyes glued to the TV game show.

Daisy sucked the last puff from her cigarette and tossed the butt in the fire. 'He won't be home now, luv, he's been paid off by Woodcock,' she observed, blowing smoke at the ceiling.

'He'd have been home at half five as usual otherwise. He'll be getting well oiled in either the Tennyson or the Lowfield now. I thought Jacky would have come home for her dinner though.'

She sighed and eased herself up out of the chair. 'I'll turn off the oven before their food dries up.'

After the main news, the regional news began and the three of them were suddenly riveted as the newsreader, looking grave, announced in solemn tones, 'News just in. A baby's body has been found in the tidal waters of the River Denny at Balchester. This is the second baby's corpse to be found in the Balchester area during the last two years. The police are not yet ready to reveal whether, as previously, satanic practices are involved. We will try to bring you more on that story later. And now . . .'

Daisy shuddered. 'Oh my God!' she gasped.

'Gory!' exclaimed Sophie, fascinated.

Rosie just felt nauseated. 'What kind of people can just dump a baby in a river like that?'

Daisy shuddered again and shook her head. 'It'll be those devil worshippers at their tricks, last time they drained that baby's blood and then flung it in the canal.'

Sophie eagerly added her bit. 'I heard at school that they drink the baby's blood and other creatures' as well, at special parties at midnight.'

Rosie leant over and slapped the child's head with her newspaper. 'Oh be quiet you, and watch your game show.' The squeaking dancing white mice in black top hats, bouncing across the TV set in the cheese advert, made them all laugh and lightened the horror of the bulletin.

But Daisy knew there would be little else talked about at the post office on Monday morning.

As he finished off his training session behind the milking parlour, Danny still thought he had a little time left before tea. With a hiss, he let Steeleye fly for the third time, and followed through. His target, an empty milk bottle which stood on top of an old milk churn, shattered into fragments. He turned quickly at the solitary hand-clapping from behind him to find Su-Ling, who was gazing at him intently. She smiled, and walked slowly up to him, her eyes roving over his dark well-muscled body. She blew a silent whistle and rubbed her delicate fingers along Steeleye.

'I've been watching you from behind the parlour wall for a full five minutes, Danny. You fight well – martial arts? I've seen many kinds in my own country.' She glanced back at Steeleye. 'But this, I've seen no such weapon in Thailand, and it looks so lethal.'

She stooped, picked up his shirt and passed it to him. 'Here, you'd better put this on, the evening air is cooling, you'll catch a chill.'

As he slipped his shirt on, Danny explained to her about his grandfather's especially adapted crowbar, and the way he'd used it in the war to kill the enemy, quickly and silently. She looked him squarely in the eyes, her beautiful face hardening. 'Have you ever used . . . ?' she began.

Danny laughed, and cut her short with, 'No, I only use it for fun, I couldn't hurt anybody with it – it's good for my training and . . .' He spun and twirled Steeleye at mind boggling speed. 'I think I'm getting the hang of the old lump of steel now.'

As she smiled, Su-Ling's gaze travelled again over Danny's body and came to rest on his thick jet-black curls. She gave a small sigh and linked her arm through his. 'I'm glad you wouldn't hurt anybody with it. Anyway, tea's ready, so I came looking for you.'

Danny packed Steeleye away into his empty rucksack – it made a handy carrying bag. 'I'm sorry Su-Ling, late for dinner, now late for tea.'

She laughed. 'Don't worry Danny, you'll get used to our mealtimes. Running the farm, we have to be punctual. By the way,' she went on, 'I'll sort out some empty cans for you from the kitchen to train with, it'll be a lot safer for the animals. Perhaps you could clear the glass up after tea.'

Danny nodded guiltily. 'Yes – sorry.'

Suddenly Su-Ling pointed excitedly aloft. 'Look! there's Horus, Ament's falcon, he's about to strike.'

Danny stared skyward in amazement as Horus flew high. But his stomach churned, as the speeding falcon swooped down, its vicious talons gripping the unsuspecting woodpigeon. A cloud of feathers fluttered away. Death was instantaneous.

Horus dropped from the sky with the kill – a perfect example of nature at its most co-ordinated and yet most savage.

Danny's voice was tinged with bitterness. 'I just hope she's going to eat it, nobody ought to kill for pleasure.'

Su-Ling cast him a concerned look. She had seen it all before and regarded it with oriental fatalism.

He shrugged sheepishly, slightly embarrassed at the way his emotion had taken over. 'I – I'm sorry Su-Ling I shouldn't have said that – after all it's your farm,' he apologised. 'Shall we go for tea now? I'm starving.'

She smiled and squeezed his arm. 'It's all right Danny, don't worry, I understand.'

As they set off, she glanced up into his fierce, hurt

eyes – admiration swept through her. 'You like nature, don't you Danny?' she asked gently.

He managed a grin. 'I s'pose so.'

'Nature can be cruel as well as beautiful,' she went on. 'Not long before you came here, a lone fox broke into our coops. It ripped the heads off twenty chickens, just for fun, and escaped!'

Danny looked at her and laughed. 'I see what you mean.'

As they reached the end of the milking parlour wall Su-Ling halted him, an uncertain expression on her face. 'Will you be going out this Wednesday night, Danny?' she asked.

'No, I don't think so. I'll be going into Balchester on Tuesday night though, I'm going to visit my friend, Freddy Haddock – why?'

'Well, it's Ament's night off on Wednesdays and George goes . . .' She paused, then giggled. 'George goes to his secret club.'

'Secret club!' exclaimed Danny.

'Yes, he has done for years now, and I still don't know what it is – probably the Buffs or Masons or something.'

'So?'

'Well, it'd be nice if you were home, neither of them come back until well after midnight, it gets a little bit lonely when the children have gone to bed so I thought perhaps we could have a drink and a chat.' The invitation in her eyes was unmistakable. 'Well – would you like to?' she murmured.

Danny hesitated, sensing danger, but her nearness

was intoxicating. He nodded in agreement. 'Okay, thanks – I only drink beer though.'

Su-Ling laughed. 'Don't worry, we have a good stock of cans in.' Pleased at Danny's acceptance she probed on a little. 'Were you ever married Danny?'

'Yep, I'm still in the middle of getting divorced.'

'Oh I'm sorry – I didn't know.'

'S'all right, it was my own fault – messing around with other women.' He shook his head and sighed. 'She was the best,' he continued sadly, 'and I didn't realise until it was too late. We got married when we were just eighteen.'

Su-Ling smiled and squeezed his arm tighter. Her exotic perfume drifted up to Danny's nostrils.

'Have you had girlfriends since your marriage broke up?' she queried.

'Not really, nothing serious.' He became pensive. 'Me Grandad Harry died recently as well, I loved him a lot.' He shrugged and gave vent to a despondent sigh. 'A lot's happened lately, with one thing and another.'

'I see.' Her voice took on a subtly caressing note. 'But surely, a good-looking, hot-blooded man like you must need some – outlet?'

She fluttered her long eyelashes and Danny felt the warmth of her body pressed fleetingly against his own. Hypnotised by her liquid dark eyes he felt his pulses racing.

Su-Ling decided to speak out. 'Danny,' she began, 'I am also in need of an – outlet. Since George's accident with the bull, he's lost interest – in me, at any rate.'

As he listened, Danny felt the sweat breaking out on his brow, Su-Ling was hard to resist and it had been a long time . . .

'Call it feminine intuition if you like, but I know he's seeing other women – young women.' Her tone was charged with bitterness. 'George lusts after young girls, he did in Bangkok. This secret club he visits is probably an illegal brothel, or sleazy massage parlour.' She gave an exasperated sigh at Danny's rigid stance. She loosened her hold on his arm and he distanced himself a little. She fervently hoped he would be rather more forthcoming on Wednesday night.

'Hadn't we better go in?' he hinted.

They walked back to the farmhouse, side by side, but not touching.

Danny had washed and changed and was leaving his room when he stopped, stunned, at his first sight of Ament's beauty. She was also leaving her room to join the family for tea. She was dressed all in red, a colour which set off to perfection her long jet-black hair, cut in ancient Egyptian style and crowned with a pure white band. Around her slender neck were strings of brightly coloured beads.

As he gazed into her long dark eyes his heart thudded. Her lovely face looked so gentle, yet, he reflected, she would command her falcons to kill just for the pleasure of it. He introduced himself politely. 'Hello, I'm Danny . . .'

'Ament! Ament!' As he painfully swung his leg to the top of the stairs Woodcock broke in on their brief encounter. 'Are you coming down to tea Ament?' he asked, somewhat breathlessly. 'The children are waiting for you.'

Ament's expression had changed, it was as if, thought Danny, the sound of his voice had transfixed her.

Ignoring Danny, she moved towards the staircase, almost as if she was sleepwalking.

'Are you coming as well, Danny?' Woodcock enquired. 'Su-Ling has prepared you a salad.'

Danny, puzzled by Ament's strange behaviour, followed them downstairs to tea.

Bobby Queen, hefty and mousy-haired, clad in blue denim dungarees, sat on the canal dump beneath the weeping willow trees, singing along to Adder's small portable radio. She'd taken her tab of L.S.D. off Miko, and was swigging lager from a can.

Adder, a small wiry youth, dressed from silly, peaked hat to booted feet in black leather, was lying on his back, drinking from a bottle of strong brown ale. He was buzzing nicely on an ecstasy pill; with Daddy owning a few tailors' shops he could well afford them. He always liked to get tuned up for a Saturday night. He shoved his dark glasses up the bridge of his bony nose and waved a gloved hand at

Bobby. His high-pitched slurred voice was threatening. 'Why don't you admit it, Bobby, you only knock around with us because you're gay and want to screw Jack.'

'Oh get knotted, Pea-brain,' she hissed. 'The difference between us is that I admit I'm a lesbian and that I love Jack. And, I admit I like a blow – but you won't tell anybody that you're a smack-head.'

Adder's long thin tongue constantly flicked in and out. He swigged again at the bottle. 'Yeah, and she doesn't want to know you because she's not gay. She'll come around to my way of thinking soon, you just wait and see – I've always fancied Jack, and I'll have her.'

Jacky cursed loudly as she pushed her way through the head-high undergrowth, which flourished in the rich dredgings from the canal. She entered the clearing beneath the giant willow trees, still swiping at the many flies that buzzed about her. She flopped down onto the grass, in between Bobby and Adder. 'Hi you two, I thought I'd find you here.' She leaned across and grabbed one of Bobby's cans of lager.

'Give us a can then Bob, I'm skint aren't I, I haven't got a bean.'

'Oh! just help yourself,' Bobby invited, her pulse throbbing unevenly at Jack's presence. 'Jack?' she drawled persuasively. 'Will you come to my bedsit tonight after the pub shuts? I've got a couple of good videos. You've promised for ages that you'll come.'

Adder stopped swigging from his bottle, raised his head, and glared at Bobby.

Jack pulled open the can tab, releasing a rush of gas, and drank. She shook her head. 'No I can't, Bobby, I'm stopping in tonight – me an' our Rosie are going to help me mam start the decorating, another time maybe.'

Adder smiled smugly to himself and dropped back down – he'd make his move for Jack now!

As Bobby sighed, sulked and took another swig, Adder gleefully kicked his legs high in the air. 'A knock-back eh Bobby? hee hee.'

Jack's eyes flashed as she turned on Adder with sudden savagery. 'Leave Bobby alone Arsehole, I meant what I said – I'm helping me Mam with the decorating.'

Adder muttered a stream of obscenities as he climbed to his feet, his head rocking in unison with the music from the radio clamped to his ear. He was already beginning to fly higher than a wild kite.

'Hey Jack, why don't you come with me for an hour?' he suggested eagerly. 'I'll take you to the "Lowfield Hotel", I'll buy you some beers.'

He dug into his pocket and brought out a wad of notes. 'See, loads of lovely bread, Babe.'

He dropped to his knees and begged mockingly. 'Go on Jack, you know I love you and all that – please!'

Bobby, who still sat sulking, suddenly cracked a smile at Jacky's answer. 'No ta, Adder, I'd sooner stop here with Bobby for a bit.'

Adder's lip curled. 'Great!' he snarled, his tongue shooting in and out. He drained his bottle and hurled it towards the canal. Then he turned sharply and spat. 'A bit, a bit, eh! – well you said it girl, dirty bitch!'

His insinuation infuriated Jacky. 'For a while, I meant,' she snapped. 'Not for sex – pervert!'

Adder wobbled away swearing fluently.

'We'll see you on Tuesday night,' called Jack. 'We'll be in town doing the usual rounds.'

'Bloody queers,' came the mumbled response. He disappeared into the undergrowth.

As Bobby's hand slid across Jack's shoulder, she smiled triumphantly. 'Thanks Jack,' she purred seductively. 'I knew you'd pick me.'

Jack pulled away sharply, knocking Bobby's arm aside. 'Leave it out Bob,' she flared. 'You know I'm not Butch.'

'Can't we just try Jack? – please! We'd make a great team us two.'

Jack shook her head decisively. 'Leave it Bobby, no! and this is the last time I'm telling you – if you come on to me again that's it, our friendship's over.'

The tense silence which followed was short-lived, and once they'd downed the final can, they set off together across the dump in a better humour.

After they'd climbed the last of the stone steps that led from the canal tow-path to the road bridge, they quickly made their arrangements for Tuesday night, and went their separate ways, Bobby to the 'Lord Tennyson' and Jacky off home.

As she paused by the vicarage Jack slowed, leaned over the low brick garden wall, and looked at the velvety red roses still in full bloom. A bunch of such pretty flowers would no doubt cheer Daisy up. Being very careful of the sharp thorns, she snapped off five, and holding them tenderly, hurried on home.

She was just turning the door key in the lock when their neighbour's front door opened. With a broad playful grin, Lance, the young man next door, proudly displayed his newest pair of coloured Hawaiian boxer shorts.

Lance was a year younger than Jacky and had always idolised her, even as a child. He worked hard at the local steelworks, dressed tidily, and didn't smoke or drink. Several times he'd tried to date her, but, being so shy and quiet, he'd never succeeded.

Many a time she'd been in Bedford and Balchester, only to find Lance not far away, as if protecting her, and she felt the familiar sadness at refusing him.

Stumpy had heard Jack's key turn in the lock and ran barking to greet her. Giving him a pat, she tugged off her boots, grabbed a can of lager from the fridge and went in the lounge.

Three heads turned quickly as she entered. She waved a welcoming hand, and going up to Daisy, thrust the roses at her. 'For you Mam, with love,' she said, and gave her a hug, then turned to leave the room again. 'Just going for a shower,' she explained.

As she went out, Daisy sighed, then sniffed at the sweet-smelling roses, while Rosie turned back to her tabloid. Sophie stared again at the TV and Stumpy settled down in front of the fire.

Chapter Six

Storm clouds had gathered over Balchester and rain was falling heavily.

It was nearly midnight, and the four Dooley females were snuggled up in their beds, asleep.

Only Stumpy stirred, occasionally scratching at his blanket, and chewing on an old bone, in his basket under the stairs.

The peace of the household was shattered by the arrival home of a very drunk Ben Dooley. He had no van, and being on foot, he was soaked to the skin and fuming. Muttering loudly, he rooted out his keys, and, after a string of savage curses, finally managed to unlock the front door. Flinging it open, he staggered into the hallway and stood there swaying, flat cap tipped back, his unshaven face distorted with rage. Turning, he kicked the front door shut, rattling the bunch of keys in the lock.

'Where, w-where is she?' he roared, 'I know she's 'ere, s-somewhere.' He groped for the stair rail. 'Breathalised! – I've been bloody well b-breathalised through that little bitch, an' I got this through her and all.' He stabbed above his sore black eye with a finger. It was obvious that Docker and company had had their fun in the Lord Tennyson.

'And I've had to walk home all the way from the cop-shop in that flamin' lot.' He flicked drops of rain from off his face. His voice rose higher with fury. 'I – I'll kill her, I – mean it, I'll damn well kill 'er.'

Dooley's loud rage woke the whole household and set everybody cringing with alarm beneath their duvets.

Jacky shot up in bed as the bedroom door crashed open. Rosie followed suit a split second later.

Dooley's fingers pounded on the wall until he found the switch and banged on the light.

Jack's eyes widened and her pale lips trembled at the spectacle he presented.

He staggered up to her bed and pointed a shaking finger. His soaking wet hair was plastered in thick black strands across his forehead, his expression was ferocious. 'I've lost m-me bleedin' driving licence through you, girl – an' me work on Woodcock's farm.'

She cowered slightly, but shouted back. 'How d'you make that out? The dirty old pervert tried to rape me!'

'He did so Dad!' Rosie bravely spoke up. 'She told me about it as soon as we were on our own.'

Dooley swayed menacingly. 'Bullshit! you're a bloody liar, same as her. She's a little thief, an' probably steals for dope anyway – slut! George Woodcock told me so.'

He advanced closer, his eyes glaring malevolently. 'I'll bloody well teach you once an' for all girl.'

He lunged at Jack with clawing hands, but she threw out a fist in self-defence, hitting Dooley full on the mouth.

He stopped, momentarily shocked, flaming eyes staring at her. He wiped his bleeding lip with his hand and glanced at the blood. 'You fuckin' little bitch!'

As his hands gripped her like a vice, she squealed and wriggled frantically, but to no avail, her cries went unheeded. Her nightie was ripped to shreds, revealing her small bare breasts, as he dragged her from the bed.

When Rosie leapt to her defence, Dooley turned on her, cupped his right hand under her chin and flung her back onto her mattress. 'It's none of your business, you!' he thundered, and grabbed Jack again. 'I'm sick to death of f-fellas in the alehouse taking the mick out of me b – because of you, Jack, – d'you hear?'

He dragged her, screaming and cursing, towards the bedroom door. 'So you want to look like a l-lad do you? – then you flamin' well will.'

Daisy suddenly appeared on the scene. 'Stop it, Ben! stop it! You'll kill her,' she cried, distraught.

As Dooley dragged Jack out onto the landing, Daisy grabbed desperately at his arm to try and pull him off.

'Get off me woman!' he roared. With a loud

smack off the back of his hand, he sent her spinning and her small frame thudded against the wall.

Rosie and Sophie, frightened but determined, came rushing to their mother's aid.

Outside, the storm had reached its peak, thunder crashed and lightning lit up the house like a disco.

Stumpy was going wild, yelping and barking furiously, as he leapt hysterically up and down the stairs.

Sophie was white-faced and staring, she'd heard her father in a temper before, but she'd never seen him like this. As she looked at Jack, she burst into tears. 'Stop it, Dad! stop it,' she wailed. But her pleas fell on deaf ears.

Dooley gripped the stair rail with one hand, and with the other, grabbed Jack by her long wavy hair and dragged her, fighting and screaming, down to the hallway. He heaved her into the kitchen and punched on the light switch. His gaze settled on a pair of sharp scissors dangling from a brass hook. He tore them from the hook and rammed Jacky down hard into a chair. She was icy cold and huddled down, covering her breasts with her arms.

'S-so you wanna look like a l – lad do yer? Then the fuck! you will.'

He swayed, grinned devilishly and started snipping.

Daisy held Sophie back in the downstairs hallway, as Jack's beautiful dark tresses fell to the floor.

'Take – your – hands – off – her, you filthy pig!' she yelled at Dooley, sobs almost choking her.

Rosie pushed in front of them and gazed, horrified, at Jack.

'You lousy bastard,' she attacked Dooley. 'You rotten drunken swine!'

Jacky had now realised that her bullying father wasn't going to beat her to a pulp, so for the sake of the others, she bravely composed herself. She sat up rigidly, raised her head high and spat defiance. 'Don't worry, Mam, I'm all right – you and Rosie take Sophie back to bed – I'm okay, Soph' don't worry.'

Her voice hardened. 'Go on, Father,' she goaded, 'go on – cut the bleeding lot off.'

Dooley, taken aback by her contempt, grunted and snipped off one last chunk of hair. Tossing the scissors onto the table, he staggered back a couple of paces, and admired his handiwork. 'There!' he growled. 'Now you look like a bloody lad.'

Turning, he snarled at Rosie and then tottered off into the lounge, leaving a trail of muddy boot prints behind him. He flopped down into his favourite TV chair, stretched out, and fell into a drunken stupor.

Rosie heaved an exasperated sigh, quickly slipped off her dressing-gown and wrapped it around Jack's chilly shoulders, fastening it gently to cover her breasts. 'There you go, Sweetheart,' she whispered, and stroked a tender hand over the jagged mess of what was left of Jack's hair. Sliding a comforting arm around her sister's shoulders she spoke soothingly to the girl who by now, had drifted into a state of mild shock. 'Don't worry, love, it's not that bad, come on to bed, I'll have a go at it in the morning. I'm sure I can make it look something like.'

She helped Jack upstairs and tucked her in, like a child. Sophie sobbed herself to sleep while Daisy lay in bed, staring into the darkness, wondering what on earth was to become of them all. Outside, the storm rumbled on – and on.

The following Tuesday evening found Danny Black wielding the large iron knocker on Merlin's front door. While he waited, he gazed around the small garden of the three-storey terraced house. The roses were certainly flourishing and the foot-high wall of yellow rose of Sharon was like a burst of sunshine. After a few minutes, Danny knocked again. He grinned as he noticed next door's net curtain twitch slightly. He heard an irritable muttering from within, 'I don't want double-glazing and there's no slates missing off the roof.'

Merlin opened the door a crack, puffing hard. 'I've got the best encyclopedia money can buy, and I'm an atheist, so you might as well . . .'

When he saw that it was Danny, and neither a salesman nor a Jehovah's Witness, his face lit up in a smile and he flung the door wide open. 'Ah, Danny Black, isn't it? – Harry's grandson,' he exclaimed, and added hurriedly. 'Fredrick Haddock, Merlin, army number 36 . . .'

Danny put up a hand and laughed. 'S'okay Freddy, I know who you are.'

'Of course you do.' Merlin beckoned him inside

and slammed the door shut behind him as he entered. 'Well, well, dear boy, take off your jacket and make yourself at home.'

He waited impatiently while Danny slipped off his anorak, and hung it on the tall wooden coat stand. Noticing an old brass barometer on the wall, next to a long mirror, Danny gave it a tap.

Merlin tutted and led the way upstairs. 'I suppose the old faggot from next door was nosing through her window,' he remarked, lingering on one step. 'I'm damn sure that old battleaxe fancies me. Anyway, come along, we can talk in my den.'

As he trailed up the second and final set of thickly carpeted stairs after Merlin, Danny stopped to study one of the many framed photographs from the old man's younger days. Many had been taken during his army service.

'Freddy!' he exclaimed, in some excitement.

'Yes, yes, what is it?'

'Is me Grandad Harry on this photo with all the fellas on it?'

Merlin stopped, puffed hard and tutted. 'Yes, dear boy, second from the left on the front row – sitting next to the good-looking one on the end.' He chortled. 'That's me by the way, in my prime, it was taken in Egypt in the last war.'

He sighed and carried on down the narrow hallway towards his den.

'Damned hot sticky country, Egypt,' he observed, opening the door of the den and letting out a blast of tobacco-stale air. 'It's no good,' he went on. 'I'll have to move my den downstairs and pack up the cigarettes.' He switched the light on, as Danny squeezed past an eighteenth century coffer and followed him into the small, low-ceilinged room.

Danny's brows lifted and his mouth gaped open, as slowly he gazed around Merlin's cramped dimly-lit den. The room was a treasure trove of old books. In the centre stood a large desk cluttered with objects, and on one side was a sizeable globe.

Danny lovingly fingered the dusty spines of the volumes on the nearest shelves, while Freddy produced a bottle of Scotch and a couple of glasses with the air of a conjuror. As he flicked through one of the many tomes on witchcraft, Danny politely turned down the offer of a drink. He replaced another large book about Egyptian mythology and turned to face Merlin, who was licking his lips after sampling his first mouthful of whisky.

Danny had only ever seen Merlin wearing his deerstalker, so he was quite surprised at his abundance of wavy silver hair which matched his moustache. His gaze travelled on over the small manual typewriter, and beaker full of pens and pencils, to rest finally on the beautifully engraved silver-topped walking cane, that hung from a small hook at the end of the desk. He remembered the cane from when he'd met Merlin at his Grandad Harry's funeral.

Merlin coughed, thumped his chest and took out a cigarette from a small fancy wooden box on top of the bureau. He pushed it into his cigarette holder, lit up and cleared his throat.

'H-hmm, I see that you like my walking-stick, dear boy, it's an oddity I picked up in Europe years ago.'

He unhooked it, rammed his cigarette between his teeth, then twirled the cane in his right hand like a magician. After sword-fencing, briefly, to Danny's amazement, he flicked up the top of the cane with his thumbnail and pressed a small button.

Danny stepped back quickly, as a thin six-inch blade shot from the end of the walking-stick.

Merlin again sword-fenced brilliantly with an invisible enemy, before finishing him off with a phantom lunge through the heart.

As Danny watched, wide-eyed, his mouth slowly curved into a grin.

Merlin's bright eyes twinkled dangerously. 'Ha!' he laughed. 'So you think it's funny do you, young fella?' With his cane still cutting air, he danced across the room to the old untuned piano, on top of which stood an antique candelabra. With his wrist flicking at the speed of light, he swished the blade, slicing each candlestick into six pieces. Turning sharply, he pressed the tiny button and the blade shot back in. Taking the cigarette from his mouth, he leaned with both hands on top of the cane, puffing heavily. 'Well, what d'you think dear boy? Mind you, when I was fifty I could slice 'em into ten. I'll have to double up on the cod-liver oil.'

Danny applauded heartily. 'Brilliant, Merlin! You're full of surprises.'

The two of them spent a full two hours in the den,

and Danny found Merlin's knowledge of Egyptian mythology and witchcraft fascinating.

In his turn, Merlin was interested in Danny's information about Ament and her red-tailed buzzard, called Horus.

Before they left the den, Freddy Haddock kindly leant Danny twenty pounds, to tide him over until he received his first week's pay from Woodcock.

Merlin swung open the Victorian front door to darkness, and a rush of chilly, late summer, night air.

'Now don't forget to call next week, dear boy – and if you move on at all, you must let me know,' he instructed.

As Danny stopped at the front gate, Merlin raised his glass.

'Cheers, bye now – take care young fella,' and he closed the door.

Danny smiled to himself, he'd enjoyed the evening. He pulled up the hood of his anorak, and set off at a brisk pace.

It was late night shopping in Balchester, so the streets were still busy and well lit.

Danny stopped fifty yards up the hill, before he reached the Fox and Hounds and peered intently ahead. He was sure that the slim girl, leaving the pub with the hefty one, was Jacky Dooley.

As she swaggered boyishly, he knew it was her. He was puzzled though, if it was her, what had happened to her hair? It was very much shorter.

He quickened his pace, and as he got closer to them he called out. 'Hey! hey! Jacky, Jacky Dooley!'

Two bright beams of light, turning out from a nearby side-street, suddenly dazzled him. By the time he'd recovered his eyesight the girls had disappeared behind an oncoming tide of happy, laden shoppers. He cursed his bad luck and stopped outside the Fox and Hounds. Someone in there must know her, or have some idea where she might be going.

Inside music blasted loudly and pool balls rattled, but the room itself was fairly empty, as always during the week.

There was a handful of rough-looking workmen drinking up at the bar, unwilling to tear themselves away from their well-earned pints. A group of young mums were just out on the town, after drawing their weekly allowances.

Danny glanced around at the smoke-stained flowered wallpaper, his gaze reached the pool table in the corner where Adder, who was always flying high, was playing pool with the Fat Man and a couple of others.

Danny had learnt his pool as a kid, in the bars and clubs of Liverpool, and by the time he was fifteen, he was the best stick in Toxteth. He decided he wouldn't mind a stick or two. He ambled up to the bar, thinking that there were a lot rougher pubs in Liverpool.

As he reached the bar, Adder broke up the balls by cracking the pack hard with the cue-ball. He squealed with delight, as a red instantly rocketed into a side pocket. He was still slouched over the pool table when Danny caught his evil eye. He looked up at Danny and tipped back his badge-covered baseball cap. 'Well,' he drawled, sarcastically. 'Look what the cat's dragged in. It must of been hot today, see the colour of him.'

There was a cackle of laughter from the corner.

Adder half-glanced at the others. 'Well, what d'you lot think, a mongrel – or what?'

'Where's the dog warden then?' chipped in Miko, as he swigged from a bottle of strong lager.

Danny held his twenty pound note on top of the bar and slowly looked around, to make sure that the snide remarks were being aimed at him. He raised his eyebrows, and even Phil, the barman, looked puzzled, as his face assumed an expression of amusement.

The pub had quietened, and the giggling mums had hurried to the safety of an alcove – they knew what Adder and his mates were like when they were high on stuff.

The barman walked up to Danny and greeted him warmly. 'Take no notice of them, mate, their bark's worse than their bite – what'll it be?'

Danny sniffed the heavy aroma. 'I'll have none of that shit for starters, but yous can gi's a pint of lager please.'

Phil smiled, nodded and pulled him a pint. 'You new around here then? – from over the water are you?'

Danny lifted his drink and sipped. 'Yeah to both questions. I've just got a job on Woodcock's farm on the other side of the meadowland.'

Phil handed Danny his change. 'I know the farm well, it's a fair old spread. He's got a tasty young missus as well – a Chink or something.'

Danny nodded as he drank. 'Thai actually, and she is very nice.'

He cocked his head thoughtfully, and stretched out his hand shoulder-height. 'Oh by the way, does a girl about so high, called Jacky Dooley, come in here?'

The record on the jukebox had finished, making it easy for Adder's pixie-like ears to prick up. He curled his top lip, and smacked his cue noisily on the edge of the pool table. His voice held a threatening note. 'What d'you want to know about her for, mongrel?'

As Danny slowly turned to face him, Fat Man came waddling up towards him. He carried a double gin and tonic in one hand, his other hand waved daintily in the air.

'Hi, you big chunk of mixed paint,' he tittered. 'D'you want any drugs?' He swayed his head smugly. 'I'm the dealer in here – amphetamines, cannabis or heroin, you name it, sweet, and I'll deliver.'

He blew Danny a large kiss – Danny felt like puking, he could have ripped his head off – he'd seen his mother die from a massive overdose of scag. His flashing eyes and gritted teeth were enough to send the Fat Man packing. He twirled about and waddled back to his corner like a flapping duck. 'So-rry, so sorry for asking, oooh, we are a nasty mongrel aren't we, a very bad doggy indeeeeeeed!'

Adder stepped forward a few paces, at the same time twirling his pool cue threateningly.

Danny ignored him and turning back to face Phil the barman, he swigged from his pint.

Adder held his cue upright and angrily banged it on the sticky carpeted floor. 'I said, mongrel, what d'you want to know about Jacky Dooley for?'

Danny lowered his pint onto the top of the bar, gripped the tainted brass bar rail with a strong hand, and turned round on Adder. His voice was cool, yet firm. 'Danny – the name's Danny Black. I've met her a few times when she's been with her ol' fella, I thought I saw her leaving here as I was coming down the road, that's all.'

Phil lifted Danny's glass as he wiped the bar. 'You did pal, she was in here with her mate, Bobby Queen, but they moved on elsewhere. Try the Bedford estate if it's urgent, they've probably gone to a pub there, it's nearer home for them – it's only a bus ride away, or a couple of quid in a taxi.'

By now, Adder had openly rolled himself a joint, and with his intake of strong lager, he was beyond fear and ready to fight the whole world.

His flour-white face twisted with rage and hatred. He flung out his hand to send a half-full glass of beer off a nearby table, it smashed on the floor and shattered into pieces. Shouting loudly, he lunged forward, stopped, and pointed at Danny.

'You keep away from her, half-caste, she's mine, d'you hear? – she's bleeding well mine!'

He slipped off his dark glasses and tucked them into his leather jacket pocket.

A couple of nervous men hurriedly drank up and left, while others eagerly ordered more beer. They enjoyed a bit of fun, as long as they weren't involved.

Adder's voice was now a high-pitched squeak, and his tongue was flicking like that of a cobra's on the attack. He dropped down onto all fours and started barking like a alerted guard dog. Then he scuttled across the floor sideways, like a demented crab, screaming loudly.

'Mongrel, who's a mixed breed then.'

A tall slim thirty-year-old man, standing on his own at the bar, watched in silence. He was dressed in a red lumberjack-style coat, jeans, and soft leather shoes. He had a definite Red Indian look about him. His hair was shoulder-length, straight and dark, framing a hard, lined face, that resembled the head of a totem-pole. He heard all and said nothing throughout the whole affair. All that Danny's ears had latched onto was that his nickname was Cochise.

Danny stayed cool, his hawklike eyes locked with Adder's, while he tried to fathom his enemy's doped mind. Adder suddenly sprang to his feet, flashing a quick-drawn blade at Danny. 'Listen mongrel,' he hissed. 'we'll play pool for Jack – what d'you say, eh, or are you a scaredy-cat.'

The pool table chorus joined in. 'Scaredy-cat, scaredy-kins.'

Cochise stood rigid, silent, with hand on glass.

An old mangy dog, belonging to nobody, cocked its leg up the one-armed bandit, before ripping open the bag of crisps someone had thrown it.

Outside, parked in a side street, was the police drug squad. They sat in an unmarked van, and had had the pub under surveillance for some time – for the moment it suited them to have all their eggs in one basket.

Danny sighed heavily, turned back to face the bar and downed his beer. He looked Phil in the eye and shook his head. 'Give us another pint will you mate, please – it looks like I may be here for quite a while, yet.'

Bobby Queen and Jacky were totally bored, as they sat in the large room of the Bedford estate social club. Usually, on a Tuesday night, things were humming and it was a fun place to be, but, with the present recession deepening, the number of customers had dwindled rapidly and the room was nearly empty.

They'd called into the Lowfield Hotel for a couple, after the Fox and Hounds so by now they were quite tiddly.

Bobby heaved herself up, walked across the room and dropped a coin into the jukebox, putting on a few of their favourite records. She flopped back into her seat, straightened her green hooded jogging top, and then twirled her delicate stemmed glass and idly watched the slice of lemon spinning in her gin and tonic.

Suddenly she raised her head. 'Hey Jack! I've got a couple of tabs here off Miko – what d'you say, d'you want a buzz – or what? Anythin's better than this dump.'

Jacky carried on swaying her head to the music. 'Nah, you know I don't like drugs.'

'But Jack!' Bobby was determined. 'We're skint now, and one of these each will keep us buzzing for ages. Come on, it'll cheer you up.' She rubbed a hand over Jack's cropped head.

'You've had a rough time lately with that perv' Woodcock and your old man – go on give it a whirl, it's only kids' stuff, honest.'

Jack sat there for a little while, looking through the high windows to the twinkling stars outside, one foot tapping in rhythmic tempo on the tiled floor, then she turned abruptly. 'Hell shit, go on then Bob, give us some stuff then, you're right, it'll probably cheer me up.'

It wasn't long before Jacky started feeling good. She giggled, and tossed down the last of her Bacardi and coke. She sounded a trifle drunk. 'B-Bobby shall we go up to Oldhall Village n-next Wednesday and have a – party at the old broken-down abbey in Bluebell Wood?'

Bobby threw back her head and laughed. 'But we haven't been there since we were kids, Jack.'

Jack tittered loudly. 'I know,' she squealed. 'It'll be great – you, me, Adder and the rest.' She danced in her seat, shaking her head vigorously from side to side. Bobby leaned back. There was a triumphant look on her face, a smug smile on her lips.

She folded her arms, Now my girl, she thought, now Jacky Dooley, you'll be mine.

Jack felt good – Jack was buzzing, and Fat Man would be very pleased with Bobby Queen, and Mister Fixit would be pleased with the Fat Man.

Chapter Seven

Titch, a four foot high dumpy youth, wearing a red beret scampered, bow-legged across the room, clambered onto a stool in the Fox and Hounds and slotted a coin into the jukebox – it needed music to break the tension.

Adder snapped his knife blade shut and faced Danny.

'Well, do we play pool, or not?'

A tall nervous girl with glasses goggled at Adder and Danny, she'd never seen trouble in a pub before.

The barman's fist slammed down angrily on top of the bar. 'Leave it Adder, can't you see that the man's peaceful. If you don't you're barred for good.'

The cords in Adder's long thin neck swelled up and stood out as his fury mounted. 'Get knotted, crawlbug,' he hissed. He flicked a wet tongue at Phil who was now wiping a glass. 'You know what happened to the last pub that barred me.' It gave Adder some satisfaction to try to harm and scare Danny off Jacky Dooley.

It was a crazy set-up. Phil dearly longed to wring Adder's neck, but with the landlord on holiday abroad, he just couldn't risk the relief manager getting the windows smashed in.

His complexion was still an angry white when Danny addressed him. 'Thanks a lot for trying mate, but I'm okay.' He nodded to Adder, who was now only a couple of feet away.

With a deadpan expression, Danny went on, in grim tones. 'We'll play pool.'

Adder gave a menacing squeal of delight, whispering rose to excited chatter, and people hurriedly bought fresh beers before taking up their positions by the pool table.

As Danny coolly chalked his tip, Adder banged his cue handle down hard onto the floor. 'Right Mongrel, now for the rules. If you win, you leave this pub in one piece, but you keep away from Jacky Dooley.' He sniggered into his gloved hand. 'But if you lose – oh yes my old bow-bow, if you lose, you'll have to fight me to get out of here – an' I'll kick your half-chat arse all the way back to Liverpool.' He leaned drunkenly on his cue tip, bent forward and swayed his head, like a horse at a stable gate. His voice was becoming slurred. 'That okay then?' He squealed again, to the delight of his drugged followers, as Danny nodded his approval.

Phil, the barman, feared the worst either way, and shook his head morbidly, everyone's gaze was firmly fixed on the pool table.

Adder won the toss, and quickly decided that his brilliant break-offs wouldn't fail him now, so with his usual squealing battle-cry, he sent the white cue-ball smashing into the pack. As the balls split, a yellow ricocheted like a bullet from out of the mouth of the top pocket, to roll speedily around the table and finally settle back down on the cush.

Adder let out a hissed curse. His break had failed and he'd set Danny up well.

Danny, calmly and ruthlessly, with perfect positioning, knocked in four reds, and so Adder was well on the way out in front of his own crowd.

Danny doubled the next red easily into a side pocket.

Adder drew in deeply on his joint, as Danny cued up to tap in the red, hovering on the edge of the pocket. Adder's tongue was furiously active, he was well on the way to being seven-balled.

Danny smiled to himself – it was time to miss.

The crowd erupted as the white ball missed the red by a good inch. Fists rose high in salute and chants of 'Adder, Adder,' filled the room. Adder had a simple table and cleaned up swiftly. And as he hurled down the black ball, screwing the white cue-ball back up the table, like an eel fighting backwards, he leapt into the air, screeching loudly with glee. Grinning with vicious triumph, he tossed his cue onto the table. He nodded to Miko and shook his clenched fist, before turning to face Danny, with wild glassy narrowing eyes.

'Right then, what's-your-name, let's away to the bogs to sort this little lot out.'

As the toilet door closed behind them to shut out the excited mutterings, Danny glanced in the facing mirror and glimpsed Adder's knife blade flashing behind him. At the same time, Miko squeezed in through the door, and smashed his empty bottle on the dirty white tiled walls. He waved the jagged glass edges dangerously.

Danny stared at them and the rage exploded in his gut like gunpowder. An animal-like roar came from him as his temper took over. He blocked Adder's lunging blow with his arm, and drove a brick-hard fist onto his chin. As Adder groaned and sagged, Danny crunched his knee in, hard between his legs. Adder howled and slumped towards the floor. Danny helped him on his way by giving him a hefty kick.

Adder's knife flew from his hand and skidded over the quarry-tiled floor. He tumbled across the toilet and landed on his backside with a splat, in the overflowing urine trough. The blood dripped from his mouth to mingle with the floating cigarette ends in the smelly yellow fluid.

Miko rushed at Danny, bottle at the ready, but Danny's fast high kick met him full in the face with a loud smack. His bottle flew up in the air and bounced into the trough. As he sagged, Danny gripped him firmly by the lapels with both hands, and after hoisting him off the floor, crashed Miko's head against the condom machine. With a loud rattle, two packets of condoms were ejected.

Danny turned and flung him towards Adder. Miko thudded against the splashback and slowly slid, moaning, into the trough. 'Ugh, Oh God,' he groaned as his hands sank below the rippling substance. 'Piss!'

Danny grabbed the two packets of condoms and beamed. He read out the label aloud. 'Strawberry flavoured and lubricated, very tasty.' He waved them at Adder and Miko. 'I could have a good use for these, lads.' He prodded the air with a teasing finger.

'We can't go around spreading Aids, can we?' He tucked them into his anorak pocket. 'I wish I could stay lads, but . . .' he sighed, and forced a pleasant smile.

Halfway out of the toilet door, he turned and snarled at Adder. 'There's a certain lady called Jack who's on my mind! Oh, and by the way – the name's not Mongrel, it's Danny, Danny Black, see you chaps!'

Adder splashed around in the sea of piddle as he tried to bring himself upright. 'You shitbag,' he fulminated, slamming his wet hand against the tiles until his delicate palm stung.

He was shaking with rage as he pointed a threatening finger at Danny. 'We'll have you for this, chocolate drop.' His voice began to quaver, emotionally. 'Oh yes, my little bow-bow we'll have you. Nobody, but nobody, does this to Adder and team and gets away with it.' His voice rose to a hysterical shriek. 'Wait till Mister Fixit finds out, Black!' He flopped back down into the urine, simmering. 'The hell fuck he'll have you.'

Danny squinted as he looked down on them.

'We'll see,' he ground out, his lip curling. 'We'll see, gutter-skunk.'

He grinned derisively and left the toilet, closing the door behind him.

Danny glanced around the bar, somebody had drunk his beer. His searching angry gaze fastened on Cochise, who still had the Fat Man well pinned by the throat, to the wall just outside of the loo.

Cochise looked hard at Danny, with a deadly fighting man's eyes. He dropped the Fat Man's squirty of mild acid, with which he intended to blind Danny in the toilet, onto the carved stool beneath him.

After he had squeezed the Fat Man's throat for the last time, sending him a deep purple colour, he silently and expressively loosened his grip, looking deadpan at Danny, then casually strode back to the bar to finish his drink – Danny realised that the mute was a friend.

The room had fallen silent, as Phil the barman spread his large hands on top of the bar and gazed up at Danny with blue-eyed surprise. His mind worked overtime, trying to suss out the goings-on, his heavy jaw dropped, and he asked, nervously, 'Are you all right mate, where's where's . . . ?'

Danny stopped in mid-stride near to the closed heavy oak exit door. He tossed back his head and laughed. He gesticulated with his thumb towards the toilet. 'If yous mean the two divvies, they're just pissin' about in there,' he drawled, shrugging his shoulders.

He pulled open the solid door, and walked out, leaving a puzzled silence behind him.

The night air was cool and a heavy mist was hovering over the River Denny. Halfway across the road bridge, which spanned the river, Danny stopped. The hustle and bustle of the city was now far behind him, and the frothing water rushing over the weir below was a harmonious sound in the night. He switched his gaze to upstream, and noticed glowing city lights reflecting on the smooth surface. As the happy laughter and voices coming from the floating nightclub drifted away into the thick mist, he put up his hood, shoved his hands in his pockets, and set off briskly for Woodcock's farm.

Danny suddenly stopped in his stride, and his ears pricked up, as the faint tinkling sound continued to follow him. When he stopped, the tinkling stopped. He stood listening intently for a moment and then carried on his way.

The fog had now fallen thickly as, once again, the eerie tinkling reached Danny's ears.

After stopping and starting a few more times with the same result, he leapt over the low lepers' graveyard wall. He knelt on some sleeping daisies behind an unreadable tombstone and waited.

The fog was now dense, and Danny could only see greyness and feel the clammy cold on his face. The tinkling came alongside him. His heart raced as he crouched to pounce. Bracing himself, he leapt into the unknown, fearing the worst. He met nothing. As his feet spread at the ready on the York-stone pavement, and his right fist drew back behind his left arm shield, there came a sudden loud tinkling at his feet. He almost jumped out of his skin.

'You little git, yous,' he gasped, and burst out laughing as he scooped up the soaking wet little she-cat.

By her pitiful condition, he assumed that she had either fallen in the river or been thrown in by some bored owner. As he stroked her, Danny smiled to himself and thought back to his grandad Harry's Welsh cottage. He had been six years old at the time, and fell foul of Harry's temper for trying to teach his cat to swim in the garden water barrel. Jolting himself back to the present, he tucked the cat inside his anorak. He carried on home, hoping that the Woodcocks would give houseroom to his new found little friend.

Danny came to an abrupt halt in the dark lane near to the farmhouse gate, as a rustling sound grew louder. After pushing its way through a gap in the hedgerow, the young red dog fox froze. It stood, ears pricked and eyes wide, white chest and mouth standing out in the foggy darkness.

For now, he was still roaming his parents' territory, but by the coming autumn he'd have left home, and by next spring found his own patch.

For a brief moment, Danny was surprised by the fox's boldness. He gave a small bark of laughter. 'So you're one of the rascals who bites off chickens' heads,' he muttered, under his breath. The disturbing noise was enough to send the fox bolting back through the thick gorse hedge.

Smiling, Danny scratched behind the little cat's ears and swung open the farmyard gate.

Panic gripped Ben Dooley, as Docker and Boots suddenly reached out from the fog and hauled him into the pitch-black alley-way at the side of the Bedford estate Social Club. He wasn't frightened – he was paralysed. He still had the bruising from his last encounter with Docker and company.

'Evenin' Dooley,' Docker growled. 'We heard on the estate grapevine about your little drunken driving escapade – or should I say, Mister Fixit did. He's sent us with a nice little proposition for you.'

He pulled out his steel comb and twisted it threateningly between his fingers. He squared his jaw at Dooley, and Dooley was under no illusion, Docker meant business. He stared at his adversary, numbness sharpening into fear. 'I – I don't know Mister Fixit,' he mumbled.

While gently combing Dooley's face, Docker turned to Boots and Brown Trilby and gave a sadistic chuckle. 'What d'you reckon Boots, he's never heard of Mister Fixit.'

Boots laughed squeakily as he turned to Brown Trilby. 'D'you hear that Trilby, he's never heard of Mister fixit.'

Brown Trilby pulled his hat down over his chinese eyes and tugged at his droopy moustache with nervous fingers. His long thin lips parted. 'Well I think he has.'

Boots glanced back at Docker. 'Well we think he has.'

Docker showed his teeth in a snarl and cocked his head. 'Well they think you have Dooley, and so do I.'

His mocking tone changed, along with his expression, to one of cold hard stone. 'From now on Dooley, you work for us. Brown Trilby here'll drop off all of your materials and be the driver for anything that you need. You pay us, well, I mean Mister Fixit, half of everything after expenses, you'll give me the money. I want a list of all of your usual insurance customers.' He shuffled, beckoned with his head and pressed the steel teeth harder into Dooley's cheek. 'We'll sort out 'bout knocking over the odd garden wall and the other mishaps – you just repair 'em – got it!'

Dooley nodded his head frantically. 'Yeah, yeah, I've got it Docker, I've got it.'

Docker ran his comb through his pony-tail. 'Good! Look on the bright side, Dooley me old son. At least you're guaranteed work this way, it's better than being laid off until you get your licence back. And make sure you're in here tomorrow night at nine with your clients' names and addresses. Oh, and by the way, that's a lousy haircut you've given your girl.'

Docker and company backed away. Docker slipped his comb back into his inside pocket. 'Have the rest of the week off, Dooley – but you'll have lots of work to start, on Monday morning. Come on lads, let's hit the bright lights.'

Once they'd disappeared into the swirling fog, Dooley shakily lit up a cheroot and set off for home. He walked straight, his encounter with Docker and company had certainly sobered him up. His damned women would suffer if his supper wasn't ready and waiting when he got home.

Merlin sat hunched up beneath his desk lamp, puffing deeply and thoughtfully on a cigarette. He poured himself another whisky, as he slowly moved his large magnifying glass over the page of small print he grunted, and cursed his fading eyesight.

He took a sip, put down his glass, and stroked his pen slowly over the coloured picture of Ament and Horus. The gentle background music on his old radio was being performed by The London Symphony Orchestra – he found classical music helped him to concentrate. 'Ah! of course, Ament,' he sighed. 'Goddess of the West and associated with Hathor as Goddess of the Underworld.' He tutted, and touched Ament's hawk head emblem with his pen-nib. He transferred his gaze to Horus. 'Mmm it appears, young Danny,' he muttered, 'that your lady falconer has named her bird after the Egyptian god, Horus.'

He took another swig of whisky. 'Mmm, God of the skies and the hunting people, a fitting name I suppose. She does seem an interesting lady, I must admit.' He pulled out his pocket watch to check the time. It was late. He reached for the whisky bottle, and then a thick book on witchcraft – it was going to be a long night and if Danny was living in a house of evil, as he'd sensed by what Danny had told him about Ament and Horus, he intended to be ready, if ever his help was needed.

George Woodcock heaved his straight leg around the door and entered the kitchen, to join Danny and Su-Ling, who were fussing over the little cat.

She'd been well-fed, had drunk a full saucer of milk, and was now rubbing her head affectionately against Danny's arm, purring contentedly.

Su-Ling had at once fallen in love with the cat.

The small stray's eyes were of the palest yellow, and her white-splattered black face made her an instant hit even with Woodcock.

Her little bell tinkled every time she moved.

'She'll make a fine little pet for the girls,' he remarked. 'But she'll have to keep a good eye out for Ament's falcon.'

Su-Ling looked worried. 'Oh, don't say things like that George, she's such a pretty little creature.'

The cat seemed to have no intention of leaving Danny's strong gentle hands. As she shifted position in his arms, Danny looked at Woodcock and Su-Ling with childish glee. 'Lotty!' he exclaimed. 'I'll call her Lotty, because she's had a lot of luck.'

It was agreed that Lotty should be introduced to Sweep and the ducks gently, and Su-Ling arranged a snug little quilted box in the kitchen corner, which was to be the stray's new home.

As Danny lay in bed, he could hear soft music drifting down the hallway from Ament's room. He leaned over and pushed his door shut, he would be rising at five in the morning, he needed his sleep.

As the wind outside rose, rustling in the orchard's fruit trees, he drifted into slumber.

Rosie and John had been into Balchester for a meal. John had driven Rosie back home and they were now sitting together on the living-room couch, sipping coffee, and chatting to Daisy about their forthcoming wedding.

Ben Dooley had arrived home before time, so it wasn't surprising that John, who detested him because of the way he treated his wife and daughters, had been a trifle withdrawn until Dooley, who'd been on his best behaviour, had retired to bed.

It was nearing midnight when Jacky came home. She slammed the garden gate shut and jigged up the path, throwing her arms in the air like a victorious football supporter. She swung out a boot at the overgrown grass and fuchsia, and was still giggling loudly as she announced her presence by rapping sharply with her knuckle on the living-room window, startling the three inside.

The drug Jacky had taken in the Bedford Social Club was now flowing through her bloodstream, mingling dangerously with the alcohol she'd drunk. She was still bouncing around, snapping her fingers and singing, when Rosie opened the front door. Jacky pranced into the living-room, Rosie following, casting a puzzled look at Daisy and John.

Daisy put her cup down and stared – Jack certainly seemed to be behaving oddly.

She rocked across the carpet, humming noisily. She switched off the late TV news, and slotted her favourite tape into the midi system, and then continued cavorting in the middle of the living-room floor.

'Jacky!' exclaimed her mother. 'You're drunk!' Daisy was concerned – Jack could sometimes be a bit of a handful, but her love for her daughter remained as deep-rooted as Jacky's was for her.

John Andrews tossed a worried glance at his fiancèe. 'Drugs Rosie,' he whispered urgently. 'It looks like she's been on drugs.'

'Rubbish,' Rosie denied through gritted teeth. 'Jack doesn't touch that stuff.'

'But look at her, Rose.'

Rosie buried her head against his shoulder. 'Shush up John, Mum'll hear you.'

To Daisy, her daughter definitely seemed strange and a lot more lively than she would be after only a few drinks.

Jacky suddenly bent forward and grabbed Stumpy, who had just hopped into the room to warm himself by the fire. She snatched him up, kissed him full on the nose and hugged him tightly, as she did a short smooch to the tape's next record, 'The Lady In Red.'

Suddenly she stopped, eyes popping, dropped Stumpy and flung her arms straight up towards the ceiling. Her voice rose high with a hint of anger. 'Hey! everybody, what you all lookin' so miserable for – misery buggers, misery buggers.' She twirled, hands out-stretched like a wobbly spinning top. 'I'm gonna take Stumpy for a walk into Balchester to get a carry-out from the Chinky's – anybody comin' – or what?' she demanded. She scooped up a bewildered Stumpy and danced, head rocking, out of the room, through the hallway and into the kitchen. She fumbled with Stumpy's lead as she clipped it onto his thin leather collar, before slamming out of the back kitchen door, muttering a mouthful of unrecognisable gibberish.

Daisy rose from her chair. 'Jacky,' she cried in agitation. 'What – what's wrong with you, Luv?' She sank down again, tears in her eyes.

Rosie exchanged glances with John, then got up and placed a comforting arm around her mother's shoulders. 'Don't worry, Mum,' she said, in soothing tones, 'she's just a bit tiddly, that's all. John and me'll fetch her back, you just sit there and finish your coffee.'

They set out in the swirling fog, John could hardly see a yard in front of him as he peered through the windscreen. At last he spotted the dim shapes of Jack and Stumpy on the through road which led to the tidal waters of the River Denny. Rosie, at boiling-point, flung open the passenger door, leapt out and gripped her sister firmly by the shoulder. 'Okay!' she exploded. 'Pick up bloody Stumpy and get your butt into the back of this car – now!'

Jacky flapped her arms violently, like the wings of a startled chicken. 'Misery bugger, misery bugger,' she taunted.

Rosie wasn't amused and trying not to startle John, she dug her fingers hard into Jack's neck and ordered, 'get – in – the – bloody – car – now – Jack!'

Her sharp claws seemed to bring Jack to her senses a little.

'B-but . . .'

'Never mind "but" and never! mind "misery bugger", get in.'

She pushed Jacky onto the back seat. Stumpy wagged his rudder half-heartedly and jumped in after her. Rosie flopped down next to Jack and slammed the car door shut. 'Take us back to Mum's John, please,' she snapped. John nodded and obeyed.

'Right, my girl,' Rosie hissed, at the befuddled Jacky. 'I want to know if you're touching drugs.'

Jack felt bruised, numbed by the shock of her sister's attack on her. She lowered her head and mumbled. 'Course not – I've h-had one too many, that's all. Adder bought me a few Bacardi and cokes.'

She shrugged and added in slurred tones. 'That's all Rose – honest!'

Rosie's lips tightened into a thin line, she was unsure if Jack was speaking the truth. 'You'd better be honest, my girl,' she threatened. 'I thought we both loved our mum. You know as well as me she's had a shit life with that bastard of a father of ours. Mum looks to us for support.' Her voice trembled with emotion. 'I love you a lot, Jacky, but if I find out that you're touching drugs . . .'

Woodcock's farm was deep in sleep, and as the tawny owl's eerie call echoed through the white blanket outside, Danny grunted, flung out an arm and shifted his head on his pillow. He gave a choking snore and slept on, dreaming. And as the gunfire and shells exploded, dressed in full camouflage gear, he spun Steeleye, sniffed the chill night air and crept through the undergrowth and up the hill towards the German outpost.

Chapter Eight

Sweep's sudden loud barking at the postman, early on Wednesday morning, woke Danny with a jolt. He yawned, and turned off the alarm clock before it began rattling noisily.

Heaving himself out of bed, he did a series of sit-ups and press-ups and finished with a brief practice with Steeleye. Dragging on his jeans, he went for his regular morning shower. He was in time to meet Ament coming out of the bathroom, clad in a long blue dressing-gown.

'Hello Ament,' he greeted her, smiling, 'I saw your falcon the . . .' He was stunned when she slowed, gave him a hard look of resentment, even hatred, and swept past him hurriedly. Danny watched, open-mouthed, as she disappeared into her bedroom and slammed the door. He shook his head mystified and entered the bathroom.

Dawn was breaking and the night wind had dropped, when Danny and Sweep brought up the cattle from the meadow to the milking parlour.

Vic, the cowman, was still off sick, so Danny

knew it would be Woodcock he would be helping again.

The ducks were already swimming about, and one by one, birds were joining in with the early morning chorus.

Once milking was over and the parlour hosed-down until it was squeaky clean, Danny and Sweep herded the cows back along the lane, while George Woodcock took the large metal jugful of fresh warm milk back over to the farmhouse for the breakfast cereals.

Danny had breakfasted with Su-Ling and Woodcock, and was leaving to start work again, before Ament and the children put in an appearance.

It was all right for some, he thought wryly. After driving the two girls to school, the rest of the day belonged to Ament, which, Danny guessed meant hunting with her falcon – for pleasure! And after dark she would probably be going out.

As Danny poked his head out of the tractor's cab ready to reverse the trailer load of manure alongside the back of the house, Woodcock came rushing across, his lame leg swinging. Sweep followed him barking excitedly. Woodcock waved his arm frantically, and shouted, 'Move her over Danny, move her over – tip it under your bedroom window, as near to the allotment as you can.' He rubbed a hand agitatedly through his thinning hair and pointed. 'I've got plans for that spot.'

Once the cow muck was tipped, Danny wiped his

brow and drove the tractor back towards the farmyard – there was still an electric fence to erect up on ten acre.

Jack Dooley sat in the personnel manageress's office in Goodporks sausage factory, glancing nervously around. As the clickety-click of Mrs Coot's high heels grew louder, Jacky squared her shoulders and tidied her hair with a quick flick of her fingers.

Mrs Coot was a tall slim forty-year-old, stylish, in a well-cut mauve suit, blonde highlights in her hair. She smiled at Jacky as she sat down and began to read the CV Rosie had typed at work.

Meanwhile, Jacky studied Mrs Coot. She was fascinated by the large breasts which filled the white silk blouse and mentally compared them with her own small, but firm ones.

Mrs Coot nodded approvingly as she read the references from Jack's two previous employers – a bakery in the town centre and a pop factory on the local industrial estate.

Goodporks sausage factory had been built recently on the other side of the industrial estate, and had advertised for labour in the local papers.

The interview was fairly brief, Jacky was taken on and Mrs Coot took off her large red-framed spectacles and shook hands. Jacky left the factory, floating on a cloud of satisfaction – she'd got the job. She was to start the following Monday morning at eight o'clock, and the extra money would certainly help Daisy out with the household bills.

As Danny's razor buzzed, he watched the headlights from Woodcock's new gold Mercedes, as it swung out of the farmyard gate and accelerated towards Balchester.

He drew the bedroom curtains and switched off his razor. The man certainly liked to live in style, he reflected. Ament had gone out earlier, and the children were now tucked up sound asleep – the next few hours, thought Danny, were for Su-Ling and himself.

He was liberal with aftershave and combed his thick hair carefully before the dressing-table mirror then, with nervous anticipation, he made his way downstairs. He heard music coming from the lounge and the distinctive voice of Roy Orbison.

He caught his breath when he saw Su-Ling standing beside the cocktail cabinet in the mellow glow of lamplight – she looked stunning in a sleek black minidress and sheer black stockings. Long gold earrings added to her exotic allure.

She flashed a quick amused glance at Danny, then asked in throaty tones, 'Would you like a drink, Danny?'

He nodded, not trusting himself to speak.

She raised her eyebrows slightly and moistened her lips with the tip of her tongue, an erotic gesture that raised his temperature even higher.

'Please sit, Danny. And don't look so nervous,' she smiled and handed him a tall slim glass of lager. 'We won't be interrupted, so let's just relax and enjoy the evening.' Danny sank into the deep leather couch and sipped his beer. Su-Ling slid down next to him, nursing a large gin and tonic. Her dress rose high above her knees. 'I chilled your drink for you,' she murmured, giving him a tantalising smile over the rim of her glass.

Danny swallowed hard and muttered awkwardly. 'Thanks, it's fine, just fine.'

She laid a hand on his thigh. Her perfume drifted enticingly under his nose, he could feel the warmth of her body and could hardly contain himself.

Su-Ling reached out, took his glass away and drew his head down. He ignited immediately at the touch of her lips, his tongue thrust into her mouth, his hands explored, her nipples sprang into life, his probing fingers plunged into a moist waiting vagina. Suddenly Su-Ling drew away.

He watched, aching with frustration, as she tidied away their glasses, turned off the music and neatened the cushions. Then she turned and held out a hand to him, her eyes glowing with a triumphant hunger. 'Come,' she invited. 'We'll shower together – make it last.'

He couldn't speak, his need too intense, but followed her upstairs in silence. She took him into the master bedroom.

He glanced round temporarily distracted by the luxurious furnishings. His gaze lingered on the magnificent carved four-poster bed, with its black silk sheets. A vision of Su-Ling in bed with Woodcock flashed into his mind – it was gross, and he tried to banish it as he followed her to the en-suite bathroom.

He felt drunk, not with alcohol, but with lust, as Su-Ling turned to him and pressed herself against him. They kissed open-mouthed, her tongue alternately darting in and out, teasingly, against his lips. Slowly, sensuously, she undressed him, revealing his huge, throbbing penis.

'No – not yet,' she whispered as he reached for her, 'cool down lover.'

With a roguish smile she switched the shower on and Danny gasped as the water hit him.

Giggling, Su-Ling slid out of her dress and stood naked, except for the black stockings and lacy suspender belt. Slowly, provocatively, she peeled them off, dropping them to the floor. She stepped under the shower with him and began to soap him all over. Their mouths locked in a frenzied kiss and her fingers closed around his pulsating erection. Tearing her lips away, she bent and tongued his nipples, sucking, flicking her tongue over them.

Danny shuddered and groaned as she knelt and flicked her tongue at his penis. She took it into her mouth and sucked, teased, and tormented him into a state of exquisite pleasure. Excitement was choking him. 'God! Su-Ling, you're wrecking me – you're wrecking me woman,' he moaned.

She gripped his shaft with both hands and sucked him harder, rhythmically, in tune with Danny's uncontrollable thrusts. He felt a beautiful rising inside him. He gripped her hair frenziedly and pushed harder. 'Stop it Su-Ling,' he gasped desperately, 'stop it, or I'll come – it's too early.'

She responded by slowly sliding her lips back up the last three inches of his pulsating solid flesh. She flashed her tongue over him and then slowly rose to her full height, kissing his body lightly all the way up. They kissed again as the hot water sprayed them, somehow creating the illusion that they were in a world of their own.

Su-Ling looked at him yearningly and, willingly, allowed him to gently manoeuvre her body around until her buttocks faced him. She automatically bent over.

Danny recollected himself sufficiently to reach for the small foil packet on the ledge and slip on a condom – better safe than sorry, he reminded himself. Inflamed again, he slid slowly, voluptuously, inside her. She was wet and ready, taking him eagerly, it was long, deep and lasting.

Su-Ling cried out, as he gave one last final ram! He had brought her to a shattering climax of sensation, and no man had ever done that to Su-Ling before – certainly not in the brothels of Bangkok.

Lance was glad that from his bedroom window he had spotted Stumpy, hopping exuberantly down the road in pursuit of Jack. He rushed out of the house and gave chase after the little dog. Jack was just entering the Lowfield Hotel when Lance caught her up, carrying Stumpy in his arms. 'Hi Jack, I'll take him home, shall I,' he offered, puffing.

'Would you? thanks,' she responded, with a smile, giving Stumpy a brief cuddle.

As far as Lance was concerned, it was contact well worth the trouble.

Miko and some of his friends barged past him rowdily, pushing him out of the way, as they followed Jacky Dooley into the bar. As Lance carried Stumpy back home, memories of Jack and himself, when they were small, flickered through his mind. He recalled the odd occasions when they had visited the museum and Balchester zoo together. He could never understand why she hung around with the horrible crowd she now seemed to prefer. But he would always be there if she wanted him, no matter what she did – he loved her.

He sighed and quickened his pace. It was Wednesday night and Lennox Lewis, boxing for the world heavyweight title, would be on the TV at 10 o'clock.

At about half past ten, Jack and Bobby Queen rolled out of the pub into the warm night, which was still and moonlit. Their pockets were packed with bottles of strong lager. Jacky had now doubled her drug intake, and they were both high on methodine syrup, which they had obtained that afternoon from Fat Man in the Fox and Hounds. He'd been smarmy and gloating over finally hooking Jack. 'My finest catch this year,' he had bragged, as he slowly slid the notes from her eager fingers. He had swayed his head cockily from side to side. 'And without a freebie as well.'

He'd leered and winked at Bobby – she was cheap and good groundbait to use.

There was a taxi standing idle on the car park, and it was only a fairly cheap ride to Seahill village, which was about a mile from Bluebell Wood where the old abbey ruins stood.

Once Jack had paid the driver off at Seahill crossroads, they passed the old Swinging Rope pub. It was a cottage now, but had once been the stopping off point for condemned criminals before they were to hang, after treading the Bridge of Sighs, which spanned the narrow canal through the city of Balchester. The two of them went on to cross Seahill Road and took the nearby footpath across the fields towards the historic abbey.

They chatted happily about how they all played there when they were kids, including Lance and agreed it would be nice to see the old place again after so many years, and enjoy a few beers at the same time.

As usual, Bobby's hungry eyes kept roving over Jack's trim tight buttocks. Her rapid breathing and nervous movements meant she was aroused, and had ideas other than exchanging childhood reminiscences.

As Jacky wove in and out of the trees and wild rhododendrons, her slurred words were lost on Bobby's inattentive ears.

Stepping through the trickle of water that passed for a brook, Jack was chattering on about their childish games of tig, and kiss chase, when suddenly she stopped dead.

Bobby stopped too, as the strange drawled chanting of men and women's voices reached their ears and grew louder.

The chanting was coming from the steep grassy hill which stretched in front of them.

Jack turned and gawped at Bobby, then her strong inquisitive streak took over. 'Come on Bob,' she whispered, excitedly. 'Let's 'ave a nosy.'

The sudden calling of the hunting tawny owl in gliding flight pricked them with fear. Jacky quickly recovered her nerve. 'Ooooh,' she waved her arms like a ghost. 'Come on Bobby, it's only a daft bird, let's go.' She set off to climb the grassy slope. Once at the brow of the hill, she crouched down and looked across towards the ancient abbey.

Bobby Queen dropped down beside her, panting heavily.

The moon was full, so the ruined abbey could be seen clearly. Jack blinked and peered harder. She pointed a slim finger towards the building. 'Who the hell are they!?' she muttered, in astonishment.

The dark hooded figures floated about mysteriously in the dim flickering lights of the ruins.

Bobby rested her chin on her fist and giggled like a schoolgirl.

'Perhaps it's a party of some kind?' she speculated, adding mischievously, 'or even, an orgy!'

Jack scowled. 'Don't be daft Bobby, who'd 'ave a party all the way out here?' She shoved a cigarette into her mouth, pulled out her lighter with a jerk and mumbled, 'anyway there's no music – who the shit'd have a rave with no tunes. And!' she finished emphatically, 'who'd 'ave a leg-over dressed like that!?'

Bobby shivered. 'Dunno, but it sure looks a weird set-up.' Jacky drew deeply on her cigarette, flicked off the ash and started creeping forward towards the abbey.

As fate would have it, Jack and Bobby had had a miraculous escape, the working coven's lookouts had failed to notice them – on the way in, anyway.

Suddenly the eerie chanting ceased.

Bobby followed reluctantly. Reaching the old ivy-clad walls, they peered inside one of the gaping holes. Jack gripped and ripped out a tuft of grass which grew in the weed-infested walls – it was bugging her.

They could see the cloaked figures clearly now – they counted eleven of them. There was a makeshift table, which was a large rotting balk of timber. The table was ready, laid with much food, bottles of wine and elaborate goblets, this was for the festivities which were to take place at the end of the ritual.

The members were in pairs and the sexual activity was great.

Although Jack and Bobby didn't know it, partners had been allotted by means of numbers drawn from a secret pouch. Tonight, the pairings were particularly good ones. Although they couldn't see each other, because their faces were hidden, youth had drawn experience.

A middle-aged wife was being thrilled while being serviced by a lusty young man, while an elderly grandfather was mounting a nubile girl.

Bobby and Jack Dooley watched, speechless and wide-eyed, as some revellers openly masturbated, another couple copulated in a variety of positions, nothing it seemed, was off limits. The final three consisted of a threesome, as there was one male free.

As the member rode the female feverishly, his fingers clawing deep inside her rectum, he eagerly sucked the solid erection of the groaning, spare male – he didn't hesitate in gobbling up his spurting slimy sperm, like a half-starved bloodsucker.

The fascinated girls picked out the men by the grey robes they wore, although their eyes were masked. Each of them had a brooch, with a precious stone, a 'cat's-eye', pinned over the heart, to symbolise membership of the coven – the newly formed Hell Fire Club. They were naked beneath the robes, and while some wore them for sex a couple had chosen to discard them, the women likewise. The women, who all appeared shapely enough, except for one obese figure, wore black nunlike habits, and they too were masked. They also each wore a white band round their heads, with a veil, to help shield their faces.

In the centre of the floor, large fallen stones had been erected to form a makeshift altar.

At the head of the altar there rested a small blood-red cross. Below it was spread a large black sheet, with all the signs of the zodiac embroidered into it in gold thread. Near each corner of the altar stood an ornate candelabra with black candles, which were alight and flickering.

Jack heaved in a gulp of air and prodded Bobby. She nodded towards the altar. 'That sheet with the zodiac signs on it, and that red cross – I saw something dead alike at Woodcock's farm. It was hidden in the outhouse where he tried to . . .' The bad memory caused her words to fizzle out. It was then she saw a lean figure slowly limp into view from the darker side of the room. He swung out his stiff leg once more and stopped.

'Oh fuck!' she gasped, shattered, 'Woodcock!'

Bobby swallowed what felt like a marble. 'You mean, you mean that's him who . . .'

'Yeah, the ugly big-eared bastard.'

Both girls were glued to the spot, staring, as Woodcock, a lustful glint in his narrow piercing eyes, raised his long arms aloft to bring the worshipper's boisterous foreplay and intercourse to a halt. They all stood, clasped hands, and gazed up at him silently. He looked down his eagle-beaked nose and surveyed the gathering. As he folded his arms, satisfied that those expected were present tonight, his lips parted in a wolfish grin, revealing a row of misshaped yellow teeth. It was obvious, to Jacky, from his mauve silk robe to his mitre, that he was the High Priest of the outfit. In the centre of the mitre there was a large 'cat's-eye', and around his neck he wore a diamond-studded crux ansata, the Egyptian symbol of immortality.

Woodcock's very presence transformed as he was, exuded power and generated fear.

Woodcock nodded to a follower, the man hurried away and returned carrying a lamb. A knife blade flashed as it was laid on the altar.

Bobby turned to Jack, nauseated. 'Stuff this, Jack,' she muttered. 'T-this is bleeding black magic, devil worship. Call it what the fuck you like but I'm off, now!'

Jack too, was squeamish, and the sight of the harmless little lamb being slaughtered before her eyes was too much.

Both of them recognised that this was an evil gathering, although they had no idea it was a revival of the Hell Fire Club, first formed amongst the wealthy, way back in the 1700s.

Once it had been a coven of thirteen but it had now increased due to the rapid growth of Balchester and its surrounding estates. But tonight there was only twelve members present, the High Priestess was missing, and with Balchester being a conservative stronghold, the coven was a wealthy one.

Bobby was so engrossed that she didn't notice the large black slug. As it started to slither coldly onto her hand she let out a sudden scream.

Jack turned sharply. 'Shut it, Bob, or d'you want us to end up on that stuffin' altar?'

Bobby knocked the slug off her hand. 'C-come on Jack, let's piss off.'

It happened that the nearest male worshipper to them had overheard Bobby's scream, and his eyes focused on them.

He recognised only Jack because Bobby was already turning away. Jack would have to be silenced, he decided. She was a virgin, as well, which would make things more enjoyable. But Jack and Bobby were already hotfooting it as fast as they could, back through Bluebell Wood, towards the safety of Seahill village, with the alerted lookouts hard on their heels.

They were blissfully ignorant of the fact that they had been spotted.

They dived breathlessly into the back seat of a cab. Thank God, thought Jack, there was one handy on the Red Lion's car park. She coughed and spluttered. 'Bedford please mate, anywhere by the parade of shops'll do.' Her heart was still thumping.

The smart taxi-driver glanced up into his mirror. He cleared his throat, discreetly, as Bobby was just about to bite the top off a bottle of lager. 'Sorry luv,' he snapped, 'not in here.' He half-glanced back over his shoulder. 'Nor that Luv,' he drawled, adamantly, as Jack lit a cigarette. 'Can't you read?' Jacky cursed and stubbed it out. She was starting to feel grotty and by the look of her, so was Bobby. Tonight was going to stay in their memories for a very long time.

Chapter Nine

Merlin passed his hand over his mop of silver hair and scratched the back of his neck. He tutted irritably as Woodcock's phone burred and burred, unheeded. He had found the telephone number of the farm in the Yellow Pages, and dearly wanted to speak to Danny. The fingers on his silver pocket watch were dead on midnight. 'Mmm,' he muttered, quietly, to himself, 'perhaps it is a little late to be phoning the place now, milking and all that to be done early morning, best I phone him tomorrow.' He pursed his lips thoughtfully and put down the phone.

Since Danny's visit he had spent much of his time looking into the history of Ament and her falcon, Horus, and now felt sure that there was a lot more to Ament than just being a children's nanny, with a bird of prey as a pet. After all, Woodcock had spent several months in Egypt – a mystical country, and he'd returned wealthy, very wealthy. It was old Merlin's suspicion that Woodcock, and maybe Ament, could well be involved with the dark forces. He smoked, sipped at his drink, and tapped his bony fingers against his wrinkled forehead. Something was wrong, he knew it; he sensed evil. It would be stimulating to have a last run-in with wicked old Lucifer at his time of life – a final victory, if you like.

Danny and Su-Ling had no intention of answering the phone, they hardly even noticed it in fact.

Beneath the black silk sheets of the four-poster bed, they were deaf and blind to all but each other.

'Mmmm,' Su-Ling murmured, blissfully, easing her lips away. Hungrily she travelled down his body, kissing, caressing tantalising, until he was hard again. She tenderly helped roll on a condom, then Danny took over.

Laying Su-Ling on her back with her legs spread wide, he teased her clitoris for several minutes with his tongue before he entered her – her juices flowed.

Unbearably excited, she shuddered, tugged at Danny, and screamed as she climaxed yet again. Panting, groaning, wanting more, she clawed his back and wrapped her legs high around him. As Danny burst inside her with, 'Oh my love! yes!' Su-Ling cried out with ecstasy.

It took a moment to realise what had happened.

'Oh God, Su-Ling,' he gasped. 'It's burst, the condom, it's damn well burst!'

Thoughts of Aids and Su-Ling getting pregnant were speedily banished from their minds by Sweep's loud barking out in the yard and the sound of a car approaching.

Oh God, thought Danny, one catastrophe after

another. 'Who is it Su-Ling?' he hissed. 'You said George wouldn't be home until at least 2 o'clock.'

As he quickly rolled off her, and peeled off the shredded condom, he glanced at the clock radio. It was only twenty-five past midnight. As the car's engine silenced, Su-Ling, with a scared expression, hurriedly turned off the radio.

Danny pushed the soggy condom under the bed, grabbed his clothes and fled towards the door. 'Don't forget to move it,' he flung over his shoulder.

She nodded, and gave a sharp intake of breath as the front door slammed. Her heart beat like a drum. After a few minutes, she heard Woodcock's slow tread on the stairs – Danny would be safe in his room by now, she thought, relieved.

She suddenly realised how wet and sticky she was and hurriedly grabbed a handful of tissues. Still dabbing at herself with them, she rushed to the en suite to flush them away, completely forgetting the evidence under the bed. She just managed to grab her weekly woman's magazine and dive back in bed before her husband angrily stomped in.

The interruption by Bobby and Jack Dooley had disturbed the coven, and he was not in a pleasant mood.

In his own room, Danny hurriedly dressed in case he needed to make a quick getaway. He could only hope there would be no disastrous consequences from the burst condom, like Aids for instance – but, after all, he reflected, Su-Ling was a married woman. She would be clean, wouldn't she? But what about other farmworkers she could have slept with, the possibility couldn't be ignored, and what about all those years in Bangkok? Hell to her being pregnant, he could handle that, but Aids . . . As things seemed quiet, he assumed that it was safe to undress again and get into bed. He was unlacing his boots when Woodcock bent over to shove his slippers under the bed.

Su-Ling froze, her gaze fixed on her husband – he was only inches from Danny's condom.

A puzzled look crept over Woodcock's face as his fingers touched the slimy rubber.

Su-Ling trembled, knowing what his temper was like.

Woodcock slowly stood up. He shook with rage, as the crumpled red condom hung limply between finger and thumb.

'Well?' he growled.

Su-Ling drew the sheets tight up around her neck. Her eyes were wide with fear. She tried to say something but no words would come. Even a rapist wouldn't leave a used contraceptive under the bed, that tale wouldn't serve, her terrified thoughts ran.

Danny almost jumped out of his skin as Woodcock's voice boomed throughout the house. 'I want a fucking son don't I, so whose rubber is it, Su-Ling?' He leaned over her, gripped her jaw tightly and squeezed with his long, strong fingers. 'Whose? You two-timing little cow, and after I brought you to England, away from those whore-houses.' He hurled the condom against the dressing-table mirror, his voice roaring. 'Whose!?'

Suddenly, he stopped and fell silent. He slowly turned towards the door and clenched his fists. 'Black!' The name shot out like a pistol-shot. 'Danny – fucking – Black! I'll kill him – I'll kill him!'

He slung back the mirrored sliding door of the wardrobes, hard. He looked up, eyes blazing, to where his shotgun cartridges were hidden at the back, out of his daughters' reach. He tore out a pile of clothes and hurled them at Su-Ling. 'I'm going to blow his half-caste ballocks off!'

Danny had heard enough, he was already up and frantically retying his bootlaces. His few belongings were stuffed into his rucksack on top of Steeleye.

The girls were awake by now and crying at the disturbance. Ament, who had followed George Woodcock into the farmhouse, was trying to comfort them.

Danny threw open the bedroom window and looked down, determined to escape, with his balls intact. He heard the snap of Woodcock's gun and his muttered threats as he approached the bedroom door. Danny leapt out and the huge pile of cow muck below greeted him odorously. 'Oh shit!' he groaned, and then grinned ruefully at the aptness of the word.

The frogs from the nearby pond set up their croaking as if laughing at him.

As he desperately pulled his legs free from the

smelly manure, Woodcock burst through the bedroom door, shotgun at the ready. He cursed, stepped quickly to the open window and levelled the barrels at Danny.

In that instant, Danny finally broke free and ran for his life. The night air was shattered by the double explosion from the shotgun. As the speeding lead pellets whistled past Danny he ducked, weaved and quickened his pace.

Woodcock's roar echoed after him. 'I'll have you for this, Black! By the Devil, I'll have your guts – Devil I will.'

Danny heard him slam the window shut, and knew there were going to be ructions in the farmhouse.

The stink of the cow manure on himself and his jeans was making Danny's eyes water so, once he was safely away, he made for a sheltered spot by the river, undressed, and dived into the water. Emerging after a quick bathe with chattering teeth, he dragged on the one and only change of clothes he had in his rucksack, scrubbed his boots as clean as he could with handfuls of dewy grass, dumped his discarded garments in the undergrowth of a small copse, and carried on his way at a brisk pace, relieved that he now smelled rather more sweetly than before.

He sheltered for the rest of the night in a derelict terraced house on the outskirts of Balchester, only a mile from the Bedford housing estate. Most of the next day he spent at the D.H.S.S. office, securing the advanced payment he would need for one of Dilly's bedsits.

The young girl behind the desk at the dole office sat red-faced and squirming, with her eyebrows arched high, as Danny casually explained the circumstances which had cost him his job, and no doubt this wages, at Woodcock's farm. Later, he scanned the attic room and nodded approvingly; at least it was clean, neatly furnished, with a cleaning lady coming in once a week and the linen changed fortnightly. Now all he needed was another job, and to learn how to use the large communal kitchen's cooker and washing-machine.

Ben Dooley reluctantly handed over the hundred and fifty pounds to Docker in the Coach and Horses pub. He had finished rebuilding the new garden wall that morning, and was already sick to the teeth with the working arrangements he now had with Docker and company, also he was still looking at a year's driving ban at the very least.

Mister Fixit, whoever he was, was going to make a tidy sum out of him. If only he knew the man's identity he could tell the police but on reflection, perhaps he'd better not probe. The pressure he was getting from the local mafia was also making him even worse to live with.

Alex, the stockily built landlord of the pub, winked at Docker and company as he placed their beers on top of the counter. The beer was free – the cheap Karaoke equipment Docker had sold him was well worth the money. On a Thursday night, Alex could draw in the crowds by putting on his own show. And, he could sing a bit as well.

As the small dark-haired girl swayed back and forth eating the mike, doing her version of Shirley Bassey's Goldfinger from the James Bond film, Adder, Miko and Fat Man suddenly barged their way through the doors into the room and pushed through the crowd up to the bar.

Alex grinned and welcomed them warmly, with a nod of his head and a confident smile. His facial scar, suffered at sea in the Falklands War, twitched.

Rumours had been spreading like wildfire throughout the estate about a fearful figure running a smallish, but effective mafia-style syndicate, and with the gathering of rogues about him, all eyes in the bar room were on Alex.

Jacky Dooley still had no steady boyfriend, and she didn't need one – her ecstasy tablets were her first real lover. She wanted it the whole time, it made her happy and she loved dancing to rave music now, more than ever. She had rapidly moved up the drug scale from her first tab of L.S.D. She was now on two ecstasy tablets, plus a wrap of speed a night, and it was costing her a lot of money for every trip.

But as she was addicted she was still only getting the same buzz – she needed more – she needed something stronger now.

She climbed off the bathroom scales and muttered

irritably, 'Bloody hell, that's another two pounds I've lost.'

She was already slim and the weight loss was beginning to tell. Her fast rising run on drugs had cost her dearly – she'd even sold her two gold rings, one of which had been a birthday gift from Daisy, to help finance her habit. She was now flat broke, and without cash there was no hope of any 'E' or speed. Jack Dooley felt grotty, she was coming down from up high to a nadir of depression. Flopping on top of her bed, she buried her head into her pillow and burst into tears. Where the hell was she going to get some money from? Even a lousy tab of L.S.D. would do.

She sat up and wiped her eyes with a tissue, then with trembling fingers, lit a cigarette. God! She thought as her mind momentarily clicked into gear. I've got my new job to start on Monday as well. She puffed out an exasperated burst of smoke, as she silently demanded, 'Where the hell am I going to get some bread from!?' She gnawed her lip reflectively for a few seconds and let out a sudden short, sharp laugh. 'Ha! I think I know,' she muttered, and a wise evil smile grew on her face.

Rosie and John were out, they always went to 'Flamingos' nightclub on a Thursday night, and from there to one of the Indian or Chinese restaurants in Balchester city centre. They wouldn't be home till gone 2 am.

Jack poked her head around her bedroom door.

The hall light was always on, for little Sophie's sake, she had a thing about the dark.

Jack's heartbeat quickened, as she slipped past Sophie who was soundly sleeping. She crept up to Daisy and Ben Dooley's open bedroom door. As she peeped in and slowly surveyed the room she allowed herself a small grin. The hall light cast a beam onto her father's work pants, which lay crumpled in a heap on the carpet. Jack eased the door wider open. Ben Dooley was grunting and snoring like a pig. Daisy was curled up on the other side of the bed.

With calm determination, Jack inched forward cat-like, towards her father's pants.

Dooley's loud snore suddenly stuck in his throat and he lurched, as Jack's nimble fingers rattled his coins slightly. She held her breath and froze.

Dooley snored on, and so in a matter of seconds she had slipped two crisp notes from out of his wallet, returned it and backed safely out of the room. She pulled the door to and stole quickly away.

At the bottom of the staircase, she eagerly checked the money – a ten and a twenty, that would do nicely. She had never stolen before and it had been easier than she'd expected.

As Stumpy hopped up to her, his short tail wagging excitedly, she gave him a pat, and whispered. 'Shush, shush Stumpy, I'm going out but I won't be long.'

Jack gently clicked the front door shut. She knew where Fat Man lived – she needed some stuff now! and she just prayed that he'd be home.

Getting out of the taxi, Lance paid the driver, and in generous fashion, added a tip. He had been sent home early from his shift at the steelworks, as he was feeling off colour. The driver thanked him and drove away.

As he looked up the road, Lance's keen eye picked out Jack's distant shape as she passed beneath the bright street-lamp – he'd know that bobbing walk anywhere. He glanced at his watch, it was 12.30 am. He stood pondering for a second, after a quick glance through the gap in the row of conifers towards his parents' house, he thrust his nausea to the back of his mind and set off to follow her. He kept a good distance behind her, and trod lightly so that his footsteps would not alert her. He could not explain why he felt so uneasy, except that she seemed somehow vulnerable. He trailed her to Fat Man's luxury pad, on the edge of Balchester, and waited patiently outside. From the nearby alleyway, he could watch the front of the place. At last, after about a quarter of an hour the front door swung open and she reappeared. He could see clearly into the lighted hallway. Fat Man lifted his hand and drew his gross fingers slowly down her pretty cheek to the corner of her relaxed lips – she'd got what she wanted.

Lance gasped, he went ice-cold and felt like puking – surely not, he thought, not a girl as lovely as Jacky.

As Fat Man tried vainly to coax her back inside, an evil sneer distorted his features. He mouthed a few obscenities, waved a despondent arm and slammed the door shut, recognising that the last thing on her mind was sex.

Jack squealed as Lance suddenly stepped from the darkness of the alley and gently gripped her arm.

She panicked until she saw who it was. Then her fear turned to puzzled annoyance. 'Shit! Lance,' she snapped. 'You frightened the bleedin' life out of me – what the hell are you doin' here anyway?'

He let go her arm and muttered somewhat sheepishly, 'I – I'm sorry Jack I didn't mean to scare you.' He hunched his shoulders and kicked a few early fallen leaves off the pavement. 'I saw you when I was coming home from work,' he explained. 'I was sent home because I felt bad. So – so I followed you to make sure that you . . .'

His words had sunk in quickly and her eyes darkened and glittered with temper in her white face. 'What! d'you mean you followed me, Lance?' Her voice rose sharply. 'You've got no right to do that, you live next door, you don't own me. Shit man! are you a cabbage or what – well, are you?'

He raised his head and shot back, 'I can't think what you bother with him for, he's a . . .'

Jack rammed the ecstasy tablet and tab of acid that she was clutching in her hand into her jacket pocket. She lunged out her arm and screamed at him. 'It's got fuck all! to do with you, arse-hole, now piss off!'

She was getting intensely ratty, she wanted to fly,

she'd been grounded long enough. She rushed away like a blast of March wind.

Lance stood speechless, mouth hanging open. This wasn't Jacky Dooley, this wasn't the girl he'd grown up with – the girl he loved. He was hurt, and he knew there was something very badly wrong.

It wasn't long after she'd crept back into the house, before Jack sat in pure bliss on the toilet seat – legs crossed and stretched out. The tab had taken hold and she was tripping. She giggled continuously as she looked across the bathroom to the pink pot hippopotamus ornament, that lay between the bath taps, amidst the talcs and lotions. Its bowler-hatted head rested cheekily on its right foot. As it waved its other leg in the air, and cocked its head from side to side, the hippopotamus's fat face swelled and burst into a broad grin.

Jack dragged deeply on her cigarette, glanced up at the light shade and shuddered. The pattern on the shade had become the distorted face of the Devil. As the shade spun around quickly the room twirled, and from the fun with the hippopotamus, her visions had turned to terrifying nightmares. She shook uncontrollably, leapt from the toilet seat, and fled through the door, as blood and live cobras spat at her from the Devil's mouth. She slammed her hands over her ears as the words exploded in her head. 'Welcome to hell!' they boomed. 'Welcome to hell, Jacky Dooley.'

By six o'clock in the morning, Jack lay on the

settee, singing in tune with the rock band, her demons vanished. Her heartbeat was rapid and her pupils were dilated – she was relaxed and happy as with sweating hands she lovingly cuddled Stumpy. She introduced her own words to the song. 'Ecstasy, I love my ecstasy . . .' She was up high with the skylark.

Danny Black had settled into his new bedsit well, and he had relished his first supper there of vegetable curry.

He left the one small window over the tiny white hand-basin open, and two early morning sparrows from the rooftop had taken advantage. They fluttered and twittered merrily as they enjoyed his leftovers.

Danny woke and cocked a wary eye smiling at the disturbance. Once he had risen, washed and dressed, he playfully shooed the small excited birds back through the window – he hoped that Lotty would share amicably with his feathered friends.

Knowing that Woodcock would be working out on the farm at that time, he'd chanced a quick call to Su-Ling to see how she was after her bedroom ordeal. After telling him of her severe beating from Woodcock, she hurriedly explained that she'd send Vic the cowman, his friend, to meet him to give him Lotty. She went on sobbing deeply, 'I still . . .' She dropped the phone, Woodcock's tractor was drawing up to the house – Danny felt sadness for Su-Ling, he sighed as he hung up.

Mrs Dilly, who lived with her husband in the largest house in the street, had agreed to look after the little cat while Danny settled in. Danny was to meet Vic later that day in Balchester to pick Lotty up. Before that, he would see if his rent had been sorted out by the D.H.S.S. – he had already found the Dillys likeable landlords.

He stood looking up out of the window at the streams of traffic on the overhead motorway as he swigged from a carton of milk – he would train later today, he decided Steeleye needed twirling and the strap leather-soaping as well.

His eye turned to the old iron guttering that was fastened just below the Welsh slate roof.

The busy birds had formed their own little garden in the gutter of grass, weeds and even a spreading rockery plant. The seeds which they had carried there had thrived well in the rich soil and moss. There was also a shallow stream just managing to trickle through the garden and into the downspout when pushed along by wind or rain.

Danny let out a satisfied sigh – the new bedsit was OK. He turned to the cupboard and switched on his small portable radio to listen to his favourite DJ.

As Jack bounced jovially into the hallway, Daisy had already descended the stairs and was picking up the mail. Strangely though, the dark red envelope which she held in her hand had no address, only 'Jacky Dooley' written on the front in large black letters. She fingered the letter curiously before handing it to

Jack who, in her exilarated condition was frantically squeezing her around the waist.

Daisy gave her a look of uncertainty. My God! she thought, her daughter was acting oddly these days. She disentangled herself from Jacky and escaped to the kitchen to start preparing breakfast.

Jack sang raucously as she slit open the envelope with a thin finger. Her version of one of the top ten pop songs, however, fizzled out when her fuzzy gaze settled onto the large words written in blood on white paper. This was no L.S.D. drug hallucination, this was real.

She gripped the letter in a spasm of terror and clenched her teeth. The words engraved themselves on her mind. 'YOU SAW NOTHING AT THE OLD ABBEY – NOT A WORD, OR ELSE!'

Jack didn't know if she was tripping, or not – all she did know was that she was scared rigid.

Chapter Ten

On the following Monday, on a wet windy morning, Jacky Dooley arrived punctually at eight o'clock at Goodporks sausage factory. She felt terrible – she was coming down after a heavy head-banging weekend on booze and drugs.

Whilst being shown around the factory and given the run-down on jobs on the production line by Janet, the supervisor, she shook continually. But she knew she had to settle herself down, for Daisy's sake, she must keep the job.

She detested the hairnet, long shapeless white overall and daft hat that she had to wear.

By dinner-time, she had done well, all things considered. She was getting into the swing of things, and after a few minor hiccups, had more or less latched on to doing the simplest of jobs on the production line.

By the end of the day, Goodporks' van drivers and warehousemen had realised that there was nothing down for them as far as Jack's neat little body was concerned. She hurriedly clocked off and rushed home.

'Cor! don't panic Luv,' shouted a fat red-faced van driver, as he backed his vehicle into the depot. 'I'll give you a lift home in a min' when I've cashed in. The way you're goin' you'll boil your water.'

As she sped by, Jack flashed a sideways glare at the lecherous slob. 'Don't worry arsehole,' she hissed. 'You won't get your grubby bleedin' fingers burnt.'

He gulped and his flabby jaw dropped.

After his sweet-talking on Thursday morning at the D.H.S.S. office, Danny managed to secure a payment. On the following Monday morning, the giro dropped through the letter-box. After cashing it, he'd tucked the twenty pounds he owed Merlin safely under the mattress. That evening he intended to go out for a drink and have a look around the Bedford Estate pubs. He needed to ask around for work, and maybe he'd bump into Ben Dooley, who always drank on the estate, he might be able to put him on to something.

On Monday night, after leaving Lotty her food and milk, Danny set off from his bedsit to walk the short distance into Bedford. He left the road at the small hump-backed bridge and ran down the stone steps onto the narrow canal tow-path. It was twilight, and the day's strong winds had blown themselves out, leaving the evening still, with a slight nip in the air.

On the tow-path, the large white barge horse, Snowy, snorted and quickened his pace, while Tony, its owner, held on to the harness. The long thick barge rope tightened to let loose a shower of water, and the boatful of chattering, camera-clicking tourists cut smoothly through the dark waters of the Shropshire Union Canal.

Danny nodded silently to Tony and stood aside to allow them through, before carrying on his way.

After passing beneath the iron railway bridge, which always seemed to send a shower of miniature raindrops into the water below, he halted.

The sight of the small wild group of dark blue forget-me-nots took his breath away – they were one of his grandfather's favourite flowers. He sighed, smiled and walked on. His head rocketed to the left, as the ravenous pike struck to send a shoal of small fish leaping skyward, their gills flapping hungrily for life. He shook his head and strode on – mother nature's cruelty was hard to take.

As Jack entered the bar of the club just in front of Bobby, she stopped abruptly. Taken aback, she stared across the smoke-filled room. Her heart gave a little lift of joy, when she thought she could see Danny Black tipping back a pint. She fumbled distractedly for her cigarettes, lit up and inhaled deeply. The stream of smoke which escaped her lips matched the drab-coloured walls. For a few seconds she stood wondering if it really was him, then he turned his head slightly – yes! It was definitely Danny. She felt Bobby dig her fingers into her back. 'Come on Jack, 'urry up, I wanna drink.'

Jacky ignored her remark, she was just glad that

she'd shampooed her hair that day. Even though it was a lot shorter after the scalping from her father, with her sister, Rosie's, help it was now a short, curly style which gave her features a certain piquancy.

As she approached the bar, Danny's thick black eyebrows rose in surprise, and a certain amount of pleasure.

He hooked his thumb into his anorak pocket and smiled at her, warmly. 'Aaah, at last, I've managed to catch up with the elusive Jacky Dooley. How are you? Would yous like a drink?'

To Bobby's annoyance, Jack accepted with a broad grin and a firm nod. A little colour arose in her cheeks – she felt an instant magnetism about this dark-skinned man.

As Jack and Danny stood near to the bar chatting, Bobby sulkily bought her own drink. 'Rip off!' she hissed into Jack's ear, as she stalked away to invest in the one-armed bandit.

The ecstasy which Jack had taken earlier was now affecting her, and Danny noticed. He had seen enough of drugs right up the scale to heroin injection, enough to last him a lifetime. His eyes darkened with disappointment and his voice was accusing. 'You're on the shit aren't you? – yous must be crackers to hit that stuff.'

Normally, when challenged so abruptly she would let fly with a verbal assault, this time she didn't. Just by looking into his unblinking caring eyes, she felt a little ashamed. She wanted to deny it, as she did to her sister, Rosie, and to John, but she couldn't. She sipped her lager, lowered her eyes and chewed at her bottom lip. Then, raising her head and looking at him sideways, she demanded, 'What's it to you anyway?'

Bobby had lost on the bandit and was slumped at one of the empty long narrow tables, drumming her fingers to the music filtering through from the disco room – she already hated Danny Black.

Danny's fingers tightened around his glass. 'It's got lots to do with me if yous must know,' he replied sternly. 'I used to be on the stuff meself when I was a kid, I saw my ol' woman die from a massive heroin overdose. You seem like a nice girl, yous should leave it alone.'

Jack shuffled uneasily and knocked the rest of her drink back with a swift gulp. She shrugged her shoulders apologetically.

'I – I'm sorry man – I'm sorry, I didn't know, did I?'

His expression stayed hard, even a trifle fierce, his piercing eyes seemed to burn deep as he asked. 'How long have you been doing it?'

'Not long – I dunno, maybe two or three weeks. I only smoked joints for a few months before that.'

'So what are you on to, speed, "E" or what?'

She nodded as she proudly paid for her own drink – Danny had waved her offer away. 'Dead on, man,' she snorted defiantly, 'both of 'em.'

As Status Quo exploded on the jukebox, she began to bounce around in an energetic, high-powered fashion.

Danny's facial muscles tightened, as her head swayed madly from side to side – his stomach churned, sickened by her state.

'How d'you get off it anyway?' she queried, almost casually, bursting into an hysterical giggle.

His patience was cracking and he snapped. 'Because I wanted to, and so the hell should you, before yous destroy yourself – got it!?'

Her response was to throw her wild arms up to the stars. She was feeling good. 'But I love my blockbusters' they make me . . .' She twirled and faced him again.

Her beautiful innocent bewildered look burnt into the roots of his heart. Her voice was excited, yet tinged with despair.

'They make me feel great!' She puckered her lips at him, and added, in husky tones, 'and sexy.'

Danny desperately wanted to try to keep the conversation going. But, he didn't want sex with her, and he quickly changed the subject.

'I thought I might have seen your ol' fella in here? I wanted to find out if he could fix me up with a bit of work, yous know what I mean like?' He deliberately swept the room with his hawk-like gaze. He politely waved her stream of smoke away from his face – he hated smoking, as much as she hated flies, spiders, and other creepy-crawlies. Because of his concentration on her drug addiction, it took time for him to notice that her hair looked different. He leaned over and scrutinised her springy dark locks. 'I see you've had your hair cut then,' he remarked.

Jack's mood changed rapidly to one of depression. She dropped her head like a falling stone and rammed her boot hard into the bar step. 'Yeah man, good style don't you reckon?' She shrugged her shoulders savagely. 'Eh!'

Suddenly, she exploded into a burst of violent temper. Danny hastily stepped back a pace. 'My old man scalped me – OK!' She wobbled, and glowered furiously at Danny. 'Yeah D-Danny b-bloody Black, your mate did this to me 'ead, – me dad, Ben Dooley, when he was w-well pissed.' She sagged, just as suddenly as she erupted. 'So there,' she mumbled.

He sighed deeply. 'I'm sorry Jack, I didn't know, I should learn to keep me big mouth shut.'

She dug her hands into her hips and swayed slightly.

'S'okay, no sweat man,' her tone was gentle.

'You weren't to know anyway.' She fingered her forehead thoughtfully. 'They're looking for a couple of blokes at the sausage factory where I work, if you're interested?'

'What for like?'

'Just labourin' and loadin' the vans, and that.' She shrugged. 'You know what I mean.'

Danny nodded eagerly, any job was better than none.

He looked at her and smiled, then nodded towards the empty pool table. 'D'yous fancy a game, girl, or what?'

Jack forced a nervous giggle. 'B-but I've never played it in my life before.'

He wrapped a loving arm around her small shoulders and eased her away from the bar. 'Come 'ead, girl, I'll teach yous to play.' Bobby Queen just sat, grinding her teeth and looking daggers at them. She'd latched on quickly to the fact that Danny and Jacky had some feelings towards each other.

The room quietened as Adder, Miko and the Fat Man barged through the single glass door at the far side. They always paid their subscriptions and didn't push drugs on the premises, so were permitted, but under watchful eyes. As the trio made their way to the bar, Jack glanced across to them and nervously discarded her cue.

Danny's animal instinct reacted immediately. He scowled, but respected the fact that Adder and friends wouldn't take kindly to Jack playing pool with the man who'd turned them over in the toilets of the Fox and Hounds.

Bobby Queen glanced from Adder to Danny and Jack and waited smugly for the fireworks to start. Let's see what you're going to do now Jacky Dooley, she thought.

Danny's keen gaze rested on the drug troop. His mind moved fast and he knew the only way to help Jack was to make a quick exit. After hurriedly finishing his lager, he hurled the last six pool balls into the pockets, flung a pleading glance at Jack and hissed, through partially closed lips. 'Listen Jack! s'best I shoot off now but I'll meet yous down the river where Stonewall House used to be, tomorrow night at seven o'clock, if you want. We'll walk an' talk, and I'll find ways to help yous fight against the shit.' He spread his calloused hands pleadingly. 'Will you come – please!?'

She glanced worriedly towards the crowded bar where Bobby was pointing at them, her lip curling.

Adder and mates were not amused.

She looked at Danny again and covered her mouth with her hand. 'OK man, OK, I'll see you there.'

Danny zipped up his anorak and moved towards the double glass doors. 'And keep off that shit kid, drugs a' no good to anybody, I'll see yous.' He left the club, feeling that he'd made a special date with a special person.

The following Tuesday morning saw Ben Dooley slouched in his usual position over the breakfast table. His dark whiskered face broke into a broad grin as he slowly scanned the neatly typed letter.

Excitedly, he slammed the flat of his hand on the table. 'Got it, Daisy,' he burst out. 'I've got the bloody council contract for the new paths and walkways.' He slurped his tea, banged down his mug and grinned at her. 'I'll be able to take on a few men and give you . . .'

Daisy sighed despondently, shook her head, and started to clear the breakfast table as he rambled on. She'd heard it all before, when he'd had a partner and built a few houses. Rather than invest in his own property, and try to work his way up the ladder, he'd blown the cash on a string of slags he'd picked up in his second-hand jag. His ex-partner was now Councillor Robins – Fat Man's father? He had spent his money much more wisely. He had bought a large plot of land and built and sold a dozen, hundred thousand pound houses. He was a distinguished figure in the masons!

Rosie just slumped a little, sighed, and dropped her cup in her saucer – she was far more interested in her tabloid than her father's bullshit.

It had all flown high above little Sophie's head, as she eagerly scooped up her cornflakes – Sammy Smith had promised her faithfully that he would show her his private collection of pictures of football stars in the park.

Jack was up in the bathroom vigorously flossing her perfect teeth. She was finding the going tough, trying to work while doing drugs. She was as fed up as the rest of the family of Ben Dooley, and his terrible drunken tantrums. To make matters worse, for the first time in her life she had discovered that she could have loving feelings towards a man – Danny Black! So, her emotions were at sixes and sevens.

As Merlin picked up his phone, Danny dropped the shiny silver-coloured coin into the house's communal pay phone, which hung on the flower-papered wall at the foot of the stairs.

Merlin coughed with annoyance, he always did when he was disturbed. 'Yes! Haddock here, Fredrick Haddock, army number . . .'

'S'me Freddy,' Danny broke in sharply – he already knew Merlin's army number off by heart.

There was a slight pause as the penny dropped.

'Aah, and about time too, young man, I've been trying to get hold of you for ages.'

'Why?'

'To ask you about this Egyptian woman, eh, what's her name, Ament! Yes, yes, Ament and her falcon, Horus isn't it?'

Danny's laugh echoed down the long wide hallway. 'Ask away Freddy, but I don't live there any more.'

'What!'

'That's why I've phoned you, to tell you I've moved. I – I – er – had to leave Woodcock's farm, I . . .'

'Why?' asked Merlin with a trace of annoyance.

Danny's eyebrows rose, as he thoughtfully fingered his bottom lip. 'Well – er – well, he fired me, he said I wasn't up to the job. I just kept getting it wrong, like going to the wrong places for stuff, an' putting things where I wasn't s'posed to – you know how it is Freddy.'

'Well, you really should try harder Danny,' Merlin said, grumpily. 'This is the worst recession for fifty years, jobs are hard to come by.'

Danny sighed, then smiled to himself. 'Yes Freddy,' he drawled. 'I know.' He went on to rattle off his new address and telephone number.

'And Freddy,' he added. 'I've got the twenty pounds I owe you, I'll drop it off later this week if that's okay?' He gazed up, absently, at the fancy plaster moulding that surrounded the white ceiling. 'Oh! by the way, don't worry too much about the job, I've got an interview later today at Goodporks sausage factory.'

'Good, I hope it goes well for you, and how's the training with old Steeleye doing?'

'Fine, just fine.'

'Useful tool, isn't it?'

'Very!' agreed Danny.

He turned, startled, at the harsh cough which carried sharply down the red-carpeted stairs.

The tubby little spotty bank teller stood leaning on the banister, rattling her change and tapping her foot impatiently. It looked as if she was waiting to phone in sick again, thought Danny.

The previous tenant had been one of Jack Dooley's friends – she had overdosed on heroin and had had a sad and humble funeral.

The bank teller had looked down her nose at Danny ever since he had moved in, she obviously considered that living next door to a labourer wasn't good enough for her.

Danny tried to ignore her as he listened to Freddy. Serve her right if she choked on her cough, he told himself.

'Right, dear boy,' Freddy, too, was coughing at the other end of the phone. 'Damned cigarettes, they'll be the death of me. I must be off, I've got a million things to do. I'll see you towards the weekend then, and please try and bring me some interesting news.'

Danny chuckled. 'Ha! Righto Freddy, I'll . . .' The phone cut off. Danny realised he was talking to himself and hung up.

Spotty stomped angrily down the stairs, complaining loudly.

'You have no right to hog the phone, you've only lived here for . . .' She barged past him so forcibly that he lost his balance and accidentally trod on her foot. She squealed with pain.

'You stupid black bastard,' she howled, stooping and rubbing her injured foot.

'Whoops!' exclaimed Danny, as he placed a sympathetic hand on her shoulder. 'I'm sorry Luv.'

Her response was to quickly straighten up, and try to slap him hard across the face.

His reactions were instant and he managed to grip her wrist, stopping her vicious blow just inches from his cheek.

She reddened, wriggled, and squealed, as Danny gently lowered her arm. His apologetic laugh, followed by, 'I said I was sorry Luv, honest!' only made her worse. As she quickly stooped again and carefully took off her slipper to inspect her sore big toe, Danny bounded up the stairs with a stream of abuse ringing in his ears, there was an interview to prepare for.

The office door clicked and swung open. Mrs Coot's bespectacled smiling face peered out into the small waiting-room. She nodded at Danny, her large short-sighted blue eyes studying him hungrily. Passing an agitated hand over her forehead, she murmured, in seductive tones, 'Come in, please, Mister Black, I've been expecting you.'

He tossed his magazine back on the small dark polished table, rose and followed her beckoning finger into her office, closing the door behind him.

She waved him to the chair on the opposite side of her cluttered desk. 'Please take a seat Mister Black.'

He thanked her and sat down, very much aware of her long slender legs, as she glided across the carpet to the shelved wall. He watched, with raised eyebrows, as she reached up on high heels to return some papers to the top shelf, then let out a silent rush of breath as she came back to sit at her desk, and peer through her bifocals at her notes. Looking up, she sighed and leaned forward. 'Right, Mister Black,' she said, clasping her hands and nodding at him, benignly. 'What ideas do you have about the good old British sausage?'

Danny was momentarily at a loss, wondering if the woman was sending him up. He hid a grin, at the thought that his views on sausages of any kind and nationality would probably make her carefully styled hair stand on end.

'Let's say I'm always ready to learn,' he replied, finally.

Mrs Coot treated him to a beaming smile. 'You'll do,' was all she said. Danny heaved a sigh of relief, it looked as if he was going to get his chance to become well acquainted with the vagaries of the Goodporks sausage.

Chapter Eleven

After about ten minutes, Danny re-entered the waiting-room, closing Mrs Coot's door behind him. He stood still for an instant and breathed another huge sigh of relief – he'd got the job.

The pulsating sex appeal of Mrs Coot had aroused him, but responsive though he was, he had not done anything that might jeopardise his job interview. Anyway, the thought of meeting Jack Dooley was wrapped around his mind like a silken web. His feelings for her were different. Strong feelings, which were more than sexual, such as he'd never had for a woman before.

A pleasurable smile spread across Mrs Coot's face, Danny Black was a handsome man and she was a very determined lady, when it came to bedding the men she fancied.

Late July daylight had merged into cool, scented dusk. As Danny sat rocking gently back and forth on the children's swing, in the small park near to the Stonewall House site, he glanced at his watch, it was five past seven – Jack was late. As a sharp breeze rose, with the rolling salted tidal wave of the River

Denny, he pulled up his anorak hood and shivered. There was no sign of Jacky, and he was beginning to get a disappointed sickly feeling in his stomach. He nodded and mumbled a disgruntled 'evening' to the stooped old man who passed with his grey-faced tottering mongrel.

Then, the gentle swaying figure approaching caught his eye. His heart lurched, as he concentrated his gaze – even the darkening night couldn't hide the shape of Jack Dooley.

The evocative scent of log fire smoke from the nearby fisherman's cottage chimney drifted up his nostrils as he waited. His mind raced, Jack was coming. He quickly slid off the swing seat, hurriedly tidied the bunch of red roses he'd bought that very afternoon and stood waiting, his heartbeat quickening with her every step.

When she reached him, he gently gripped her hand before giving her a firm loving hug. Then holding her at arm's length he said, huskily. 'Hi Jack, God I thought yous wasn't going to come.' Before she had time to answer, he picked up the bouquet of sweet-smelling flowers and gave them to her. 'I bought them especially for you!' he murmured.

She gave a startled smile as she took the flowers and dropped down onto the seat of the swing. 'Phew man I'm knackered, it's a fair walk from Bedford to 'ere,' she said, distractedly, then gazed at the flowers, inhaling their fragrance. She couldn't believe it, she was touched but embarrassed – no man had ever given her flowers before.

'D'you like them?' he asked.

She shook her head. 'But – they're just daft flowers,' she blurted out, momentarily incapable of receiving them graciously.

Danny scowled, hurt. 'They're not just daft flowers. They're roses and I thought you'd be pleased.' He reached out to grab the cellophane wrapping. 'But if you don't like them I'll . . .'

Her fingers clasped around the flowers like a vice, and her face hardened. 'I never said I didn't like them, did I?' she snapped, snatching them away from him and hiding them behind her back, furious with herself. 'They're all right.'

He smiled and touched her soft cheeks with his fingertips.

'Good,' he said, in kinder tones. 'I'm glad you do want them.'

As he gripped the chain to stop the swing moving, and lowered his face towards hers, she averted her head, she didn't want him to realise how miserable she felt because she had no money for drugs. She needn't have worried, he had already noticed.

Catching him unawares, she slipped off the swing, and suggested, 'come on then, let's walk.'

They hadn't gone far when they were surprised by a distant fisherman's screams coming from well down river. 'Bore! the bore's coming.'

As fishermen threw their tackle to safety, and scrambled up the bank, the speeding tidal wave roared past Jack and Danny, and the river rose sharply. They, too, scrambled back up the bank and

Jacky skidded on the slippery ground. She fell on her face and, screaming, slithered swiftly towards the swirling water. Danny's head shot round and he panicked.

'No! Jack,' he yelled, 'no!' He turned, crouched, and gripping hold of a small sturdy shrub with his left hand, lunged forward, his right arm outstretched, his fingers clawing frantically for hers. As the cold, racing water engulfed her feet their fingers locked together. 'Hold on Jack!' he shouted, 'hold on to my hand.'

Danny heaved, inching her body back up the bank, while she let loose a volley of verbal abuse. 'Fuckin' Stonewall House – I should have known I'd fall in the bleedin' river by where that dump used to be, I . . .'

Back safely on top of the bank, she climbed exhaustedly to her feet and threw her arms gratefully around Danny's neck.

They both panted for breath, she hugged him tightly and kissed him thankfully and firmly, full on the lips. 'Thanks Dan – thanks man, you probably saved me life, I don't know what me Mam would have done if anythin' had happened to me.' She hugged him tighter. 'I love you man.'

Danny held her close, he could feel her heart racing as she still panted heavily. Suddenly, she turned her head and gazed back down at the river, it was quieter now, the bore had hit the weir and the waters were ebbing. Despair momentarily swamped her, as memories of the terrible time she'd had whilst attending Stonewall House School flooded her mind. She used to see the bore regularly through her classroom window. At this moment, even being with Danny was no substitute for her need to swallow a tablet of ecstasy – blind to all else but her craving she didn't notice the lone rat, watching her wary-eyed from behind a nearby slimy rock, taking its chance as it scampered away leaving a trail of tiny footprints.

What breeze had risen with the speeding bore had now dropped and there was quietness.

Danny smiled and gently cupped her chin in his fingers and gazed into her uplifted face. 'Hey come on Jack, don't look so sad, things aren't that bad.'

Jack suddenly realised that she was smeared with mud, and some had rubbed off on Danny's clothes.

'I – I'm sorry man, I'm sorry,' she stuttered, apologetically.

'Forget it Babe, it doesn't matter.'

He laughed as he gazed at her grimy hands and face and produced some tissues from his pocket. 'Here, let me . . .' He did the best he could to clean her up then she did the same for him, catching his mood, making a joke of it.

Afterwards, he wrapped his arm around her waist and coaxed her to walk with him slowly down river. They passed by the drooping, whispering weeping willows and the string of anchored salmon fishing boats.

Danny respected Jack's silence, sensing that her spirits had drooped again. He was right, she didn't feel good at all and a cool blanket of mist now covering the river made her shiver with cold. She raised the collar of her leather jacket and fastened the top button. Then, lifting the bunch of flowers which Danny had retrieved for her to her nose, she sniffed at them again. A small smile crept around the corners of her pale lips, and she looked up at him with tired eyes and mumbled. 'Thanks for the flowers Dan they're OK.'

He watched as she lowered the bunch of roses and with her free hand brought out a clean blue comb from her pocket.

She ran it through her dark curls tugging at the tangles and, studying her, he felt a melting in his heart.

They wandered on for a hundred yards or so, then halted near to a large dead elm tree. The day's last beautiful notes of a lone bird, high up in the branches of the tree, echoed across the river.

Danny pointed to it. 'A song thrush,' he exclaimed. 'Just listen to her, she sings because she's happy and contented. No beer, no drugs and no ciggies. She's just grateful for life, yous know what I mean like?'

Jack never replied, just stood, rigid and silent, looking skywards. Her wide eyes stayed glued to the bird and her ears took in the sweet notes. She never even noticed that Danny had quietly stepped back several paces – she was mesmerised. Maybe she thought, just maybe, there was a flicker of truth in what he'd said, but only a flicker.

After a brief spell, the thrust fell silent. Jack suddenly noticed that Danny had moved away, that it was getting dark and cooler. With her shoulders hunched, she turned after him, rubbing her hands vigorously. She twined her fingers in his.

'Can we go back now, it's getting chilly? Anyway,' she added, 'I need a drink, or somethin.'

Freeing her hand again, she yanked out her cigarettes and lit one up – stuff the song thrush, the one thing she did need was her cigarettes.

As they walked back, they halted by the fisherman's old cottage. Danny needed some of the light from the living-room window to write down his address and phone number on a scrap of paper for Jacky. He handed it to her and they strolled on.

'Just ring the buzzer if you call,' he instructed, 'mine's number seven, the attic conversion.' He nodded skywards. 'I'm up there with the sparrows and house-martins.'

She raised a small laugh. 'Sounds OK.'

He arched his eyebrows and his voice was tinged with speculation.

'It's a tidy place, it's got everything I need.' He smiled. 'You'll have to pay me a visit.'

'Mmm, I'll see about that,' she replied, thoughtfully.

By the time they arrived back at the Stonewall House site, Jacky felt a little brighter. Darkness had fallen completely, and the river was now deserted of fishermen.

As they had walked across the small park, past the

wooden see-saw, the conversation had touched on Woodcock, brought about by Jack's puzzled queries as to why Danny had left his job on the farm. He was caught on the hop. He gulped and cleared his throat, nervously. He was going to find it harder trying to lie to her than it had been to old Freddy Haddock, or Merlin, his nickname, which Danny preferred.

Danny's crafty tale about crashing Woodcock's new Ford tractor into the barn seemed to carry him through, however, the last thing he wanted was for Jack to find out about his brief affair with Su-Ling. His gaze dwelt on her face, he couldn't stop looking at her. There was no way he could prevent himself, apart from throwing himself in the river. He just had to meet her again – soon, his feelings for her were tearing at his heart.

'Woodcock's a weirdo,' Jack observed bitterly. Then, with a sudden burst of relief at having Danny beside her, she gripped his hand and swung his powerful arm high in the air. 'I mean it, Dan, he's dead weird.'

Danny stopped, let go her hand and fixed her with stern eyes.

'How so? What d'you mean, a weirdo? I mean, I lived there for a while, and the only thing I noticed was that he seemed to be loaded. I found the Egyptian woman, Ament, and her falcon, a bit strange, but that's about it.'

Jack waved her arms about in sudden high excitement – she wasn't going to be frightened by the Hell Fire Club's threatening letter any longer, she had found someone that she could really talk to about Woodcock and his evil goings-on. Danny gently gripped her arms and eased them down to her side. He nodded and grinned. 'OK, OK, Jack, just take your time, wind down a bit an' tell me what yous know about Woodcock.'

She sent a stream of smoke pouring out to mingle with the thickening mist. 'What 'appened was, the other week, me an' Bobby Queen went up to Bluebell Wood, to the old broken-down abbey, and saw Woodcock an' his mates doin' all this black magic stuff.' She sniffed and took a deep drag. 'There was a crowd of others there in hoods and cloaks.' She shook her head disbelievingly. 'They were all screwin' each other man – honest.' She dropped her cigarette-butt and stamped hard on it. She handed the roses to Danny, reached inside her jacket pocket and pulled out the red envelope. She extracted the Hell Fire Club's note and shakily passed it to him. 'One of 'em spotted me an' sent me this. I've been shit scared since.' She took out her lighter, and curling her hand around it managed to muster a faint flickering gleam for him to read by. A shocked gasp escaped Danny's lips. 'Nasty,' he drawled. 'Very nasty.'

The large blood coloured words were vivid to his keen eye in the dancing flame. 'NOT A WORD OR ELSE'

'And don't you remember that day at Woodcock's farm?' she went on fiercely. 'When I ran past you – well he'd tried to rape me in one of his outhouses. I found some of his weird black magic stuff in the outhouse as well, it's probably all been shifted now.'

Danny handed her back the note and she tucked it inside the envelope and shoved it back in her pocket.

Danny was taken aback, he had never imagined Woodcock was into Devil worship, despite Merlin's suspicions about Ament and Horus. He looked at Jack and asked, with a certain amount of surprise. 'Didn't you tell the police about any of this?'

She threw back her head and laughed loudly. 'A' you kiddin'? Woodcock's probably one of the biggest names around here. We've got no proof – anyway, who's going to believe the likes of me an' Bobby?'

Danny glanced towards the gliding water, his jaw clenched hard.

'I believe you, Jack, and I'm – I'm sorry for what Woodcock tried to do to – well, you know . . .'

She slipped a hand beneath his elbow. 'S'okay man, no sweat, come on you can walk me to the bus stop. I'm not walkin' all the bleedin' way back to Bedford as well.'

Danny smiled and suddenly his eyes lit up. He stopped dead in his tracks, and exclaimed, 'Freddy Haddock! I've got a friend called Freddy, well, Merlin, I call him, because he's a clever old smart-arse. He knows all about that sort of stuff. You know, witchcraft an' Devil worship an' that. I'll have a word with him if you like. Better still I'll take yous to see him if you want.' She nodded her head eagerly.

'Yeah, yeah man, I'd like that. It'd be nice to get back at that perv' Timberdick.'

He threw his arms around her shoulders and squeezed her.

'Okay I'll fix it up. Come on I'll take you back to Bedford and buy you a drink.' He gazed down at her face. A face pale, drawn and free of make-up. He felt sorry for her, but only a little. So, she had no drugs and was suffering, cruel maybe, but . . .

It was the first Monday morning in August, when Danny clocked on behind Jacky Dooley for the very first time, at the Goodporks Sausages factory. By the morning break time, rumours had already swept through the workforce that Mrs Coot had left suddenly.

'Probably run off with that Bert,' muttered Janet, the supervisor, into Jack's ear. 'You know, the hunky one she was having it away with. If you ask me she . . .'

'Could Jack Dooley please come to the manageress's office,' interrupted the booming voice over the Tannoy. 'Thank you.'

'Come!' the voice ended on a bellow.

Jack was startled, surely she knew that voice. Her mind tumbled. No, it couldn't be. She walked the short distance to the door and gripped the handle dubiously. 'Come on Jack,' she exhorted. 'Where's your bottle now? it can't be her.'

She entered and clicked the door shut behind her. Turning, she took a step forward, then suddenly stopped and winced. She couldn't believe her eyes, it couldn't be her – but it was.

The woman standing with her back to Jack was huge, with her oak tree like legs astride. Her black brogues squeaked as she rocked to and fro. She looked as if she had walked into the factory straight from the set of H-Block Prison. She slammed the grey filing cabinet drawer shut and turned slowly, her chubby ringless hands were clasped behind her back. She grinned maliciously, and fixed small piggy like eyes on Jacky. Jack's heart thudded as she stared back at the woman. The new supervisor was Miss Bull! Her ex-teacher from Stonewall House!

Miss Bull had pulled strings to get the job after Mrs Coot's sudden exit from the factory. Mrs Coot's husband, Harry D. Coot, along with Woodcock and Miss Bull, was a member of the coven. He was also a partner in Goodporks Sausages, a very good friend of Bull's, and a very unhappily married man – his wife was noted for being free with her favours.

Miss Bull stepped heavily forward and stopped at the side of her desk, resting her hand on the desk top, immobile as a monument but for the small darting eyes in her fat face. They were photographing the size, shape and features of Jack Dooley.

'Well Dooley,' she rapped out, in the steely tone which Jacky would never forget. 'I see you've still got your – er – trim little body.' Her brows arched in disquieting appreciation. 'Sexy, and very appealing. Tell me Dooley, do you still head-butt people in the stomach as well?'

Ripples of apprehension crawled up Jacky's back. God, she needed the job. There was Daisy, and her own 'deadly desire' to think of, and they both required every penny she could earn.

Bull ran a hand through her short brown hair, before picking up a pen and twisting it between her fingers. She stepped over to where Jack was standing. Jack tried not to flinch as tall and looming, Bull circled her slowly and menacingly, scrutinising her carefully from head to toe.

'So, Dooley, we meet again, it's been a long time, a very long time. But this time, Jack Dooley, you can't head-butt me and run away – well you could, but you'd be out of a job.' She lowered her head and stared in Jack's face. Jacky stayed tight-lipped, trying not to tremble. She already had a gut feeling of what was about to follow. As Bull's excited chubby fingers started to travel over her shoulders and breasts, Jack shot out of reach and glared at her.

Words spat from her curling lips. 'Get your dirty! fucking! hands off me Bull, you perverted old cow. I told you at Stonewall House that I'm not butch, I'm still not, so piss off.' She moved smartly towards the door, side-stepping Bull, whose flabby jowls were shaking with rage. 'Can I go back to work now – please?!'

Bull swivelled round speedily for such a large woman. 'You'll go back when I tell you,' she snapped. 'You're still a maladjusted brat I see.' Malevolently, she approached Jacky and stabbed a finger in her chest. 'We've a party at my house this

Saturday night. Be there at eight o'clock sharp, and on your own, or else! I still live in the same house in the road by Stonewall.' Jack's eyes flashed as she gripped the door handle. 'Or else what!' Bull rocked back and forth on the balls of her feet, a snarl on her lips. 'Or else I'll make your life here hell! My dear little Jacky. Didn't you know? I'm here at Goodporks permanently now.' Her voice changed to a low growl. 'I'm going to have you, Dooley.' She ogled Jack's body, hungrily. 'One way or the other, I'm going to have you, finger you, suck you, and fuck you – now get out.'

Jack stared at her with repulsion. 'Well,' she drawled, sarcastically. 'You've started work in the right place haven't you? I mean Good – pork! you fat slob of a pig!' She gripped the door handle tighter, her bony knuckles forcing her skin taut. 'There's no way you'll ever poke my fanny, fat slag, not with your fingers or slobbering tongue – I've fuckin' told you, I'm dead on and the only person who's gonna break me, is the person I love, and fat bastard, I know who the man! is, and I love the man a lot, so go fuck your blow-up doll.' She stormed out of Bull's office, slamming the door hard.

'Think about it Dooley!' Miss Bull roared. She hurled her pen across the room. 'Just think about it.'

Jacky stalked angrily through the small waiting-room and away. She managed to think about it all right. Even with the lovely idea of Danny like sunshine in her mind, she'd thought about it.

Stuff Bull and stuff her job at Goodporks Sausages

factory. She only hoped that Danny would believe her when she told him why she was leaving.

Bull would convince her superiors that Jack wasn't right for the job, she always had been a liar, even as a teacher at Stonewall House.

Chapter Twelve

After the full red sun had slunk away behind the sea of dark rooftops, darkness swiftly fell.

It was Tuesday night, when Bobby Queen and Jacky Dooley silently and speedily made their way over the muddy, toy cluttered back garden. Once they had reached the rear of the place, they hot-footed it down the entry which ran between the row of terraced Victorian houses. They stopped at the end of the alley and leaned against the red brick wall, breathing heavily.

Bobby pointed to the row of bright house lights across the road. 'We can go through that passage there and across the garden on the left. That backs onto the Edwards's back garden and we . . .'

Jack produced a packet of cigarettes, gritted her teeth nervously and interrupted. 'You're dead sure they're still on holiday?'

She handed Bobby a cigarette and they lit up, sending clouds of smoke drifting into the glow from the nearby streetlight.

'Yeah, yeah of course I am, for another week yet – come on.'

Bobby was a pro, but Jack had never before robbed someone else's house. She deeply regretted becoming hooked on drugs, but she was up to her silly neck in the stuff now, and this seemed the only way to get the money for them. She hadn't even considered going on the game, it just wasn't her style. She dug deep into her mind and tried to psych herself up, get her act together, for the burglary. As she looked at Bobby's determined face, she felt a stab of annoyance, even jealousy, at her toughness and experience when it came to antisocial exploits like thieving.

Bobby had already sussed out beforehand that the Edwards's house had no alarm system, foolish in this day and age but . . . In a matter of seconds she had covered the dining-room window with heavy adhesive tape and, with a hushed dull thud, smashed the single pane of glass. It only took a moment to strip the glass from the window and lay it stealthily on the concrete path. All that was left were the sharp pieces protruding from the putty at the edges.

Jack hurriedly lit another cigarette from the smouldering butt which had been clamped between her teeth.

'Put that damn fag out Jacky,' Bobby rasped. 'We're on a bleedin' job 'ere, not the back seat of the bus going to bleedin' Balchester.'

'Sorry, so sor-ry.' Jack stamped on the two cigarettes.

Bobby nodded towards the window. 'Go on then,' she whispered crossly. 'Hurry up, you go first.'

'I – I'm not ready yet,' stammered Jack, sweat breaking out on her upper lip.

Bobby snarled at her. 'Go on bloody hurry up. You want the piggin' money to buy some gear don't you?'

Jack wiped the back of her hand across her mouth. 'All right, all right, I'm going.' She placed her hands on the stone sill and started to climb through the window.

Bobby poked her in the back. 'Watch your hands on the glass.' She then gave Jack an extra heave up.

Jack scrambled in through the window, and after a look around, Bobby was quick to follow her.

Jack clumsily knocked over a footstool, making what sounded to the girls like a tremendous clatter.

'Watch it,' Bobby hissed. She turned her head and held out clutching fingers. 'Torch!'

Jack fumbled in her pockets. 'I – I thought I'd got it,' she dithered.

Bobby became exasperated. 'Fag lighter then, matches, any bleedin' thing as long as it lights.'

Jack dug in her pocket, brought out her lighter and passed it over. Bobby snatched it and flicked it on, shielding it with her hand. With Jack tagging along behind, she speedily scoured the dining-room and lounge, saw the lighted time and date on the video and pounced. She also swooped up the nearby radio cassette, they were the easiest things of any decent value to get rid of, Docker and his cronies would always do a 'phone call and buy.

Jack was quick to learn, and in the dim light, aped

her and swept up an expensive Midi Hi Fi which stood near to the TV.

'What about this Bobby?' she asked, feeling pleased to get one over on her.

Bobby nodded and smiled. 'Well done Jack! You're learning.' She puffed hard as she walked to the dining-room window and put down her pickings on the thick grey carpet. 'Come on Jack,' she urged. 'I've got to screw the place for money an' rings and that yet.'

As she held the Midi Hi-Fi in her hands, Jacky, stayed rooted, breathing heavily and moistening her lips.

Bobby's patience snapped. 'Come on Jack, move it. We'll be able to buy the best with this little lot. You name it, speed, smack, coke, whatever drugs we want.'

Jack swallowed hard and walked towards the dining-room window.

Bobby brushed past her. 'Wait here,' she ordered. 'I'll only be a min.'

It wasn't long before she reappeared. 'Thirty quid and some rings an' that Jack,' she bragged, 'it's better than nowt – come on let's piss . . .'

Suddenly a key clicked in the front door lock sending a spasm of panic tearing through them both.

Jack dropped the Midi Hi-Fi onto the windowsill, and hissed at Bobby. 'Hell shit Bobby, I thought you said that they were away on holiday.'

'They are!' Bobby muttered, shaking her head.

'Miko's old woman got a card off them this mornin' and Adder said they're still in Spain.'

'Then who the fuck is that!?'

Old Freddy Haddock hadn't wanted the Edwards's key, he hadn't even wanted to keep an eye on their house while they were away. Maybe it was a good thing, but he was beginning to find the new Homewatch scheme a pain in the butt.

He would much rather be up in his den, drinking his Scotch, deep in his study of Egyptian Gods such as Bast, the benevolent cat-goddess of Bubastis, who, interestingly enough, was a distant relation of Horus, both sacred in their own right. Horus, a god of hunting and Bast the cat, a goddess of kindness, were both answerable to the beautiful Ament, goddess of the West of Egypt, and identified with Hathor, likewise a most powerful presence in ancient Egypt.

Freddy also enjoyed a tipple while pondering over the Devil and witchcraft. 'They're nothing but a flaming nuisance,' he grumbled, as he opened the door into the lounge and reached for the light switch.

As he switched on the light, he was surprised by the sudden presence of the Edwards's ginger tom-cat as it shot past him, and ran out through the open front door. He glared after the animal and grunted, 'huh! only give the cat the tins of salmon, she said, wasting good money, if the damn creature was mine it'd eat ordinary cat food, or scraps.' He went on grumbling. 'I'd sooner be up in my den studying Bast – now there's a real cat!'

'It's an old bloke on his own,' whispered Bobby, after a quick peep into the lounge.

To Jack's horror, she picked up a large porcelain vase from the sideboard. 'Bobby!' she gasped. 'You can't – you musn't.'

'Shut up, d'you wanna end up in the nick or what? Just hide behind the door an' don't let him see your face.'

Bobby had already covered her own features with a dark kerchief. She placed a finger to her lips as Merlin checked the lounge. 'My God!' he spluttered. 'The place has been . . .'

Bobby suddenly burst through the living-room doorway, leaving Jack with her heart lurching uncontrollably.

Merlin was fit for his age, but barely had time to turn before Bobby let out a ferocious roar, and sent the vase smashing into his bemused face, with her full ten stone behind it. It shattered.

Freddy Haddock screamed, as fragments of razor sharp porcelain tore into his wrinkled flesh. Other pieces shot across the room landing on the cream suite and pale brown carpet. Blood spurted from Freddy's deep gashes. He staggered trying to claw the embedded china from his face. Whimpering, he crumpled onto the settee, bleeding freely on the pale upholstery. With a groan, he rolled off onto the carpet and lay still. Three large pieces of porcelain protruded from his face like darts in a dartboard.

His long silver hair and moustache were streaked dark red.

Bobby stared at him for a moment and then gave an uneasy smirk.

'Silly old bastard shouldn't be here anyway.'

Jack wiped traces of vomit from her mouth with a tissue, she felt violently ill – she didn't mind the robbery bit too much, and she could handle herself as well, but this . . .

At that moment Ginger Tom slunk back into the house, crouched by Merlin, shivering, and gave a low yowl, as it nuzzled, his wounded face.

Bobby grunted and hissed, as she shooed it out. 'Piss off, you blood-licking moggy.'

Jack groaned, and heaved again from her guts. 'God, shut it Bob, will yer – I feel bleedin' bad enough as it is.'

Bobby started to clamber out through the window. 'Come on, come on pass the stuff out to me, let's get to Docker an' Boots. Someone's bound to have seen the light, come on.'

Once they had crossed back over the gardens, Bobby stopped for a breather. 'I'll need some bleedin' speed after this little lot.'

Jack couldn't help but agree.

As they hurriedly approached Bobby's flat, Jacky suddenly stopped by the public call-box. 'S'no good Bobby, stuff it. I'm going to give 999 a ring an' get an ambulance to that house to help that old geezer, I can't leave him like that, it's not right.'

'No, no! We can't,' Bobby burst out. 'They'll trace the call.'

Jack paused, gave her a defiant determined look, and swung open the call-box door. 'I'm 'phoning, Bobby, I won't give them time to trace it.'

'Oh no you're not!' insisted Bobby.

'I am Bob, you don't own me,' Jack's voice was low and driven. Aghast, Bobby cursed and stormed off towards her flat. Jack dumped the Midi Hi-Fi on the 'phone-box floor and dialled. She stayed on the line only long enough to say that there was a seriously injured man, who might be dead, at a house in Carter Street. 'And hurry!' she urged, and hung up.

Grabbing the Midi Hi-Fi she ran to catch up with Bobby.

As they breathlessly reached Bobby's flat, she turned on Jacky.

'If you've dropped me in it, Jack, I'll ... I'll ... Oh what the hell!' She did her best to balance the video recorder on her knee while she struggled to open the door with her key, and pushed it open with her foot. 'Come on, and close the door.'

Once they had stashed the stolen goods in Bobby's bedroom, they both gulped down a can of strong lager, Jack felt she would need a gallon of the stuff to drown out the repugnance which she felt over what Bobby had done to old Merlin.

A few moments after Brown Trilby and Boots had walked away from the jukebox, Paul McCartney's voice burst through the speakers. Later that night, heavy cloud had moved in from the west. Jack and Bobby entered the Coach and Horses with their hair wet, and rain streaming down their coats. The sudden downpour had been heavy. After Jack had bought their drinks, they sidled across the bar to where Docker and company were.

Docker's mean eyes locked on to the two girls, his hand tightened around his pint glass and he took a long slow swallow. Then, leaning on the bar, he ran a hand down his greying pony-tail. Brown Trilby and Boots stood either side.

'Well,' Docker drawled. 'If it isn't Little and Large, and what can I do for you pair?'

After Bobby had told him what they had on offer, he put down his beer and went to the bar's pay phone. As he spoke, Docker looked across at their desperate faces and nodded his head firmly. They both let out a gasp of relief – at long last, it was nearly time for a pick-me-up off the Fat Man. But, the pay-off did not come up to expectations.

Bobby flicked through the banknotes, and gave a disgruntled shake of her head. 'Huh, enough for a few days stuff, the bleedin' gold sovereign ring's worth that much on its own.'

Jack angrily thrust herself forward. 'She's right, Docker, and you know it. There's eight hundred quid's worth of gear there, with the video an' that.'

Boots clicked his heels and straightened to his full height. He was a big negro.

Brown Trilby smirked, and tugged lightly on his long droopy moustache.

Docker made a faint movement of his head and ordered three more beers. Jack turned and stared at Docker directly, hatred burning in her eyes.

'But it's second-hand, Jack' he reminded her. He cheekily cocked his head sideways at Brown Trilby. 'Isn't it Trilb?' Brown Trilby pulled down his hat over his blinking, slit-eyes.

'Yep, and after Mister Fixit's bought it off you, it's got to be sold again, hasn't it Boots?'

Boots gazed down at Jack and Bobby, a provocative glint in his chestnut eyes. His rough voice tailed off with its usual high squeaky laugh. 'Sure has Trilb, I guess that's the way the cookie crumbles girls. Hah hah.'

Docker leaned forward with a hard glint in his eyes. 'Well, have we done a deal, or what?' he whispered. 'You do want your "Blockbusters" or whatever shit you take, don't you?'

Jack nodded frantically at Bobby and thrust out a sweating palm. She eagerly snatched her half of the money and necked the last of her beer. 'Up you, arsehole, and tell Mister Fixit, your so-called boss what he can do . . . oh, forget I said that, man.' Her glass rattled as she dropped it on the bar, and clasped a hand on Bobby's shoulder. 'Come on, Bobby, let's just get into town and see the Fat Man – I need it.'

As they left with their money, the mocking laughter of Docker and friends echoed in their ears.

'Brothers in Arms' by Dire Straits was playing

softly, as Jack and Bobby lurched into the Fox and Hounds. Jacky was on a real downer, she wasn't meeting Danny until Friday night, and the flashbacks of Merlin lying there moaning, covered in blood, tormented her – she just hoped the ambulance got there in time. She had given up her job, and her half of the robbery proceeds was going to have to go on drugs.

Cochise happened to be standing by the bar, tall and straight, his hard eyes glued to the mirror behind the row of optics. His multicoloured lumberjack coat, with its reds and blacks, stood out vividly beneath the coloured bar lights. Being a mute, he usually kept himself to himself, and Danny Black was the only person in the pub with whom he had ever associated. He was always acutely aware, however, of the seedy goings-on around him.

His gaze slid to the left, as Fat Man wove daintily through the crowd towards Bobby and Jack. The long-stemmed glass of gin and tonic was held high above his carrot-topped head. He rammed a hand into his fat hip. 'Hi sweets.' He slurped down the last of his drink, and tapped out the rhythm of the music on his glass with his long fingernails. 'I've got some bad news for you, darlings, the drop off fell through, there was a slight intervention by the law.'

'What!' Jack moaned. 'You mean you've got no drugs at all?'

Her heart executed a wild turnover. She felt sick in the pit of her stomach. She needed, she had to have something. Bobby spread her hands despairingly. 'Hell shit! Fat Man, you must have something.'

He looked at them with a sudden gleam in his eyes. 'Smack! that's all I've got.' He gave an evil grin and waved a fat ringed finger in the air. 'But, it's the best heroin you'll find.' Cochise read his lips well, and moved swiftly to intervene. Like Bobby and others, he had sussed out that Danny Black had a soft spot for Jacky Dooley, and he liked them both. He left his beer, strode quickly across to Jack and gripped her wrists, his lips tight and his eyes fierce. Fat Man stepped back quickly, he hadn't forgotten his last run-in with Cochise. Cochise shook his head vigorously, at the same time desperately trying to force out words, but only urgent grunts left his lips. Jack squealed and tugged her wrists free. 'Leave it out, man! I need the stuff, just fuck off! eh.' She laid hands on Cochise's chest and pushed him away.

It was getting towards nine-thirty, and many in the Fox and Hounds were either high on drugs or drunk, so in seconds, Cochise found himself surrounded by Adder, Miko and several angry revellers. Adder poked him hard. 'Leave it out mate,' he hissed. 'Watch my lips – carefully. You, live your life, and we'll live ours, got it.'

Cochise could lip-read well, his hard lined face became twisted with bewilderment, and his eyes wide and ablaze with anger as he glared at Jacky. He couldn't understand why she hit the shit – to him, Danny Black was the best thing for her. He forced out several furious grunts and swung a wild arm, knocking Miko aside.

He stormed from the pub, and the heavy oak door slammed to on its large iron hinges with a loud bang. He certainly had the spirit within him, but to try and fight so many on his own would be stupidity.

The transaction between Bobby and Fat Man was over within the blink of an eye.

Jack had already broken away from the amorous advances of Glo', the gorgeous butch blonde whom any normal man would love to bed, and made a beeline behind Bobby to the ladies' powder-room. The door swung to behind them.

Jack's hands shook convulsively as, under Bobby's supervision, she emptied her first ever wrap of heroin onto the piece of tinfoil. Excitedly, she flicked her lighter and held the low flame beneath it. She knew about it, she needed it. And at long last, she was going to do it.

Bobby urged her on. 'Come on Jack, come on, I wan' it as well.' Jacky trembled, as she inhaled the wisps of smoke which curled off through a short tube of thick paper – Jack Dooley, was 'chasing the dragon' and she was relishing every suck. She let loose a surge of relief then allowed Bobby to take her turn. After a few minutes, she was experiencing a sleepy, pleasant euphoria and life's anxieties were swiftly subsiding. As the drug entered her system she felt a surge of pleasure – Jack Dooley was 'monging'. She sat slumped against the wall, gazing at the tiles through reddening eyes. 'Chasing the dragon' was what she wanted, to smother the thoughts of her job loss, Merlin's battering from Bobby and her burning feelings towards Danny. She squashed a fly settled against the toilet wall, and gave an evil laugh, as she flattened a peaceful moth.

'Fuck you! Danny bleedin' Black. And up your bloody flowers!' She raised her voice. 'I hate your silly fuckin' flowers and nature crap anyway!' Then her tone softened, dramatically. 'I hate you, you black bastard.' Jacky Dooley loved Danny Black, but she was 'chasing the dragon'! She rammed her boot into the flower-patterned wall tiles and vomited over the quarry tiled floor and slumped forward. 'God! I hate you Danny, and your stupid thrush!' she suddenly wailed, heartbrokenly.

Chapter Thirteen

Danny Black glanced down at his watch, kicked up his heels, and ran faster.

The strong gale sweeping in from off the high Welsh mountains stung his eyes and tangled his long black curls. His heart raced as the blood pumped through his veins. As he ran, his mind flashed back to his secret visit to Woodcock's farm, a couple of days before. He'd kept watch on the farmhouse to see if Su-Ling was all right.

After Woodcock had found out they had been to bed together, he had feared the worst, knowing the violence of the man's temper. Danny had managed to sneak a word with Vic, the cowman, who had told him that Su-Ling was virtually a prisoner, kept under lock and key, and that also, from a distance, whilst glancing through the kitchen window, he had noticed that her eyes appeared to have been blacked.

He tried to put thoughts of Su-Ling to the back of his mind, it was ten to six on Friday evening, and he was to meet Jack Dooley at seven.

Throughout his jogging stint, he had also been recalling and enjoying in retrospect, his dates with her. Now, bursting eagerly into the kitchen through the back door, he briefly nodded to Spotty, who was cooking tea, and sped on to pound up the stairs to his room.

Stripping to the waist, he worked out for several minutes on his basic self-defence.

He cut the air, viciously, in a succession of lightning moves with Steeleye, before unstrapping the heavy crowbar and tucking it safely beneath his bed.

After showering, he slipped on a clean ice-blue sweatshirt and a pair of jeans. Laughingly, he swept up Lotty, who kept winding herself around his legs purring, with her tiny bell tinkling. It was kind of Vic, the cowman, to have brought Lotty to him, he reflected. He cuddled her as he looked through the dirt-streaked attic window at the screeching seagulls. They circled high above – it must have been rough at sea to send them so far inland.

Danny smiled happily to himself, he was going to meet Jack.

After hurriedly devouring a hefty sardine salad, Danny fed the rest of the fish to Lotty. Then he bounded down the stairs, and was the first to grab the free local newspaper that dropped through the letter-box. He gasped at the picture of Freddy Haddock on the front page, beneath the stark black headline. 'LOCAL PENSIONER VICIOUSLY BEATEN UP ON CRITICAL LIST' Stricken, he read on. When he had finished, he clawed at his forehead. The thought of old Merlin beaten up, possibly dying, wrenched at his heart.

Merlin was special, he was his Grandad Harry's best friend in the war, and now he was one of his own best friends – he just had to go and see him.

He tossed down the newspaper, and fumbled in his pocket for some change.

He phoned Balchester Royal Infirmary, to confirm that Freddy was there, then rushed up to his room for his anorak and the box of chocolates he'd bought for Jack. He was to meet her in the Lowfield Hotel, and he made up his mind he would ask her to go with him to see Merlin.

He found her sitting at the bar, sipping from a glass of lager, and drumming her fingers to a Tina Turner hit. She accepted Danny's chocolates with a warm smile – they would come in handy with a bottle of sweet pop, when she was craving for heroin. 'Sure I'll go with you,' she agreed, to Danny's request, and after stubbing out her cigarette, and swallowing down the last of her beer, they set off for the hospital.

Danny soon managed to find out which ward Freddy Haddock was in, and as he and Jack rushed on at top speed, the panicking nurse desperately rushed after them, trying to tell them that he was not allowed visitors.

A policeman stepped over, to stand astride across the doorway leading to Merlin's ward. He shook his head adamantly, his voice decisive. 'Sorry, no visitors – not without the doctor, anyway.' As Danny stood rigid, defiantly, the nurse cast pleading eyes at the officer. 'I – I'm sorry, I did try to tell them. It's his best friend, he's worried, I tried to stop them, but . . .'

The policeman aimed his stern gaze at Danny, then nodded towards a bench nearby. 'Why don't you just wait over there sir, the doctor's due shortly to see Mister Haddock – we'd like to speak with the patient too.'

Frustrated though he felt, Danny respected the policeman's authority and clasping Jack by the hand, went to sit down.

Doctor Warren arrived soon afterwards, swept past Danny and Jack, stopped at the door of Merlin's ward, and spoke briefly with the nurse and the policeman, glancing occasionally at Danny and Jack as he did so. Then walking over to Danny and Jack, he explained quietly that Danny's old friend appeared to have been battered by a heavy object, and by the wounds and splinters in his flesh, something made of porcelain, but they were on the whole hopeful of his recovery. 'He's a strong old guy,' he added, as he led Danny and Jack past the officer and into Merlin's ward. 'You may see him, but only for a few minutes.'

The old man who was attached to a drip lay still. With his face swathed in bandages, he looked like a mummy.

Danny gazed at the inert form and close to tears, swallowed hard at the lump in his throat. Clenching his fists he turned to Doctor Warren and the nurse. 'Christ! is he that bad?' he demanded, hoarsely.

Jacky put a comforting arm around Danny's waist, as the doctor replied, gently, 'It could have been fatal for a weaker man of his age.'

Danny's guts burned for revenge. 'Fuckin' bastards,' he hissed. 'Bet your bleedin' life it was drugos' stealin' for the shit! I'll have them for this – no sweat man, I'll have them.' It was plain to them all that he was in deadly earnest.

Suddenly, it hit Jack like a brick on the head. The long silver hair, the heavy vase, the size, age, everything! Bobby had done over Merlin, Danny's best friend.

She went icy and bile rose in her throat, that wasn't simple nervousness. This was fear, cold and solid and strong, catching at her breath, chilling her blood. She did her best to keep her expression calm, but her heart was banging like a hammer against her ribs. All Danny had told her in the pub was that Merlin had been badly hurt, and now here she was, with the victim of the robbery she and Bobby had committed, and the police outside the door!

As Jack gazed at the injured man, she struggled with a deep sense of shame as well as fear. She gently gripped Danny's fingers. 'I'm sorry man,' she whispered. 'The fuck shit, I'm so sorry about your old friend, you've always said what a nice old geezer he is.'

She felt sick to the stomach. Stuff you Bobby Queen, she thought, bitterly. Stuff you, you butch cow, and I only wish you'd stuff your bleedin' drugs an' all, you cruel bastard. She glanced back at Danny. His face began to crumble, and for one awful second she thought he would burst into tears. She was grateful for the sudden interruption by Doctor Warren. 'You'll have to go now, I'm afraid, your friend needs plenty of rest.'

'But – he'll pull through, won't he?' Danny's voice was hoarse, his expression pleading.

'He's holding his own, Mister Black, that's more than we'd hoped for when he first came in. Like I said, he's a tough old gentleman. Give Sister a ring tomorrow and she'll report on his progress.' He ushered them out. Danny cast a despairing look back at Merlin before trudging down the corridor away, gripping Jack's hand.

The gale force wind howled and whistled through the telephone wires.

Little Sophie Dooley gripped her pillow tightly and sobbed, as her father's angry voice carried up the stairs. She didn't notice the noise of the three ridge-tiles, when they took off from the roof, and crashed into the front garden.

As Ben Dooley ducked from the flying chipped mug, Daisy screamed abuse at him. Enough was enough. He'd barely started the council house contract when, whilst out shopping at the local parade, rumours had reached her of his womanising. This was after he'd secured the HP deal on a flashy second-hand red convertible – rumours were correct, because the reclining seat had already been well used.

Dooley swayed drunkenly. He swung out his arm and the back of his broad hand cracked into her face, hard. 'Stop yer naggin' woman.'

Stumpy hopped around barking frantically.

The loud knocking on the front door saved Daisy from further beating.

Dooley's eyes blazed, as he met her defiant gaze. He growled and turned sharply to answer the door.

Daisy leaned on the table and sobbed. Blood trickled from her nose, and her lip was already swelling.

Lance stepped back a pace, as Dooley threw open the front door and rammed his jaw at him. The theme music from News at Ten drifted out from the lounge. 'Yeah, what d'yer want?' Against his sallow skin, his stubble of beard stood out.

Lance's gaze swept past him and locked onto Daisy's bloodied face as she walked slowly towards the stairs.

He glanced back at Dooley. 'Eh, I – I just came to see if your Jack wanted to come to the pictures tomorrow night, to see Robin Hood.'

'I dunno, you'll 'ave to ask her. She's not in. Anyway she's seein' someone.'

'Uh!' came the open-mouthed gasp. 'Who!?'

'A Danny Black, he's an 'alf chat who I used to work with – now piss off.' He slammed the door hard in Lance's face.

Taken aback, Lance stood staring blankly at the door. He was dumbstruck – he'd known Jack Dooley nearly all his life, and she'd never had a steady boyfriend before. He'd seen Jack and Danny together occasionally but this – this was a bolt from the blue, a severe body-blow. He felt bruised, numbed by the shock that Jack was finally courting steadily after all these years, and that it wasn't with him. He kicked a nearby fuchsia shrub, turned, and ambled away despondently. His face had crumpled into a picture of bitter disappointment.

Ben Dooley's attitude softened instantly when his daughter, Rosie, and fiancee, John, arrived home after a meal at the Flamingo club.

Rosie glanced around. 'Where's mum?'

John raised his eyebrows questioningly as Dooley drunkenly stuttered. 'Daisy's g-gone to bed, she's got a – an 'eadache.' Rosie met her father's sheepish eyes with a hard knowing stare. Dooley swigged the last drops of bitter from his can. Rosie, tight-lipped and trembling with anger, relieved him of the empty tin. If John hadn't been there, she would of rammed it down his throat.

Her father looked edgy, and made a hurried excuse. 'S-stroll on, I'll 'ave to go to the – the bog, I'm bleedin' burstin'.' He staggered towards the stairs.

John's face expressed repugnance – thank God, Ben Dooley had never worked the building sites where he was the site agent.

As the drunken screeching Karaoke singer tortured Cliff Richards's 'The Young Ones', Danny and Jack left the Lord Tennyson, arm in arm, in lighter mood.

The beer they'd drunk had temporarily taken both their minds off the vicious injuries inflicted on Merlin.

Lance halted in the shadows and tightened his lead on Bimbo, his cocker spaniel.

As Danny and Jacky reached the Dooleys' garden gate and stopped, Lance watched, with an unblinking gaze. Bimbo's attention was riveted by the slow progress of a creeping slug. He sniffed it, his tail wagging slightly.

Danny gently gripped Jack's narrow shoulders and eased her round until she was facing him. She didn't resist as he drew her close to him. As his arms encircled her waist, she slipped her hands up onto his broad chest and looked at him lovingly. His gaze rested on her lips, and she began to tremble. She didn't know why, for she had hoped and prayed for ages that he would kiss her.

Lances's eyes widened, he tugged on Bimbo's lead. 'Heel!' he whispered sharply, his tension mounting.

Jack was now held tightly in Danny's arms. He stared down at her in silence.

She met his eyes, which seemed to glint against his dark skin, like a cat's in the night. 'I think I love you Princess,' he said, softly. 'In fact I know I do.'

Her breath quivered, emotion had robbed her of speech. His dark head came down towards her and she reached up to meet him, her lips moist and eager.

The kiss was gentle at first, then deepened, until she could hardly breathe. Exquisite pleasure shot through her. She half expected a flashing tongue to penetrate her mouth, but it didn't. The pressure of his long pulsating kiss eased at last, but her heart still raced wildly.

Lance's grip loosened on Bimbo's lead. His face had drained of colour, his shoulders sagged. Bimbo whimpered and he looked up at his master impatiently.

As Danny's lips finally eased away, Jacky shuddered, blissfully.

'I love you too.' She whispered, shakily, 'a lot.'

In the dim streetlight, he was looking at her tenderly and she smiled at him, happiness catching at her throat.

Danny gave her two fairy-light kisses on the lips, then held her off at arms length. 'Will I see you tomorrow night then?'

'OK, I'll meet you in the Coach and Horses at eight. I'll wait there for you if you're going to see your friend in hospital.'

Danny nodded. 'I'll make sure I'm there.' He smiled. 'I'll see you then.'

Jack tore herself away from him, unlocked the front door, waved and disappeared inside.

The pleasure of the evening and Danny's words of love were tarnished for her, however, by returning thoughts of Merlin, of her guilt, of her deceit in not confessing to Danny.

Meanwhile, as Danny was walking away, Lance

yanked on Bimbo's lead. 'Come on you,' he snapped. 'Let's go home.'

Once indoors Jack had 'chased the dragon' with the heroin she had bought off Fat Man, and she had a feeling of warmth and drowsiness.

Rosie was sleeping soundly by the time Jacky turned off the horror movie. Christopher Lee had been at his brilliant best. She didn't know that inside the remains of the old abbey, deep in Bluebell Wood, Woodcock and his coven were at work.

As she slept Jack twitched, and twitched again. Forks of blue lightning flashed across her brain. The evil smiling faces of Woodcock, Miss Bull and Adder, appeared menacingly, as if on a screen, before her.

Ament, the High Priestess of the coven, suddenly rose up to confront her.

Their eerie chanting grew louder in her ears. They allowed their robes to slip to the ground and cavorted naked. Woodcock's huge genitals jutted out in a massive erection. The ugly fat Miss Bull looked more grotesque and wrinkled than ever. Her repulsive coils of flesh and her massive breasts bounced obscenely as she gyrated.

Adder's slim shining body moved like a trained cobra's.

Woodcock raised his arm skyward. His loud menacing tones rose high above the coven's chanting. His large beckoning hand seemed to smother her face. 'Welcome to hell Jacky Dooley, welcome to hell!'

Ament thrust her long slender finger forward as she screamed an order to her falcon. 'KILL!' Horus left her gauntlet at speed. He came at Jack's face, talons first. His claws dug into her eyes, tearing them from their sockets, blood spurted through her mind. Sweat poured from her and she twisted and writhed continually.

'Aaaaah!' with a sudden scream, Jacky shot up in bed. Rosie, startled, leapt up and flew across the room to her. Jack trembled uncontrollably, white-faced, wild-eyed. She gripped the duvet tightly with both hands and fought for breath. Rosie hugged her. 'What's wrong Jack – what's wrong love?'

Jacky shuddered and shook her head vigorously. 'Nothin' nothin', Sis honest, I'm all right. I just had a bad nightmare, that's all, a bad nightmare.' She lay down again and Rosie tucked her up, kissed her forehead, and went back to her own bed.

Jack lay awake for a long time, her eyes were wide open, her mind was being torn to pieces.

The one person who might be able to help, she thought, despairingly, was old Merlin, Danny's friend, the man she had unwittingly helped Bobby Queen to almost kill. She felt tormented.

In the room down the hallway little Sophie hugged Pooch, her favourite cuddly toy and peacefully slept on. The Dooley house once again fell silent.

Chapter Fourteen

On the second Saturday in September, the early morning news on the local radio station rocked Balchester to its very foundations.

'The severed head of a local factory manageress has been found in the River Denny, by a diver searching for relics close to the ancient Roman barracks.'

The news, an hour later, declared that her mutilated torso had been discovered by police divers who had joined the search. Devil worship in the area was now believed to be widespread.

Harry D. Coot viciously stirred his tea as he listened to the statements. He rubbed a chubby hand over his balding head, and pushed the gold-rimmed glasses back up the bridge of his stubby nose as he reflected on what he had heard. His wife, Mary, had left him a while back for one of her toy boys from the local sausage factory where she worked. 'Ha!' he gave a bark of laughter. 'The old cow deserved what she got.'

He had been a member of Woodcock's coven for a year, and had revelled drunkenly and masturbated lustfully as the members copulated which included the most obscene sexual practices. Then he watched, goggle-eyed, as Woodcock raised his arm aloft to order the first lunge of the sacrificial knife, to frenzied chanting, blood had spurted out.

He laughed again harshly, at the memory and then, with sadistic pleasure, tore their wedding photograph from its frame and ripped it into tiny pieces.

Su-Ling eased her foot off the Land-rover's accelerator and leaned forward, peering urgently, with wide-eyed surprise, through the dirty windscreen – she felt as if someone had waved a magic wand.

With a racing heart, she swung the vehicle over and brought it screeching to a halt on the double yellow lines. Leaning across, she quickly rolled the window down and shouted. 'Danny! – Danny Black!'

Danny stopped abruptly, outside the entrance to Balchester's market. He turned sharply, glancing keenly around him, until his startled gaze rested on Su-Ling. They smiled at each other warmly, memories of past pleasure surfacing for both of them. Swinging his carrier bag, Danny made his way through the crowded street towards the Land-rover. She was as alluring as ever, he thought, looking down into her pretty, welcoming face, recalling the feel of her pliant body in his arms. But then Jacky's image arose in his mind and he knew that nothing in this world, or the next, would ever have the power to turn his heart away from her.

'Hello Danny, it's nice to see you again,' Su-Ling exclaimed, stroking Sweep, who was sitting by her, wagging his tail excitedly at the sight of Danny. 'Are you well?' she went on.

'Fine, fine,' he replied. 'I'm working at the sausage factory now.' His face broke into an involuntary smile. 'And I'm courting now as well – her name's Jack Dooley, she came to your farm sometimes with her ol' fella, Ben.'

Su-Ling gaped at him. 'Jack Dooley?!' she echoed, on a note of pain. The thought of a girl with Jack's background capturing Danny's heart bugged her – even if she was a good-looker.

Danny poked his head through the open window and nuzzled Sweep. The sheepdog responded, and as he showed his affection with a wet tongue, Su-Ling wrapped her arm around Danny's neck.

'We could still meet again, couldn't we?' she purred, seductively. 'I could always pick you up in the Land-rover. Remember how it used to be? and anyway, you do owe me something after my husband found out about us.'

Danny was startled. 'What d'you mean?' he demanded. 'Vic, your cowman, did tell me that it looked as if you'd had a rough time, but you can't blame me for that – we both wanted it, didn't we?'

'It was worse than just a beating, Danny.' Her face hardened. 'Far worse.'

'Worse? how?' he pressed her.

She was silent for a moment, then, her face pale and taut, she said, 'He made me do things.'

Danny frowned. 'What things?'

She closed her eyes, momentarily, as if trying to shut the world out. Then, sighing, she told him. 'Despicable things, in bed and – and other places.'

Danny's face was grim, his voice cutting. 'What things Su-Ling?'

'Vibrators, and – and – you, know, sex toys.' She almost choked on a sob. 'He boasted he could satisfy me better than you could, and he – he degraded me. He kept reminding me of what I used to be.'

'Su-Ling, I'm sorry, I'd no idea,' Danny burst out. 'I'll go back an' beat the shit out of him if . . .'

'No Danny.' She laid a placating hand over his arm. 'I can handle it.' She gave a wry grin. 'After all, I'm used to dealing with men.' She sighed briefly. 'But you – well you were special, Danny. Are you sure we couldn't get it together again?' She looked up at him pleadingly, but he steeled himself to resist the temptation of those voluptuous lips, that he well remembered.

'Su-Ling, you're a very lovely woman,' he began gently. 'And if it wasn't for the fact that . . .'

'That you're in love with Jack Dooley,' she broke in, and laughed ruefully. 'Ah well, you lose some, you win some. At least Danny, we'll always be friends.'

'Always, Su-Ling,' he responded, squeezing her hand. 'If ever you need help . . .'

'I'll call on you,' she promised. 'Well, good luck with your lady, Danny. I've a feeling you're going to need it.' She started the Land-rover, waved, and drove away, Sweep's nose pressed against the window.

Danny watched her go with a faint nostalgia and regret. But his destiny was tied up with Jacky now.

The fortnight which followed passed swiftly for Danny and Jack.

Jack was still acting normally – up to her neck in heroin. The loan which Docker had handed her from Mister Fixit had now all gone. A thousand pounds didn't go far when one was well hooked on smack. She paid Boots and Brown Trilby back regularly every Friday night in the Coach and Horses, before meeting Danny, so that he didn't know about it.

Meanwhile Danny's mind was in turmoil. He felt a sense of guilt over Su-Ling, but his main worry was Jack's drug addiction. The memory of his own mother's death from a massive overdose of injected heroin, in conjunction with a heavy bout of drinking, preyed on his mind. One bright spot though, was that Merlin was on the mend. After being moved to a main ward, he was already notorious as one of the grumpiest patients they had ever had to contend with. Orange juice was rejected with an arm-folded grunt, and being refused a cigarette provoked a stream of unanswerable abuse in Latin – Freddy Haddock was definitely recovering.

Merlin's housekeeper, Mrs Witton, had sorted out a varied selection of his books on witchcraft and Egyptology for Danny to take to him in hospital.

Jack had smiled warmly at Merlin, as she sat down beside Danny. While he and Danny talked her eyes were intent on the old man's thin face, with its lines of stitches.

After her previous visit, when Danny had told her so much about him, she had taken a liking to Merlin and felt bitterly sorry for what Bobby Queen had done to him. She had delved deep into her mind and heart – and finally decided she wouldn't tell Danny she had been with Bobby when she attacked Freddy – perhaps she should let sleeping dogs lie? Yes! her mind clicked, she would do just that.

She realised that Danny was asking for Merlin's aid to protect her from Woodcock's coven.

Merlin's eyes shone with excitement, although he winced as he moved, his wounds were still very sore.

'By golly,' he exclaimed. 'I'd love to help. Just give me a couple of more weeks and I'll be with you.' He rubbed his small bony hands together. 'The Hell Fire Club, eh!' He pointed a shaky finger at the stack of books piled on top of his bedside cabinet and nodded at Danny. 'Pass me that book there, dear boy. The thick one by Dennis Wheatley. What a writer! He gives me so much inspiration at times like this.' He tutted and smacked his thin lips together. 'God! the sooner I get out of this place for a drop of Scotch and a cigarette, the better I'll be.'

Yes! Jacky was really feeling for old Freddy Haddock. It was just a pity, she thought, that he couldn't help people get off drugs, the way he could help them in their fight against the Devil.

The phone call to the Bedford estate Social Club, just before closing time, wasn't friendly.

Boots and Brown Trilby leaned outside the telephone kiosk door.

Boots slid a hand over his black shining head and then scrutinised the delicate stitchery on his highly polished cowboy boots. Brown Trilby tweaked his long Mexican moustache thoughtfully. He nervously sipped at his beer and eased his hat down over his eyes.

Docker stood inside the kiosk, fingering his ponytail and nodding frantically as he spoke to Mister Fixit.

'Yeah, yeah, I've got it boss. If that arsehole, Ben Dooley, doesn't come across with your four grand from the council contract you fixed for him, we're to do him good style.'

He blew out a rush of air and squeezed his eyes tightly shut. 'How long d'you say? – one week. Right boss, it'll be sorted.' He eased the phone away from his ear as Mister Fixit raised his voice. 'Yeah, yeah Boss, I heard you, you want his balls sliced for breakfast, then you want him eliminated if he doesn't come across.' Docker hung up, and breathed a huge sigh of relief, the boss was fuming about Dooley.

Meanwhile Ben Dooley drunkenly led Blondie, the young mini-skirted girl, towards his parked car, he hawked noisily and spat out a ball of phlegm. With a lecherous smirk, he ogled her shapely legs and slid a grubby hand across her firm buttocks and up around her waist. He felt his erection pushing against his jeans – he'd paid for her, and the reclining seat of the convertible would be well used tonight.

As Dooley and Blondie turned into the dark sidewalk, leading to the small car park, they were startled as Brown Trilby materialised from nowhere and grabbed the girl. He slapped a firm hand across her mouth, and gripped her firmly around the waist with his other arm.

The glinting machete blade sliced through the air before Dooley's astonished eyes, and slammed into the nearby wooden garden post.

Boots chortled and twisted his powerful wrist, splitting the post straight down the middle.

Dooley let loose a whimper of terror at the sight of the giant negro's snarling face, he knew what this was about. 'I – I'm gettin' Fixit his money, 'onest I am. I'm just waitin' for a cheque that's all.'

Docker emerged from the night's blackness, stood, his legs spread like two small oak trees, and rammed a finger at Boots. 'Do it, Boots,' he growled. 'Do it now!'

Dooley gasped and shook with fright as Boots gripped his arm and slammed it down on top of the four inch wooden post. The giant negro gave an evil grin, his eyes glinting like cat's eyes on a road.

Dooley's bowels loosened and the still air stank. Blondie's skirt had slipped higher up her thighs, when Brown Trilby grabbed her, leaving nothing to the imagination. Her desperate squeals were muffled by his smelly fingers – he panted and grunted as he pressed against her body.

Dooley's eyes were horror-struck, his voice quavered.

'For fuck's sake Docker, I'll get Fixit's money, I – I mean it – just call this fuckin' black bastard off me will yer?' His words tumbled out rapidly, as he desperately sought a reprieve. 'L-listen Docker I – I can't work if 'e cuts me arm off, can I, well – can I?' He screamed. 'Well the fuck shit can I, Docker?'

Docker smirked and slid his steel comb down Dooley's right cheek, just hard enough to leave a long thin trail of blood.

'Aaaah!' Dooley's head shot back with pain. 'P-please Dock,' he whimpered. 'I'll get the bleedin' money.'

Docker curled his thick lip. 'Shurrup, snivelling bastard.' He nodded to Boots. As the machete cut the air, Boots suddenly released Dooley's arm.

Dooley wrenched it away a split second before Boots slashed his second garden post of the night – Boots threw back his head and gave a loud laugh that died into a high-pitched squeal. Docker touched noses with Dooley and hissed, 'One week Dooley. One bleeding week for the four grand – or else!' He pretended to slit his own throat with a thick ringed finger. 'Got it Dooley?' Dooley held his painful wrist, and blew out frightened gasps of air.

'Yeah, yeah, I've got it Docker, I'll have the money.'

Docker turned and nodded to Boots and Brown

Trilby. 'Bring that blonde slag over to the old garages. We might as well have some fun with her, after all, Dooley did pay for her with the boss's money.'

Trembling, Dooley hurriedly waved Blondie and Brown Trilby away.

'She, she – she's yours Docker, do what you want to her, she's all yours.'

Blondie gave muffled squeals as she desperately tried to pull up her knickers, while with his free hand, Brown Trilby pulled up his zip – he'd certainly need to wash himself, and Aids hadn't even crossed his drunken mind.

Dooley was already running towards his motor, fumbling in his pocket for his car keys.

Blondie had no more fight in her, and in the rubbish infested garage she gave her neat body up to Brown Trilby again, and to Mister Fixit's henchmen.

That night, whilst little Sophie slept, Daisy worked busily. She couldn't pack Ben Dooley's suitcase fast enough. There was no way he could pay Mister Fixit back – the cash was long gone on prostitutes and booze.

Driving around in his convertible whilst being banned for drinking and driving, was nothing in comparison. Daisy slammed the front door shut behind him and his luggage and raised her eyes heavenwards.

Have the dirty bastard back when things had settled down? – he must be joking, no chance. She clasped her hands together and exclaimed joyfully.

'At long last the bullying bastard's gone, thank you God!'

She would get around to telling her daughters somehow, not that Rosie and Jacky would care. It was going to be harder to explain to Sophie though, that her father had gone, he could still pull the wool over her eyes – Sophie still had feelings for her dad.

Within minutes, Ben Dooley was on the motorway and heading South.

In the Fox and Hounds, Adder sent the final black ball slamming into the bottom pocket with his usual victory squeal. He tossed the cue against the rack, grabbed his glass of lager from the nearby table, and sat by Jack.

It was six-thirty on Monday evening, and Jacky was meeting Danny in the Lowfield Hotel at seven.

The re-release of Buddy Holly's 'Peggy Sue' had set Jack's foot tapping, as it echoed throughout the bar.

Adder sucked hard on his joint and spat out a stream of sweet-smelling smoke. 'Well, come on Jack, what d'you reckon?' he asked. 'Will your ol' woman put me up now that your old fella has gone – or what?'

It was the third time he'd asked her and Jack was adamant about her decision, she knew him well enough. Anyway, her mother had enough to contend with keeping the home together, without Adder's drug addiction and violent tantrums. One drug addict in the house was enough, not to mention the fact that he was a randy swine, and there were her two sisters to consider. She moved her head to the music and shrugged her shoulders, carefree – she was feeling nice on heroin and her words were slurred. 'Nah, I've already bleedin' told yer, she doesn't want any more blokes there, it's because of me ol' fella in it.'

'Come on Jack, I bet she could do with the bread?'

Jack ignored his remark, and glanced up at the large wall clock hanging behind the bar.

A wasp was perched above the minute finger, as it shifted onto the hour – it was already seven, she'd have to get her skates on.

The wasp took off and zoomed towards her, buzzing purposefully, she swiped at it with an angry arm to send it veering off course. 'Get lost wasp.'

Cochise, standing at the bar, was studying Jack. He smiled to himself at her evident dislike of wasps. Again, he wished he could speak, so that he could remind Jack, that wasps are God's creations, just as dogs and flowers are. But, he thought, I'm sure, knowing my friend Danny's appreciation of nature, in time he'll bring her around to his way of thinking. Jack caught his eye and smiled, Cochise responded with a friendly nod of the head. He liked Jack Dooley and Danny Black.

Jack stood, swayed, and nodded to Adder. They still remained friends, even though Danny and Adder hated each other's guts.

If Jack had had any idea that Adder was a member of Woodcock's evil coven, however, she would have given him short-shrift. As Bobby Queen took over the pool table, Jack gave her a hard piercing look. Startled, Bobby stared back. 'What the bleedin' hell's up with . . . ?' she began, then watched as Jack stalked silently towards the door – she was late for Danny.

Adder was working undercover for the Hell Fire Club. They needed a fresh young virgin for their ceremony on All Hallows' Eve, and Adder knew who he wanted to mount, before the fatal sacrificial blow was struck. But, wriggling his slimy way into the Dooley's house to get near to Sophie, was going to be trickier than he had thought.

Everyone was expected to attend on this night, from rats like Adder, to the middle-class Harry D. Coot, to the very wealthy and high-ranking George Woodcock.

Failure to attend, without a worthy excuse, meant expulsion from the club.

Mary Coot, though, would be absent for evermore, thought Adder, with a leer, you don't give away the Club's secrets and get off lightly, not when the police are getting warmer, thanks to her continual blabbering to her toy boys.

Danny had taken Jack home at eleven-thirty, and then headed back to his bedsit.

He, too, like Adder, had suggested to her that perhaps he could move into Daisy's house after Ben Dooley's departure. But, Jack, after Daisy's insistence about not having another man in the place was compelled to decline his generous offer of weekly cash, along with his promise to look after Daisy, take care of the house, and also sort out the front and back gardens.

Their Rosie was the boss hen, and there was no way she would sleep under the same roof as John, unless they were married, old-fashioned maybe, but ... To Rosie, Adder was just one of Jack's friends, not a lover, and his weekly money would help Daisy out – Jack was now sorry, that after a few drinks, she had blurted out to her that Adder had asked to stay. Afterwards, she'd lied through her teeth to cover her clumsy tracks to convince Rosie that Adder had now found other accommodation, hoping and praying that they didn't bump into each other.

Rosie lived in a different world from Jack and thought Adder was OK!

The inevitable happened, accidentally on purpose, Adder managed to bump into Rosie whilst she was shopping at the local Bedford parade. Putting on his baby boyish face, he explained to her that as he was such a great friend of the family's, especially of Jack, perhaps she could persuade Daisy to let him rent a room, and of course he would pay rent!

Rosie soon gave in to his sweet-talk and told him to come around with his things that very day. And! she'd certainly give Jack a good ticking off for lying to her – as for Daisy, she would soon convince her that Adder would be an acceptable lodger.

Adder gleefully rubbed his skinny gloved hands

together, when his mate passed on the phone message from Rosie, confirming that Daisy had agreed that he could move in.

Sophie's single bed was shifted into Jacky and Rosie's room, and by midnight on Tuesday, Adder was high on coke and settled in.

His eyes glinted viciously and his pointed tongue shot in and out. He could feel his small penis throbbing, as it rose to prod his red striped briefs. He opened the girls' bedroom door a touch wider, to get a better look at Sophie – Rosie and Jack were well hidden by quilts. But Sophie's young shapely bare leg was hanging out of her bed, right to the top of her dimpled thigh.

Adder hungrily gripped his testicles, savagely tempted by the young girl's body. Trembling with lust, he flashed his wet tongue back and forth between his lips. He craved to enter her body, but he knew that only the High Priest of the coven had that privilege – and that was Woodcock. He longed to masturbate at the sight of her, but repressed the urge. Instead, he retreated to his bedroom, to devise ways of debauching Jack, now that he was so close to her, also, he knelt before his lord – Lucifer.

The Dooley women slept on, none the wiser, and downstairs, Stumpy pricked his ears at a sudden passing owl's screech, and whined uneasily.

Chapter Fifteen

The late summer night air was crisp, and Jack was glad to get warm in front of the gas fire.

Danny himself was downstairs chatting on the telephone, smiling happily as he talked and listened.

It was Thursday night and the call was from Tommy, an old mate from Toxteth, Liverpool, who had finally managed to track him down. It was good to hear his voice again, thought Danny.

Tommy invited him to go over the water to Liverpool for his stag-night party the next day, and his wedding on Saturday afternoon. They had arranged everything just as Tommy's pips went.

'Yeah, yeah Tommy,' Danny hurriedly confirmed. 'I'll see yous in the Lion at eight tomorrow night, ta-ra.'

He hung up and bounded up the stairs, his face was still set in a broad grin and he closed the door behind him, Jacky smiled in sympathy. 'You look chuffed, old flame was it?' He laughed and told her about Tommy and his invitation. As she listened, she switched the stereo to soft music and carried on pouring two cans of lager into glasses.

'So, going to Liverpool without me are you?' she teased, as they snuggled close on the small grey settee.

'You don't mind if I go, do you Jack?' he asked, worried for the first time, 'You can come too if you want, 'onest you can.'

Jack smiled mischievously to herself, swigged her beer and stubbed out her cigarette in the ashtray. She derived a schoolgirlish satisfaction from winding him up – like a pretty girl baiting two boys in a playground. She tightened her arm round him and flicked a straggling lock of dark hair out of his eyes, the music changed to the beautiful voice of Jennifer Rush, singing 'The Power Of Love'.

They forgot everything for a moment as they nuzzled each other, whispering the tender words that lovers have exchanged since time began.

'No, you lovely great hunk, of course I don't mind if you go to your mate's wedding,' Jack murmured, eventually. 'I'll be all right. It's only a couple of days, anyway I've got to look after me mam.'

Danny kissed her gratefully, but already the heroin and beer were having their effect on her. 'I love you, Princess,' he whispered. 'I'll love you forever.'

She smiled blankly and her words were forced out. 'I – I love you too Dan, I – I'll love you w-when you're thirty, forty, sixty or even a fuckin' hundred, you – you lovely black bast . . .' Her voice faded as she keeled over, her head dropped down onto the arm of the settee – Jack Dooley was out of the game.

Danny sighed heavily and gazed at her in distress – he was finding Jack's addiction to drugs harder to handle by the minute. He cursed aloud, got up and grabbed the pillow and quilt from his bed, and tucked her up where she lay, out for the count. He knew she was going to encounter a physical and psychological battering when she started withdrawing, that when she was roused from her stupor she would be weak, and bad-tempered, and trembling uncontrollably.

Tears welled up in Danny's eyes, as his mind flashed back to his own mother and her heroin addiction. He knew that when Jack surfaced, she would be hunting high and low for a substitute, anything would do, bottles of cough mixture, or medicines containing mild opiates, even alcohol. At this moment he was worried sick in case he, too, flaked out. Supposing Jack woke and tried to rob the bedsits in the house for 'H', he reflected.

He kissed her lightly on the cheek, turned off the fire and light, then curled up on the settee beside her. It was going to be a long night – but it was going to be harder over the water in Liverpool, because Jack would be continually on his mind. He just hoped that the likes of Cochise, Rosie and John would keep their eye on her, and he knew that Lance, who lived next door, was a devoted watchdog.

The early Friday morning radio show, run by Terry Wogan, sometimes made Danny livid, but he still enjoyed the Irish blarney which rolled so easily off Wogan's magnetic tongue.

He pushed open the small top light of the rain-lashed window, to a serenade from the rooftop birds. He breathed in the bracing air, glanced at Jack, and then admitted Lotty, who was mewing at the door. The little cat quickly devoured her breakfast and then, purring loudly, she nuzzled Jack's face.

Jack opened bleary eyes and swung her arm at Lotty irritably. God, she felt terrible! She groped for her cigarettes, then peered around the room, with half-closed foggy eyes, until she made out Danny's figure. 'Shit Dan,' she croaked. 'You got any tea, or what? – sweet man, dead sweet, I love me sweet tea.' She dragged herself upright and buried her head in her heads. Her voice suddenly came sharp, like the crack of a whip. 'Danny! – a' you the fuck deaf, or what?! Do us a drink will yer. I'm dyin' of thirst.'

Danny reacted angrily at first, he hated it when she was snappy, he hated even more to see her fling Lotty aside, hated her being on heroin with the inevitable aftermath.

He swept up Lotty in his arms and confronted Jack. 'Leave my bleedin' cat alone,' he ordered. 'She's only being friendly, it's your fuckin' fault you feel rotten, taking the shit!'

Looking up at his glowering face, Jack felt ashamed. 'I – I'm sorry man, OK, I'm sorry,' she muttered, adding defensively, 'your cat's all right, I only gave her a bit of a shove, me mam's got a dog you know. I'm used to animals. I just feel . . . well what the . . .' She stubbed out her cigarette, buried her head in the pillow and groaned. 'Okay, okay,' said Danny, and he went to switch the kettle on.

After downing two cups of sweet tea, Jack felt better and tidied herself up.

Danny had showered, trained lightly with Steeleye and eaten breakfast. It was the first time Jack had seen Danny and Steeleye in action, and she was quietly impressed.

As she and Danny waited for the taxi which was to take her home and him to work, she gazed hungrily at the delicate silver necklace he had given her then tucked it away in her jacket pocket.

As Danny's buzzer sounded, announcing the cab's arrival, Jack threw her arms around his neck, reached up, and kissed him hard on the mouth. 'I won't get a chance to give you a nice goodbye kiss in the taxi, Dan, have a great time in Liverpool. I'll see you at seven in the Lord Tennyson on Monday night.' She hugged his firm waist. 'I love you a lot Dan.'

The taxi horn blared outside in the road.

Danny kissed her back, tweaked her nose tenderly and gripped her hand.

'I love you too, Princess, come on or I'll be late for work.' Hand in hand, they went out to the waiting taxi.

On the evening of that same Friday, Danny sat, his head gently rocking to the rhythm of the train to Liverpool, as it thundered through a long black tunnel. He would take some flowers to his grandad Harry's grave, he decided, then his thoughts returned to Jacky and his worries about her weighed on him.

Lance commanded Bimbo to sit beneath the overhanging willow tree, and stood watching Jacky and Adder as they staggered across the car park towards the Coach and Horses. He gazed with pained attention as they barged in through the doors – he knew Jack was out for drugs.

The Fat Man waddled across the smoke-filled room, beaming – he was always grateful for the custom. He nodded a welcome, and clamped a heavy arm around Jack's shoulder. His breathing was laboured, he'd piled on the weight lately. His councillor father had his fingers in many pies, and had lately upped Fat Man's allowance. With his drug deals increasing by the day, Fat Man was living well and showing for it.

He brushed a chubby ringed hand through his mop of red hair and chuckled, a note of dominance in the sound. 'Coke, or for you, my sweets, purest heroin, the very latest stuff on the market, it's delicious, what'll it be? That's all I've got so . . .' He spread his arms and leered.

Adder swayed and clumsily dragged out some notes. Suddenly, his blurred gaze caught Cochise's hard gleaming eyes, lit with a pale fire – he was leaning on the bar watching every move Jack Dooley made.

Adder prodded Fat Man in the gut. 'Come on, g'is some of that pure stuff you fat bastard, come to the bog.' He turned to Jack. 'You wait here Jack, that fuckin' dumb half-breed at the bar is watching us.'

His tongue flashed in and out, occasionally running along the full length of his thin lips.

Cochise stared at Jack, who was swigging lager, clicked his tongue and grunted with dissatisfaction. His brow darkened, as he remembered how Danny had managed to explain, by means of crude mime, and by mouthing words, how his mother had died from a massive overdose of heroin. Jack Dooley was already in the worst state that he'd ever seen her, and it was still only eight-thirty in the evening.

There was no sign of Danny, nobody to look after her, and Cochise was worried, he didn't like poking his nose in but . . .

Jacky and Adder didn't stay after the deal, and as they tottered back across the car park, Cochise peered anxiously through the small paned glass window. He could see Lance and Bimbo standing across the road near to a streetlight. His lips tightened and his jaw hardened, as Adder and Jack fell into a taxi which was ranked on the car park. He wished desperately that his friend, Danny, had been there right now.

By eleven pm, in Miko's grotty flat, high up on the eighth floor of the high-rise block, Jack was higher than a kite on beer and drugs, and the heavy metal music shook the room.

Adder and Miko, who were slumped in a world of

oblivion, flopping their heads to the music, didn't even notice that Jack had over drunk, and over chased the 'dragon'. She was suffering respiratory depression, low blood pressure, and had drifted into a coma.

Cochise had found it impossible to settle after Jack had left the pub with Adder. He'd collared the same taxi-driver, when he finally returned, after several trips, to the car park rank. It took the cab-driver a few minutes to suss out what Cochise was trying to say.

Cochise spent a further half-hour touring the high-rise block. The small crowd of angry neighbours gathering in the passageway, listening, and hammering on the door to complain about the noise of the deafening music coming from Miko's flat, ended his search.

After a full minute's fruitless banging on the door, Cochise stepped back and let fly with a hefty boot.

With a sharp crack the door flew open. He rushed inside, and ignoring the slurred abuse from Adder and Miko, he towered over the body of Jack Dooley, which appeared lifeless.

He was shocked by her appearance, and his eyes burned with hatred for the two yobs.

A scraggy-haired Irishwoman poked her head around the door. On seeing Jack's state her words came hurriedly. 'I'll get an ambulance me dear, I'll phone one right away.'

Lager splashed everywhere, as Miko heaved himself to his feet and clumsily swung his bottle at

Cochise. The back of Cochise's long hand met him full on the nose. Miko squealed like a pig, and reeled back, blood pouring from his nostrils. He gripped his reddening face, his words were muffled. 'Yer dumb bastard! Yer've broke me fuckin' nose. We'll have you for this, you long-haired shitbag.'

Cochise couldn't hear him, in any event, he was more concerned about Jacky, who was still lying motionless and silent.

Adder also climbed to his feet and wobbled about, spitting obscenities at Cochise and the onlookers. 'W-what's – what's the marrer with – with you lot, she's always getting high, sh-she'll be all right, she always is.' He lurched towards the small group of spectators, flapping an arm and swigging beer. They disappeared at his violent outburst. 'Go on, you – you interfering gits, p-piss off, she's OK.'

Within ten minutes, Jack was in an ambulance and on her way to Balchester Royal Infirmary, the siren blaring, and blue light flashing.

As Rosie frantically hammered on the neighbours' front door the hall light flashed on. The catch clicked, the door swung open, and Lance's face appeared.

Rosie heaved a sigh of relief and asked, worriedly, 'Can I use your phone please, Lance? The police have been. Jack's been rushed into hospital, they said she's bad, very bad.'

Lance looked alarmed. 'Yes, yes of course you can,' he gestured her inside. 'What's happened to her?' His guts churned. With the state Jack was in, when he saw her outside the Coach and Horses, anything could have befallen her, more so when he knew she hit the drugs so hard. Rosie pushed her hair out of her eyes and dialled the number with unsteady fingers. In her panic, she hit a five instead of a six. The slurring male voice that answered wanted to know how much she charged. She slammed down the receiver button and redialled.

'I don't know yet Lance, honest,' she replied to his anxious question, and put up a hand to silence him as the sister at the hospital came on the line. With relief, she learned that Jack was alive, but in the intensive care unit – she and Daisy could go to see her.

She hurriedly put Lance in the picture, while his invalid mother shouted from upstairs, and banged her cane on the floorboards, eager to know what was going on. 'Oh it's only Rosie, Mother,' Lance called up, brusquely.

As Rosie was leaving, she paused and turning, asked, 'Lance, will you do us a favour and try to contact Danny Black?'

'Yes, yes Rose, of course I will, but where . . . ?'

'Liverpool! Toxteth to be exact. He's gone to a mate's stag-night. Jack said he was meeting him in the Lion, at eight o'clock. Try directory enquiries and take it from there, there's a good chance someone will know where they've gone, anyway, they might still even be there. Oh, could you phone me a taxi straight away, there's a love?'

'OK Rose, will do.' He dug out the yellow pages while Rosie thanked him and hurried off.

Back home, Daisy was frantically pacing the room, watched by a bemused Stumpy, who huddled by the fire.

As Rosie re-entered and told her tale, Daisy responded anxiously, 'You go down the hospital now love, I'll have to wait for Adder to come in, I can't leave Sophie on her own.' Just then, they heard the cab beep outside.

Meanwhile, next door, Lance was trying to get hold of Danny Black, so far without success.

Chapter Sixteen

The night sky was cloudy and not even a glimmer of moonlight relieved the darkness.

The door of the Toxteth nightclub, the Purple Parrot swung open to reveal a Mike Tyson look-alike bouncer. He gave an ugly scowl. 'Yeah man,' he growled. 'What d'you want?'

Carl tipped back his head cockily and stepped forward from the small group of men. He was coloured, and stood a good inch taller than the six-foot bouncer. He was smartly dressed for Tommy's stag-night. 'It's me, Carl, you stupid fuckin' gorilla. Is Danny Black here? He left the Castle before us with Tommo, said he was coming here.'

Club bouncer or not, Gorilla dare not mouth back to Carl, he was top dog on the Toxteth streets, and the only man he'd ever had any respect for was Danny Black. They had gone to the same school together, and for the rest of his days, he would sport the broken nose that Danny had given him many years before. Likewise, every time Danny looked in the mirror he could see the small scar on his right cheek left by Carl's teeth. Gorilla still carried the memory of a fellow bouncer being blown backwards through a plate glass window with a sawn-off shotgun. Nobody had ever been charged for the shooting but . . .

Carl rammed a slender cigar between his teeth and flicked his lighter. He sucked hard, and before long a stream of cigar smoke engulfed Gorilla's face. 'Well!' Carl queried.

Gorilla hid his fear and stoutly kept his face expressionless. Nodding his head, he beckoned the group forward. The three inch knife scar down the left side of his face twitched. 'Yeah, he was here ten minutes ago when I went for a hit an' miss – he was talking to Tommo and the Ballerina, by the dance floor, he's half pissed, man.'

The group brushed past him and went inside.

As the mass of coloured bodies danced to Bob Marley, beneath shooting beams of flashing lights, and rising clouds of wacky backy, the Ballerina threw back her mass of black frizzy hair and laughed. She gave a flippant little wave of her hand. 'So, now you don't want me any more, eh, Danny Black? Now that you're going out with a honk, well, well.'

The Ballerina was small and slim, almost skinny. She was mad keen on different shades of pink, even if they clashed, and tonight she was a dazzling spectacle in a shocking pink trouser suit, pale rose high heeled sandals, and a cerise hair ribbon. She'd been one of Danny's on and offs for the last three years, and they were still good friends. Danny grinned and went on gyrating to the music. 'Come 'ead girl, you're not jealous, are you!?'

She fluttered her lashes and giggled. 'Course not, why should I be when you're stopping at my place tonight.'

Danny's grin widened and he shook his head. 'Uh, uh, I've told you, Ballerina, I love the woman, anyway I'm stoppin' at Tommo's.'

She hooked her finger under his chin and tickled him confidently. 'We'll see, we'll see my love, when you've had a few more drinks – I'll look like a Page Three stunner to you then.' She giggled, provocatively.

Danny turned sharply when he was suddenly prodded in the back by the stocky bearded Negro. 'Hey man,' the Negro exclaimed. 'A' you Danny Black?'

'Yeah, why?'

'Phone man, for you.' He indicated the glass door near to the bar with a thick nail-bitten finger. 'Over there.'

'Cheers mate.' As Danny walked away, he said, over his shoulder, 'I won't be a min' Ball . . .' The Ballerina, though, was already flouncing off in search of another partner.

Danny picked up the receiver. 'Yeah, who is it?'

'It's me, Lance, Danny,' Lance's voice trembled slightly. There was a pause as Danny tried to recall who Lance was.

'Lance! I live next door to Jack – Jacky Dooley.'

'Oh that Lance.' Recognition dawned on Danny, 'What's up then lad, something wrong?'

Danny's face grew grim as Lance blurted out the story of what had happened to Jack.

Lance was nervous, scared even, maybe, of Danny, even at the end of a telephone line twenty miles away. Rumours sweeping the Bedford Estate to the effect that Danny was no man to mess around with, had already reached his ears. Nevertheless, he was determined to put him in the picture. 'It – it could be drugs again, Danny.' He knew damn well it was.

The Fat Man had been spreading his net lately on the estate but nobody dared say a word about him. Windows had been smashed before, one house had been torched. His mind briefly flashed back to the terrible incident of the blazing house – he had seen it himself whilst out walking Bimbo, a child had been badly burned in the fire.

Lance went on talking, his stomach churning. 'I just happened to – to be passing the Coach and Horses, and I saw Jack going in there with that cretin, Adder. She's in a bad way, Danny, honest, that's why Rosie asked me to try and track you down.'

By the deathly silence that followed, Lance realised that perhaps he had said too much. His words tumbled out frantically. 'D-don't get me wrong, I'm only guessing, it could be . . .' Too late! Danny was already completing the sentence in his mind.

Above the distant beat of the soul music drifting

down the line, Lance heard a harsh groan. He gawped at the mouthpiece. 'Danny? Are you there Danny?'

There was a click as Danny dropped the receiver. Anger and grief were exploding inside him like gunpowder, but his training in martial arts had taught himself to restrain himself. He had to get back, he had to see Jack, he'd have to make his excuses to Tommy and leave. 'If those fuckin' drugo bastards have hurt her I'll screw their . . .' The threat died down into a muttered curse.

Tommy was standing near the bar talking to Carl and the Ballerina as Danny approached. He walked unsteadily and his face was thunderous.

Carl winked at the busty barmaid, snapped his fingers and pointed at Danny. A pint of lager quickly appeared in exchange for a crisp banknote.

At that moment, a purple high-collared shirt approached, it was covering a small but muscular male torso. The large sun-glasses, resting on his wide nose, hid most of the young man's dark face. The tempo of the music and song had changed to heavy rap. Purple Shirt's head rocked from side to side with the rhythm. With a finger and thumb he raised his sun-glasses, looked at Danny and asked. 'You after drugs, man? I've got the best on Merseyside. I can even get . . .'

Suddenly his bubbly voice became a squeaky little croak, as Danny's lightning grip tightened around his stubby neck.

Purple Shirt had picked on the wrong man at the wrong time.

'H-hey, what the fuck's up man, you're bleedin' chokin' me?'

Danny's face twisted with hate as he pulled Purple Shirt's weasel face to within an inch of his own. 'Fuckin' little arsehole, I ought to screw your knackers off!'

A burly bouncer appeared from nowhere and stepped forward. Danny's thick black eyebrows drew together, he hissed, and took on an attacking stance.

Carl flicked out a hand and gripped Danny's wrist. 'What the fuck's up with yous Dan' leave it out man. Yous know the score here, a' you listening, what's up with you?' He flashed a hurried glance around the room. 'D'yous want half this bleeding lot on your back, or what? Most of 'em are on the shit.'

Momentarily, Danny's eyes met Carl's and he knew his friend was right. Sanity prevailed; with a snarl, he released his powerful grip.

Purple Dealer's face was the colour of his shirt, he coughed and spluttered before staggering away clutching his throat.

'Bastard,' he croaked. 'S'lucky I'm busy or I'd . . .'

He was quickly submerged by a group of larger revellers who were eager for his wares.

The bouncer's mean face showed disappointment, he'd have relished a punch up – even with Danny Black, or the chance to prove himself against Carl.

Danny crossly took a large swig of lager and

wiped a hand across his mouth. He looked at Carl, and his fierce expression crumbled into one of apology. 'I – I'm sorry Carl, mate.' He raised a hand to his brow. 'But I'm up to 'ere with pissin' drugs.' He hurriedly blurted out his story to his three friends. God forbid! He wanted to enjoy Tommy's wedding festivities, but Jack came before anything and everybody, even childhood mates.

Danny spread his hands. 'I'm sorry Tommy la' honest I am.' He glanced from one dejected face to another, then went on, briskly, 'Come 'ead Tommy, yous know I wouldn't let you down, even if yous wus hanging, but she's bad Tommy, and I've gotta get to Balchester Royal Infirmary straight away, I wanna be with her, that's all.'

Tommy, Carl and The Ballerina all gazed at him with a certain amount of respect. Tommy nodded. 'That's fair enough Dan, s'okay, just give us a bell, eh, to let us know how yer lady is, all right?'

Carl, one arm around The Ballerina's waist, dragged hard on his cigar, and nodded emphatic agreement. 'And don't forget Danny la', if yous need a hand with this Fat Man and his mates just give us a bell,' he put in, his eyes serious as he glanced at The Ballerina and Tommy. 'We don't know nothin' about this Woodcock geezer and black magic stuff, but if we can help, well . . .'

Tommo stepped forward and gripped Danny's hand. 'Thanks for coming anyway, Dan, and don't forget to ring us if yous need us – any time. D'you wanna a taxi man?'

Danny shook his head. 'No ta Tommy, I need some air.' The Ballerina broke away from Carl's grip and planted a deep pink smacker on Danny's lips. 'I'll catch up with you again, you fuckin' evasive hunk.'

Danny gave her a big squeeze, then gently eased her away and nodded his thanks to Tommy and Carl. 'I'll see yous all again, no sweat.'

As he passed by Gorilla at the club entrance, the great goon just had to say the wrong thing. 'The pink lipstick suits you man, nice guy was he?'

Danny stopped, growled, then thrust two lightning fast elbows into his rib cage.

Gorilla grunted and slumped to the floor, clutching himself in pain and gasping for breath. Danny tidied his jacket. 'Sorry, ugly bastard, just slipped.'

He wiped The Ballerina's lipstick from his mouth and barged through the club doors to hail a taxi – he had more important things than silly bouncers on his mind.

He melted into the night's thickening Mersey mist, with hatred for Fat Man, Adder, and any other mother fuckin' smackhead or drug-dealer, burning like fire in his guts.

He was drunk, and with his fists clenched, he screamed into the swirling fog, 'What the fuck is wrong with this pissin' world of yours God, when yous do things like this to Jacky!'

There was nothing but an eerie silence – no answer came from the void.

He half fell in front of the taxi, flapping his arms like a windmill. At last he was bound for Balchester.

When they arrived at Balchester Royal Infirmary, Danny climbed clumsily from the cab and handed the driver a twenty and a five. 'Keep the change pal, and ta for the rush job, it's appreciated.'

He dived inside the hospital, the automatic doors sliding to behind him. The cab driver was glad to be rid of his passenger, he'd carried edgy characters before, but this one, well . . .

Danny had napped for a couple of short spells on the way back, and sobered up a little.

He enquired about Jack at reception and was directed to a nearby waiting-room. There he found Daisy and Rosie, Lance having been roped in to babysit Sophie.

'That Adder didn't turn up,' Daisy complained to Danny, 'just when he was needed.'

Danny could have told her a thing or two about Adder, but saved it for later. 'Have they said anything to you about how Jacky is?' he asked of Rosie, worriedly. It was Rosie who seemed the calmer of the two women. 'Only that they're doing all they can,' she replied.

'They won't let us see her,' mourned Daisy, plucking at the pages of a tattered magazine. 'Goodness knows what they're doing to her.'

Rosie brought them cartons of coffee from the machine, and they went on waiting.

A screeching child, bouncing up and down on her mother's knee, was giving Danny earache.

Meanwhile, only a few wards away, Freddy Haddock was lying awake listening to the start of the three a.m. radio show on his headphones. After only a few minutes he switched off, not eager to hear another Beatles record. 'Huh, pop music,' he muttered, disgustedly.

He leaned over and groped in his bedside cabinet for his small stash of cigarettes. He was gasping, and would have to have a swift drag leaning out of the window to avoid the smoke alarms – the night nurse would be reading her book now, anyway. Mentally, he was already drawing up plans to try and help Danny and Jack Dooley in their fight against Woodcock's evil coven. But, at this present moment in time, he needed a cigarette.

It was shortly after half past three in the morning when Olga, the bossy night nurse who wouldn't let him smoke, shivered, put down her Stephen King horror novel, and realised that Merlin was missing from his bed. Leaning out of the window, the night air had been chilly, so Merlin had beat a hasty retreat to the toilet to finish his smoke. After a fleeting search of the small empty lounge, she pounded along to the toilet.

At the loud knocking on the toilet door, Merlin took a last quick puff and flushed the butt-end down the loo – anyway, the smoke alarm had already given a sharp beep as a pre-warning of what could follow.

Cursing quietly to himself, he opened the door

slowly and smiled ingratiatingly. 'Eh, eh, just using the toilet, nurse, that's all,' he said, straightening his pyjamas.

Olga, arms akimbo, gazed at him suspiciously. 'Was you Fredrick Haddock?' She puckered her nose and sniffed the aroma. 'Wonder you haven't set yourself on fire. One of these times I'll catch you at it,' she threatened.

Merlin assumed an expression of innocence as she escorted him back to his bed. She'd have to be quick about it he reflected, he was to be discharged the next day, and Danny had promised to collect him from the infirmary himself, and take him home in a cab.

It was twenty past five in the morning, when a nurse came to tell the weary trio in the waiting-room that they could see Jacky, just for a few moments.

'Is she going to be all right?' Rosie burst out, agitatedly.

'She's still very poorly,' the nurse replied in gentle tones. 'It seems it was a pretty bad overdose of alcohol and heroin.'

Daisy covered her face with her hands. 'Oh my God!' she groaned.

Danny laid a comforting arm around her small shoulders.

'Please don't worry, Mrs Dooley,' the nurse added, sympathetically. 'Your daughter's in no immediate danger.' Her glance took in Danny and

Rosie, as she went on, 'Doctor is hopeful she'll pull through now, if you'll follow me, please . . .'

At the sight of Jacky, grey and exhausted, Daisy burst into tears.

Rosie, herself shocked, gently pushed her mother into a bedside chair, and tucked some tissues into her hand.

As for Danny, he'd stopped at the end of Jack's bed and was staring at her; dismayed beyond words at her condition. Anger, that had never been far beneath the surface, flared inside him, but he knew he must control it at present. Moving to the side of the bed, he gently stroked her limp hand. 'How are yous Jack?' he whispered.

She tried to smile. 'I'm okay Dan,' her voice was so weak he had to bend close to hear her. 'I'll be all right man, 'onest.'

Rosie sat grim-faced, she'd always had her suspicions that Jack was on something, and now she knew it for sure. Daisy, still tearful, was in a state of confusion. 'What's wrong with you, love,' she kept saying. It was obvious to the others that the nurse's mention of heroin had been something she couldn't face so she had subconsciously blotted it out.

Rosie tried to calm her down. 'Don't worry Mum,' she said, consolingly. 'She just drank too much beer, that's all.' She tossed an urgent glance at Danny Black. 'Didn't she Dan?'

Danny nodded. 'Yeah, yeah that's right Daisy, too much lager an' that. She went to a party in the high-rise flats, that's all.'

Jack's cheeks were whiter than the pillows and hollowed. She shifted her head so that she could look at Danny. She glanced at the drip, curled her lip, and whispered, hoarsely. 'I feel bleedin' awful, the bastards, God! Never again Dan, 'onest, never, ever again.'

She gripped his hand with sudden strength and gazed at him with pleading eyes. 'Help me Dan,' she begged, 'I just wanna get off this fuckin' shit man.'

Danny held on to her tightly. 'You've got my promise on it Princess,' he vowed, still struggling to keep his rising temper under control.

As they were speaking, Rosie managed to divert Daisy's attention with remarks about her wedding, how it looked as if Jack would be well in time.

Later that morning, Danny arrived back at his bedsit, tired, but profoundly thankful that Jack was going to pull through.

One of the other tenants must have let Lotty in through the front door, because she was sitting on the top of the stairs, her tail swishing. She rubbed herself against his legs in an ecstatic welcome.

Danny unlocked the door and she rushed in ahead of him for her milk and food, her little bell tinkling.

He switched on the radio, fed Lotty, and dropped down onto the bed. Burying his head in his hands, he heaved a sigh. It had been a bad spell. Whether or not it had all been caused by Woodcock and his coven he didn't know – but it had been a diabolical spell!

He shook his head vigorously, enough was enough, the drugos just had to be stopped. Reaching under the bed, he drew out the bundle containing Steeleye. Rising to his full height, he strapped the deadly crowbar to his wrist. He started to spin Steeleye. Then he tested his reflexes by attacking the small glass cabinet. He succeeded three times out of three, stopping the whirling length of steel a hair's breadth from the leaded glass. He was containing a deadly anger, he was ready. He nodded with satisfaction at finding his reflexes as sharp as ever, then dropped back onto the bed.

As the London Symphony Orchestra provided a background of Rod Stewart's 'Sailing', he lay down with his feet hanging over the bed end. He was weary and needed some sleep after the long night – he would visit Jacky later that afternoon. The next morning he remembered, he was to pick up Merlin from hospital and take him home.

As Lotty snuggled up, warm against his legs, Danny fell into a deep sleep.

His mind drifted into the past. Pictures of his grandfather Harry teaching him to whittle wood flashed before him like a film show. His tight lids flickered with movement, as the rippling brook swirled through the small glade where they sat. As the rays of sunshine pierced the broad green leaves, the scene faded, and his mind once again fell dark. Danny slept on, and not even the squabbling pack of angry dogs who roamed the nearby alleys disturbed him.

Chapter Seventeen

Freddy Haddock swung open his own heavy front door and with a little help from Danny, stepped inside.

Danny smiled warmly. 'I'll bet it feels good to be home, Merlin, doesn't it?' He put Freddy's small suitcase down and added, 'Go easy on the Scotch though.'

Freddy nodded as he hung his deerstalker on the hatstand.

'I shall be prudence itself, dear boy, thank you for bringing me home.'

The house was spotless and the smell of a floral aerosol was so strong that Freddy sneezed once or twice. He cursed loudly, having told his cleaning lady a thousand times that he hated the stuff. 'You can't beat the aroma of tobacco smoke, Mrs Jenkins,' he would say grumpily. 'All this modern stuff just isn't healthy.'

The only place she dare not spray was Freddy's den. In fact she wasn't allowed anywhere near it.

Danny was still very concerned over Jack's state of health, but somewhere behind his troubled look there lurked a little smile – it was good to have Merlin home, scarred for life, but well again. In any case, the way Merlin had joked about always wanting to grow a beard made Danny feel rather better.

In the dim light of the hallway Freddy Haddock tilted his head and peered up at Danny's face. 'Thank you again, dear boy, you've been very kind.'

Danny's expression became stern as he responded, 'And you, Freddy Haddock, are very lucky to be alive, so no more heroic home watch schemes. Just keep your eyes open, and phone the police if yous see anything suspicious, eh. Anythin' more, leave to the younger blokes, OK!'

'Yes, yes dear boy, I take your point.' Suddenly he wagged a finger skyward. 'Oh and by the way, I've started work on this devil worship stuff for your friend, Jacky. Please do give her my regards when you see her again. Don't worry, I'll be in touch, and now for a drop of Scotch.' He smacked his lips. Danny opened the front door ready to go. He didn't want Merlin to know how bad Jack was, just in case it upset him. At the moment, he didn't even know Jack was in hospital.

'I'll see yous soon, Merlin,' he said and resolved to keep a watchful eye on his old friend. The front door clicked shut, as Danny passed through the small front garden he stopped to smell, and gently caress, one of Merlin's pure white roses. The scent was magic. He bowed his head briefly, he remembered how white roses had been his mother's favourite flowers. With a sigh, he shut the garden gate and hotfooted it towards home – he was starving, but first he would enjoy a pint.

On entering his den, Merlin breathed in the deep musty air with a certain amount of satisfaction. He dumped the books he'd read in hospital back onto his cluttered desktop, slid open the drawer and reached for the whisky bottle. He poured a man-sized shot and tossed it down, straight.

'Right!' he muttered, determinedly, 'The Hell Fire Club!' He pushed a cigarette into his fancy holder, lit it, and turned on his ancient radio. Frank Sinatra singing 'My Way', brought back recollections of how Danny's grandfather, Harry, and himself, had tackled things their own way, during the war, so many years before. He filled his glass with more whisky and raised it aloft. 'Cheers! Harry.' His voice softened, with a certain sadness. 'Cheers, my old friend, you've got a marvellous grandson.' He shook his head. 'Ah, the good old days.'

Flicking open the cover of the book on Egyptian mythology, he cleared his throat raspingly. 'Right!' he muttered. 'Time for some work.'

On the following Thursday night, Danny called into the Lord Tennyson for a drink, after visiting Jack in hospital. He was happy because she was on the mend, and tipped back his beer in a celebratory mood.

The pretty dark haired landlady was cheerful and

Danny enjoyed talking to the landlord, who like him, was a keen Liverpool football supporter.

Rumours had spread like wildfire about Jacky Dooley being in hospital. The estate was like a beehive, buzzing with gossip, and not all from women either, some of the men were just as bad.

The pretty landlady placed her elbows on the bar and cupped her chin in her hands. 'How's your girlfriend Dan? Is she all right?' she asked.

Suddenly, to a loud and arrogant request from a drinker, the jukebox rose to ear-splitting pitch – Bruce Springsteen was exploding with 'Born In The U.S.A.'

Pretty landlady's face became a picture of wrath. Her head shot round and she glared at the guilty, tiny, long-haired barmaid. 'Turn that bleeding racket down will you, I'm trying to talk to Danny.'

The jukebox immediately quietened to a gentler tone. Danny gave Pretty Landlady a grateful smile. 'Jack's doin' fine, ta, she's well on the mend.' Then picking up his beer, he ambled away to talk to one of the pub's footballers. Later, feeling satisfied, Danny left the Lord Tennyson, and soon reached the wooded footpath that came out near to the Lowfield Hotel. He threw an arm around the trunk of the smooth grey beech tree, as he heaved himself to the top of the hilly hard-packed mud track, which was close to the barely used railway line, that now only carried the steel freight from the steelworks where Lance worked. As he stepped forward onto the slabbed pavement, a red double-decker bus changed gear and roared past him. He stopped halfway across the railway bridge and stared towards the Lowfield Hotel, which lay only a stone's throw beyond.

Not a muscle in Danny's face twitched when, in the lights from the pub window, he spotted the Fat Man selling drugs on the car park to two boys no older than twelve years of age. But his eyes were smouldering, like those of an alert dangerous animal – he just had to do something, he gritted his teeth and smacked a heavy fist into the palm of his hand – he would keep his emotions under control and wait, wait until the time was right!

'Fat man,' he breathed softly. 'I'm gonna have your fuckin' guts.'

He let out a small hiss and set off briskly for home. It was at least a mile and the walk would do him good, wind him down a bit, perhaps!

Danny sat drinking lager in the Winchester Arms, which was only a couple of hundred yards from his bedsit. It was near to closing time and he was tipsy. He'd been drinking on his own and brooding over the Fat Man, hardly noticing the bar emptying around him. Anyway, he'd been engrossed in watching brilliant, high-scoring dart players, who'd seemed to do nothing but slowly pace up and down the black rubber mat for the last thirty minutes. Finally, the two players cased their darts, drank up, and left.

Danny struggled slightly to find his feet, downed

the last of his lager, and without a word left the premises. He was the last customer, and as the large wooden door slammed shut behind him, he heard the bolts being drawn.

It was just past midnight, when Danny stood in his bedsit and twirled Steeleye. He felt ready, and the trayful of chips and curry from the Seaview chippy had tasted good. In addition, the beer he had drunk had drowned any butterflies churning in his stomach. A fierce glint kindled in his eyes, as he rubbed his thumb over the two points at the end of the crook.

'I'm sorry Grandad,' he muttered, 'but . . .'

He made sure that Steeleye was strapped securely to his wrist and then, with a spine-chilling chuckle, he smacked the crowbar's jaw-breaking disc into the palm of his hand – Fat Man and his shitty friends were gonna get it!

He showed his teeth in a tight smile, and then shoved Steeleye up, beneath his black anorak.

Lotty had just come in and was yowling for milk. He put a saucerful down for her, petted her, then strode out of the bedsit, locking the door behind him.

It was chilly lurking in the darkness of the alley-way but at last Danny was rewarded for his patience. A five-seater black cab turned into the street and drew to a halt outside the Fat Man's drug-financed luxury pad.

Danny's lip curled as he focused his vision on the tubby red-headed drug dealer. 'Good,' he muttered, with a note of satisfaction, as Miko led two long-haired heroin addicts, along with a sexy little miniskirted, purple-haired bimbo, up to Fat Man's front door.

As Fat Man slapped a fiver into the cabbie's palm, he twirled his bunch of keys in his other hand. 'Keep the change my man, keep the change.'

Danny's strong grip tightened around his steel friend, irritation was gathering inside him, he was already keyed up. He gently nudged an inquisitive little mongrel aside with his foot and carried on eyeing up the group of addicts. 'S'better than I thought,' he whispered to himself. 'A hoard of the druggy bastards!' He shuffled uneasily, he'd give them a few minutes to get nicely settled down, and then . . . ?

Fat Man was having a drugs party – fine, just fine, it suited Danny, right down to the ground!

He was just about to make his move when he froze suddenly. The Yamaha 250cc motor bike roared into the street, and screeched to a halt outside Fat Man's flat.

The motor cyclist raised the visor and removed the fancy striped helmet.

Danny's eyes nearly bolted from his head. 'Su-Ling!' he gasped, astounded.

Su-Ling got off the machine and placed her helmet on the black seat. She shook her head, causing her long dark hair to fall down past her leather-clad shoulders.

Rave music was already drifting out into the street, through Fat Man's heavily curtained windows.

Danny shook his head in bewilderment and put a distraught hand to his brow. 'I – do – not – believe – what – I'm – seeing!' he hissed, between gritted teeth. 'I just don't fuckin' believe it!'

Su-Ling unzipped her jacket and pulled out a small package. As she approached the flat, the front door swung open to reveal Fat Man's smug round face. He hurriedly ushered her inside and quickly closed the door again.

Inside, Su-Ling stiffened, but she schooled her voice to be casual. At this level of drug dealing Fat Man was usually on his own, not with a group of deadheads. With a touch of vexation she said, 'Hello Fat Man, I have the delivery. Perhaps we'd be better talking in the kitchen.'

Fat Man shrugged his shoulders heedlessly. His side of the business was going well, and he was getting too cocksure. 'It's OK Su-Ling we're among friends.' He waved a hand at the company. 'I trust them, darling, OK?' He spread his drunken arms wide. 'I love them my sweet,' he drooled, 'I love every one of them, while they buy our goodies.'

As Danny strained his eyes, peering through the small gap in the curtain, he managed to see Su-Ling hand Fat Man a package. In return, Fat Man passed an envelope to her with a sickly grin. Danny had seen all he needed, and the revolting sight of Su-Ling taking drug money nauseated him. 'Fuckin' drug money, the cow's taking drug money,' he spat the words out. 'And to think I slept with that bitch. I should scrub meself down with disinfectant – shit! – The cow's got kids of her own!'

For a short while, shock silenced him, but his blood still boiled and he shook with rage. His mind flashed back – he'd never seen a motor bike at Woodcock's farm while he worked there. He thought on. A lock-up somewhere? Yes! yes Su-Ling must have a lock-up.

He desperately wanted to unleash Steeleye on Su-Ling, and her drug-running machine, but something from deep down inside him restrained him. He just silently stood in the shadows as she left Fat Man's flat, tugged on her helmet, started up her machine, and roared away at speed.

Danny shook his head again with disbelief and snarled bitterly.

'Su-Ling eh! Su pissing Ling into drug pushing.' He felt as if he was burning up, yet his thoughts were clear. Things were now beginning to slot together, he remembered what Ben Dooley had told him about George Woodcock suddenly arriving back in Balchester from Bangkok, with Su-Ling, and thousands of pounds to buy 'Meadows Farm'. The gold Merc' must have cost a bomb as well.

Words and incidents jostled frustratingly through Danny's tortured mind.

George Woodcock wasn't just a farmer, he realised, but a dangerous, deadly man, with a sly wife, just as deadly! There was Ament, too, that strange nanny. He recalled Ben Dooley's words. 'She'd just disappear Danny.' He'd snapped his fingers. 'Disappear, just like that. And every time she took just a small brown case, and was gone for only a few days. I mean,' he'd added, 'this happened when I was working here – how many other times did it happen?'

Danny's muddled mind desperately tried to piece the strange jigsaw together quickly, but he was searching for the final picture that probably wasn't on the front of the box – a pornographic picture of a neat little threesome. Ament doing Su-Ling, Su-Ling doing Ament, and horny Woodcock doing them both at the same time, utterly – sordid!

Danny's heart seemed to be beating so fast he felt as if he would choke. Every nerve screamed for action – now he was ready. They're a team his mind shrieked, a weird perverted team. He split from the alley-way like a sprinter leaving the starting blocks. He crouched, hugged Fat Man's flat wall and ripped out the telephone wire.

He pulled the blue Balaclava over his head, having made up his mind earlier in the day to wear one – if he was really going to sort the Fat Man, he certainly didn't want to be recognised. Within a matter of seconds, he'd run around to the back of the flat, which was well hidden by a tall brick wall. All that lay beyond was a school playing-field.

With a fierce snort, Danny smashed the glass-panelled back door with Steeleye, and burst into the kitchen.

From within there came a squeal of terror, mingled with a cry of pain, as the wafer-thin dying heroin addict suddenly withdrew the point of the syringe from his leg. The 'track lines' were clearly visible – there wasn't much more of his abused body left to use.

He gulped. 'What the hell fuck . . . ?' He wobbled to his feet, wide-eyed with fear, as Steeleye glinted fearsomely in the light.

With an angry bark, Danny stormed into the flat and rammed Steeleye against Heroin Addict's head, forcing it back against the kitchen wall. The metal wall hook, from which a wooden key-ring holder hung, slammed into the drugo's cheek. As blood flowed freely, he screamed with pain and hurled the syringe wildly at Danny, missing him by at least a couple of feet. Danny's response was instant. Wild eyes blazing, he gave two short rapid stabs with Steeleye, and Heroin Addict doubled up and slumped to the floor, clutching his broken ribs – a chunk of his flesh was left hanging with the keys.

Danny said not a word, he just let loose a vicious hiss, and tearing open the oak-grained door, advanced into the lounge with Steeleye spinning at the ready.

Drugged eyes widened, as his very presence filled the room.

Miko's gaunt face still held its silly satisfied grin,

as he withdrew two sticky fingers from inside Bimbo's slippery vagina. He turned over and climbed onto his elbows. 'What the shit is . . . ?'

Smack! – his left eye exploded as Steeleye butted him – he was a hospital job, and, for a long time.

Danny dodged the empty lager bottle which the blond straight-haired smackhead threw at him, before he jumped up and fled for his life through the hallway door. Danny couldn't give a toss if Miko was at death's door, his mind was flashing back to his beloved mother pumping heroin into herself, and the love of his life, Jack, overdosing on the purest 'H' which had ever hit the streets of Balchester.

Remorselessly, he advanced and with Steeleye, shattered the bottles and glasses on the coffee-table. Fat Man and Bimbo shielded their faces as fragments of glass and beer sprayed the room.

Bimbo screamed and frantically tugged on her knickers over well-shaped white thighs – she was scared witless! Fat Man cowered, terrified, nevertheless, with him the heroin came first. He scooped up the merchandise and let out a blood-curdling yell of frustration. 'No! Please, not the drugs, please don't touch the heroin, it's the best, there's a small fortune there.' He hugged the small bags of off-white powder tightly to his heart.

Whimpering like a baby, he turned and tried to run. He screamed, pathetically, and sobbed. 'I'll be fucking dead – d'you hear? dead! if you take this, what'll it cost me for you to . . . ?' With a vicious hiss, Steeleye lashed out and the cold deadly crook of the crowbar locked onto his neck, stopping him and holding him fast.

He stood hugging the junk, trembling violently, his flabby butt twitching. 'P-please, I don't know who you are, but just leave me alone, please!' he croaked. 'L-listen I'll pay you whatever . . .'

Nature had flown out of the window for Danny now – stuff Grandad's owls, fuck his river's fishes and up Merlin's sweet-smelling roses. This was nature's business, at its most lethal.

Blood spurted out as Steeleye twisted Fat Man's neck around, took quick aim and bust his nose in good style – Danny Black, and his mate Steeleye just didn't like drugs!

Fat Man screamed and dropped his treasure, the pain was excruciating and he smothered his face with his hands. 'My face, my fucking face you bastard!'

Danny didn't speak as he sent a karate-style kick thudding into Fat Man's testicles. Fat Man's eyes went wide and blank as stone. His mouth dropped open, his bloodied hands grasped his wounded genitals, but only a faint squeak escaped as he spun and slumped to the floor to wriggle, and finally settle in a lifeless heap.

Danny bent forward and scooped up the bags of heroin. 'This is one batch yous won't be cuttin' and mixin' you fat ugly bastard,' he muttered, furiously. He made a beeline for the toilet, there was only one place this shit was going, where it belonged, and he'd shove Blondie Addict down the bog with it.

He ripped open the bags and tipped the white powder out. As he flushed the chain, thousands of pounds of drugos' most luxurious shit swirled, frothed up, and disappeared down the brown-stained toilet with a rapid suck. The window just swung back in the stiff breeze. Toiletries from off the window-sill littered the thick pink pile – Blondie Addict was well gone.

Bimbo's small face was a picture of terror, as Danny stomped angrily back through the flat.

He stopped in the middle of the lounge and cut Steeleye loose. In a matter of seconds, he'd smashed the large coloured TV, and video to pieces. The rave music ceased as the glass door of the stack stereo, and the mantelpiece ornaments were left a wreckage of razor-sharp fragments. With a last defiant gesture, he sank Steeleye's two teeth into Fat Man's most prized possession, a three foot original oil-painting of a country cottage by Ronaldo Lancastrio.

Little Bimbo cringed as Danny stared at her piercingly from behind the balaclava. She tugged her miniskirt down over her knees as far as she could and tried to wriggle backwards, as if hoping that the wall would open up and let her free. She looked like a rag doll that had been tossed around.

Her bloodshot eyes were tearful as she pleaded. 'P-please, please mate,' her Scottish twang became stronger. 'Dunni hurt me, I – I ain't done nothin' to you!' She burst into sobs as Steeleye spun rapidly in Danny's hand. 'Please!'

Danny wasn't one to hit a woman, and as far as he was concerned Scottish Bimbo was safe – she'd probably fallen into the same trap as Jack had done anyway.

He merely grunted, turned on his heel and he and Steeleye left for home.

Bimbo gasped with relief, and dived for the phone – the telephone was dead, so she dashed out into the silent street and screamed. Danny was coolly making his way home through the back alleys, it had been a good night's work.

Chapter Eighteen

A little after 5.30 am, on the following windy Friday morning, Adder slipped silently out of Daisy's house by the back door. He hurried towards the call-box at the end of the street. Letting the door slowly swing shut behind him, he picked up the telephone and punched out the digits. He clutched the instrument between his long thin jaw and shoulder, and while listening to the dull burring he lit up a joint, sucked hard, and then waited.

Woodcock was awake, and sat drinking tea from his favourite mug. He was working the farm's milking parlour today, because Vic the cowman was on his day off.

Ament, the nanny, had also risen early, it was her job to prepare breakfast for the family when milking was over. She intended to clean out the mews where her falcon, Horus, was kept at night.

Horus would then spend the rest of the day in the adjoining ground – he thrived on the natural elements. Usually, Su-Ling was up at the crack of dawn too. But she had had a busy late night, delivering the merchandise.

George Woodcock snatched up the 'phone. 'Yes, "Meadows Farm", Woodcock speaking.'

Dropping his cigarette butt and stamping it out, Adder gripped the telephone in his bony gloved hand. 'S'me Boss, Adder. I'm sorry to phone you so early but . . .' Woodcock's upper-crust voice broke in on a note of annoyance.

'Ye – es Adder,' he snapped, sweeping an irritable hand through his grey thinning hair. 'What is it? Please be brief, I've cattle to tend too.'

Adder was well gone himself, as he twiddled the wino's empty sherry bottle left on the small shelf. He was oblivious to the stench of stale urine that rose from beneath his jingling boots. Gathering his wits together, he began, urgently. 'Tina Bell has just . . .'

'Who!'

'Tina Bell, Boss – she's always buying off Fat Man – or was.'

'What d'you mean Adder, was? Go on, enlighten me.'

'Well, she's just come to me digs. I was making something to eat in the kitchen and . . .'

Woodcock's patience was fast running out. 'For God's sake Adder,' he roared. 'Spit it out, man.'

Adder took a deep breath and the words came out in a rush. 'She's just come from the cop-shop. She says some hooded maniac with a crowbar has done over Fat Man and Miko in good style.'

'How bad?'

'Boss! I meant what I said – good style! They're both hospital jobs, and another buyer as well. Not only that, Boss, the fucking nutter flushed the heroin down the bog, the bleeding lot of it.'

For a split second Woodcock was speechless. His hand tightened with rage around his mug, nearly crushing it. At last, he snorted and demanded fiercely. 'What! The full two ounces?!'

'That's right, Boss,' Adder confirmed, in a state of mounting tension.

Woodcock leapt to his feet, slamming his mug down. 'There was fucking thousands of pounds worth there Adder,' he bellowed.

Ament drew back, spilling her own tea. Woodcock gripped the 'phone tighter. His voice took on an ugly rasp.

'Who was this maniac, Adder, have you any idea?'

Adder shook his head rapidly, as if Woodcock could see him.

'Uh, uh Boss, Tina just said he was a bloody nutter, wearing a Balaclava and using a crowbar. She said he spun it like some sort of trick or somethin' and that he used it like a pro.'

Su-Ling had risen earlier than expected, and entered the kitchen, wrapped in a purple-patterned kimono, just as the Balaclava and crowbar were being discussed. Picking up the teapot, she flashed a false smile at Ament – it was a case of two seductive women competing for one very powerful man. Ament, for his insatiable sex drive and supremacy over the 'Hell Fire Club', Su-Ling, for a home and the sake of her children, sadly aware that she had no future with Danny.

Woodcock continued his conversation with Adder in cantankerous tones, scarcely acknowledging his wife's arrival.

'A crowbar you say Adder, and nobody knew who he was?'

'No Boss, like I said, he wore a Balaclava.' Adder paused briefly, and then went on, thoughtfully, 'The only person we've had any trouble with, but it wasn't worth botherin' you about, was a geezer called Danny Black. I suppose it could have been him – he's an anti-drug nutter. And, by the way Tina describes his shape and size, and the way he uses karate, well . . .'

'Danny Black!' echoed Woodcock, sharply. He clenched his fist, driving it down onto the large wooden table. 'Danny Black! you say? God! that man used to work for me, I caught the black bastard in . . .' He broke off as unwelcome visions of Su-Ling and Danny Black making love in his bed invaded his mind again, after he'd tried to push them away.

Both Ament and Su-Ling glanced nervously at Woodcock on hearing mention of Danny Black.

Ament had been hostile to Danny from the start, while Su-Ling quickly put two and two together. She remembered seeing Danny practising with Steeleye behind the milking parlour on the farm. Her hands trembled slightly as she poured herself a cup of tea. She had already made up her mind not to breathe a word to George Woodcock about Danny and his crowbar.

Ament merely looked sour, as far as she was concerned Danny Black had been an intruder, who somehow spelled trouble.

'Adder,' said Woodcock decisively, long eyebrows arched. 'There's a handsome reward for the man, or men, who give him a damn good hiding.' He shifted his tall body to take the weight off his lame leg then, with a grunt, carried on the conversation.

'Mind you, I don't want him killed, or anything like that. Just a flaming good hiding will do, we don't want any unnecessary hassle at the moment.' He gave an evil chuckle. 'Anyway, if anyone is going to eliminate Danny Black, it'll be me.'

Beneath the pretty oriental robe, Su-Ling's heartbeat rose to a violent crescendo, with the fond feelings she still cherished for Danny, she couldn't bear to think of him in danger. 'George!' she exclaimed, involuntarily, then stopped short, as Woodcock's eyes suddenly gleamed with a ferocity that she knew only too well. She remembered the look from the time when he had blown the bull's head off, with his shotgun, after it had maimed him. Gathering her robe around her tightly, she rushed from the kitchen – at this moment in time, or at any other, she knew it was not safe to try to defend Danny Black in front of her moody husband.

Woodcock's voice sank to a grim whisper and he gripped the telephone as fiercely as if it had been Danny's neck. His face wore a look of sheer evil as he raised his head and levelled a lustful gaze at Ament.

'Remember, Adder, the "All Hallows Eve" ceremony will soon be here, so we don't want any hitches – do we?'

'No – no Boss,' came the nervous reply. 'Of course we don't.'

Woodcock carried on talking quietly, his cold penetrating eyes staring through the window at the vegetable plot beyond.

'How is our immaculate little maiden, Adder, is she ripe and ready?'

'Yes Boss, whenever you give me the word – she's as pure as the driven snow.'

'Good,' Woodcock gloated. 'You've done well Adder, very well indeed, you can be the one to follow me, after her virginity has been taken.' He chuckled, evilly. 'That's if she's in one piece.' Adder's penis was already rising, pressing hard against his briefs. The very thought of entering Sophie's small curved body, from the front and the back, caused his tongue to flash in and out feverishly.

Woodcock bade Adder goodbye, adding a stern reminder. 'Remember Adder, keep me informed about Danny Black, bring me some good news eh, for a change.' He rang off and swigged down the last of his tea.

A few seconds later, after drumming his fingers reflectively on the tabletop, he reached for the telephone. Docker wouldn't be amused being woken so early, but it had to be all hands to the mast to get Danny. Woodcock hurriedly dialled his number.

Three days later, Rosie and John brought Jacky home from the hospital. While she had been in there, Jack had been unable to get her hands on any drugs. She had even started to eat decent meals, and her pixie-like face was beginning to take on a slightly healthier look.

Danny had called to see her at Daisy's home, after work, that same Monday evening. He was totally unaware of the fact that the word was out on the estate streets to turn him over – there was a horde of drug-starved addicts, who knew how to spend the handsome reward that Woodcock had placed on his head.

Danny hadn't gone into the Dooley's lounge, hearing Adder's voice above the noise of the TV, was enough for him. He thanked Daisy for giving him permission to go up to Jack's room, and bounded up the stairs, hugging a box of her favourite chocolates.

Adder heard him and sniggered quietly, his face taking on a fiendish expression. His mind had veered away from the TV and Sophie's cute backside.

'You're gonna get it Mongrel,' he muttered under his breath. 'Oh yes, my son, you're gonna fucking well – get – it!' He continued to swig from his bottle of strong lager and puff at cigarettes like they were going out of fashion. His revolting burp, which seemed to go on for ever, was enough to make Rosie throw down her daily tabloid in disgust. Tight-lipped she scowled at Adder, then stalked out to the kitchen. She'd rather dry dishes for Daisy than sit opposite that slimy arsehole. She snatched up the tea towel, wiped a plate and sent it onto the drainer with a clatter.

'God Mum,' she blasted angrily, 'I hate that flipping creepy-crawly in there, can't you get shut of him, we're not that desperate for money are we?'

Daisy sighed, as she washed the last dish and shook the warm soapsuds from her fingers. 'You know we need the money, pet. Anyway, when you are married and you've gone, I'll probably have to take in another lodger as well, unless I get an exchange for a two bedroomed flat, or something.'

Rosie finished racking the cups and mugs, and a shudder ran through her, as she remembered overhearing Adder sweet-talking Sophie.

Meanwhile, Sophie was stretched out in her favourite place on the rug, in front of the fire's leaping flames – Stumpy shared the same spot. As she wriggled her neat little body to a more comfortable position, Adder's gaze slid from the TV to lock on to her chubby little bottom. His ogling eyes were wide, and his voice was hoarse as he promised, 'I'll get you some more of that chocolate tomorrow Soph' – you know, the fruity nutty sort that you like.'

His lecherous glance travelled slowly over her slim body, he lusted over her neat round butt, and leered at where her small knicker-line showed through her tight white pedal pusher pants.

Sophie, all innocence, went on watching TV. 'Thanks Adder,' she replied trustingly. 'I love it.'

Adder's flashing tongue darted back in as he tore

his randy stare away from her back to the prancing figures on the screen.

So do I, Sophie darling, he thought. So do I!

The following Wednesday night, Adder came back to Daisy's home earlier than expected, and unusually for him, he seemed strangely sober. He had his evil scheme well prepared, however, he was carrying a bagful of strong lagers.

Jacky had told him that Danny was playing pool that night at the Bedford Social Club, so he'd be out of the way for the time being. Daisy and Sophie were watching TV and Rosie and John were dining out at the 'Flamingo Club'.

Adder made his way up the stairs with the aid of the handrail. Tonight, he wasn't drunk or high on drugs, so he didn't have to crawl up them to find his bedroom the way he usually did. The light from Jack's small bedside lamp glimmered into the hallway, as he gently pushed open her bedroom door. He flicked a glance around her room to make double sure that she was alone, and then, pretending to be drunk, wobbled across to her bed.

Jack jerked up startled, as Adder laid a hand on her shoulder.

'What the fuck a' you doin' in me room Adder?' she snapped, glaring at him. 'Our Rosie will go bleeding nuts if she finds out.'

'Look, Jack,' he hissed. 'I've got you some beers, and a pick-me-up.' He proudly displayed the tablet of ecstasy. Jack rubbed her eyes and heaved herself up onto her elbows. She'd been off drugs for some days now, and she was furious at his careless disregard for her health. 'Piss off, Adder,' she snapped. 'I'm trying to leave the shit alone.'

Adder dropped down on the bed and dug into the off-licence carrier bag. He drew out a can of strong lager. 'Here y'are then Jack, have a lager.' He ripped off the tab, shoved the can into her hand, and opened a can for himself, tossing the looped tabs carelessly onto the carpet. He was familiar with her drinking habits, knowing that when she had one, well . . . anything could happen.

'Oh – all right,' she agreed, after a brief hesitation. 'But then you'll have to go in case our Rosie comes home early. Anyway, our Sophie 'll be coming up soon.'

Adder only pretended to swig from his can, he had to keep his mind sober and alert, whilst with Jack, one can led to another, and another, and with her defences now at rock-bottom, she easily succumbed to temptation.

Adder watched, with evil satisfaction, as the tablet of ecstasy slid down her throat – Jack was well back onto the drugs. Sophie had gone straight up to her own room not wanting to disturb her big sister, and was soon soundly sleeping. Normally, she would go into Jack's room for a cuddle, but tonight she decided that her sister needed her rest.

Three-quarters of an hour later, at about ten o'clock, Jack was bubbling over with false energy, so much so that she was up and dressed and ready for action.

Sophie shifted restlessly in her bed, as Jack turned up her radio and babbled away to Adder – it was good to be back on a high, she kept repeating, feverishly.

Daisy could hear Jack and Adder holding a slurred conversation as they descended the stairs, and hurried out into the hall to confront them. At the foot of the stairs, kneading her small hands together, nervously, she pleaded with Jacky. 'Please! Jack, you can't go out yet, the doctor said . . .'

Jack's maladjusted emotions, confused by drinks and ecstasy, exploded into violent rage. Defiantly, she dragged her grey leather jacket from off its peg and struggled into it, scowling furiously at her mother. 'For fuck's sake Mam, I'm okay,' she snarled, fire in her eyes – 'I'm not a kid you know, I'm bleedin' seventeen, I can look after me pissin' self.'

Daisy's pretty heart-shaped face went white. Her eyes swam with tears at Jack's harsh words. Not knowing what to do, she shook her bemused head and blurted out, 'Jack! – I only wanted to . . .'

Adder stepped forward quickly, and spread his hands, then giggled childishly. 'Don't worry Daisy, she'll be fine, I'll look after her, I always do.'

As Jack swayed slightly, a silly grin spread over her face. Her mood switched rapidly to that of a pleading schoolgirl. She shrugged her narrow shoulders. 'I'll be all right Mam.' She threw her arms around Daisy's neck and hugged her. 'Onest I will, we're just goin' out for a few late beers – that's all.' She gave her mother a firm smacker on the lips, and releasing her, with loving eyes said, truthfully, 'God! I love you Mam.' Adder wasted no time in swinging the front door open and ushering Jack outside into the dark chilly night.

His false smile masked his vile motives. 'I'll look after her Dais' don't worry.'

As the front door slammed to, Daisy called out worriedly. 'Please be careful Jacky, and don't stop out late.'

Stumpy was hopping around yapping noisily, until Daisy shooed him back into the warmth of the lounge. Jacky and Adder's chatter drifted away to mingle with the stillness of the night – Daisy's anxious caution had fallen on doped ears.

It was just after half past ten when Adder led Jack out of the Lowfield Hotel, after they'd each downed a quick half of lager. Outside, on the spacious car park, he eagerly flicked his lighter and lit up a joint. He and Jack passed it from one to the other hungrily, sucking in the heavy substance, like children enjoying a sweetshop mix.

Adder's warped and agile mind shifted into overdrive. As he blew out a stream of drugged smoke, his brain cells triggered phase two into action. He tossed down his joint butt, he'd enjoyed his blow, but enough was enough, his mind was geared for the job in hand. Too much, and he might spoil things.

He glanced at Jack. 'Tell you what Jack, let's go to the club for a drink. I wanna see Tina Bell about somethin – you could see the mong . . .' He thought better of it and substituted 'you could see Black while we're there.'

As Jacky eagerly agreed, Adder tossed a sly grin towards a bright sky – his diabolical little plan was going nicely.

After walking for a few minutes, Adder stopped by a 'phone box. 'Won't be a min', I just wanna make a call.'

'Hurry up then,' she snapped. 'I want to see Dan.'

Adder entered the kiosk muttering. 'Fucking black bastard.' He dialled and covered his mouth, at the same time keeping a watchful eye on Jacky, who was lighting up a cigarette.

'That's right, Tina girl,' he said, in low tones. 'Just be outside the club in two minutes, got it!' He hung up.

A couple of minutes later, Adder peered down the dimly lit street. Yes! Tina was outside the club. And Dead-leather, a tall thin gaunt-looking young man, with skin like a well-used football, was standing across the road in the shadows. Dead-leather's back was humped, so he walked with a permanent stoop – he was a user, turned dealer, who had taken over the Fat Man's role. Neat! really neat!

Adder lit up a cigarette and sucked hard. He gave Jack a nudge. He fumbled for her hand, and pressed some crumpled notes into her palm, then nodded towards Dead-leather. 'Go on,' he urged. 'Go and get the stuff Babe, we'll have a good night after – a real rave.'

She hurled an anxious look at the club. 'But, but I wanna see . . .'

'You need the stuff as much as me,' he barked. 'Now go on, I'm fuckin' paying aren't I?'

Jack shrugged despondently and sighed. 'Yeah man, yeah – I need the fuckin' shit!' She went weaving across the road to meet the new man.

Adder turned sharply and waved a hand at Tina, who, in turn, quickly re-entered the club through the heavy Georgian glass doors.

Adder dug into his inside pocket, and pulled out the short heavy metal, stone chisel. His eyes blazed as he tapped the chisel on his thigh. 'You're gonna get it you bleedin' arsehole,' he muttered hoarsely. 'Oh yes! my little chocolate drop, you're gonna bleedin' get it.'

Inside, Tina poked her pretty face into the bar. 'Hey! are you Danny Black?'

Danny stopped his shot, still gripping the pool cue firmly, and turned his head sharply. 'Yeah! why?'

'Jack Dooley wants you outside, she said hurry up will you.'

She disappeared, the door swinging shut behind her. Danny turned to Cochise and handed him the cue. 'Do us a favour, will yous Coch', and finish off the game for me, I'll see what . . .' He mouthed the last two words fully to help Cochise understand him. 'Jack wants.'

Cochise smiled and nodded, and Danny went out.

In the street, Jacky cringed at Dead-leather's muffled request. 'Go on then,' he urged. 'Kiss me, on the mouth.' Dead-leather definitely worked differently from Fat Man. He'd recently moved back up from London, to keep the heat off, he owed his supplier at lot of money. In the Kings Cross area, the passing of drugs had to be done discreetly, from mouth to mouth. Jacky would have done far more than cringe, if she'd known that he'd just taken the tiny package from its hiding-place up his rear end – Dead-leather was now a very cautious man. Reluctantly she reached up and pressed her mouth against his, wincing at Dead-leather's vile breath as he passed her the drugs.

As Danny swung open the door of the club and stepped outside, he froze, utterly astonished to see Jack, her mouth pressed firmly against the dealer's. He groaned, and quickly recovering himself, went charging forward. Reaching Jack, he gripped her shoulder and spun her around. The tiny package fell from her mouth. Danny swooped it up and tore it open. He didn't have to examine it closely, he knew what it was. He glowered at them both. 'Drugs!' he roared, 'I thought yous was trying to get off this shit!'

He gripped Dead-leather by the throat and

snarled. 'You drug pushing bastard, I'll rip your f...'

With a dull thud, Adder sent the steel chisel crashing into Danny's cheek from behind. The world went black as he was lifted off the ground by the force of the blow. He didn't utter a word or even groan, just hit the hard pavement like a sack of grain – he was out for the count. Danny had neither heard nor seen anything – Adder had lived up to his name.

Chapter Nineteen

Not much blood flowed from Danny's small wound, but he was knocked unconscious.

Adder cackled, and flashed a lizard-like tongue. 'Got you, got you, you bleeding half chat mongrel bastard! got you at long last.' He laughed again, then kicked at Danny's limp body with a classy jingling leathered boot.

Jacky gasped, shocked and angry. She dropped to her knees and cradled Danny's head, flinging a furious glance at Adder.

'Why?!' she yelled at him, 'what the fuck did you do that to him for?' She paused, feeling a sickness in the pit of her stomach. 'You've killed him, you bastard! you fuckin' killed him!' She felt choked with rage and fear for Danny, as she stroked his face and head with trembling hands.

Dead-leather was already racing off down a nearby alley-way.

Adder tucked the chisel back into his pocket and spread his hands, all innocence. 'I thought he was hurting you babe, honest I did – you've gotta believe me,' he lied, his venomous expression contradicting his words.

Jack turned a tear-stained face towards him. 'Get stuffed Adder, you lyin' bastard.' Her words were harsh and bitter, 'You always wanted to do him in, all because I won't sleep with you, you cretin, you pervert!'

Bending over Danny's prostrate body again, she rocked him in her arms and murmured long forgotten prayers, tears falling on his face.

As people at the club entrance suddenly showed interest, Adder, breathing heavily, rubbed his thin face anxiously.

'Look!' he blurted out. 'Someone's gonna recognise us and phone the law, let's get out of here.'

Jacky held Danny even closer and shook her head defiantly. 'No! I'm staying here with Danny, you do what the hell you want!' Adder glanced towards the gathering audience and then turned away. 'Up you then girl, I'm off.' And away he went, with Jack's screaming farewll ringing in his ears. 'An' get out of our house you murdering slimy bast-ard!'

By now, Cochise, realising something was going on, came hurrying to Jack's side. Adder, like Deadleather, was already racing off down the nearby alleys and across the gardens. He knew the estate like the back of his gloved hand, so Cochise didn't attempt to give chase. Instead, he gave his full attention to Danny.

Grunting and gesturing urgently, Cochise managed to prise Jack's hands from their grip on

Danny's head. She dropped back onto the pavement and sat, head bowed, sobbing hysterically. Cochise hurriedly checked Danny's wrist and neck pulses, gnawing worriedly at his thick bottom lip. Suddenly his rugged face broke into a wide relieved grin. Looking at Jack, he happily shook a clenched fist and did his best to signal to her that Danny was alive.

Jack, weeping now with relief, laid her head on Danny's chest to listen to his heartbeat.

Cloud had thickened from the west and rain began falling heavily, but Cochise and Jacky Dooley hardly noticed, they had other things to worry about.

Jack leapt to her feet. 'I'll 'phone an ambulance from the club, Coch',' she exclaimed. 'If we get him straight to . . .' She turned sharply, as the loud blaring of a police car siren echoed across the estate – so someone had telephoned them from the club – Adder was right.

Another siren from the speeding ambulance blared in unison. Danny gave his head a little shake and opened his eyes. After a few seconds, his blurred gaze focused on the intent faces of Jacky and Cochise.

He tried to sit up and fell back with a groan. 'God, Princess, what the shit happened? I feel like I've been whacked by a sledgehammer, I . . .'

He grimaced and tentatively touched his left cheek. 'Ouch! that bloody hurts,' he moaned through gritted teeth. 'Hell shit! that – hurts Princess.'

As he gripped Cochise's hand, his beaming friend nodded eagerly with satisfaction – if Danny could feel pain, he would at least live.

Danny again felt at his cheek and broad unshaven jaw. He shook his head in bewilderment. 'What the – ouch! – hell happened?'

Jack leant over and gently kissed him on the lips, while Cochise stood up and let loose a sigh of relief.

'It was that slimy bastard Adder,' Jack told Danny, with a scowl of disgust.

'He whacked you from behind with a steel chisel and then did a runner, the cowardly arsehole.' She took out some tissue and gently dabbed Danny's cheek where the blow had struck. The lightning downpour, however, had washed away most of the small amount of blood.

The storm had now eased, and was drifting away towards Wales. Jacky shook the raindrops from her hair and wiped the moisture from Danny's face, the three of them were soaked to the skin.

The police car and ambulance both tore noisily into the street, and screeched to a halt near to where Danny lay, trying to regain his battered senses. Two young police officers rushed across to him.

Danny's mind moved fast for such a shocked and injured man – his natural fighting instincts carried him through. He raised his head towards Jack, his dark eyes hard with challenge. Gripping her hand, he warned quietly. 'Tell 'em nothing' Jack, do yous hear, nothing. I'll sort it out meself.'

He groaned as she helped to ease his head back

down. His voice had the low growl of a cornered beast. 'I've told yous, I'll sort that bastard Adder out myself.'

Perhaps, thought Jacky, in her emotional reaction to Danny's survival, she shouldn't have blurted out to him that it was Adder who had hit him.

She eyed the policeman briefly, flashed a glance at Danny and nodded her understanding.

As the ambulance swiftly pulled away, the policeman unwrapped a chocolate bar and turned to his mate. 'Same old story, Terry eh!? Nobody sees anything.' He bit off a chunk and mumbled, with his mouth full. 'That's the third time this month nobody's seen anything after a punch-up outside this club.'

Terry sighed, and tipped back his cap. 'Yeah mate, I know what you mean.' He re-started the car, just as a call came through about a domestic quarrel on the Lord Tennyson side of the estate. He glanced at his partner. 'Here we go again! You know, sometimes I dunno why we bother.'

The police car sped away with water spraying from beneath its tyres.

Five days later, Jacky brought Danny back home from hospital. His smashed cheek-bone had been repaired, bruising was healing, he had supposedly been checked over for any other injuries. The only visible sign of his ordeal was the small stitched wound, covered with a plaster, on the side of his head where the surgeon had done his work.

On their way home in the cab, Jack hugged him from time to time, as if he was a giant cuddly teddy bear. At one point she pulled out her ciggies, but received a sharp reprimand.

'Sorry luv.' The driver pointed at his small label. 'I'm a no smoking cab.'

'Shit!' Annoyed she rammed the fags back into her jacket pocket. With her left hand, she gripped Danny's leg tighter. She felt so very sorry for him, but then reminded herself that her man was tough, he'd certainly been tough with her over using drugs.

Her heart seemed to ache endlessly – she loved the man so much, hell shit or high water.

She pecked his cheek, and above the low background taped music of the cab, murmured in his ear. 'Let's get your gear, Dan, Mam meant what she said, you can live with us, Adder's gone, we've kicked the rat out for good.' Her face took on a look of hopeful expectancy.

Danny smiled and nodded. 'Sure Jack, I'd like that, very much.' She squeezed him harder still.

On the following Friday morning, Danny awoke in Daisy's house to sunshine. He also awoke with a blurred left eye, nothing serious, he decided, probably a touch of migraine. After breakfast, he and Jacky set off along the canal tow-path towards Balchester, to visit Merlin and discuss the Hell Fire Club affair. Suddenly, Danny stopped short and shook his head, his eye was now completely blind. He rubbed it with his finger, blinking hard, and tried again, still blind. It was an enormous shock. Jack was looking at him anxiously but said nothing, it wasn't necessary, she knew that Danny was no wimp and that something was wrong.

'It's me eye Jack, I can't see a bleedin' thing through it an' I dunno why.'

She squeezed his hand tighter and studied his face sympathetically.

'Come on Dan', we'll call at the chemist's on our way to Merlin's, maybe he can help.'

Danny glanced across at a group of trees swaying in the breeze, colourful with the reds and golds of late autumn. He closed his right eye, nothing, only blackness. His heart was thudding fiercely, a sudden fear gripped him, holding him motionless and silent. The thought of blindness was terrifying. He flicked open his eyelid just in time to glimpse a swooping seagull which had flown inland. It then rose up again, a feathered acrobat, gliding and soaring against the sky. Tormenting thoughts tumbled through his frightened mind. How terrible it would be if he couldn't see the flowers, the birds, woods and fields and the tints of sunrise and sunset – the chemist had to come up with something.

The chemist was a tall middle-aged slim man, who spoke English with a slow comforting Welsh accent. 'Use the drops for one week, and if there's no improvement go and see your GP.' Danny and Jacky thanked him and left feeling hopeful. Danny had to see Doctor Millward, anyway, to renew his sick note.

Meanwhile, up in his den, Freddy Haddock reached for another cigarette, slotted it into his holder and lit up. Then he carried on with his research into the Hell Fire Club. Flicking over a page, he stroked a hand reflectively over his new short silver beard – his facial scars were now well hidden. The old flirt from next door hated beards, and so had stopped chatting him up, thank God! He was finding things difficult, so he topped up his whisky glass, took a mouthful, then banged the glass down with frustration.

There seemed to be no way to defeat the cult. He muttered irritably to himself. 'Huh! no magic spells, no silver bullet, not even a lousy stake through the heart, how painfully boring.' He slid a slender finger and thumb down his bony nose. Suddenly, his silver eyebrows shot up. 'Got it!' he shouted. 'By golly I've got it. Fire! – the Hell Fire Club, we'll fight fire with fire, Danny, my dear boy, yes we will.'

Docker, Brown Trilby and Boots sat despondently in the Four Wrongs public house. A strange name indeed, for the new pub recently built on the fringe of the estate. It had been christened after four historic wicked deeds, which had happened on that very spot from as far back as 1500 A.D.

Docker and company were in sombre mood and worried, very worried. The All Hallows' Eve ceremony was rapidly approaching, and the last thing they needed at the moment was a pair of young smart-arse twins moving in from Liverpool to try and take over Woodcock's reasonably small, but profitable empire. The word was out that they also used shooters – something not seen on the estate as yet. They'd picked on the right man though, George Woodcock had had a lifetime of guns and certainly knew how to use them.

'They seem to think that they're the fuckin' Kray Twins,' Docker growled, running a rough hand down his greying pony-tail. 'But we'll stop 'em, you watch, the boss'll see to that.'

Danny had settled into Daisy's cosy home well, and like Adder, got on just great with Sophie, except he was sincere, and not a villain.

Jacky loved having Danny under the same roof, but she was finding it increasingly difficult to feed her habit with him around, keeping a watchful eye on her – she'd even thought it would be easier when he was well enough, after the cheek-bone operation, to go back to work. She'd make any excuse, lie through her teeth, to get her hands on drugs, any drugs would do, she needed them desperately.

She was regularly shoplifting with the best, to keep her supply going. She now had a steady arrangement with Dead-leather, even if he was a bigger creep than Fat Man.

It was the last Friday in September when Danny visited his GP – the eye drops had failed to work. After a quick assessment, Dr Millward telephoned the hospital and made an urgent appointment for Danny to be seen immediately by a consultant. The eye surgeon, a Mister Dutton, gave his verdict after his examination, and the report was grim enough to make Danny feel faint and require a glass of water.

'I'm sorry Mister Black,' the consultant said, gently. 'But I'm going to have to do microsurgery on your eye. The retina has a serious tear, and there is also a hole at the back which needs sealing.'

Danny shook his head, and gave a deep sigh. 'Do I have to have it done?' he pleaded hoarsely.

The tall, bespectacled surgeon gazed at him earnestly. 'Mister Black, believe me, the operation is necessary to preserve your eyesight, so that you can still see in your old age,' he replied, his tone compassionate but firm. 'I want you to make all necessary arrangements and be back at this hospital by half past five this evening. I will operate tomorrow morning.' He waited an instant in case Danny had any questions but, realising he was shattered by the news, he rose to his feet, patted Danny's shoulder encouragingly, and left him to the care of the nurse.

Meanwhile, Jacky Dooley had sold her stolen goods for enough money to secure a supply of heroin, and by the time Danny arrived back home for his belongings, she was blown out of her mind.

Danny could ill afford to waste time, he just grabbed his things and threw them into a sports bag, borrowed from Sophie, kissed Jack, hoping she had understood what he had told her, pecked Daisy on the cheek and left the house – the bus into Balchester was due in one minute.

It was nearly midnight, the next day, when Jack entered the nearest call-box, dialled and slurred into the mouthpiece.

'S'that the – the 'ospital, I wanna talk to Danny Black, is he OK?'

'What ward is he in?' came the brisk response.

'How t-the bleedin' hell should I know?'

'Who's speaking please?' was the next question.

'S'me in' it? his girlfriend.'

'Are you a relative?'

'I've j-just fuckin' told you, woman, s'me, Jacky Dooley, his girlfriend. Just tell, tell the black bastard I love 'im will – will you.' She let the 'phone drop. It jerked to a halt at the end of the wire. She pushed open the booth door with the aid of her desert boot. 'St-stupid bleedin' cow!'

The girl on the switchboard who had answered the call raised her neatly plucked eyebrows and tutted as she disconnected. She heard practically the same thing every day from one person or another.

The combined pressures of heroin and of Danny being in hospital were beginning to tell on Jack, she was rapidly becoming a potential time bomb. The final additive, alcohol, lit the touch-paper. She stormed into the lounge, the room was dark, and in the glare of the TV her eyes were wild and staring. She stopped, swayed, and clumsily swigged lager from a can, spilling most of it on the carpet.

She was high on heroin and dangerous, to say the least. She swung out a booted foot at random and sent the glass-topped coffee-table and cups flying.

Daisy, Rosie and John, leapt to their feet.

Jack's gaze was like that of a wild animal, her voice was slurred and angry. 'W-where the shit – is Danny?!' She glared around the room and screamed. 'Where the fuck is the bast-ard?!'

Rosie and John pounced on her, and after a brief struggle forced her down onto the settee.

Rosie's eyes flashed as she yelled, furiously. 'You daft bitch!' She gripped Jack by the hair and pulled hard, at the same time swiping a hand at John, who was trying to intervene. 'You bloody behave yourself, mum's had enough to put up with.' She tugged harder, jerking Jack's head back further. 'If you're going to take drugs, then damn well take them, but keep them out of Mum's house, OK!'

Finally, to Daisy's relief, John managed to separate the two sisters.

Lotty whose feet were still well buttered to keep her from straying, fled, with a yowl, across the room. She had found Danny's bedsit a lot more peaceful than her new home.

Jacky staggered up and tossed her empty can into the hearth. She whirled round, scowling. 'Don't you ever lay a hand on me again sister, d'you hear – never!' She barged out of the lounge, leaving a trail of mumbled threats behind her. 'I'm goin' ter find Danny, I – I love the fuckin' man.' She screamed louder before slamming the front door behind her. 'S-stuff the bleedin' lot of you.'

Stumpy re-surfaced, with a timorous wag of his tail, while Lotty tapped a playful paw at the large spider which she'd cornered by the skirting-board – the whole household breathed a sigh of relief.

Sophie felt her way downstairs, holding onto the rail and rubbing bleary eyes, she'd been woken by the disturbance.

'Danny! have you heard?' Lance exclaimed, as Danny paid the taxi-driver outside the Dooleys' residence.

It was Sunday afternoon and Lance was bringing Bimbo back home from a walk across the fields.

Danny stopped dead by the garden gate, and with a finger raised his shades off his wounded eye.

'Heard what Lance? he queried.

Lance shuffled nervously, and tapped his forehead with a slim finger.

'Jacky's hitting the heroin – hard! She's smashed out of her mind nearly all of the time. I – I just thought I'd better warn you, that's all.'

Danny heaved a despairing sigh. 'Thanks Lance, I'll see what I can do, she's been back on the shit for a while now.' He flicked back his shades, dug deep for his key, and walked briskly up the garden path. He already felt bad enough, because Jack hadn't visited or come to bring him home from hospital. Lance shook his head sadly and trudged on his way.

Next morning Freddy Haddock was sitting in his den, swishing his silver handled walking cane, when the telephone rang. At the foot of the stairs, while he spoke to Danny, he cut the air with the deadly six-inch blade. 'Hello Danny, how's the eye? I'm sorry I couldn't visit you in hospital but I've a touch of flu.'

'S'okay Merlin,' came the anxious reply. 'They told me that you'd phoned, they told me the eye should be OK. I'll lose a bit of vision, but . . .'

'Good, good,' answered Merlin. 'What can I do for you dear boy? You sound a little upset.'

After a short pause Danny responded. 'It's Jack, she's back on heroin hard, Merlin, I need your help.'

'Yes, yes, go on dear boy, go on.'

Danny hurriedly explained to Freddy that he wondered if he could bring Jack to his place for a while, to try to get her off drugs. It would mean her being locked up in Freddy's den.

'I know it's a lot to ask,' he concluded.

'My dear boy, calm down,' said Freddy. 'Of course you must bring her here. When?'

'Tonight! I've already explained things to Jack's family, they trust me,' said Danny. 'Jacky doesn't know anythin' about it, we'll have to con her into it. I'll bring her to see yous about the Hell Fire Club and then . . .'

Freddy was already scheming, even at his age, he still loved a challenge.

'Right! dear boy, I'll expect you at around seven o'clock. Oh! I must 'phone the cleaning lady and tell her not to bother for a couple of weeks. I'll tell her my sister from London is coming up, they hate each other anyway. Our Ruby always insists she could do a lot better for me.'

After ringing off, Danny walked away from the

telephone with mixed feelings. Adder, Woodcock, Su-Ling and the Hell Fire Club, were all playing on his mind, but the biggest fight now, bigger than any bout of karate, was getting Jack Dooley off heroin.

Chapter Twenty

Jacky Dooley couldn't climb any higher, she'd hit the needle and it was good. Aids, or any other diseases, were the furthest thing from her confused mind, all she wanted was the kick from heroin.

She was higher than a kite that Sunday afternoon, as Freddy Haddock puffed and hammered home the last three inch nail. The small window in his den was now securely sealed up. He'd obeyed Danny's request to the letter. The lock on his den door was sound, so there would be no escape for Jack once she was coaxed into the room by Danny and himself.

Old as he was, Freddy had managed to rig up his spare single bed in the corner of his den for Jack's use. He hummed along, as he worked to the words of Maurice Chevalier's frisky rendering of 'Thank Heaven For Little Girls'. Hearing Danny's loud banging on the large brass knocker, he stubbed out his cigarette in the glass ashtray, pocketed his holder, and hurried to answer the door.

Opening up, he eagerly beckoned Danny and Jack into the hall. With a beam on his face and his halo of silvery hair, he had the look of an elderly cherub.

'Hello Danny,' he exclaimed, casting a keen eye on Jack, he held out his wrinkled hands in a gesture of welcome.

'Hello to you too, Jacky,' he greeted her, a touch too effusively. 'Come in, come on in dear, it's good to see you again.'

Once they were both inside, he flashed a wary glance up and down the street – all clear! No nosy neighbours about. He heaved back the heavy door, clicking it shut then led the way upstairs and ushered them into his den.

He switched on the low watt bulb, and discreetly nudged Danny in the back – it was Danny's pigeon now. Making a hasty excuse about fixing them both drinks, he beat a swift retreat along the narrow hallway.

Shock kept Jacky silent for a moment, as, with a doped gaze she apathetically scanned Freddy's den. It was a case of books, books and more books. They were married to his globe and mound of pens, notes, and literary works which littered his dusty desk. Danny stayed silent as she ambled over to it, stopped, and bemusedly turned the globe around. She looked up at the smoke-stained artexed ceiling, stared at the dim unshaded light-bulb and her pretty mouth curved into a faint smile. Heroin was still oozing through her, and as she sucked hungrily on her cigarette, she didn't notice Freddy's deadly silver-topped walking cane, with the automatically operated six inch blade, handing from its hook on the side of his desk. Instead, her roving glance left the light-bulb and fell on the boarded up window. She quickly smelled a rat and, with a startled glare, swung round on Danny.

He bit his lip edgily and lowered his gaze. Then, slowly, he looked up again, straight into Jack's eyes. He knew what was coming, that he had to deal with it. She cocked her head, and squinted at the window, her lip curling. 'What – w-what's the window boarded up for Dan' is it broke or something?' she forced the words out with an effort. Danny shuffled uneasily, then braced himself, aware that there was worse to come. Placing a gentle hand on each shoulder, he took a deep breath and answered, 'It's for yous, Jack.' Wrapping his strong arms around her, he went on in firm, but compassionate tones. 'I'm sorry Princess, you're gonna have toos stop here until you're off the fuckin' shit.'

He felt her trembling violently and held her tighter, tenderly kissing her brow. His voice sank to a loving whisper. 'Jack, I love yous babe, I've already sorted it out with your mum, and she agrees – yous a' comin' of the junk lady.'

Jack gave a hoarse cry and pulled away from him. She beat at his broad chest with her small fists and exploded. She whirled about the room like a dervish, her face distorted with rage.

'The shit I am man! You said Merlin was going to help us fight against the Hell Fire Club. You're not fuckin' lockin' me up in this bleedin' grotty dump.' Running a hand through her dark hair furiously, she made for the door. 'I'm goin' home you lousy lyin' arsehole.'

He stepped sideways, barring her way, and placed a strong brown hand on her shoulder. 'Uh, uh, yous a' going nowhere's, Jack. Me an' Merlin are going to help you fight the heroin and Woodcock and his poxy Hell Fire Club – got it!' He gently eased her away from the door, stepped quickly out of the room and began to close it on her.

'You lousy bastard!' she screamed, white with anger, as she lost her footing and staggered back. 'You stinkin' – fucking arsehole. I trusted you – you big black shit!'

Danny winced at her verbal assault as he turned the large iron key in the lock, making the door secure.

'I'm sorry Princess, honest I am, but it's for the best – it's for yous, because I love you,' he called.

Even as he spoke, his heart sank, he knew junk, and he knew his battle against heroin had only just begun.

Jacky pummelled fiercely on the heavy pine door with her clenched fists. 'Let me out, you bastard,' she shrieked. 'I want me hit, I need me hit off Deadleather.'

She hammered on the door until her hands were red and sore, then she collapsed into a heap on the floor. Suddenly, it was as if Lucifer had stepped in, an image of Woodcock, baring his uneven yellow teeth, passed before her, and then disappeared quickly into a wall of flame. Her voice changed to that of a pleading little schoolgirl begging not to be given detention.

'Please – please! let me out Danny. Woodcock, George Woodcock, I've been dealing for him, I owe him a lot of bread man, shit man, a lot!' She raised her voice again, desperate at the lack of response, and yelled venomously. 'The nutty bastard 'll have me if I don't come across. For Christ's sake you cruel get! – help me!'

Danny sagged and sighed with frustration. He buried his head in his hands. 'I am helping you, Princess,' he murmured to himself. 'I am helping you sweetheart.'

Shaking his head sadly, he left her still cursing and pleading by turns and went downstairs. At this moment, more than any other, he needed Merlin to talk to.

Jacky clawed at the multi-coloured carpet and sobbed hysterically.

'Oh God! oh – my – fuckin'! – God!'

About an hour later, Jack exploded into violence. Danny and Merlin were watching TV desultorily in an attempt to relieve tension, when they heard a loud crash as she swept Merlin's precious books thudding to the floor from off the dusty shelves. Danny leapt to his feet. 'I'll have to stop her, Merlin,' he exclaimed, 'she's wreckin' yer room.'

Freddy Haddock pushed himself up from his favourite chair by the fireside. Unlike Danny, he stayed calm, even though his books were a most important part of his own world. 'Not a good idea, Danny,' he warned. He stroked his small silver beard and despite the pain he felt at having his treasured books despoiled, managed to say, quietly, 'Best leave her alone, dear boy, let her blow off a little steam, let her wear herself down a bit, then, hopefully she'll rest for a while.'

After the nine o'clock news, peace was restored to Freddy Haddock's home, Jacky had fallen into a restless slumber.

Danny, relieved at the calm after the storm, remarked, 'I'll just nip an' see how she is, Merlin, yous know what I mean, like.' Merlin's expression was wary as he took a sip of his whisky.

'Be careful dear boy,' he warned, in concerned tones. 'As you well know yourself, heroin is evil, the devil in a different form. It is the brother of young Jacky's deadly enemy, Woodcock, and his wicked Hell Fire Club.'

'I'll be okay,' Danny assured him.

As soon as Danny entered the den, Jack jolted awake and started to plead pathetically, her face tear-streaked. 'Please! Dan' if you love me you'll fix me a hit with Dead-leather.' She shook her head despairingly, and sobbed out piteously. 'Please! Dan' you don't understand, heroin and other drugs keep me going.'

She tugged out another cigarette from the packet, and with a shaking hand lit up, blowing out a stream of smoke. 'Can't you see it, man? they help to keep us in love.'

Danny stepped back towards the door. He felt as if he'd been hit by a verbal bullet. He gawped at her in disbelief and walked out. He turned the key to a mouthful of vicious abuse.

'You – black! – shithouse!'

Merlin's globe smashed against the door.

'Get – me – my fucking – junk! I need the stuff.'

Danny leant against the wall for a brief moment, feeling shattered. He quickly regained his poise, however, realising that behind her verbal assault, deep down in her swimming drugged mind, she did love him – it just hurt, that was all. He ignored the wounding words that followed on and made his way back downstairs.

Merlin handed him a fresh can of beer, having heard Jack's drugged outburst. He swept a hand through his mop of hair.

'I did warn you, dear boy.' He gave Danny a fatherly pat on the back and persuaded him to sit down.

When Danny was settled, Merlin flicked over the TV stations.

'Ah good,' he observed. 'Snooker. That's better.' He knew a bit of snooker would probably cheer Danny up a little.

Meanwhile in a quaint country pub called The Headless Woman, several members of the Hell Fire Club were secretly meeting over drinks. Their main topics were the 'All Hallows' ceremony, and the well-being of their sacrifice, Sophie Dooley.

Harry D. Coot gave a plummy chortle, as George Woodcock responded to a suggestive remark of his with a wide sick grin. Miss Bull's flabby jowls wobbled with excitement, as Adder's sneaky little fingers searched beneath the table and slid up her fat thighs, to slip beneath her bloomers and up her huge sweating vagina. She giggled and reluctantly pulled his hand away. 'Stop it, you filthy little beast, you disgusting, lovely little urchin. I'm sure such a randy creature like you would rather give the same treatment to Sophie Dooley on the big night – with your tongue!' She swigged the last of her red wine, and let out a revolting burp. 'And perhaps?' she added, her eyes lustful, 'we may get the chance to do the little virgin together.'

Adder laughed boisterously, licked her secretions from off his sticky fingers then gulped down his Bacardi and coke – it was always tidy dress and the best drinks when he was in the presence of Woodcock.

'Yes, and you never know. If our master, Lucifer, is kind, he may present us with the chance to fuck Jacky Dooley as well.' The very thought of him heaving himself in and out of Jack, whilst holding her legs high in the air, with Bull forcing her forest of pubic hair against Jack's mouth, had his trouser-zip bulging, and his tongue working overtime.

Ament, sitting with ladylike grace, sipped delicately from her glass of pure orange juice. She was a health fanatic, dedicated to keeping herself fit and well. It was she who initiated all new male members to the coven, sometimes two at a time. A High Priestess had an important role to play.

Freddy cursed and topped up his whisky. He liked Steve Davis, and at the moment he was two frames down against the unsmiling Scots kid, Stephen Hendry.

Danny, finding it hard to concentrate, was glad of the excuse to take Jack a glass of iced mineral water.

Nursing the glass, he pressed an ear to the door. Silence! He braced himself, unlocked the door and went in.

Jacky stood up, swaying a little, as he held out the glass to her. There was a sour bitter taste in her throat which needed sweetening, heroin would do the trick, but... her breath quivered, and she erupted like a volcano. She snatched the glass of mineral water, and swigged a large mouthful quickly, and then spat it out, straight back into Danny's face. Taken by surprise Danny couldn't avoid the vicious spray, and gasping, took in half a mouthful of the cold liquid.

Jack's words stormed out at him. 'Water!' she screamed, 'You bast-ard! I don't want fuckin' gnats' piss, I want a fuckin' fix! God damn you, you arsehole!' As she lurched at him frenziedly, Danny swiftly stepped back and locked the door. He sighed heavily, leaning his head against the heavy pine panels.

'I – I'm sorry Jack, I'm sorry, Princess. I just love you and want to get yous off the bleedin' shit, that's all.'

Freddy Haddock loved 'The Sky At Night' programme on TV, and watched Patrick Moore's eager antics with great enjoyment. When Danny reappeared, however, his gaze left the screen and he asked, sympathetically. 'How is she, dear boy? Suffering I suspect.'

Danny nodded, as he grasped a new can of beer and peeled back the tab. Grim-faced, he drank it down, not feeling much like talking.

Freddy appreciated his mood, poked the fire and tossed another log onto the leaping flames. Then his attention returned to Patrick Moore, excitedly prodding the next diagram with his thin baton.

Later, Danny again turned the key, swung open the den door, and switched on the light.

Jacky was huddled up on the bed, shivering. She was naked, except for the checked blanket wrapped around her shoulders and her small white panties.

As Danny dropped down on the bed beside her, she threw her arms around his neck and cried out, in short, choking bursts. 'P-please Dan' get me a fix, eh! – I need it man.' She clawed frantically at her forehead, and tried the Devil's own wiles on him. Her tears ran freely. She used dulcet tones, and snuggled her near naked body against him. 'P-please! Dan', I've lost Bobby, me best mate. Me ol' fella's pissed off down south and I've lost me bleedin' job.'

She gazed at him with wide, reproachful eyes. 'Come on Dan' I need the shit, I'll do anythin' you want for it – anything.'

Danny felt a surge of desire, a naked longing to succumb, let her have what she craved, and take what she offered so temptingly. But he knew what the result would be and summoned up all his strength, all his resources, to resist. He tore her hugging arms away. 'Eh, eh, Jack, no way, Princess, no drugs.' His tone admitted no argument.

She lurched at him, in the grip of a diabolical rage. Her stomach heaved, her face contorted and she spat a mouthful of phlegm directly into Danny's face.

In silent disbelief, he touched the slimy substance on his skin with his finger. He felt nauseated as he stared, speechless, into her malevolent eyes.

'Fuck you! fuck you,' she hissed. 'You lousy mongrel, you bastard, you whore-master! I hate your fuckin' guts!' As Danny sat dumbfounded, Jacky reared up and rained blows on him.

He reacted instinctively, grabbing and holding each of her slender wrists, in a vice-like grip. Anger came to his aid, he drew himself up and, eyes flashing, berated her. 'Bullshit! Jacky, you're talking the fuck bullshit.'

Releasing her wrists, he got off the bed, and stalked around the room, picking up Merlin's littered books, stacking them on his desk. He discovered that Merlin's globe was broken, wrenched away from its spindle.

He glared indignantly at Jack, who was shakily lighting a cigarette.

'Bobby Queen got you hooked on the junk,' he fumed. 'She's a butch cow, an' she's been no mate to you!'

Jack winced – Danny's anger subdued her, and she thanked her lucky stars that she'd never told him that it was Bobby who'd put Merlin in hospital.

Danny continued, forcefully. 'Get your stupid head straight woman – there's – no – more – shit! And as for your old man . . .' He paused and stabbed at his head with a tense finger. 'He's a dickhead, a dumbo, yous know what I mean like, girl?' Jacky hurled her cigarette onto the carpet, her temper rising again. But Danny was already pounding out of the room. He slammed the door and locked it to a barrage of shrieking abuse.

'I'm 'ungry as well, you mother-fucker,' she screamed. 'An' I wanna go ter the bog an' all, all right!' She grabbed a book and squashed out the smouldering fag-end.

Danny stopped on the landing, breathing heavily – he would provide her with both in a moment but he needed to wind down first.

A little while later, after Danny had escorted her back from the toilet, Jack eagerly tucked into the rich gateau which Merlin had prepared, and left by the door for her – he was leaving the main business to Danny.

It was Jack's first food for a long time, and she even drank the mineral water as well.

Danny stood silently watching her, as she ate like a starved street urchin. He was a man through and through, but he felt no shame as he wiped tears away with his hand – things were beginning to look up, he told himself, she had the drug demon on the retreat. Lucifer does not give in easily however. He speedily resurfaced to inflame Jack's drugged senses. Suddenly, she sent the plate flying, dropped to her knees, gripped Danny's legs, and gazing up at him, cried out frantically. 'Please Dan', I'm decaying man, rottin' away, you've gotta help me. Get me a fix off Dead-leather – please!' She sucked hard on a fresh cigarette, practically eating it.

She leapt to her feet and ran across the room to the boarded up window. She clawed at the wooden bars, and screamed, as splinters dug deep into her delicate skin. 'Let me out of here, you shitbag, you half-chat twat!'

She stubbed out what was left of her cigarette on the boards, and turned furiously to face him. She licked the blood from her wounded fingers. She cowered, snarled and hissed like a wounded animal. 'Out! Get the fuck out of here, you slimebug, you . . .' she yelled.

Danny locked the door to the sound of her once again tearing Merlin's den to pieces. Heavy metal music suddenly exploded from Merlin's old radio.

Jack dropped onto the bed and curled up. She tried to sleep but couldn't, pictures of herself getting the rush from the needle into her arm clouded her mind – she wanted junk – she wanted a syringe – now!

Chapter Twenty-One

The birds' dawn chorus echoed in the stillness, and one lone crow, perched on top of Merlin's TV aerial asserted his authority with a harsh grated cawing.

Danny stood with his back turned as Jacky bathed in Merlin's small, pink-tiled bathroom. She grabbed the bar of soap from off the soap-tray, splashed her hands into the hot water then angrily hurled the soap at him.

Danny swivelled sharply as the missile thudded against the towel rack fixed to the white-painted door. He cursed as it hit the carpet.

'What the shit d'you do that for Jack?'

Clenching her two small fists together, she pummelled her forehead, shook her soaked hair and sobbed hysterically. 'I can't go on Dan – I need junk, I need you. Don't you understand you arsehole? I need you to fuck me man, in every way, you half-chat bastard!'

She sagged beneath the white foam, held her head under for a few seconds and gurgled. 'Somebody's got to bleedin' save me – Jesus Christ!'

Danny reacted instantly. He took a pace forward,

snatched at her hair and yanked her head back above water.

'You little shit!' he growled, 'what the fuck a' yous trying to do to yourself.' Memories flashed before his eyes, Jacky's face was suddenly transformed into that of his mother's. He winced, and choked from the pit of his stomach. He grabbed her hair fiercely and battled with an insane urge to rip her head off. Shuddering, he let her loose, she fell back limp and slapped wearily at the suds. A sob broke from her and she cried out pitifully. 'I – I'm sorry Dan, I'm not the mother fuckin' Devil, 'onest I'm not man.' She grasped his wrists in her little, helpless hands and her voice softened to a whisper. 'I love you Dan – more than anythin' in the world.' Slowly her trembling fingers slid free, she lowered her tired head onto the back of the white fibre bath, and suddenly fell asleep.

Danny's face crumpled – it was his lovely mum all over again, as she had been, not long before she died. He ground his teeth, forcing back a storm of emotion which he knew would not help either of them.

Outside, a stiff breeze had risen and Danny could hear the postman whistling cheerfully. He held Jack's naked body tightly in his arms, she was limp, and still moist from her bath. He dried her on the pink bath towel and tucked her, unresisting, into bed. He quickly flicked through the radio channels until he found Radio Two – Terry Wogan was giving away another clock and then Pavarotti hit the turntable.

Danny looked warmly at Jacky. At least while she was sleeping maybe her aching joints would cease, but he knew that the stomach cramps would wake her up.

After a brief spell Jack, hugging her stomach woke, grumbling. Unexpectedly, she lurched up from the bed and threw her arms around his neck, pulling his face down to hers.

Pressing her lips against his, she sucked at him avidly. 'Give me your tongue, and your tosser,' she purred, in would-be seductive tones. 'Come on man, give it to me, fuck me hard!'

Danny winced, shook his head, tore her clinging body away, he felt like vomiting. 'Leave it out, Jack!' he snarled. 'What the hell's got into yous girl, a' yous sane, or what?' Jacky dropped back against the pillows and began to ramble about long-ago days.

She lifted a tired arm, and drawled, sorry for herself, 'I've rammed that fucking needle everywhere, Dan.' She quickly ran her fingers over her arms and legs, the 'tracking lines' were clearly visible. 'Before long there'll only be me neck left to shove it.'

Danny clenched his fists and yelled at her. 'Stop it, Jack! you can beat the stuff, I know yous can. You're already halfway there.'

Furiously she brought up his own past. 'God! Danny, you know it's not easy, you used to hit stuff yourself when you was a kid.' Danny's eyes glittered dangerously, he leapt to his feet.

'Come 'ead girl, you know that ain't fair. I was only little then, and anyway, I managed to get off it.'

Memories flooded through his mind again of his mother, her dreadful death from that massive overdose of heroin. Feeling he could bear no more for the moment, he left Jacky on the bed, stormed from the room, and pounded down the stairs.

Merlin had risen early, and the house was already filling with the aroma of toast and frying bacon.

After a brief conversation about the state of Jack's health, Merlin smiled and handed him the large silver tray, which was crammed full with a hearty breakfast and two mugs of steaming tea.

Usually, at this time of the morning, after jogging, Danny would be training with Steeleye, but under the circumstances, that would have to wait.

Jack and Danny had both cooled down by the time he arrived at her bedside with the tray. He smiled and nodded his satisfaction as he watched her eating everything in front of her. They were winning the battle.

It was two days later, on a Wednesday afternoon, when Jacky flicked through the radio stations until she came to Radio One. Steve Wright was hosting the show. She dropped down onto the bed, and while head banging to Guns N' Roses, drew deeply on her cigarette.

Danny was up and dancing in tune with the rhythm. He stretched out his hands and beckoned

Jack to him. 'Come on, Princess,' he coaxed. 'Come and dance with me. You're looking a lot better, I bet you feel it as well?'

She nodded, stubbed out her cigarette and swayed seductively towards him. Dancing close to each other, they gazed lovingly into each other's eyes.

As the music echoed through his usually peaceful home, Freddy Haddock cast a disgruntled glance at the ceiling and tutted.

'Youngsters today,' he muttered, wiping another plate with the tea-towel. 'Mad music, drugs and joyriding, God! where will it all end?' He sighed and added resignedly, 'Still, youth must have its fling.' He glanced at the wall clock, it was five to nine. He had time to catch the bus to buy supplies on the market and escape from that thudding music. He banged loudly on the door of his den and roared over the din. 'Danny! Danny, dear boy, I'm off into Balchester shopping, I'll see you in a couple of hours.'

'Bye Merlin, I'll see yous,' came the muffled reply.

'Bye Merlin,' echoed Jacky, with a loud giggle.

Freddy sighed, shook his head, and collecting his canvas holdall, went off on his errands.

Jacky had been feeling really good until, looking over Danny's wide shoulder, she had fixed her gaze on Merlin's white bust of Charles Dickens. She suddenly felt faint, and shook her head; a surge of dizziness swept through her frail body.

Charles Dickens had, luckily, withstood her

drugged onslaught on Merlin's favourite room, but was now changing form before her very eyes.

Danny gripped her narrow waist as she gasped, gave a groan, and sagged.

'What's wrong Princess, what's wrong – eh!?'

She didn't look at him or reply, she just stared at Charles Dickens, who had now turned into the form of the falcon, Horus but with two heads. One head was that of a lecherous looking George Woodcock with his leering mouth. The other was that of Ament, her long searching tongue tipped with a razor sharp talon, that reached out and sliced the air only an inch away from Jacky's terrified face. She screamed and clung desperately to Danny, burying her head against his chest. When she fearfully glanced up again, Charles Dickens was back to normal.

Danny gently shook her. 'A' you all right Jack?'

A long sigh escaped her pale lips, then she suddenly responded to the pop group, Abba, by breaking back into dance as 'Dancing Queen' burst out from the radio. She nodded and smiled nervously. 'I'm fine man, just fine.'

They danced on together and finally kissed passionately as the Abba voices trailed away.

To the sound of Bryan Adams' voice singing 'I'll Do It For You', they dropped down onto the bed a little tired after the rigorous dancing.

Jack bowed her head and tried to think clearly, at least her mind seemed to function a little better now. Looking up, she gazed at Danny, her expression one of warmth and tenderness. 'You really are determined to get me off the junk, aren't you Dan?' she murmured.

He took her in his arms and cradled her. 'Yep! I am Princess, I definitely am, because I love yous Babe,' he declared, emphatically.

Her eyes glistened with tears. She nuzzled him and whispered lovingly, 'I know you do Dan.' Her face flushed with warmth as she went on. 'And I love you too, I'm sorry for everything, I know you're only trying to help me.' A solitary tear slid down her left cheek – Jack Dooley was becoming a different woman, a caring, gentler lady, and to hell with the Devil. She raised her face to Danny's and her lips met his. This time, he responded eagerly.

After a little while he eased himself away from her – he was becoming aroused.

'Phew,' he gasped, 'you shouldn't do that, Princess, yous really shouldn't, I mean . . .'

'Why, you enjoyed it didn't you?'

'Of course I did, you know I did.'

As they embraced again, Jacky took hold of his hand with trembling fingers and guided it slowly over her knee and up the inside of her shapely thigh.

She kissed him again hungrily, and by now he was sure that it was with genuine love.

As his hot tongue responded to hers, he took control and gently guided her hand to his thickening penis.

She squeezed and stroked it through the denim of his jeans until he had reached a massive erection. He groaned with satisfaction, thrust his tongue deeper, and massaged her small firm breasts, their nipples already swelling. With one hand he unfastened and took off her trousers, then stripped off his own jeans. In seconds he'd removed her panties and top. He had seen her naked in Merlin's bath, but in the dim light of the room, her shining body looked so much more beautiful.

He moulded her breasts again, then took each nipple in turn between his lips, sucking them.

Jack clawed at his long curls, shivering in ecstasy at the sensations he was evoking.

Danny, too, was finding the foreplay more loving and arousing by the minute. As his fingers slid inside Jack's wet vagina she whispered urgently, 'please do it Dan, God, please!' She was impatient, yearning to surrender her virginity to the man she loved.

Danny licked his way down her waiting body, and as his long searching tongue flicked against the sensitiveness of her clitoris she groaned and climaxed – her yearning to experience the pain that would be like pleasure as he took her virginity, increased.

Danny hoisted himself back up the bed, lay fully on top of her and gently eased her legs well apart. He whispered lovingly in her ear. 'I want to take your beautiful virgin body, Jack, and make you mine forever, in every possible way, I won't hurt you I promise – I love you.'

He slowly hoisted his body up until he could comfortably rest, legs spread, and tease her mouth with his large bulbous organ – she took it with both hands and sucked him eagerly and firmly, until he begged her to stop. He slid back down her quivering body. He closed his fingers tightly, even slightly painfully, around the base of his penis to swell it to its extreme; she drew in a deep breath, and her heart pounded, as he probed her slippery cleft and penetrated her. She gave a small squeal as his throbbing thickness stretched her. She gave a hoarse cry.

'Oh my fuckin' God! Danny.'

With a long sliding thrust he broke through the hymen, making her his woman.

She clung to him, marvelling at their oneness, that the pain had been so slight because she had wanted it to happen so very much.

'God! I love you man,' she sighed.

He pushed again, delving deeper, grunting, as he did so. She gasped loudly, and gripped him tighter. 'I really do.' He didn't hear what she said, he was on a different planet, high on the purest drug of all – real love.

Cupping her rounded buttocks in his strong hands, he urged her into rhythmic movement with him as he thrust deep inside her, pausing, almost withdrawing from time to time, teasingly, only to add to the thrill when he drove his manhood hard within her again.

Her legs round his waist, she gripped him firmly as he rode her, continually.

After another orgasm rose and exploded inside her he disregarded the soaking wet discharge of sperm. 'Hold me tightly, Jack,' he gasped. He gripped her shoulders and started to roll her body over, making sure he stayed locked inside her. She clung to his lips, sucking his saliva and swallowing it greedily.

Danny hoisted her on top of him, pushing hard to make sure she swallowed him right to the hilt. She whimpered, then groaned, as he thrust violently, at the same time working her buttocks up and down on his solid manhood.

Jacky slowed down, something was happening to her, the loving feelings seemed lost, drained away by an alien force. Woodcock, and his coven – she knew instinctively that they were trying to come between her and Danny.

Thriving on the wonder of her first full sexual experience, Jack did her level best to fight a mental war with Lucifer, but the Devil was already lying in wait within the long mirror on Merlin's dressing-table.

Gritting her teeth, Jack tossed back her hair defiantly and rode on Danny's penis, hard, fast, and furious, determined to try and rid herself of the evil power.

But as Danny came, disappearing into a paradise of his own, Jack glanced across at Merlin's mirror. She wanted to climax again at the sight of their two bodies engulfed in love-making, but found she couldn't. She suddenly tore herself away from him and shook an angry fist towards the grubby mirror.

The face of the Devil was there, his eyes, slanted

and large, glowed deep red and blazed with unholy excitement as he drooled over the sight of their naked, beautiful bodies. Yes, many a man within the coven would like to bend Danny's masculine physique over the sacrificial stone and mount him.

For Satan to appear himself the preparation by the whole coven must have been great.

Then Ament's haughty features also appeared in the mirror followed by a mass of hooded figures.

Ament's mouth twisted into a sickening grin as she ogled Jack's body.

Danny gasped, and sucked in an angry breath. 'What the hell d'you do that for Jack, why d'you stop?' He was peeved, it had all been so wonderful.

She whimpered and bravely raised her eyes again to the mirror. She shuddered at the scenes before her.

Wrapping her arms around Danny's waist, she hid her face against him and sobbed. 'S'okay Dan, 'onest, I'm okay. It – it's just these stupid bleedin' pictures that I keep seeing in the mirror – that's all.'

They turned together to face the long mirror. Jacky breathed a hugh sigh of relief, the only picture now was of her and Danny sitting naked on the bed. Danny hugged her tightly, warmly and tenderly. 'It's all right Princess, the pictures are all part of the stuff, before long yous won't see any more, it'll be all over and you'll have won.'

Wrong! this was the Devil at his most devious.

As his lengthening tongue stretched out, snake-like, in the mirror, dripping saliva, Jack's terrified shriek once again burst through the boarded-up window of Merlin's den.

Merlin drew in his breath sharply and snatched up his bags.

'My God! what's happening up there?' he exclaimed aloud. 'Jacky!? – Danny!?'

He made his way hastily to the front door, unlocked it and rushed inside.

Danny had managed to regain control after the sudden shock of seeing the Devil's grotesque form for the first time in the mirror – this was real, no drugs. It appeared as if the Devil was trying to break free from Merlin's mirror. God! he thought. I could do with Steeleye right now.

As Lucifer's tongue seemed to reach further and further towards them, Danny quickly gripped Jack's arm and dragged her to the door. He turned the knob and tugged frantically, the door was jammed fast.

Satan gave an evil cackle, he was now in his most revolting form. The fiend's eyebrows had risen until they were like two pointed ears, and there was a sickening crack as his skull split, to allow two goat-like horns to rear themselves. His deep red eyes blazed, his nose swelled, and he belched forth a blast of fetid air in their direction.

Ament's face once more slowly appeared in the mirror, but this time she stayed in the background. Alongside her, again, were many cloaked figures. Above all, there was visible the bronze coloured statue of Bast, the benevolent cat-goddess of Bubastis. Bast was highly sacred to the coven; whilst many other creatures were freely sacrificed and their blood drunk eagerly, cats were spared. Ament raised her arms aloft and intoned a string of Latin words. As a sound of humming from the cloaked figures grew louder and louder, Bast and Ament slowly merged into one, until her body was that of a woman, with the head of Bast. Her cat-like eyes were yellow, and as she scrutinised Danny and Jack she hypnotically moved her head from side to side and hissed, the sinister hiss of an enraged feline. She, too, started to seep through the glass mirror and out into the den.

Suddenly, a wind rose, picking up speed, until in a matter of seconds it reached hurricane force.

Danny clung desperately to Jack, as they were battered ferociously by the wind. With a loud, splintering and snapping of wood, bars were wrenched off the sealed-up window and hurled about the room.

The radio went dead as it was flung to the floor, along with other stray items – the white porcelain bust of Charles Dickens was smashed to atoms. A loud eerie humming of many voices came from the mirror, growing until it reached fever pitch.

Danny and Jacky longed to cover their ears, but they dare not let go of each other.

Loose papers tore around the room like a berserk snowstorm. Ament tossed back her cat-like head and her evil shrill laugh pierced through the humming. A heavy book smacked against the side of

Danny's face, nearly thrusting him away from Jack, but he bravely held on to her with one strong arm, whilst gripping the doorknob firmly with the other hand.

Lucifer's mouth gaped open, saliva flowed freely from his long thin fangs. Suddenly, as the whole room shook, Merlin's silver-topped walking cane flew from its hook, and its six inch blade shot out.

With a wave of his claw and a surge of mental power, Satan sent the blade hurtling towards Danny – Danny was a persistent nuisance to the coven, and had to be eliminated.

Somehow, Jacky's deep love for Danny helped her to respond instantly. She swept up Merlin's fallen stool and used it as a shield for Danny.

As the shining blade thudded into the stool's seat, Danny was sucked towards Satan and Bast – the coven was determined to destroy him.

Jacky Dooley was intended for Satan's sexual gratification on the stone altar at the old abbey.

Outside the room, Merlin tugged frantically at the door of his den.

'Danny! Jacky! are you both all right?'

Jack screamed continually, while Danny yelled above the din. 'The damn door's stuck, Merlin – for fuck's sake do something or we'll both be killed.'

Merlin yanked even harder at the doorknob. 'What is it Danny, what's happening?'

Danny yelled a brief explanation of the evil visitation. As Merlin hurried away for help, Danny and Jack, together, managed to pull themselves away slightly from the occult influence.

'Come 'ead, Jack,' Danny screamed, 'help us to try an' open the door.'

One by one, the Devil's cloaked and hooded disciples slid out of the mirror and squirmed across the floor towards the young couple.

Satan tossed back his head and roared.

Jack shook uncontrollably, dread overwhelming her. She'd paid Danny back for saving her from the surging waters of the River Denny, by stopping the cane's blade from killing him, but now total fear had taken grip of her. Out of sheer terror she bit into her shaking fingers.

Danny held onto her, wide-eyed. He looked at the advancing incubus and went rigid with horror.

Within seconds the Devil had expanded, his mouth an obscene dark cavern.

Suddenly, with an ear shattering crash, the mirror exploded, showering Danny and Jacky with glass – Satan and Bast were free.

At that moment, Merlin's axe crashed into the door. Again and again, he struck, until finally the door was free. His long silver hair was swept back by the raging gale, as he tried to force himself into the room. A vase smashed over his head, but he went on relentlessly, at the same time pulling a large silver crucifix from his pocket. 'Are you all right Danny!?'

Danny clung to Jack and managed to gasp out, 'yes.'

The fiend gurgled and sent multi-coloured vomit spraying over them – the room smelt revolting.

Merlin pushed himself forward into the wind and raised his cross aloft.

'Get thee away Satan!' he shouted. 'Get thee away!' Blood suddenly burst from the tap, which was on top of the small sink in the corner of the room – a tap which hadn't worked for years.

The lights flashed on and off repeatedly, the old wardrobe door banged open and shut time after time – and above it all, the wind howled.

Merlin pushed forward another yard.

As Danny tried to move to assist, Merlin waved him back, yelling. 'No! No dear boy, you can't fight him with violence.'

Jack was on her knees, sobbing bitterly, and hanging on desperately to Danny's legs.

Merlin pushed his cross ahead of him, and called out a line from his wartime motto. 'Dum spiro vivo (while I breathe I live) Get thee away! Satan, get thee away!'

The Devil and Bast were stopped in their tracks; fearfully, they turned their gaze away, Bast squealed and Satan put up his talons to shield his face.

He shook his head from side to side, then spewed out another stream of vomit.

Merlin was but feet away and holding his ground. 'In pace inveniro caelum! (in peace I find heaven) Get thee away! Satan,' he called out, above the din. 'Get – thee – away!'

Suddenly, the terrible wind began to die down,

and Satan and Bast retreated back towards the mirror.

Merlin drove himself on, implacably, until he was nearly charging forward. 'Dum spiro vivo, get thee – away Satan!' he cried. Chunks of glass suddenly began to rise from the carpet and floated towards the mirror.

The black-cloaked figures squirmed and whined pathetically, as they slithered back from whence they had come – the Devil's takers had gone, rotted away, to leave nought but lifeless shadows.

With one final roar from Merlin of 'In pace inveniro caelum, get thee away Satan!' the last of the winds were sucked up by the mirror, taking Satan and Bast with them. Very gently, the pieces of glass settled down and slotted together, like a giant jigsaw puzzle, until the mirror was complete. The faces of the Devil and Ament faded away, all that could be seen were the reflections of Danny, Jacky and Merlin. The room was once again as peaceful as a country churchyard.

Merlin stumbled across to where Danny was nursing Jack, who was still sobbing bitterly – he was now a tired, drained figure of a man, Satan was tough opposition.

'Are you both unharmed?' he asked, wearily, as he tucked the cross into his jacket pocket.

Danny eased Jack up in his arms and nodded, they both looked utterly exhausted after their ordeal.

'I guess we're OK Merlin,' he replied, gratefully. 'Thanks to you, that is.' He helped Jacky to the bed, where she lay down, shaking in every limb, her hair wet through with sweat. She was as white as a ghost and felt sick and faint.

Danny and Merlin gazed at her with concerned faces. Danny held her little hand tightly in his own warm one, willing strength into her. 'D'you think she'll come round all right?' he asked Merlin.

'I think she'll be just fine now, dear boy. The way she has been beset by the Devil, she has been through a terrible mental ordeal. Maybe now she's finally beaten heroin, we'll just have to keep our fingers crossed.' He lowered his voice to a whisper. 'But, whatever the outcome is, we must let her think the whole thing has been a hallucination, is that understood?'

'Yeah, sure, Merlin.'

Merlin's eyes smiled, confidently, into Danny's, as he reached into his waistcoat pocket for his silver pocket watch.

'Now! dear boy, whilst she rests we'll have a tot or two. And, when she is refreshed and with a sharper mind,' he swung the pocket watch gently, 'I'll use a bit of hypnosis on her to add a little weight to your own excellent work in trying to save her. Hopefully, together, we'll rid her of the Devil and his drug forever.'

As Jack's eyes became heavier, Danny gently released her hand. He shook his head with disbelief at Freddy Haddock. 'Yous never cease to amaze me Merlin, 'onestly, you don't.'

'Just a little trick I picked up on my travels, dear

boy, along with my trusty walking cane, that's all. But if it will help Jacky, well . . .'

A little while later, back downstairs, after Merlin had treated Jack with light hypnosis, he was preparing a hot tasty meal for them all.

Jack and Danny cuddled close on the settee in front of the glowing fire.

Their lips met tenderly and stayed caressingly together for several minutes. Finally they parted and Danny said softly, 'I love you Jack.'

'I love you too.'

Danny and Merlin had at last freed Jacky Dooley from drugs and the Devil, but – was it forever?

Chapter Twenty-Two

It was the last week of October and a mild Friday afternoon. Adder lounged against the old brick wall near to the exit gates of Sophie's school. He kept well out of sight of any prying eyes, and only occasionally peeped around the corner, to see if Sophie was coming.

At around three forty-five, she appeared at the gates with a school chum. After a brief, cheerful conversation, her friend departed to join a group of other girls who were heading in a different direction – Sophie ran towards the old brick wall, innocently, and alone.

Adder let loose a satisfied hiss, and a smug boyish grin broke out on his thin, drawn face. It was the grin which held a terrible inner evil, it was the grin that had always kidded Sophie.

The only people it could never fool were Danny Black and Rosie Dooley, Rosie detested him.

Adder stepped out a little way, and waved his hand.

Sophie, smiled broadly, and waved back happily. She'd seen him – good, he thought, sexy little bitch!

As she reached the wall, Adder held up two packets of her favourite chocolate munchies, and stepped back a little further into the shadows.

'Hi Sophie, how you doing?'

She approached him eagerly. 'Hello Adder, what are you doing here?' Giggling, she reached for the chocolates. 'Are they for me?'

'I was just passing and thought, well, just thought you might like some munchies, that's all.'

She tossed him an artless, look of admiration. 'Ta Adder, I'm doing OK.' She shrugged her shoulders. 'Just fine, especially now that it's the weekend – how are you anyway, how's your new flat?'

Adder's grin widened, she was making things easier for him than he'd expected.

'It's great, you'd like it, I've got it just the way your mum did the room for me at your house.' His villainous scheme was going well. He raised his eyebrows questioningly.

'A' you going home right away?'

'Yes, why?'

'I'll show you the place if you like, it's on the way to your house.'

Sophie considered briefly, as she rammed some more munchies into her mouth. Her answer was slightly muffled by the stickiness of the sweets. She shrugged her small shoulders again. She'd never had any reason up to now to fear him, so why worry. 'OK s'fine by me,' she agreed flippantly, 'let's go.' She grinned happily.

He slid his leather-clad arm around her small waist.

'Righto then Soph,' he said, eagerly. 'We'll take the short cut down the alleyways, it'll be quicker.' And less conspicuous, he added to himself. He playfully tweaked her nose, she'd always like that, and continued, coolly. 'Then, when you've seen my flat, you can tell your mum how nice it is, can't you?'

'Yep, sure, sure.'

He quickly led her off down the nearby cobblestoned alley. As they went he cast a searching glance over his right shoulder – good! the coast was still all clear.

After walking briskly for a few minutes, he brought Sophie to a halt by an old weathered backyard gate. He'd need to use the back way so as not to be seen.

Sophie popped another munchie into her mouth, and waited while Adder eased the broken gate open by just lifting it up on its faulty hinges and pushing it. He climbed the single step.

'Come on, Soph' we'll use the back door.' He waved a casual hand. 'We don't want to disturb the old boy who lives here, do we?'

She put a finger to her childish lips and whispered, 'OK,' then followed him eagerly. She was dying to see his flat, so that she could take a report back home with her. She cast a rueful glance at the overgrown garden, if that was anything, to go by . . . , still, she thought, their own garden was nothing to write home about.

As Adder followed her up the stairs, his lustful, beady eyes stayed riveted to her tight little backside. His skinny tongue shot in and out and then slid slowly and avidly along his bottom lip.

The sight of her pale shapely legs, fringed with a short red skirt, and her neat white bobby socks set his sexual appetite seething.

When they reached his flat, on the first floor, he deliberately leant over her to feel the warmth of her body as he unlocked the door.

Sophie, blissfully unconscious of his intentions, stood waiting, humming a pop tune under her breath.

He pocketed his key, swung open the brown-stained door and ushered her inside.

Sophie's expression was one of shock when she saw the revolting state of the place. But it quickly turned to one of surprise, as Adder gave a huge sigh of relief and locked the door. He quickly withdrew the key and pocketed it again. As Sophie glanced around the untidy room, her nose twitched – the place still stank of joint smoke. Empty beer cans littered the floor. The room was dark and dingy, with just a mattress and a couple of grubby blankets on the worn carpet for a bed. There was only one chair, and a dusty sideboard, with a small portable radio perched on top, for furniture. And he had said it was like her mum's place, she remembered – no way, her mum's place was clean and tidy, and certainly better furnished. Sophie looked up into Adder's leering face.

'W-what d'you do that for Adder?' she asked with the first stirrings of concern. 'Why d'you lock the door?'

Adder nervously lit up a smoke, and snatched a half-empty can of lager from the sideboard. He took a long swig and then wiped his mouth on his jacket sleeve. 'To keep you here my little lovely, that's why.' he replied.

Sophie stepped back a little, uneasily, she was beginning to feel scared. 'Why Adder!?' she exclaimed, her voice trembling. 'What have I done?'

Adder peered down his thin bony nose contemptuously. Pulling open the top drawer of the sideboard, he took out a length of thin rope.

'Nothin' Sophie Dooley, you've done nothing my little sweet.' A harsh dry laugh came from him as he looked her up and down.

'It's what we're going to do to you on "All Hallows Eve" that counts.'

Sophie was bemused, even mystified, Adder had always been so nice to her – she even liked him, or had up until now. He pushed her down, hard, onto the mattress, she squealed, loudly. As she fought him furiously, kicking out her legs and scratching him, Adder sent the back of his gloved hand smacking into her face. Her lips swelled up almost immediately, and blood trickled from the split in her lower lip. She fell limp and sobbed bitterly. In a matter of seconds, he'd bound her hands and feet tightly. Her eyes were wide with terror, as he rammed the valium tablets into her mouth, before gagging her firmly with a dirty kerchief – a steady stream of the tablet would keep her quiet right up until the rite. She lay there helpless, able only to utter a muffled squeak which nobody would hear. Whilst drifting, with heavy eyes into a strange calmness, Sophie tried to puzzle over what Adder had said about the 'All Hallows Eve', she knew nothing about devil worship, or the Hell Fire Club, and she had no idea what he meant.

Her heart gave a frantic lurch as Adder slipped off her socks and tossed them onto the carpet – she could just, still sense what was going on.

He pulled off his gloves slowly, finger by finger, his small snake-like eyes glinting lecherously. He dropped the gloves, placed a hand on each calf, and slowly slid his fingers up and over her soft thighs. Somehow she managed to muster the strength to slam her knees shut, shaking her head and whimpering in horror.

Adder shuddered, and breathed heavily, as his penis became solid. His hands moved quickly over her body until they came to rest on her tiny firm breasts, he moulded them eagerly. Her skirt was now high above her waist and the sight of her well shaped thighs and small blue panties had him drooling. God! how he yearned to take her virginity there and then, but he knew he would face the full wrath of Woodcock – hell shit! He couldn't make her do oral sex to him – he dare not remove the gag, just in case she could raise a scream. He slipped his hand into his pocket, pulled out his blade, and pressed the tip firmly against her neck. With his other hand, he undid his belt and dropped his pants. He pushed his erect penis closer to her, grabbed her small, bound hands, and tried to wrap her fingers around it. 'Take it, you sexy little bitch, take it and rub it up and down – gently! Come on, come on. You've seen enough sex on the goggle-box.'

Suddenly, his mind clicked, and his stomach twisted. Christ! he was supposed to phone Woodcock at 4.15, exactly. He threw a glance at his watch, it was a minute to. In seconds he'd put his clothes to right and rushed from the room, locking the door behind him. The call-box was near by, and Woodcock would be waiting for news of the sacrificial victim.

Sophie lay still, drugged, and firmly trussed up.

Meanwhile, at home, Daisy paced up and down the living-room anxiously. She lit yet another cigarette as she wondered where on earth Sophie had got to.

It was seven in the evening, and there was still no sign of her. She'd never be this late without getting in touch, thought Daisy.

Even Stumpy, sitting by the fire, seemed uneasy as he watched Daisy pacing about.

A feeling of panic hit her. There had been that spate of murders recently. Where was the child? If anything terrible had happened to her ... Daisy's mind refused to complete the thought.

Rosie and Jacky, who had been out searching for Sophie, returned with glum faces.

Jack undid her desert boots and kicked them off. 'We've looked everywhere Mam,' she sighed. 'We've been around the subways, and through the park – nothin.'

Around quarter past ten that night, John, Rosie's fiancé, kept peering fruitlessly through the living-room window.

Lance, from next door, and Danny, were there as well, their faces grim.

Rosie wrung her hands and exclaimed. 'Well, I've phoned everyone in her diary. I think it's time we rang the police.'

'We should have done it before,' said Jack, sitting with an arm round her mother's hunched shoulders.

Daisy nodded a mute agreement. In her eyes there was torment as the time dragged by, and still her child did not come home.

By 11.30 pm the police cars were on the lookout for Sophie Dooley.

Danny, Jacky and Lance, went out again to tour the streets with John, in his car, also searching for some sign of her.

John knew several of the taxi firms – several years previously he'd driven cars for them. Each office that they called at agreed to put it out over their radios, so that their cars could keep a watch for her – Balchester's radio wavelengths were buzzing.

'She's about five feet tall, with long wavy auburn hair, and she's very pretty. She's slim and wearing a red school skirt, short white socks and a navy blue cardigan. She could be wearing, or carrying a blue and red anorak with a hood.' The search continued.

After a good hour touring the city streets and local children's haunts, they returned home – it had been a fruitless exercise.

'Hello, Fredrick Haddock here.'

Danny quickly slotted the silver coin into the telephone pay box, taken aback by the speed of Merlin's reply. For many years, Freddy had intended to have an extension to the telephone put in his attic, but just hadn't got around to it. However, after all the trouble with Jacky during her stay, he'd decided it was time to act. Anyway, he was just about sick to the teeth of clambering down all those stairs every time the telephone rang.

'S'me Merlin, Danny.'

'Ah, Danny, how are you dear boy? and how's Jacky coming along – is she sticking with it?'

'Fine, just fine.' There was a tiny pause, before Danny went on. 'It's her little sister, Sophie, we're bothered about at the moment, Merlin. She's gone missin' and we're all worried about her, yous know what I mean like?'

Merlin gently turned his new globe as he listened intently – Jack Dooley had destroyed the last one in a temper tantrum when under the influence of heroin. He'd just come to the great lakes of Canada, as he said, encouragingly. 'Yes Danny, go on – go on, dear boy.'

Danny tried to tell his story calmly, he desperately needed his wise old friend's assistance. He gave the details of Sophie's disappearance, and finished, hopefully. 'We was hoping Merlin, that maybe you could help.' Danny's tone grew agitated. 'You know, with yous living here so long, you may know a place where she could be holed up.'

Merlin interrupted sharply. 'Danny! Danny, dear boy, I understand your concern for Jack's little sister, but please give me time to think.'

There followed a long pause, while Merlin sipped at his nightly tipple of whisky, and Danny tapped the mouthpiece irritably with an edgy finger.

'Merlin,' he enquired, at last, testily. 'A' you still there mate?'

Merlin gave a chesty cough and stubbed out his cigarette, before replying. 'Yes, yes, dear boy just thinking that's all. The cogs are moving a little slow these days, old age and that, you know. Do you have a number where I can reach you?' Danny rattled off the call-box number to Merlin, along with Daisy's address, just in case it might be needed.

'OK Merlin? Bye.'

'Bye dear boy.' The line went dead.

Danny let the booth door swing to, walked a few paces, and sat on the nearby low brick wall – he'd wait for Freddy Haddock to 'phone – at the moment he needed all the help his friend could give him.

It was approaching half past twelve on Saturday morning, and still Merlin hadn't returned Danny's telephone call. Still Danny waited anxiously, shuffling his tired limbs, glancing from time to time down the street at Daisy's house. No phone call from Merlin, no sign of a police car at Daisy's home. He was beginning to feel bewildered, angry even, at the long wait.

At around twenty to one, Danny gazed thoughtfully at the moon's appearance, and despondently swung a boot at a lone discarded coke can. It only just missed the litter bin at which he'd aimed.

Merlin must have fallen asleep, he decided – he just wished there was something he could do. He cursed his luck and trudged back to Daisy's house.

It was then that Freddy Haddock's head shot up suddenly from where it had been resting on his forearm. Danny was right, he had dozed off at his desk, but he was only in the lightest sleep, his mind was still whirring. 'By golly!' he exclaimed. 'I may have it.' He sat up quickly, remembering Danny waiting by the telephone. 'Oh my goodness, Danny! poor boy.' Frantically, he rumaged around on top of his desk. 'Where's that damned number?' he snapped irritably. He finally rooted out the small piece of paper bearing the phone number and Daisy's address. He dialled. No reply. 'Damn and blast it!' he cursed. After a further two attempts, a drunk answered the phone. After trying in vain to get some sense out of him he slammed the phone down in frustration.

Freddy had pieced together what Jack had told him about the coven at the old broken-down abbey, along with her black magic discoveries at Woodcock's farm. Then there had been Jack's ordeal where the Devil and his henchmen tried to take her.

On Sunday night, it was 'All Hallows Eve' and who better for the sacrifice, thought Freddy, than Sophie Dooley – a pretty, young virgin. He grabbed the telephone and dialled again. Good! a sober man walking his dog, much better.

Danny's eyes flickered open at the sudden rat-a-tat-tat on the front door. Everyone was tired and on edge, waiting for news. Only Daisy was upstairs in bed, sedated by the doctor, to give her a few hours of oblivion. The strain had almost driven her out of her mind.

Danny thanked the man with the dog for his message from Freddy, and made haste to the call-box. Luckily for him, no-one had been to use the telephone. He swung open the kiosk door, picked up the phone, and spoke. 'Hello, is that you Merlin?'

'Ah, the man managed to find your address then, good!' exclaimed Merlin, and paused to take a swig of whisky.

'Come on, Merlin,' Danny practically shouted in his exasperation. 'Tell me, 'ave yous found anythin' out yet, or not?'

'Take it easy dear boy, I have thought it all out.'

Merlin explained his theory, that Sophie could be being held by the coven as a replacement for Jacky.

Danny listened eagerly, then nodded.

'Makes sense, Merlin,' he agreed. 'Makes sense.'

Merlin lit a cigarette and went on. 'Now I don't want you and Jack to worry too much, Danny. If the coven do have her, she will not be harmed. Sophie will be sacred to the High Priest, well, that is until "All Hallows Eve" at least.'

Danny seemed to freeze. His voice was barely above a whisper as he asked. 'What then Merlin?'

There was a brief silence before Merlin replied, in cautious tones. 'Best come to my house later today, say, around noon, we can talk things over then. Mind you, dear doy, if by any chance the coven aren't holding her it will be up to the police.' He coughed chestily as he dragged on his cigarette. 'By the way, dear boy, will it just be yourself and Jacky coming over?'

'There could be four of us Merlin. Jacky, me, Lance, from next door, and Jack's future brother-in-law, John, but don't worry, they're OK!'

'Good, the more worthy people the better.' Merlin suddenly recalled an earlier thought. 'Oh! by the way Danny, I'd have somebody stay with Sophie's mother whilst the rest of you come over here, she shouldn't be left on her own.'

'Sure Merlin,' Danny promised. 'I'll see to that.'

'And Danny' – Merlin paused a minute, then continued earnestly. 'Please trust me, as I used to trust your grandfather in the war. Anyway, we'll talk later. Good-night dear boy.'

'Yeah, OK Merlin, we'll see yous at dinner-time, bye now.' He rang off.

Dawn was breaking, and each birds song was rapidly joining the morning chorus.

It was a long time since Danny Black had donned his white karate suit, along with his black belt – a hard earned belt, due to his grandfather Harry's brilliant help.

Although Danny had trained regularly, it felt better training in his martial arts attire – his gi.

Lance, who had gone back next door earlier, was up and awake, having taken his dog, Bimbo, for a walk. He gazed in awe from his bedroom window as he watched Danny training. It was just like watching someone in a kung fu film, Bruce Lee, for instance.

Jack Dooley was also watching Danny from her bedroom window, her eyes shining with admiration.

Danny was training at his best, and with Steeleye too. His veins bulged, as he hissed and stopped the deadly crowbar just a whisker away from the strong silver birch tree-trunk. He was a professional at work, and getting ready for the most vital battle of his life.

Chapter Twenty-Three

Bobby Queen swung open the Dooleys' garden gate, and politely waited for the milkman to finish exchanging three pints of milk for the empties, whistling loudly as he did so. Passing her on his way out, he quickly looked her up and down, and stopped whistling. He curled his lips as he observed her boyish attire and as he returned to his vehicle, he muttered, audibly. 'Butch cow, she's just gotta be butch.'

Bobby shrugged and knocked loudly on the front door, trampling her cigarette-butt into the ground, as she waited for an answer – it had been a fair while since she and Jack had spoken to each other.

The battering of old Merlin had been a nasty affair, and one which Bobby had come to deeply regret. By now she was missing her friend, Jacky, an awful lot. Luckily, she'd escaped prison for the terrible deed, but that was only thanks to Jack for keeping her mouth shut about it.

It was a while before anybody answered Bobby's knock. Nobody had slept much in the Dooley household the previous night. So far, the police had found nothing to help them in their hunt for Sophie – she was still missing from home.

It was Jack, tired and still dressed, who finally opened the door, chewing on a piece of toast. When she saw Bobby, her eyebrows arched with surprise. 'Oh! so it's you, Bobby,' she exclaimed, a hint of hostility in her voice. 'What d'you want?' Her expression was one of suspicion.

Bobby nervously lit another cigarette and looked pleadingly into Jack's tired eyes.

'Hi, Jack,' she fumbled for the right words. 'L-listen Jacky, I only came because – because I heard about your Sophie going missing.' She shifted uneasily from one foot to the other.

'I – I thought that we could make it up, and that maybe I could help you find her. That's all – honest.'

Jack stood listening in silence, still chewing thoughtfully on her toast.

At that moment, Stumpy squeezed between Jack and the open door and greeted Bobby warmly, he'd always made a fuss of her in the past.

'Anyway, Jacky,' Bobby went on, patting Stumpy affectionately. 'I've seen that old geezer knocking about quite a bit lately, he must be all right now. He's grown a silver beard and he looks OK. Like I said Jack, I want to be friends – what was the geezer's name anyway?'

'Freddy, Freddy Haddock. Merlin to his friends, like me an' Danny, OK?' She added, sourly. 'It's no thanks to you he's all right, is it?'

Bobby sighed and spread her hands placatingly.

'Look! Jack, I'm sorry for what I did to Merlin, or what ever you call him. Now can we make it up – or not!?' She stooped to stroke Stumpy again and continued. 'I promise I won't come on heavy with you ever again, honest. Anyway, I'm going steady with Jenny Carter now, so what d'you say, friends again or not, eh?'

Jack considered the question, a medley of thoughts and memories churning through her mind. She and Bobby went back a long way. Her eyes began to soften, after all she was pretty sure there was no danger that old Merlin would recognise Bobby again, and she wasn't the type to bear a grudge, so what the shit! Her lip curled in a smile and she beckoned Bobby into the house.

'OK Bobby, let's forget it all. Come on in.'

Bobby's face broke into a huge beam as she stepped inside. She nodded at what was left of Jack's toast. 'All yours mate, but I could do with a cuppa though.'

Jack wrapped an arm around her friend's neck and laughed. 'Same old Bobby, eh.'

Just before they entered the living-room, Bobby stopped and gently tugged at Jack's arm. 'Is that right Jacky,' she whispered. 'You've managed to kick the drugs?'

Jack held up her hand and crossed her fingers. 'So far, so good,' she replied, quietly.

Bobby smiled. 'Good, I'm glad, after all it was me who got you on the . . .'

'Forget it, Bobby,' Jack's tone was sharp, 'I'm a big girl now, I knew what I was doing.'

'OK Jack, ta.'

They entered the room to join the others.

It was a little after noon when Merlin opened his front door to greet his visitors. He looked smart in his best tweed jacket and neatly pressed trousers. He had even sprucely trimmed his silver beard. He'd obviously dressed for the occasion. He beckoned them inside and invited them to follow him into the lounge. The only person missing from the party was Rosie. It had been decided that she should be the one to stop with Daisy, whose state of mind was worsening by the hour as there was still no news of Sophie.

Merlin offered drinks from his well stocked cocktail cabinet, but they all, with the exception of Lance, who settled for orange juice, preferred cans of cool beer. As for Merlin, he stuck to his usual Scotch.

Once everyone was seated and supplied with drinks, Jacky remarked. 'We can't stop long Merlin, we want to join the search again for our Sophie this afternoon.' She passed Bobby a cigarette and they lit up, while Merlin cradled his whisky glass and nodded, thoughtfully. 'Yes, yes my dear Jacky, and believe me I understand and sympathise with your concern, but I fear you may all be wasting your time.'

Bobby forced herself to look Merlin straight in the face – if he did recognise her, so be it, she just wanted to put the past behind her and help to find Sophie. 'How so? What d'you mean, wasting our time?' she queried.

Merlin gazed at her, but if he did know her, he gave no sign. He took a swig of his whisky before replying. 'I fear the coven already have young Sophie for their ritual tomorrow night.'

There was a general exclamation of dismay at this and Lance observed in puzzled tones. 'I don't understand, if you know that, why don't we just tell the police?'

Danny, topping up his glass from the can, looked up at Merlin and raised an admonitory finger. 'Good point Merlin!'

Jack nodded. 'Agreed.'

'Ah!' said Merlin, glancing at each face in turn, then addressing himself to Lance. 'Because, dear boy, firstly they'd think we were totally bonkers for even suggesting the idea.' He took a sip of whisky, then wagged a finger at Lance. 'Pray tell me, Lance, what the police have done about the recent wave of murders, which the press claim are black magic related.' His voice became deadly serious. 'I'll tell you what – nothing, and d'you know why?' Lance shook his head.

'Then I'll enlighten you, dear boy. Because, like millions of other people, they're frightened of the dark arts, Devil worship, damned witchcraft, call it what the hell you like.'

His eyes glinted fiercely, as if the very devil was in himself. He got up quickly from his chair, gritted his teeth and punched the air with a small bony fist. 'But I'm not afraid, and I'm sure you . . .' He gestured around the group. 'I'm sure you're not frightened either.'

Wrong! They were all frightened, very frightened, apart from him, but no-one was willing to admit it. They glanced at each other furtively and tried to pluck up their courage.

'S'fine by me Merlin,' declared Jack, squaring her shoulders.

'Me too,' asserted Bobby, clenching her fists in a manner that meant business.

Lance had gone pale, and stared into space for a moment as he fought to stifle his dread of what might be ahead of him.

John, taking care not to drink too much as he was driving, found himself hoping he would only be needed as the chauffeur. Danny had already had experience of Satanic forces when he had witnessed Jack's battle in Merlin's den. Trained to fight though he was, he was wary, very wary indeed, but he would certainly support old Merlin up to the hilt. He nodded his head thoughtfully. 'Let's go for it, Merlin, let's sort it out, once and for all.'

Merlin gave a thankful smile. 'It's good to know I have all of your support, but please let me continue.' He sat down again and took another drink of whisky, obviously gratified that he'd won them over. 'The second point I have to make is, that neither the police, nor we, have any idea where young Sophie is being held by the coven.' He glanced round at their concerned faces. 'Or whoever else may be holding her.'

He paused a second before adding. 'And thirdly, whatever is happening, I'm sure if the coven do have her, they won't touch a hair of her head until the ceremony.'

He looked reassuringly at Lance. 'So, young Lance, going back to your point about contacting the police, we may be on a wild-goose chase, which I fear would not go down too well.' He sighed heavily and downed the dregs of his Scotch. Then he made his final point. 'Don't forget, we can contact the police, so that they can intervene, whenever we want them to.'

There were mumbles of agreement from the others with Merlin's summary.

Jack stubbed out her cigarette in the heavy glass ash-tray, and then hurriedly lit up another one – her face was pale and drawn, her nerves on edge. The desire for drugs was still gnawing at her. She gripped Danny's fingers as she drew smoke deep into her lungs. She fired a question at Merlin. 'So what the hell d'you think the best thing is to do then? – hell shit, this is my little sister we're talking about here.' Danny laid a firm, but loving hand on her shoulder.

'We wait,' replied Merlin, gazing at her calmly, 'we wait until midnight tomorrow, the night of "All Hallows Eve". If in the meantime, you wish to carry on the search for your little sister, then by all means do so, and of course, I wish you well.' He waved an arm at them all. 'And that goes for the rest of you also.' He poured another small whisky, leaned back and sipped it contentedly. He felt confident, he felt good, he had spent a lifetime waiting for the chance to fight against a fully-fledged coven.

Lance still looked doubtful, however. 'Well, I still think we should tell the police,' he persisted. Merlin sighed heavily, and wondered why some people were so stubborn.

'We tell the police, young man, but not until the time is right.' He began to outline his plan for an assault on the coven at the old abbey. If the ceremony was going to take place, actual proof would help, but they had none, they had to trust to Merlin's instinct.

Providing Sophie had not been found safe and well, the party arranged to meet again at Merlin's home, at ten o'clock on the Sunday night – 'All Hallows Eve'.

After a brief farewell to Merlin, the group returned to Daisy's house for a meal, and a brief rest, before rejoining the search for young Sophie Dooley.

Sunday, the 31st of October, came in with a violent thunderstorm. Torrential rain filled the River Denny to well over bank level and sent cascades of water pouring through the streets of Balchester – fears for Sophie Dooley's safety were increasing rapidly.

Daisy's mind was tormented almost beyond endurance, but everybody about her kept secret from her the distinct possibility that Sophie was in the evil clutches of the Hell Fire Club. Neighbours offered sympathy and help, the doctor prescribed sedatives to try to calm her down, her family gave her loving support, but nothing could ease the poor woman's torture; only the sight of her child's little dimpled face would do that.

By about half past six, that evening, George Woodcock had assembled several of the coven in a small country pub. Adder was noticeably absent, he was still employed in the important business of securing Sophie ready for the ceremony.

Miss Bull and Harry D. Coot shared a bottle of red wine, as they gnawed greedily at a plateful of greasy chicken wings. Docker, Boots and Brown Trilby, exchanged lecherous glances as Woodcock explained how Sophie would be taken to the altar after he had enjoyed first turn.

Boots was a strapping negro, and an evil leer spread across his face as Woodcock promised he could have her next and from behind, as buggery was his speciality.

Woodcock paused to swill down a piece of chicken, burped and wiped his mouth on a napkin. As his hand reached out for the wine bottle, he turned to Docker. 'You will be supplying the usual sex toys Docker?'

'They're all ready boss.'

'Good, I'll be using my own Arab strap, as normal.' Docker nodded in agreement.

Cochise, the mute, stepped thoughtfully out from

the bar of the Lowfield Hotel into the darkness, then held his wrist up to the pub light to look at his watch. It was ten past nine. He glanced grimly around the half-full car park and scratched his head. Where the hell was Danny Black these days? He hadn't seen him for ages, nor Jack, and it was bugging him. He knew nothing about the battle Danny and Merlin had fought to get Jacky off heroin.

Cochise was a loner. He couldn't hear a radio and barely read the Balchester Chronicle. He still knew nothing of Sophie Dooley's disappearance. After a little while, he realised what he must do.

He strode with long loping gait across the car park – he'd find out himself where and why his two friends had disappeared from off the local scene.

As the rain tippled down, Ben Dooley sat reflectively listening to light music in his clean and tidy flat. He sipped iced water as he peered out through the small window at the dreary weather. He'd always assumed that the south-east of England was a warm sunny place to be – wrong!

It had been a hard battle, but with the help of 'Alcoholics Anonymous' he'd managed to get himself off the booze, and he'd cleaned his act up no end. He cupped his clean-shaven jaw in his hands and sighed, despondently.

He was missing Daisy and his daughters badly, especially Sophie – the apple of his eye. He realised now how much Daisy and his family meant to him –

absence does make the heart grow fonder, he thought.

Ben Dooley had learnt his lesson, and was determined to purify himself, in the hope of winning his loved ones back. Up to now, he'd had no response to the couple of botched letters that he'd sent Daisy. He'd done his best to find a bit of building work down south, but to them he had a foreign accent, and they believed in keeping the work in the village for their own lads. He got lazily to his feet and ambled across the room into the bedroom. Flopping down on the bed, he switched off the alarm clock and stretched out. He certainly had no intention of being woken by it early next morning. The clock fingers now showed quarter past ten – time for sleep. Sleep used to be whenever the booze and sex had finished, but those days were over. He had an important meeting, mid-morning, the next day, at St Oswald's, with the local vicar – Ben Dooley was definitely purifying himself.

Jack, Danny, and the rest of the party trooped wearily into Daisy's kitchen. They were completely worn out, after searching for Sophie well into the small hours of Sunday morning – their hunt had been fruitless.

Danny flopped down into the kitchen chair, more than ready for the hot drink which Jacky was making. He'd searched several miles of the canal tow-path by himself, calling out Sophie's name until he was hoarse.

Rosie served everybody with mugs of steaming tea, while Jack hurried upstairs with a cup for Daisy, who was still in bed. The doctor had called again, and given her an injection, the stress of Sophie's disappearance was becoming too much for her.

Merlin's idea of Sophie being in the hands of the Hell Fire Club was now becoming a reality. It looked as if they would all be meeting up at Merlin's that very same night.

At around two that afternoon, in Danny's flat, he was wakened abruptly from a deep sleep by Spotty, his unfriendly ill-tempered female neighbour – he'd flopped on the bed tiredly, while gathering the rest of his belongings, before handing in his keys to his landlords, the Dillys.

Spotty was banging noisily on his door, to tell him that there was a telephone call for him downstairs in the lobby. And also, that he still owed her some money for Lotty's upkeep.

'As a matter of fact,' Spotty added, looking up at him inquisitively, as he dug into his pocket for the few pound coins he owed her. 'It sounds like the same women who called here while you were away, a foreign one.'

She took the money he offered her and dropped it into her open purse. 'I gave her this telephone number because she said that she might not be able to call at the house again – you don't mind do you?'

Danny shook his head. 'No, no, – er – thanks

anyway.' He quickly headed down the stairs, wondering who could be ringing him.

'Hello, Danny Black speaking,' he said, into the mouthpiece. Her voice came small and nervously. 'Hi Danny, it's me, Su-Ling. I'm sorry to trouble you, but I need to speak to you, I . . .'

'Su-Ling! s'good to hear from you, how yous doing?'

'Not very well, I'm afraid, Danny.'

'Why Su-Ling, what's wrong?' he asked, concerned.

Her voice trembled. 'I – I have to leave George. I can't go on with all this drug business' – she broke off and Danny heard a stifled sob.

'And he's started beating me as well, once in front of the girls.' There was a tense moment while Danny choked back his anger at the idea of her being ill-treated.

'I see, have you got anywhere to go?' he asked, when he felt calmer.

'No, not yet. I – I was wondering if you could help me, I don't know many people around here, and I need somewhere safe for the children and for me straight away.'

Danny's response was speedy. 'Yeah, I think I can help yous. I've got a friend over in Liverpool. He's a good fella, he's called Tommo.' He switched the subject. 'A' yous on yer own?'

'Yes, George is out on the farm and Ament is in Balchester shopping, it's her day off. The girls are still at school.'

'Good, put the phone down and I'll get back to you after I've rung Tommo to suss things out.'

Her voice sounded faint with relief. 'Oh Danny, thanks so much.' She hung up.

Danny quickly flicked through the 'phone numbers in his diary. He redialled three times before catching up with Tommo in the Castle pub.

Tommo immediately agreed to organise a safe haven for Su-Ling and her two young daughters. He'd promised Danny he'd help him any time, and Tommo was a man of his word.

Danny explained that he had George Woodcock and the coven to sort out at his end, the arrangements were made swiftly, and he rang Su-Ling back.

She answered immediately and listened carefully to Danny's instructions.

'And take the Land-rover Su-Ling, it'll be less conspicuous than that bloody great Merc,' he advised, then he went on to rattle off the details where she and her girls were to meet up with Tommo in Liverpool.

'Just be there at five this afternoon, Su-Ling, and my mate will be waiting for you.'

She sounded more relaxed as she replied. 'Right Danny, I'll pick up the children from school first and then we'll be on our way.' She added, a wistful note in her voice. 'We will see each other again Danny, won't we? I still love you. You know that.'

He drew in a deep breath and cleared his throat. 'Please, this isn't the time, and in any case, you know I love Jacky.' There was a silence and he prayed for her to understand, he hated to cause her pain. 'Listen, I'll be in touch again as soon as Tommo has got you settled in – I promise,' he said. 'Best start packing now, I'll contact you before long.'

'You do mean that Danny, you will still keep in touch?' Her voice was no more than a whisper.

'I've already told you Su-Ling, I promise, I must go now, take care.'

'Bye Danny – and thanks.'

When he had rung off, he stood for a minute, thinking, remembering Su-Ling and her sweet and joyous love-making. There would always be tenderness in his heart for her, he knew that. But for now, his friend Tommo would look after Su-Ling and her two daughters, he himself had more urgent matters to attend to.

Just after quarter past ten at night on that 'All Hallows Eve', Adder telephoned Harry D. Coot at his home to come and collect Sophie and himself. He didn't want to miss any of the early activities.

Sophie had now been released by Adder from her bonds and gag, she had to look the part and be able to walk to Coot's car properly, although the knife, rammed discreetly in her ribs, would make sure of that.

Adder had camouflaged her well, in a dark hooded duffle-coat.

Harry D. Coot drew up in his volvo and kept the engine quietly ticking over as he waited for his passengers.

Sophie stepped out obediently into the misty October night air, her distress intensified by the feel of Adder's knife blade pressed firmly against her side. She hesitated and gave a stricken look at Harry D. Coot's leering eyes. Even though the street was only dimly lit, they seemed to glitter through his thick-lensed glasses like a beast's eyes surveying its prey.

Sophie winced as the blade prodded her, trembled with terror as she was forced toward the waiting car.

As Adder deliberately rubbed up against Sophie in the back seat of the car, his lust was inflamed by lascivious thoughts of the orgy ahead, of what he would do to her tempting young body. He clasped his gloved hands together avidly and rammed his thighs against his rapidly expanding erection. He chortled, quietly, from deep within his throat. He would be next, after Woodcock had finished with Sophie's maiden body. He wasn't to know that he was mistaken – not yet, that Woodcock the High Priest had already decided – Boots, the well-endowed negro would be next.

Chapter Twenty-Four

At around ten o'clock on 'All Hallows' Eve' night, Danny helped Merlin into the back of John's car. He just hoped that his old friend was right about the coven having Sophie – at least that would mean she was still alive.

Lance had parked his father's car just behind John's, he was taking Jack and Bobby Queen to the old abbey.

Lance accelerated gently past John to lead the way, according to Jack's instructions.

In John's car, Merlin sat upright with his cane wedged between his knees.

Steeleye lay on the floor between Danny's feet.

The night was cloudy and still, and as Cochise rushed from out of the alley-way, his breath streamed in icy puffs in the orange glow of the streetlight.

As the two cars picked up speed, he leapt into the street in front of them, waving his long arms frantically.

'God!' shrieked Jacky, 'Cochise!'

John and Lance slammed on their brakes, both

came to rest, only a yard from Cochise's legs. John's vehicle nudging Lance's rear end.

Danny raised a hand and brushed it across his sweating forehead, realising it had almost been curtains for his friend. Merlin cursed under his breath, the sudden jolt had nearly brought up the couple of double Scotches he'd downed to steady his nerves before the confrontation at the old abbey.

A second later, both Jack and Danny jumped out to greet Cochise.

'Took a chance didn't you?' Danny shouted, slapping him on the back. 'You nearly ended up as mincemeat.'

Cochise grinned mutely. He had managed to track them down by sheer dogged determination. He'd called at every pub and club on the Bedford estate, finishing up at Daisy's home. Rosie had managed to explain to him that they had all gone to pick up Merlin.

The buses were few and far between on Sunday nights, so Cochise had run the mile and a half in double-quick time, he'd deserved his stroke of luck in catching up with them. He understood their mimed invitation and quickly climbed into the back seat of John's car, next to Merlin, who treated him to a scowl. He hadn't forgiven the mute yet for being the cause of his somersaulting stomach. Cochise however, grinned at him and nodded his head excitedly.

After ten minutes of steady speed, the two cars turned into the narrow dark lane which led to the outskirts of Bluebell Wood. There they parked in the overgrown yard of a derelict farmhouse, an ideal hiding place for the vehicles, well out of view from the coven's scouts.

Merlin squinted at his wrist-watch in the faint light of the moon.

'Mmm, five to eleven Danny, we're in good time dear boy.' He quickly glanced around the stern faces. 'Now remember everybody, keep a sharp watch for any of their lookouts, we don't want to spoil things. If they do have young Sophie, one mistake could cost her her life.'

Jack shuddered at the very thought and nodded, along with the rest.

They were roughly a quarter of a mile from where the old abbey ruins lay, deep in Bluebell Wood – they would have to go on foot from here on in.

Merlin found that he wasn't as fit as he'd imagined, the years of drinking and smoking had taken their toll on his frail body. After a couple of hundred yards of brisk walking, he was leaning heavily on his cane, too proud to admit he was finding it tough keeping up with the young ones.

At the fringe of the wood, the party halted and waited for him, scrutinising the darkness for any sign of a scout – all clear, as far as they could see, but . . . ?

Merlin leaned against a giant oak tree, panting heavily. It was still a fair trek to the heart of the wood. Danny stepped a few paces back and rested a friendly hand on the old man's shoulder. 'A' yous all right me ol' mate, d'you wanna' sit down for a bit?'

Merlin stiffened and rammed his deerstalker on more firmly. 'Of course I'm all right dear boy,' he retorted, straightening up and prodding the drifts of fallen leaves with the tip of his cane.

'I've been through a lot worse than a bit of hiking and tangling with old Nick, it's chicken-feed compared with what I went through in the war with – with . . .'

His voice trailed away sadly, as his mind flashed back to his good old wartime friend, Harry. 'With your grandfather, dear boy.' He sighed heavily. 'With your Grandfather!'

Danny shook his head slightly, moved by sympathy and respect for Merlin, and loving regret for his Grandad Harry.

'S'okay, Merlin, me old mate,' he said, gently. 'S'okay, come 'ead, let's go.' He turned a blind eye as Merlin dug into an inside pocket, pulled out a small flask of Scotch, and helped himself to a good swig. Smacking his lips, Merlin set off again with renewed determination, muttering, crossly, 'these young folks! think I'm ancient! I'll show 'em.'

Jack and Bobby, pushing on through the wet, cold shrubbery, both cursed as they clawed frantically at the glistening walls of spiders' webs, which broke and clung to their faces – they both hated spiders.

Bobby wrapped her chubby fingers around Jack's elbow and tightened her grip slightly, just enough to stop Jack in her tracks.

Jacky glanced at her startled, she was already finding it hard enough to control her nerves, with the lack of drugs. Bobby, too, was twitchy. 'Let's have a fag Jack, before anything starts,' she suggested and they both eagerly lit up, taking care to conceal as much of the lighter flame as possible – the scouts were about.

As Adder and Harry D. Coot dragged Sophie through Bluebell Wood towards the far side of the abbey, Adder stifled her screams with his dirty gloved hands. In the end, to stop Sophie's ferocious wriggling and jerking, Adder and Coot swooped her up between them and carried her young writhing body the short distance to the huge, masked cloaked woman who was to dress her for the occasion. The woman stood in a small clearing by the abbey, her eyes ogled Sophie's childish figure hungrily. She was obviously one of the oldest of the coven, with her large hunched frame, and her greying hair. Her eyes gleamed with lust behind the mask and her mouth slavered as she fondled Sophie's young flesh with eager trembling hands. 'Oh yes, oh yes,' she croaked, ecstatically, 'our lord Lucifer will just love taking this little beauty.' Little did Jack know who the old hag was who was about to prepare her little sister for the ceremony – the old hag was Miss Bull.

The sky had now almost completely cleared and the moon was shining brightly overhead, throwing helpful light to the watching party. So far, so good – it seemed as if they had avoided the coven's scouts.

The giant broad-leaved trees which surrounded the ancient abbey ruins cast eerie shadows over the historic ground below.

The members of the coven were now all gathering and last-minute arrangements were being made for the buffet and wine drinking session which was to conclude the 'All Hallows' Eve' ritual.

Danny, Merlin, and the rest of the nervous group, came to a halt on the far side of the abbey. It was near to the place where Jacky and Bobby had been spotted by Adder, as they secretly spied on an earlier ceremony – it had been that incident which had brought Jack into direct conflict with the evil Hell Fire Club, and they still lusted to have her naked body spread across their foul altar, along with that of her little sister.

Merlin had dropped to his knees and edged his way across the wet grass and rubble, until he was crouched close to Danny. He pushed aside the creeping ivy and peered through a break in the wall.

The rest of them gazed through their peep-holes with mounting concern.

As the orgy commenced, Merlin glanced at Danny, his eyes expressing repulsion.

'Oh yes! dear boy,' he murmured. 'An ideal location for devil worship – a sacrilegious mockery of what the abbey once stood for.'

As the cloaked figure of a woman lit the final black candle on the last candelabra, there was a profound silence. It was a weird silence, which spread amongst the watching group in a way that caused all of them to shudder.

Jack suddenly gave a choked exclamation. 'Fuck me! – Jenny Carter! – it's Jenny Carter lightin' that candle.'

Poor Bobby's mouth just dropped open in astonishment – Jenny's face could be clearly seen, her love life certainly had its set-backs, she loved Jenny a lot, but not the Hell Fire Club.

Bobby Queen watched in horror as her lover, Jenny, thrusting out her heaving breasts, sauntered towards Docker, whom she had drawn as her first sex-partner, a goblet of wine in her hand, obviously in no need of the aphrodisiac taken by many members of the coven. There was lewd giggling and total abandon as men and women coupled and performed obscene acts.

Woodcock was already mounting his second woman in doggy fashion. His sexual appetite was clearly insatiable – the bacchanalia, before the midnight ceremony, was now in full swing.

Sophie had been bound and gagged again after being made ready to grace the altar. The old hag, Bull, was guarding her, while Adder moved swiftly, erection at the ready, into the heart of the debauch.

On that same afternoon, after the church service, Ben Dooley met the vicar as arranged. It had been a long conversation, during which Ben had told of the mental anguish he was suffering over losing Daisy and his daughters' love. He also blurted out a full confession of his evil deeds. He went on to describe the religious revival gathering which he had wandered into almost by accident. It had changed him, he explained he had suddenly seen himself as he was and it had appalled him. 'I've seen the light, honest I have,' he declared.

The vicar listened to him sympathetically, before giving him advice. His response to Ben's last question was a positive one. There was to be another religious revival meeting that very afternoon, on the local playing field, and he saw no harm whatsoever in Ben attending it. Ben and the vicar parted with smiles and handshakes on both sides. The conversation alone had already made Ben feel much better within himself, the vicar had proved to be a true man of God and had aroused Ben's respect and esteem.

At the revival meeting, in between hymns, Ben listened to the speaker, and found himself overcome with emotion. As he sang and swayed with the crowd, clasped hands held high, he could feel a glorious sense of love and belonging rising inside him. His earlier conversion was confirmed, gloriously – Ben Dooley had seen the light!

Ben drove his old battered van northwards joyfully, humming phrases of hymns, his heart light as a feather, his whole world remade.

Meanwhile, Daisy stood at the living-room window, eyes red-rimmed, her mind haunted by dread for her child. She peered out at the dimly-lit street, then turned to gaze at the wall clock. It was approaching quarter to eleven, on 'All Hallows' Eve', and there had still been no sighting of Sophie.

Suddenly though, as she was about to drop the curtain, she heard a sound that caused the muscles of her stomach to tighten, and sent shivers down her spine. It was a sound which she would never forget, it was the deep chugging of her husband, Ben Dooley's, van. She looked down the road towards the approaching headlights, her face grim, her mouth taut.

As the van shuddered to a halt, beneath the glow from the streetlight, her worst fears were confirmed, it was Ben Dooley.

Rosie had already seen her father from the upstairs window and was ready and waiting.

She stood at the front door, arms akimbo, her face set in a stern scowl. There was no way she was letting her mother, in her state of mind, have to face him!

Ben stopped at the front door, gazed intently at Rosie and smiled. 'Rosie love,' he said, in warm, gentle tones. 'It's good to see you, you're looking well.' He glanced in the direction of the half-closed living-room door, behind which Daisy crouched, listening to what was going on.

Rosie stared at her father suspiciously and made no reply. Dooley went on, diffidently. 'I – I've just come to see your mum, Rosie love, that's all.'

He spread his hands placatingly. 'I've – I've come

back home, Rosie love, is your mum still awake so I can talk to her?'

Daisy was still standing in the wings, and heard Rosie, galvanised into speech, spit out the words. 'Go away Dad! We've got enough on our plate right now.'

Impulsively, Daisy called out. 'It's OK, Rosie, I'll talk to him, he's Sophie's father, he should know about her.' As she appeared at the front door, Rosie stepped back a pace but remained there, determined not to leave her mother's side. Daisy gave Dooley a long curious stare. In the dim light, she could make out his face. It had been a long time since she'd seen it clean-shaven. She went on to scrutinise his attire. He was clad in a smart sweater, and his pants actually had a neat crease down each leg. Her gaze settled on his feet. Polished shoes instead of old working boots, another rarity. Even his hair looked clean and well-brushed.

Dooley, however, was startled at the reference to Sophie, as he knew nothing about her disappearance. 'What d'you mean Daisy, I should know about Sophie, know what?' he enquired.

Daisy's head drooped and her voice trembled as she said, 'You'd better come in Ben, and I'll explain what's happened.' She and Rosie stepped aside as Ben wiped his feet on the doormat and entered.

Once inside the living-room, what little fight Daisy had left in her quickly drained away. She subsided into her chair and, between sobs, eventually told Dooley the story of Sophie's disappearance.

Ben went white and suddenly sagged. Groaning, he sank down in a chair and buried his face in his hands.

'No, oh no, not my little Sophie . . .'

'Don't give us that,' Rosie snapped. 'You didn't give a shit for any of us when you went off and left us so don't come the grieving father now, it won't wash.'

He looked up at them both, tears glistening in his eyes.

'I've changed, love, believe me. I know what a rotten father I've been, I know what I've done to you, Daisy, but I'm different now . . .'

Rosie still stared at him hard-faced, but Daisy's lips were trembling and there was a softening in her expression as she faltered. 'Oh Ben, I wish I could believe you but – oh Ben, our little girl, what's happened to her? Where is she?' Overcome by emotion, she burst into bitter tears.

'Come and lie down again, Mum,' urged Rosie, casting a virulent look at Ben.

'He's no business turning up like this and upsetting you all over again.' She led the sobbing Daisy out of the room and took her upstairs. When she came back she spat fire at Dooley.

'Just get out of here and leave us alone – we've enough to cope with, we don't need you pratting on about being changed.'

'It's the truth, love.' Ben's tone was desperate as he tried to get through to his disbelieving daughter. 'I've stopped drinking, something's happened to me, something wonderful. I went to this meeting, see, and I found God – ' he broke off as Rosie gave an almighty snort. 'Found God!? You? Now I've heard everything.'

'All I want is a chance to prove I've changed, Rosie, love – '

'Look, all I want at the moment is news of our Sophie,' Rosie broke in, her face looking haggard with anxiety and loss of sleep.

'What about the police?'

'They're out looking for her – fat lot of good they are too.'

'Don't they have any idea?'

Rosie studied him for a long moment, as if wondering how far she could trust him. At last she made up her mind and, bending near to him, she whispered in his ear all she knew about the Hell Fire Club and the suspicions which Jack, Danny and the rest entertained about Sophie being in their hands.

'Mum doesn't know anything about that, she'd go crazy if she did,' Rosie emphasized, as she finished. 'We're not positive that the Hell Fire Club do have our Soph', but this Merlin bloke is in charge of a rescue group, just in case – Jack and the others are with him.'

'What can a tin-pot effort like that do?' Ben leapt to his feet.

'If they know something they want to get the police in on it. I've heard things about these Hell Fire Clubs, they're deadly. If they've got Sophie in their hands – it doesn't bear thinking about . . .' He stopped , hearing Daisy's feet on the stairs.

'Leave it to me,' he whispered hoarsely to Rosie.

When Daisy came in, he went towards her and took her hands in his. 'Can't you rest, love?' he murmured. 'You should try, leave everything to us, we'll have Sophie back safe and sound, just have faith.'

She gazed up at him, wide-eyed. 'You *are* different, Ben, I can see it,' she said. 'But how long will it last?'

'For the rest of my life, I swear it, please trust me Daisy.' His tone was quietly convincing. 'It was like a great warm glowing light that came over me – I could see how I'd been with you and the kids, how I'd abused myself and others, how different it could be. Daisy, love, I know it sounds corny, but this is the truth – I've found God, or rather, he's found me, like that lost sheep you read about in the good book. I've come home to try to make it up to you, for what I've done to you in the past. All I ask is that you give me another chance, please Daisy, just one last chance.'

Even Rosie looked at him more kindly, moved by the entreaty in his voice, the humility in his expression as he knelt down in front of Daisy and held her hands pleadingly in his own.

'I'll – I'll think about it – ' Daisy whispered, tearfully. 'Find Sophie, Ben, find my baby, that's all I want – find her for me . . .'

'Right,' Dooley got to his feet, determination

written all over him. 'I'm off, and I won't be back without her. Rosie take care of your mother.'

'I've been doing that without your help all these weeks . . .' she was beginning, but then, seeing the entreaty in his eyes, she sighed, and said, in gentler tones. 'All right, Dad, away you go and, good luck.'

'A prayer, or two wouldn't come amiss,' he said, already on his way out.

Rosie raised her eyes to the ceiling, shaking her head in disbelief. Ben Dooley asking for prayers, normally it was a pint of bitter, and a packet of fags, something certainly *had* happened to alter him, she thought, and her lips curved in a faint, affectionate smile.

Chapter Twenty-Five

As wise as he was, Merlin had been wrong about the police thinking that the rescue party would be bonkers about going to them over their thoughts about Sophie being in the hands of the Hell Fire Club. The police concern had been so great over the recent satanic related murders that they were only too keen to listen to Ben Dooley's determined pleas for them to immediately follow up Merlin's suspicions. And so, with Dooley adamant to tag along in search of his daughter, the police set off with great haste towards Bluebell Wood.

A damp cool mist had fallen over the old abbey causing the watching party to shiver.

The setting for the ceremony they were witnessing was not elaborate, as it had had to be arranged in haste, as usual. There was none of the glamour and pomp which was once associated with the notorious Hell Fire Club.

The club had originally been established in the 18th century by Sir Francis Dashwood, who had formed an inner circle of thirteen. There had also been many associate members, including noblemen.

But now, this latest circle consisted of drug barons, sex perverts and wastrels – these days, wealth was not a necessity, but their main aim was still the same, to worship their own lord – Lucifer, and make a mockery of the Christian religion.

A breath of wind caused the flames to flicker on the black waxed candles in the seven-branched candelabra and Merlin turned to Danny excitedly and pointed an eager finger towards the stone altar. On this there was a cat, either stuffed, or made of some other substance, which, it was hard to detect, owing to the dim light and thickening mist.

Merlin whispered hoarsely in Danny's ear. 'That cat Danny, is meant to resemble the ancient Egyptian cat goddess, Bast – a highly respected deity indeed.'

Merlin clenched his fist angrily, as his glance fell on the scarlet banner which was draped over the side of the altar – it bore the derisory symbol of a black cross turned upside down.

'Damn the blasphemous bastards!' he hissed. His gaze passed on to the blood-red cross which lay at the head of the large stone slab, and the two small chafing-dishes which contained burning oils. He shrugged, as he half-turned to Danny. 'Not exactly as fashionable as the original Medmenham Abbey in Buckinghamshire, dear boy, but I suppose it will serve its purpose just as well.' He carried on scrutinising the signs of the Zodiac and the Yin and the Yang, which were all present.

'Mmm,' he murmured. 'Everything seems to be in order for such a ceremony.'

After a brief absence Woodcock, the High Priest, reappeared alongside Ament, who was the Abbess of the coven. On her right hand she wore a leather gauntlet, which stretched a little way above her wrist. There, with his talons gripping tightly to her, and fierce eyes surveying the surroundings, sat the deadly hawk, Horus.

Woodcock and Ament both wore robes of mauve silk. Woodcock was also crowned with a mitre which had the cat's-eye stone in the centre. Round his neck, fixed to a heavy gold chain, hung the diamond-studded crux ansata, the Egyptian symbol of immortality.

Woodcock had initiated every woman of the coven himself, and with his huge sexual drive, looked forward with relish to initiating many, many more.

The sexual activities of the coven were brought to an abrupt halt by the sudden jingling of a silver bell. The men quickly straightened their monks' robes, and adjusted their masks tidily, while the women smoothed down their black gowns, and veiled their faces – silence had now fallen.

There was but one exception amongst the women, a first timer, a novice, who wore white. She, too, was masked and her veil completely hid her face.

The large cat's-eye emerald studded brooch, which Ament wore, sparkled brilliantly in the light from the moon and the flickering flames of the candelabra.

Woodcock, the High Priest, and Ament, the Abbess, held hands and bowed before the altar, turned slightly, and nodded their heads in recognition of the cat-goddess, Bast.

Turning to face the coven, Ament raised her arm and beckoned the novice and her male escort forward. At the same time, she fondled Horus, and the bird of prey responded by ruffling his feathers with pleasure.

The novice had been led into the circle by the rope from her own gown, and it was looped around her neck.

Ament spoke to the woman briefly, spelling out her fortune to her, by means, chiefly, of thought transference. She used her power of suggestion to influence the novice into considering breaking off her relationship with her fiancé, in order to wed her escort, a wealthy drug baron, who contributed handsomely to the coven funds.

The girl and her companion bowed and rejoined the gathering – it was time for the girl to make her decision, but there was little doubt of the outcome.

As Horus shifted position slightly on Ament's wrist, his hard steely eyes glittered and he appeared to be alertly scrutinising the members.

Merlin nudged Danny and whispered, excitedly. 'The hawk, Danny, represents Horus, the most powerful of all the Egyptian falcon-gods. A beautiful creature, dear boy – don't you think?' Danny just shook his head in bewilderment, wishing he could take this affair as lightly as his aged friend seemed to do. He himself was as scared as the rest of the watching party. Regarding the proceedings, wide-eyed, he curled his lip and muttered in grim jest, 'yeah, it's a charmin' bird Merlin, just charmin.'

Close behind them was Lance, who stared, mesmerised, as Ament held Horus aloft, and with her free hand tugged at the short cord which released her gown and revealed her naked dark-skinned body.

There was a hushed sigh from the gathering, and even Danny, Cochise and the rest of the watching males goggled, magnetised by Ament's beautiful body as her gown settled at her feet.

Her breasts were full and firm, and her red nipples became enlarged when stimulated by the coolness of the night air. A mass of black frizzy curls covered her well-developed pubic area. Whilst still tending Horus, she raised her free hand aloft, turned to face the altar, and called out loudly, 'Oh mighty Bast, our beloved daughter of Satan we . . .'

The members of the watching party held their breath as Ament went on with her worship of Bast.

At last, with a kiss from her full lips, she coaxed Horus from off her wrist onto a large stone nearby, where a member of the coven tethered him to a small wooden stake.

By this time, Woodcock had also disrobed and lay down, stark naked, on the altar, his long legs stretched out, and apart. Ament scanned the silent gathering with an air of importance. She then clapped her hands and, with glistening eyes and parted lips, gazed at Woodcock's large erection. She swayed towards him, threw herself on top of him and, impaled herself on his penis, and rode him with complete abandon, her expression one of lustful pleasure. The High Priest responded and their bodies heaved up and down in a frenzy of gratification.

Boots, the negro, who was extremely well-endowed, was naked, and awaiting his turn. He spread himself over Ament's back and inched his way into her rectum. She groaned with delight. As he held her apart, with strong fingers and thumbs, he rode her in rhythm with Woodcock.

Watched by a sexually aroused audience, the three writhing bodies climaxed simultaneously.

Boots exploded with several short, loud grunts and sighed with satisfaction as his penis spurted its load inside Ament. He hadn't, however completely rid himself of his lust – he would save the rest for Sophie Dooley.

As Woodcock gave Ament a final ram from beneath, he tossed his head from side to side with exhilaration, shuddered violently, and at the intense sensation of climax, Ament screamed with delight, enjoying orgasm after orgasm, until, when they were all spent, she slowly withdrew.

The Abbess had shown the coven the way to please Lord Lucifer, and that meant that, stimulated to fever pitch by aphrodisiacs and the orgiastic couplings they had just been watching, they were eager for the defilement and sexual sacrifice of Sophie Dooley to take place.

The Egyptian Gods of Bast and Horus would also be highly gratified, and would have been more so had Jacky Dooley been spread naked across the altar as well, alongside her little sister, but the devil had lost that round of the battle to Danny and Merlin.

Bobby Queen gasped, and shook her head in disbelief at what she had witnessed. She stared goggle-eyed at Jack.

'Fuck me, I'm gay, and I've had blokes as well, but I've never seen anything like this, this is unreal man – unreal.' Jack, even more upset, crouched down and scurried the short distance to Danny and Merlin. Wriggling her way between them, she clamped an urgent hand on Merlin's arm, and asked him, fearfully. 'Merlin! for fuck's sake man, they're not goin' to screw our Sophie like that? tell me man. They'll split her apart.'

Merlin gave a small cough as he nearly choked on his drop of Scotch. He hurriedly rammed on the top of the small flask and stowed it back in his pocket. His tone was confident as he responded. 'Jacky, my dear girl, have no fear. As yet we have no positive proof that your little sister is being held here, but, if she is, we will do our utmost to save her.'

Danny placed a comforting arm around her shoulders and squeezed her lovingly. 'Don't worry Princess, Merlin's right. If your Sophie is here, we'll get her out, and alive, and in one piece.' He kissed her gently. 'I love you Princess – just don't worry.'

Merlin's glance darted around the ceremonial setting. There was still no sign of Sophie and the seconds were rapidly ticking away towards midnight. Damn it! he thought, if the child isn't here, she may well be lying dead somewhere. Then, suddenly, from out of the darkness on the far side of the abbey, Sophie appeared. Bobby and Jack stared at the child, shocked and dismayed.

Sophie had been well prepared by the old hag, even to the point of having her small panties and brassiere removed ready for the High Priest. She was clad only in a white robe, which would normally be worn by a bride. On her head there was a wreath of orange blossom, but even the veil covering her small face couldn't disguise the fact that she was Sophie from the hidden watchers, she was well-known to them all, apart from Merlin and Cochise.

They watched as she was being led towards the altar between Boots and Docker.

Docker was also leading a lamb, which was attached to a length of cord. The animal was to be sacrificed first, and its warm blood drunk by the members of the coven. Then, when the coven's lust and excitment had reached its full extent, Sophie Dooley would die by the sharp blade of the sacrificial knife. The black-handled knife was similar to a large hunting knife, and was treated with respect and the greatest reverence, as a sacred object.

Ready for use, it lay at the foot of the altar. Sophie was also led by a cord, which had been knotted thirteen times, like the lamb's cord. The Old Hag, known, as The Angel Of Death, had done her job.

Jack felt as if her blood had turned to ice as she saw her little sister being led towards the altar, with the cord fastened securely around her childish neck.

'Merlin! Danny!' she sobbed, hot tears flowing down her face. 'You both promised that no harm would come to our Sophie, come on, for fuck's sake do something before that pervert, Woodcock gets his hands on her.'

As Sophie whimpered and wriggled, Miss Bull, who was also part of the escort, slapped her hard around the face, and cursed. 'Shut up! you little bitch, you should be grateful, you're about to lose your virginity to the High Priest.'

As blood broke from her lips, Sophie dropped her head, dazed. Merlin fingered the crucifix, with the carved figure of Jesus on it, which was in his pocket, along with a phial of Holy Water, together with his own mind, it was his most powerful possession.

Before Merlin and Danny had even a chance to reply to Jack's plea, the silver bell tinkled again, and within a few seconds a member appeared carrying a silver tray, laden with a varied selection of sex toys. Everything was there, including the largest and fanciest vibrators, oriental sex potions, realistic vibrating strap-on condoms – even the coven was becoming Aids conscious.

Woodcock's lips parted in a sickly, lascivious grin, which revealed his two rows of rotten, distorted yellow teeth. He stretched forward a long clawing hand and eagerly picked up his Arab-strap, a most intricate piece of sexual equipment – he wanted to be at his best to take Sophie Dooley's virginity, in front of his master, Lucifer.

As the lamb was swiftly sacrificed with a lightning slit of the throat by the sacrificial knife, High Priest, George Woodcock, let loose his mauve robe so it fell to the ground. With legs spread, he then sighed with enjoyment as one of the young female members knelt and sucked him feverishly before taking the Arab-strap from his eager hand. She then proceeded to dress Woodcock's huge erect penis with the strap, which enlarged his manhood even more.

The strap, also known as the potency-strap, often helped Woodcock to power his way to the sexual fulfilment of his dreams. It was a narrow thong, which was fastened firmly over the base of the erect penis, and helped to push the testicles forward. There was also a short strap leading off it, fastened to a tight ring which fitted just above the testicles. This helped to enlarge the bulge and thickness of the genitals in order to give maximum pleasure.

The Abbess, a fully-fledged witch, sniffed, with great satisfaction, the small clipping of fine hair that Adder had snipped from Sophie's near bald pubes. The hair helped to enhance her powers even more, and as Sophie was Jack's little sister, it could most certainly spell trouble for Jacky.

The warm lamb's blood had been swallowed eagerly by the members of the coven and they were now, all except for Ament, in a high state of frenzy.

Sophie had, by now, been quickly stripped by Bull and forcefully laid down on the altar. Her small feet had been hooked over either side of the cold stone slab, which kept her legs spread wide apart to make it easier for the High Priest to force his entry.

Sophie's face was now a picture of pure terror, as Woodcock's huge throbbing genitals approached her trembling lips – oral sex gave him the greatest gratification, by man, or woman. As his lecherous gaze roved over her beautiful young body, from head to toe, saliva oozed from between his distorted teeth – he would suck the juices from her pure vagina first, before hungrily tickling her clitoris with his long tongue, and finally take her virginity.

Rigid now with fright, Sophie cried out, 'Mummy, Mummy,' then held her breath, and squeezed her eyelids shut, as if to block out the horror of what was happening to her.

After finishing intoning the Lord's prayer backwards, Woodcock pushed the shining bulbous head closer to Sophie's mouth. Her head was being held firmly in position by a naked female member, who forced the child's top lip up by pushing her nose up hard with her fingers, while with her other hand she pulled down hard on her jaw. All was ready for Woodcock to enjoy oral sex.

Lance's stomach was still churning from the recent sight of a male member copulating with what appeared to be a dead animal, it was too dull to see properly, but they were all sure it wasn't human. But, as he turned his head away in revulsion at the sight of poor Sophie, his keen eyes spotted a lurking shadow, they'd pushed their luck too far, they had been spotted by the scouts.

Lance's nerves were already at breaking point; panicking, he suddenly leapt to his feet and blurted out. 'There's somebody behind us, Danny. Shit! I'm off, I've had enough of this lot.'

The watching scouts were ready to try and capture the intruders straight away, as the intruders had witnessed too much. If the scouts were successful, Jacky, Danny and the rest of the rescue party, or those captured, would be imprisoned and then brought before the High Priest to be dealt with *after* the ritual had taken place, because the rituals were lunar connected, so the timing would be a very important factor. There was no way Lance, or, any of the others would be allowed to leave the old abbey after what they had witnessed – alive!

But, at the sudden disturbance, the Abbess broke free from her trance, halting the ceremony abruptly. Wine goblets, some of which had been filled with urine were drunk quickly with relish, then dropped – no coven liked being disturbed.

The Abbess's eyes dilated, she turned sharply to face the hidden Jack Dooley and the others. Pointing an accusing finger, she called out, loudly. 'Silence! silence my children. There are unbelievers in our midst.' The power of the scent off Sophie's pubic hair had already worked for the witch, before the disturbance. She went on with rising anger, her flashing eyes searching out the darkness.

'Who dares to enter our coven's ceremony uninvited? You, for one, Jacky Dooley, and there are others with you.' As her head thrust forward, she pointed her finger fiercely, and shouted, 'come forward and show yourselves.' She shot an arm high into the chill air, her eyes challenging Woodcock's surprised stare. 'Hold, my High Priest! It seems we have much bigger fish to present to our Lord Lucifer.'

'Oh shit!' Bobby gasped, as she glanced round at the advancing scouts. 'The weird cow knows that we're here now.'

Jacky appealed, frantically to Merlin. 'What now, Merlin, what the fuck do we do now?'

Meanwhile, Lance had huddled closely to Danny and Cochise, the idea of trying to fight his way through the scouts had quickly left his mind.

Danny gritted his teeth and clenched his large fists. 'Come 'ead Merlin,' he gritted, swiftly scanning the marauding scouts. 'We can't go back now without a fight anyway, so let's get in there an' sort 'em out before the bastards hurt Sophie. How the shit do we fight these freaks?'

Merlin fumbled in his pocket and brought out his crucifix and the small bottle of holy water, both intended to expel the most evil spirits. In this case, it was George Woodcock, the High Priest himself, whom the Devil was working through.

Merlin's lips tightened and his face was stern. 'We fight them with these for starters, dear boy.' He held up the crucifix and holy water. 'We fight them with these!'

Chapter Twenty-Six

Merlin smacked his lips, and pocketed his flask. He flashed an urgent glance from the rear, back towards the ceremony.

'Have no fear, Danny,' he said, rather hurriedly. 'I wouldn't have let the High Priest get any closer to Sophie. It was good that the Abbess should have found us out, it gave us a touch of breathing-space.'

At the sudden interruption, Woodcock had stepped back a few paces from Sophie, but the Arab strap still kept his erection solid. Ament had beckoned a member to release Horus, and the hawk was now back on her wrist, gripping her gauntlet with his powerful talons – the Abbess and her protector, were ready for action. She had quickly donned her mauve silk robe.

At this moment in time, Cochise felt himself almost choking with rage. All he wanted was to storm into the ceremony and take his chances whilst saving Sophie, but he too, like the others, had consented to be guided by Merlin.

Little Sophie still lay there on the cold stone altar. She had opened her eyes, which were wide with terror. Her mind was completely distraught by what was happening around her.

The coven's scouts barred the way back for the rescue party with a thin menacing line, and they knew the wood well, just in case anybody did try to break away, but not quite as well as Jacky Dooley.

Once again, Sophie whimpered. 'Please, please! let me go home to Mum,' but no-one took any notice.

George Woodcock had fantasised over Jack Dooley's body for years, ever since she had come to help her father with the building work on his farmhouse and outbuildings. He remembered how once, in one of his outhouses, he'd had her trapped, and was only seconds away from raping her, but she had fought back viciously and escaped unharmed.

Like Ament, Woodcock was fastening his mauve silk robe. On hearing her reference to Jack, his face broke out into a sickly leer, and his chuckle was spine-chilling.

The Abbess once again addressed the gathering.

'A vote! I call for a vote, to see if we give Jacky Dooley, or her little sister, to our master.'

'Give Jacky Dooley to our master,' came the massed voices of the depraved gathering. And their hands were raised in unison. After all, the coven still bore a grievance against her for spreading malicious gossip about them.

The Abbess once again turned to face the watching party. At the same time, she smoothed Horus's feathers at the back of his head.

'Jacky Dooley!' she called. 'You have heard and seen our vote. Give yourself up to us, and your little sister may go free. I, the High Priestess, promise this in the name of our Lord Lucifer.'

Merlin saw Jack's terror-stricken eyes turn to him, and spoke firmly. 'Take no notice of the damned witch, Jacky,' he snapped. 'She's lying!' He grasped her hand and squeezed it hard. Glancing back at the Abbess, he went on, 'but, we must go along with her evil little plot, my dear girl. Now, be brave, and tell her you agree.'

Danny flung a glance at the menacing line of scouts behind, then leaned over and gripped Merlin's arm fiercely.

'A' yous sure about this Merlin, me old mate? I mean . . .'

'Of course I'm sure, dear boy, just trust me.'

Merlin gripped his silver-topped cane firmly, pushed Danny's hand away, and with a grunt, drew himself up to his full height.

At this moment, the members of the coven seemed to have sobered a little from the drugs in which they had indulged. They all grouped together and started to chant, insistently, 'Jacky Dooley, Jacky Dooley, Jack . . .' The scouts from the rear did the same – the party, and poor Sophie, were terrified, but, unknown to them, rescuers were being willed on by wise old Merlin.

Adder was now hooded and had swept up the sacrificial knife, if anyone was going to use it tonight, he was. He'd lusted after Jack and Sophie

Dooley for a long time, and now that the opportunity had arisen for him to have sex with them both, there was no way he was going to let his chance slip. Also, it would be sweet revenge against Danny Black, who, he knew, loved Jack dearly, as well as Jack's mother, who had thrown him out of her home – yes, revenge would indeed be sweet.

Outside, Jack was nerving herself for the ordeal. 'Okay Merlin, okay,' she said, her breath catching in her throat. Danny clenched his fists tightly. 'Good luck, Kiddo,' he whispered urgently, full of admiration for her courage. As she climbed to her feet and took a step forward, Jack could feel the sweat breaking out all over her body.

Bravely, she climbed over the broken-down wall and paused to compose herself. Then, she called out crisply the words Merlin had told her to say. 'Reverend Mother! I believe and trust you. I now bring myself and my friends into your fold. I have faith in your promise and will abide by the laws of your coven. I will give myself for the freedom of my little sister.'

Ament now stood tall and straight, her head proudly held high, her piercing eyes gleaming with triumph.

'Enter then, Jacky Dooley,' she ordered. 'Enter, and bring those who are with you also, so that the transaction can take place.'

Jack had to do, or say nothing more, and she felt assured when the familiar figures of Danny and Merlin stepped out into the dim light alongside her.

As the three of them moved, shoulder to shoulder, through the overgrown shrubbery, the rest of the party nervously followed a couple of yards behind.

Merlin was still in control, and had already passed on to Danny, Cochise, and the rest of the young party, information which they would need to use in their attempt to defeat Satan. The essence from the herbs which had been tossed onto the burning oils of the two chafing-dishes hung heavy in the air.

Meanwhile, Ben Dooley was panting hard as he pushed himself through the pain barrier. He was determined to keep up with the much younger policemen, as they charged on through Bluebell Wood towards the old ruined abbey. He was ashen-faced with worry, and repeatedly enquired of the officers what time it was – he feared, now, that it could be too late to save his young daughter, Sophie.

As they neared the old abbey, he glanced repeatedly at the sky. In the distance he could hear the very faint whirling of the police helicopter.

At the ruins the High Priest was standing with his arms folded, alongside Ament, the Abbess. Due to the circumstances, his erection had now softened and he had removed his Arab-strap.

As Jack Dooley and her friends cautiously approached into the heart of the coven, Docker, Boots and Brown Trilby, along with the rest of the gathering, formed a menacing band on either side of them. The scouts walked slowly behind them, as if to shepherd them into the heart of the assembly.

Adder stood by the altar, the sacrificial knife held

lightly against Sophie's throat, one mistake from the intruders and her pretty little neck would be slit! Her blood would be freely drunk and any excrement fearfully discharged from her neat little backside would be eagerly gobbled up by the members – men and women alike.

Now that the party was beyond return, Ament gave vent to an eerie cackle. 'Ha! so!' she mocked. 'If it isn't the one they call Merlin, the interfering wizard, and his young friend, Danny Black, who is besotted with Jacky Dooley.' She curled her lip and hurled an angry finger at them. 'The two meddlers who hindered our attempt to take Jacky Dooley for our master, Satan.'

Suddenly, she hunched her shoulders, and her beautiful face took on the hideous appearance of an aged wrinkled black witch. Her words burst from her in a harsh croak, like that of an old woman on her deathbed.

If ever there was an evil reincarnation of the ancient Egyptian goddess Ament, this woman, was it. And with her rebirth she'd gained the knowledge and the ability to use the most intricate secret potions ever used.

'You fools! you stupid Christian bastards! You didn't really think we'd let you take Sophie Dooley away from us, did you?'

At that instant, Merlin suddenly stepped forward, whipping out the small bottle of holy water from his pocket. Quickly removing the top, he advanced and hurled the liquid into the High Priest's face.

Woodcock's features twisted into horrific contortions, demons within him were tormented. He staggered backwards, uttering a series of gurgling screams.

'Devil!' Merlin roared, as he hurled the bottle of holy water at Woodcock. 'Get thee away!'

As the rest of the coven looked on in bewilderment, Woodcock excreted substantial amounts of the most foul-smelling substance, and without even opening his mouth a stream of verbal filth poured from him.

Merlin then turned sharply to face Ament, and with his cane raised high and pointing at her, exclaimed, 'You foolish arrogant woman, did you really think you could deceive us? That we were so stupid.' He tugged out his crucifix, just as the Abbess gathered her senses, and her features and voice returned to those of a beautiful young Egyptian woman.

'So,' she drawled. 'it is trickery that you use. You pathetic little creature, you believe you can defeat our coven? you are wrong!'

She again assumed the form and bearing of the enraged High Priestess. 'Fucking Christian bastards!' she shrieked. She snatched up the wooden cage which held two cocks for the sacrifice – they were the symbols of light and goodness, but were to be presented to Lucifer, and their blood drunk. As she hurled the cage to the ground, it smashed to pieces, setting the squawking, flapping birds free. She snarled at Merlin and the others, and screamed.

'You've fooled nobody, you cunting snivelling mass of after-birth.' She thrust her arm forward and barked a command to Horus. 'Kill! Horus – kill the damned wizard.'

As Horus flew at Merlin, his talons outstretched, Merlin held the crucifix aloft with his left hand, whilst in his right hand he gripped his trusty cane.

As the scouts from the rear suddenly surged forward Merlin shouted to Danny. 'Now Danny! now! Save the child.'

Danny signalled to Cochise by tapping him sharply on the shoulder and nodding towards Sophie.

Danny himself swept up one of the chafing-dishes and hurled the burning oils onto the ground, before any fatal blow to Sophie could be struck. Taken by surprise, Adder dropped the sacrificial blade and as he attacked Danny, slipped on the greasy surface, his face absorbing some of the hot oil. He screamed with pain, clawing at his features. The burning oil had splashed into his right eye causing him agony. He managed to climb to his feet, and stagger several yards before falling to the ground again, writhing with pain.

Another hooded member snatched up the knife and, with arm raised high, ran at Danny, but he, too, slipped on the burning oils which set his robes ablaze.

Jacky swiftly cottoned-on and sent the other chafing-dish crashing to the floor with a hefty kick.

As flames quickly engulfed the members' robes,

his screams echoed round the chamber as he tried to tear off the flaming fabric.

Merlin's crucifix seemed useless against Horus's talons and he had already suffered a terrible gash to his cheek.

'Kill! kill the wizard, Horus!' Ament screeched. But, as Horus attacked him again, Merlin pressed in the small button on top of the cane's handle. As the six-inch blade shot out from the tip, he thrust it deep into the bird's breast. The hawk died instantly, and dropping to the ground lay in a lifeless heap.

Meanwhile, Cochise had swooped up Sophie's naked body and was hurrying away from the fracas.

At the sight of her beloved hawk lying dead, Ament flew into the most terrifying rage. 'Kill them! gouge their eyes out, cut out their hearts,' she shrieked. Falling to her knees, she fondled Horus, sobbing bitterly. 'Kill – kill the Christian scum.'

The man whose robes were alight had managed to discard it, but the smouldering material had set the shrubbery on fire and flames were now spreading fast in either direction. A blaze by the altar, from the spilled oils, had also quickly dried any dampness on the shrubbery and taken hold.

Merlin held his crucifix high and fearlessly advanced, through the thickening smoke, towards the High Priest, repeatedly reciting prayers from the Greek New Testament, as he did so.

As Woodcock retreated, screaming obscenities and spitting a foul-smelling substance at him, Merlin turned his head, and called loudly to Danny,

'Danny! Danny, dear boy. The silver bell! find the silver bell and ring it – in the name of God, ring it!'

Danny had just felled Brown Trilby with a thunderous karate kick, but his keen ears had picked up his old friend's words. The bell had been laid at the head of the altar. Searching for it, Danny's tired eyes eventually spotted it through a break in the swirling smoke. Hurling Boots, and another member of the coven out of his way, he managed to grip the silver bell and ring it. At the sound of the loud ringing, Woodcock howled like a wolf, flung his own body about and fell to the ground, white foam spewing from his mouth. Cringing like a cornered animal, he babbled in a demented fashion, his features distorted, as vomit continued to spurt from his gaping mouth. But, the Devil departed from him, Woodcock finally collapsed beneath Merlin's crucifix, whimpering like a whipped pup.

As members of the coven were trying to escape from the flaming abbey, Ben Dooley and several policemen came charging out from the darkness of the wood. They leapt over the shattered walls and stormed into the grounds to make their arrests.

Jacky suddenly spotted Miss Bull's heavy figure making a cumbersome getaway towards the small stream which was on the far side of the abbey ruins. No way was she going to let that fat evil cow escape justice.

After lumbering the short distance to the bank of the stream, Bull hurried to the left, where an ancient fallen oak formed a bridge across the swift flowing water, Jacky though, was hot on her heels.

Bull hated heights and it was a good drop to the stream below, so she crouched on all fours and slowly, nervously, edged her way across the slippery trunk, towards freedom. But, glancing fearfully behind, she saw Jack only a couple of yards away, and about to step onto the wooden bridge.

Jacky was far more agile than the self-indulgent Bull, and in a matter of seconds she was on her, and reaching out to grip her gown. Bull would be a prime catch for the police in these circumstances, because one thing Jacky Dooley was not – was a grass.

'Come 'ere Bull! you perverted, butch bastard,' she hissed, 'you'll need your fuckin' black magic to get out of Balchester cells.'

Bull's flabby jowls were now vibrating with fear.

'Get away Dooley!' she screamed, 'get away from me before I . . .'

Too late, Miss Bull swayed uneasily, clawed frantically at the rotten bark, and with a loud screech slipped, and fell like a stone to the stream below. She groaned, gave a brief sickening gurgle, and shuddered violently, before lying lifeless, her gown fanning out in the rushing water. The upturned branch, which had been snapped from a storm-swept tree and lay in the shallow water, had pierced her heart. In a matter of seconds, downstream the water was flowing blood-red. The larger eels that lived there, wriggled easily against the current towards the tasty scent.

The old badger who had been peacefully marking out his territory, stopped in his tracks and stared, mesmerised by events – he still bore the scars from a recent battle with several cowardly Jack Russell terriers, and, the edge of a cruel digger's spade.

At the sight of Bull, Jack felt nauseated but recovered herself and hurried back to the scene of action – Miss Bull, the wicked old torment, was dead!

The police helicopter whirled noisily overhead, its giant searchlight beaming down on the interior of the fiery ruins.

While the police were rounding up their prisoners, Ben Dooley rushed over to Cochise, who held Sophie in his arms. As Ben poured out his thanks to Cochise, the mute nodded eagerly, and signed that he was just glad to have been of help.

Sophie was still terror-stricken, so her father had to gently prise her arms from around Cochise's neck. She clung to Ben's waist and sobbed bitterly, too petrified to speak. Ben stooped to kiss and comfort her. His voice was tender, as he murmured. 'My baby, you're safe now, Dad's here to take you home to your mum. You're safe now, everything's going to be all right now.'

At that moment, Lance emerged from behind the large trunk of a silver birch tree, where he had taken refuge during the worst of the violence. Much as he loved Jack, he had been scared nearly out of his wits. All he wanted to do now was clock on for his next shift at the steelworks.

When the police officer had finished talking to him, Merlin rejoined Danny and Jack, wrapping an arm around each of them.

'Come along you two, it looks like we've all got to go with the police to Balchester police station,' he exclaimed. 'There's a lot of questioning to be done and the police doctor will want to take a look at young Sophie, just to make sure she wasn't, well – er – defiled . . .'

As the helicopter still circled, looking for any stray escapists, fire-engines and ambulances could be heard in the distance. The police cars and van drew away from the outskirts of Bluebell Wood – leaving the ancient abbey in peace, at last.

Chapter Twenty-Seven

It was Christmas-time on the Bedford Estate, and the snow was covering it in a veil of white.

Daisy had decided to give her husband, Ben Dooley, one last chance, and had taken him back into the home. Both she and his three daughters had found him vastly improved, now that he had given up booze and attended church every Sunday. Also, thanks to Sophie's rescue from the fate planned for her by the coven, the Dooley household, though somewhat subdued, was nevertheless a happy one.

It was going to take time and skilled counselling for Sophie to recover from her ordeal. The formerly carefree affectionate child was now nervous and prone to nightmares, but her family's loving care, and particularly her father's gentleness with her, were her best help.

Rosie and John had brought their wedding forward to the Christmas season – Rosie realised, with surprise, that now she would be proud to have her father walk her down the aisle.

'Of course, Rosie,' Ben had exclaimed, beaming at her, 'of course I'll help to pay for your wedding.'

Daisy looked fondly at her reformed husband, she was falling in love all over again with the new, kinder Ben Dooley.

In the new year, the case of the kidnapping, the drug trafficking and other offences came to court. George Woodcock had become a babbling wreck, his mind destroyed by his own excesses and the superior powers exerted over him by Merlin. Unfit to plead, he was sent to a psychiatric ward in a mental hospital, where he was to remain for the rest of his life. His property was sold and Su-Ling, who had filed for divorce, received the residue after the state had requisitioned its share.

Adder, who leered and cavorted in the dock as if he was on a winning streak at pool in the Lowfield Hotel, changed his tune when given a stiff prison sentence and was hauled down below bellowing curses at the top of his voice. Danny was top of his hit list. 'I'll swing for you one day, Danny – fucking – Black, you mark my words you mongrel bastard, I'll . . .' He was dragged to the cells, cutting short his threats.

In the court gallery, Danny sat, stern-faced gripping Jack's small hand – they both knew Adder, and they knew whilst he was banged up he would lust after revenge, as much as he did after sex and his Lord – Lucifer.

As for the Egyptian, Ament, that evil woman had forestalled justice. Despite all precautions, whilst in her cell she had swallowed a mysterious Eastern drug she had concealed just inside her rectum. It killed in seconds and everybody present, including the police doctor, were horrified at the sight of the figure lying slumped on the cell floor – it had the face of a withered, deformed old woman, it was if as she died, her features mingled with those of a cat – maybe Bast!? – the ears were similar.

As no proof was forthcoming as to the coven's involvement in the Balchester murders, the rest of the members got off scot-free, apart from Harry D. Coot. Apparently his conscience had tormented him after the murder of his wife to such an extent that he committed suicide. He was found dead in his car with a hose-pipe leading to the exhaust. He left no confession implicating other members of the coven which left the murders still unproven – this would serve him well in the bowels of hell.

The wedding went well, with Rosie a beautiful bride and John a happy proud bridegroom. After the small family reception at a Balchester hotel in the afternoon, the evening celebration at the Bedford Social Club was a very lively affair. As disco lights flashed and the music rebounded off the walls, the Ballerina and Tommo, invited over from Liverpool, lived it up along with Cochise and Lance, while Merlin enjoyed himself after his own fashion – the Scotch, he thought, wasn't too bad, anyway, several had been free.

The Ballerina, a pretty, well-developed coloured girl, wore her favourite pink and large looped earrings. Coming up to the bar where Danny and Jack were, she ogled him hungrily and announced to

Jack, 'just warning yous girl,' she snapped her fingers. 'I'd have Danny back like that. I still love the hunk, and I don't care who knows it.' She nodded at Jacky, maliciously. 'See!' she added.

Jacky awarded her a small mocking smile that said it all – Danny loved only her, and she knew it.

Danny was disconcerted when Su-Ling phoned him and listened to her declaration of love for him with a sense of nostalgia. She was a beautiful woman and they'd had a great time together but he knew his destiny lay with Jack.

'Look, Su-Ling, I'm sorry, but I love Jacky very much, and I'm staying with her.' His voice was gentle but firm. 'I'm sorry,' he repeated, 'but if ever you, or your two little girls need any . . .'

Su-Ling had burst into tears and hung up, and Danny felt a great sadness for her. He knew she was finding his decision hard to accept, that much as she hated it, it was wise for her to stay in hiding until the hue and cry of the drug-pushing had died down. After all, she had been involved in running a courier service, so she needed to lie low.

As for the others who had helped to rescue Sophie, Cochise, the mute, a man of roving ways had disappeared after the wedding, causing a nuisance to the police who required him as a witness.

Lance was still working shifts at the steelworks, and still hopelessly in love with Jacky Dooley.

One day, around Christmas, Danny felt the urge to visit Grandad Harry's grave. Jack went with him but stayed in the background, beneath one of the giant yew trees. Snow had again fallen overnight, and Danny pushed a drift of it from off the grave before placing on it a small holly wreath. For a few moments he stood there, deep in thought, resolving in future to visit the grave regularly, then he turned, and went to rejoin Jack. They kissed, linked arms, and walked in silence to the nearest bus stop. They had no need of words, the understanding between them was perfect.

Later that night, in the bitter cold, they telephoned Merlin from a call-box. Whilst Danny waited for a reply, Jack glanced towards the streetlight opposite and glimpsed Bobby Queen, she was with a friend purchasing drugs from a pusher.

Jack bit her lip hard and started to fidget, it had been quite a while, and she could murder a joint right now. She gave a quick glance at Danny and pushed the phone booth door open with her boot.

'I – I won't be a minute Dan, Bobby's over there on the other side of the road. I just wanna say hello to her.'

Danny had already noticed Bobby Queen drug dealing, and his free hand flicked out, gripping Jack's arm firmly – he could read her like a book when it came to drugs. Glaring at her, he grated out, from behind gritted teeth. 'Forget it! Babe, you're never goin' to touch that shit again – yous don't need the stuff any more. D'yous hear me girl? you – don't – need – it!'

Jack returned his gaze with angry pleading eyes,

and for a few seconds, as the telephone burred, there was a deathly silence. Suddenly, she yanked the door shut, and, with brown eyes blazing, blurted out, 'who the fuck needs the shit anyway, Danny! fucking! Black!' She turned her face away to glance again at Bobby, and demanded in agitated tones. 'Where the shit is Merlin – is he asleep, or out, or what!?'

The slightly slurred voice finally answered, with more than a touch of good cheer.

'H-hello, Fredrick Haddock here, Merlin's my nickname, born and bred in Wellington, 28 Carter Street. I was born in 1917 and served fifteen years in the army – number 3653594 sir! Who's speaking please?'

'Hello Merlin, s'me Danny.'

'Hello! Danny, how – how the devil are you dear boy? How is everything settling down after – after our little escapade?'

'Fine, just fine,' Danny responded.

Jack dug him hard in the ribs with her elbow. 'For Christ's sake ask the man, Dan.'

Danny gripped the 'phone more tightly, his voice was thoughtful as he spoke again. 'Mmm, Merlin, me an' Jacky have got this good mate called Jamie, he's a good kid, you know? His old fella lives in a dead old house on the other side of Balchester. He's adamant that there's a werewolf in the area, he's heard howling an' seen it he reckons. In a nutshell, me old mate, his dad wants to know if yous can help – please!'

He heard as old Merlin smacked his lips, and pictured him, eyes alert, stroking his silver beard and taking a swig of his Scotch. Danny's eyes smiled warmly at Jack as he waited. 'I love you Princess,' he whispered.

'Love you too, Dan,'

Then Merlin said. 'Tell me more dear boy, tell me more, and I'll see what I can do . . .'

The moon went back inside its doors,
To weep loudly behind the wakening day.
The paths of pleasure are now closed,
For the young boy, who with the Devil does play.

Anon.

AM I THE EXPERIENCE,
THE LOVE I AM.
        JP.